"YOU LOVE ME, DON'T YOU, DEENA?" HE WHISPERED. "SAY YOU LOVE ME!"

He was on top of her, pinning her thrashing body to the bed with manic strength, silencing her screams with his mouth. With one hand, he pinioned her arms above her head.

"You're still my wife, remember? According to your precious Jewish law, we're still legally married."

He forced her nightgown around her waist and started to undo his belt. She tugged her left hand free. She groped for the phone cord and pulled it toward her until the receiver was in her hand. Then she brought it crashing down on his head.

He grunted, but he wouldn't stop, wouldn't go away. He just lay there, a dead weight, grinning at her.

She had no choice but to pound him again and again and again . . .

TILL DEATH DO US PART

ROCHELLE MAJER KRICH

AVON BOOKS NEW YORK

TILL DEATH DO US PART is an original publication of Avon Books. This work has never before appeared in book form. This work is a novel. Any similarity to actual persons or events is purely coincidental.

AVON BOOKS
A division of
The Hearst Corporation
1350 Avenue of the Americas
New York, New York 10019

Copyright © 1992 by Rochelle Majer Krich
Published by arrangement with the author
Library of Congress Catalog Card Number: 91-92441
ISBN: 0-380-76533-0

First Avon Books Printing: July 1992

AVON TRADEMARK REG. U.S. PAT. OFF. AND IN OTHER COUNTRIES, MARCA REGISTRADA, HECHO EN U.S.A.

Printed in the U.S.A.

RA 10 9 8 7 6 5 4 3 2 1

In loving memory of my mother, Sabina Tadanier Majer,
a beacon of joy, kindness, wisdom, and courage.

For their gracious assistance, I thank Detective Dan Andrews of the Wilshire Division of the Los Angeles Police Department, Dr. Jacob Fleischmann, Andrew Friedman, Dr. Michael Held, and Rabbi Abner Weiss. Special thanks to my critique group—Phyllis Z. Miller, Serita Stevens, and Anita Zelman—for showing me where to start. I am indebted to my husband Hershie and to so many supportive friends whose encouragement and belief in my story never wavered—Terry Baker, Mike Bandler, Mimi Berkowitz, Sylvia Goldberg, Wendy Hornsby, Frieda and Len Korobkin, Toby and Jack Krich, my father, Abraham Majer, Sol and Miriam Majer, Bruce Powell, Debbie Rechnitz, Debbie Shrier, Liz and Peter Steinlauf, and Sara Teichman.

Finally, I salute the heroic endurance and faith of the many *agunot* all over the world whose plight, like that of the fictional women in my story, is all too real.

RMK

Rabbi Akiva Eger, a renowned eighteenth-century Tal-mudic scholar, welcomed the man into his home.

"Please have a seat," Rabbi Eger offered. He selected a text from the volumes that crowded his bookshelves, sat at his desk, and found the page he wanted. "This is from the first tractate in laws dealing with marriage."

The man sat, stonelike, and said nothing.

Rabbi Eger began to read: " 'A woman becomes mar-ried in three ways . . . and becomes free in two ways: by divorce, or by the death of her husband.' " Rabbi Eger shut the text and looked at the husband. "You have two choices, my friend," he said softly.

The husband rose. "I refuse to give my wife a divorce." He nodded stiffly to the revered scholar, and without a backward glance, left the room.

Exiting the house, he shut the door firmly behind him and walked a few paces before he fell to the ground—dead.

THE NIGHT AIR WAS SURPRISINGLY COOL FOR JULY. DEENA Vogler hugged her arms as she hurried from her car and searched for the Alcott Street address. There it was. At the front door, she reached for the bell, then hesitated.

Tonight's appointment was probably pointless. Another tease, looking for help from a well-meaning rabbi who would listen to her in a paneled room filled with authoritative volumes of the Bible, the Talmud, and their related commentaries. She'd spent several sessions in another paneled room with another well-meaning rabbi, and the wealth of knowledge contained in the richly bound tomes that filled the air with their leathery perfume hadn't provided her with any answers.

But Alan Krantz, her summer employer and her best friend's husband, had pushed her. "This rabbi's different," he'd insisted. "He's aggressive, and I hear he has new ideas for women in your predicament. What do you have to lose?"

She rang the bell. Don't expect anything, she told herself, then smiled wryly, because of course she did, or why would she be here?

Moments later, Deena was standing inside a small room. It wasn't paneled, she noticed, but the books were there, overfilling the shelves that lined the walls.

"I'm glad you came, Mrs. Vogler," Reuben Markowitz said. There was warmth in his voice and his brown eyes. "Please, have a seat." He gestured to a folding chair in front of a wood-toned Formica desk, then noticed the Cabbage Patch doll that was occupying it. "My best listener," he told Deena as he moved the doll to his already cluttered desk and took his seat. "Never criticizes my sermons. Unfortunately, I have to share her with Tamar. She's our three-year-old." He smiled. "Let me get a pen and paper and we'll get started."

She watched dubiously as he searched under staggered, pagodalike layers of books and papers that seemed precariously close to toppling onto the carpeted floor. She pictured Rabbi Brodin's rosewood desk, always immaculate, cleared of everything except a leather-bound calendar, a brass stand that held a gold Mont Blanc fountain pen, and a pad of cream-colored, linen-weave paper that bore a calligraphied inscription in raised charcoal-gray ink: "From the desk of Rabbi Morton Brodin." *He never even gave me one of his personalized notes,* Deena realized suddenly. *But then, with all his efficiency and organization, he had nothing to tell me.*

Rabbi Markowitz was much younger than Rabbi Brodin, probably in his early thirties. There was no gray in the trim beard or the curly brown hair capped by a black suede yarmulke. He was dressed more casually, too, dark slacks and a knit polo shirt instead of a three-piece suit. Rabbi Brodin, she was sure, would not approve.

"Found it!" Rabbi Markowitz held up a pad of yellow lined paper and a ballpoint pen. "You mentioned on the phone that you're having difficulties with your husband. For counseling, it's always better—"

"My ex-husband," Deena interrupted quickly. "Well, that's the problem, really. I got my civil divorce months ago, although we still haven't made a property settlement. But Jake won't give me a religious divorce."

A *get.* Without it, she could never remarry. Rabbi Brodin had sat, swiveling gently in his beige upholstered armchair, reminding her in his carefully modulated voice that she couldn't initiate the *get,* that Jake had to sign it and hand it to her voluntarily in the presence of witnesses, that no rabbi could usurp that authority.

And the curious thing was that she'd listened with disbelief and mounting horror, as though this was all new to her, as though she'd never heard stories about women whose husbands refused to give them a *get.* The stories had troubled her, but in a detached sense, much the same way that she was troubled hearing that some person unknown to her had been stricken with a disease. "How awful," she always said. "What a bastard!" And she meant it. But now she was the woman in the story, and it was all shockingly new.

"So I'm Jake's property, his chattel, subject to his whim?" she'd demanded of Rabbi Brodin, already knowing the answer. *"Well, I wouldn't put it exactly like that,"* he'd mur-

mured. He had avoided her eyes, had doodled on the linen-weave paper.

But what other way was there to put it?

Rabbi's Markowitz's lips tightened. "Is it a question of the property division? Is he using the *get* as leverage?"

"My attorney, Brenda DiSalvo, thinks so. She says that explains Jake's demands." Eighty percent of the value of their three-bedroom house in Beverlywood, an upscale residential L.A. neighborhood adjoining Beverly Hills. True, as a real estate broker, Jake had had the inside track on the house, but without the downpayment from her parents, Jake and Deena would never have been able to buy it. He wanted the dining room set, the stereo system, the TV, the VCR. And the cobalt dishes. "But every time I've compromised—against my attorney's advice—Jake has increased his demands. And frankly, I'm angry about having to give up what's rightfully mine. It's not the things," she added quickly. "Things are replaceable. But I hate giving in to blackmail."

"You shouldn't have to," Markowitz said firmly. "No one should. Has your husband told you what he wants?"

"Jake has this insane idea that we should get married again. He claims he still loves me, but it isn't that, it's—" She stopped, searched for the words. How could she explain it to someone else when it wasn't always clear to her? "Jake doesn't like to lose, Rabbi Markowitz. He's a real estate broker, very aggressive, very successful. He never lets a deal slip through his hands if he can help it. I think he sees the divorce like that. I'm a challenge again."

"Again?" He looked puzzled.

She brushed her hair away from her forehead, as if to clear her thoughts. "I thought he loved me, at least at first. Now I'm not so sure." She sounded wistful. "I think, you know, that he saw me as intriguing, different from the other women he knew. Jake is ten years older than I am, did I mention that? He's much more experienced."

And extremely handsome, she added silently, with thick black hair, penetrating gray eyes, and a slow, sensuous smile that had invited intimacy the first time they met. Deena had never lacked dates—she knew men found her more than pretty; they always told her so, complimented her figure, her long, thick, coppery hair, her green eyes. But they hadn't prepared her for Jake. The mutual physical attraction had been immediate, intense. And he'd been funny and exciting and sophisticated and spontaneous, lavish with gifts and flowers. And incredibly charming when he wanted to be—which had been always during their courtship and engagement. She'd been caught up in the illusion of romance, had mistaken flash for substance.

"But we had a lot in common—similar backgrounds, interests. We're both only children of Holocaust survivors; we both come from Orthodox homes." Was she explaining to Rabbi Markowitz, she wondered, or defending herself?

"So where did you and Jake meet?"

"At his realty firm. Two years ago, before I started law school, my dad got me a summer job there. My dad's friendly with the senior partner, Ben Kasden." It was an arrangement that Max Novick had bitterly regretted from the moment Deena told him she was going out with Jake. *"Just one time,"* she had told her father. *"What's the harm?"*

"How long were you married?"

"A little under a year." She watched him write the information on the yellow pad.

"Do you have any children?" His pen was poised, waiting.

"No, I—no." She avoided his eyes, felt herself blushing even though she knew he couldn't read her mind. She'd felt guilty using birth control; as a devout Orthodox Jew, she knew it was prohibited. And she'd wanted to get pregnant, to have Jake's child. But Jake had insisted, and she'd given in. Even then, he'd been irrationally worried about her becoming pregnant, frequently demanding assurances before they made love that she was using her diaphragm.

At the time, she'd been hurt, disappointed, puzzled by his reluctance. Now, she was thankful. A child would have made everything so much more difficult.

"Mrs. Vogler, why did you want the divorce?"

Irreconcilable differences, Brenda DiSalvo had told the judge. Usually, that was a vague, catch-all phrase; in this case, it was absolutely true. "I'm very committed to being Orthodox. It isn't just something I grew up with. It's what I am. Jake didn't want to be religious anymore."

"That's rough," Markowitz agreed. He tapped his pen against his palm. "This was a sudden change?"

"Not exactly. Jake gave up religion in his teens. When he met me, he became observant again, but after we were married, he became lax—about daily prayers, about keeping kosher, about *Shabbas*. Everything. He mixed meat and dairy dishes, brought home food he knew wasn't kosher. He stopped going to *shul* on *Shabbas* and did things he knew would upset me. He turned on lights, watched TV, drove his car.'' All of which are forbidden on the Sabbath.

"Did you talk to him about it?"

She nodded. "We argued constantly."

"What did he say?"

"I'm tired of all these goddamn rules, sick of this anti-quated crap! This is the twentieth century, or maybe you haven't noticed. And I'm fed up with having you look over my shoulder, spying on me. Saint Deena."

"Jake, you knew from the start how important this is to me. We had an agreement. You promised—"

"Yeah, well, it's time to change the agreement, sweetheart. You don't like it, sue me."

"Basically, that he wanted to live in the modern world," Deena told Rabbi Markowitz. "He said that I could live the way I wanted, but that I had no right to force my life-style on him." She hesitated. "Sometimes I had the feeling he did it all to annoy me, to get even."

"What do you mean?" He frowned.

She felt her cheeks getting hot. It was difficult discussing this with a stranger. "He . . . uh . . . was very unhappy with our . . . sex life. He resented the restrictions." According to the laws of *taharat hamishpacha,* family purity, a husband and wife have to separate each month from the onset of her period. After her period, she counts seven clean days, then immerses herself in a *mikvah,* a ritual bath.

Deena still remembered in detail the first time she'd gone to the *mikvah,* the night before the wedding. Pearl had accompanied her, and Deena had been nervous yet excited.

The attendant had led Deena to a private room outfitted with a full-sized tub and separate tiled shower, a commode, and a sink and vanity area attached to a mirrored wall. Neatly folded thick, white towels and disposable slippers sat on the counter next to a large tray holding shampoo, nail polish remover, baby oil, and acrylic containers filled with cotton balls and Q-Tips. One drawer revealed scissors, emery boards, and pumice stone; another, combs, brushes, and a blow dryer.

The *mikvah* itself was in a separate tiled area. Deena walked down the steps to the center of the heated pool. She immersed herself completely for a few seconds and bobbed up. The attendant nodded her approval. Deena recited the blessing in Hebrew, and it seemed to her that her voice echoed in mystic resonance. She immersed herself again, recited another, longer blessing; she stumbled a little on the words, but the attendant smiled her encouragement. Then Deena submerged herself a final time. When she climbed out of the pool, the attendant stood, her face modestly averted, extending a robe to Deena.

Deena had felt special. Pure, somehow. Convinced that this would start their marriage off right.

Rabbi Markowitz said, "But he knew about these rules before you were married?"

"Of course! And I told him it was something I'd never compromise on." Was that why she'd given in on the birth control? Probably. "The first few months, Jake was fine. Then he became more and more difficult." He'd been alternately demanding, cajoling, insulting, petulant, a spoiled child who couldn't have his way. Twice, she'd had to physically fight him off and spend the night sleeping on the den couch.

"Being Orthodox involves continuous commitment and faith," Rabbi Markowitz remarked. "And enormous self-control. Even then, it isn't always easy. We follow rules that govern our daily actions, tell us how to dress, what to eat, when to have sex. Some people can't handle that."

"But Jake didn't even try, Rabbi Markowitz! And I should have known it wouldn't work. That's what really bothers me. Everybody warned me—my parents, my friends." She paused. "I was worried too. I told Jake it wouldn't work if he was doing it just for me, but he said he was committed, and I believed him." She studied her hands. "I know what you're thinking, that I believed him because I wanted to. I see that now."

"Listen, I don't know anyone who hasn't done that at least once. Including me. You think your husband fooled you? Maybe you're right. But he probably fooled himself too, or he wouldn't have married you. You made the terms clear, right?"

She nodded.

"And you know, there's something awfully compelling and romantic about saving someone's soul. I should know." Markowitz grinned.

She flashed a half-smile. "Maybe." The thought had crossed her mind. "But I still feel pretty stupid."

"You have to put that behind you," he said firmly. "So okay. Things weren't working out and you separated?"

"No." She shook her head. "No, I went to Rabbi Brodin for help. He's the one who instructed Jake when he was becoming Orthodox again. He married us."

"And?"

"He told me to be patient. He said Jake was probably going through a phase; everything would work out. I wanted to believe him. I wanted more than anything for the marriage to work. And then . . . and then . . ." She felt a familiar tightening in her chest. "I found out Jake was having an affair."

"I'm sorry," Markowitz said gently. "That must have been very painful."

"I was devastated," she said softly. Even now, the hurt and humiliation were still there, and the sense of inade— too. Because of course she'd asked herself c— what had driven him to Annie.

She shifted in her seat. "But i— happened, learning the truth— Jake was a terrible m— the divorce wo— wasn't ha—

sp—
tra—
thi—
well

"R—

"R—
until w—
and it w—
ment. N—
will see —
Rabbi." S—
encounter.

"According—
Nothing the j—

[overlapping page fragment, partially visible and rotated:]

get
that m—
I'll ma—
"But I—
"No. I—
her very ess—
Reuben M—
yellow pad. To—
spoke.
"I'm not going
situation," he said
expecting an immedia—
"No, of course not,
ning after all? For a wh—
blinked back tears.
"But it isn't hopeless."
desk, and half-sat on the edge—
judging from what you've told m—
I can't tell you how long it'll take—
everything I can to help you."
"Thank you." Her voice quavered
"Don't thank me yet." He smiled—
what the Talmud calls an *agunah*—literal—

another man, let alone marry someone.'' A note of triumph had crept into his voice.

''Why are you doing this, Jake? What can you gain by refusing to give me a get *besides making me miserable?''*

''I told you. I want you to take me back. That's all I've ever wanted! Not the house, not the money.''

''That's not going to happen! You're living in a fantasy.''

''Maybe. But I'm in no rush.'' He paused. ''Are you?''

''What?''

''What's the matter, Deena? Is there a boyfriend I don't know about? Some cute law student who carries your books?''

''Don't be ridiculous!''

He got up and made his way to the front door.

She followed him. ''What about the property settlement?''

''Make me an offer, Lady Dee.'' He smiled jauntily and left.

Deena leaned forward. ''Rabbi Markowitz, I can't tell you how helpless I feel, how . . . trapped. From the time I wake up until the time I go to sleep, all I can think about is the ⸻ Sometimes—'' She stopped. ''Sometimes, I'm so angry ⸻ I just want to walk away from it all. I tell myself that ⸻ rry without it, that God will forgive me.''

⸻ you can't.'' It wasn't a question; it was a fact.

⸻ wish I could, but I can't.'' She would be denying ⸻ ence. She took a breath. ''So can you help me?''

⸻ rkowitz capped the pen and placed it on the ⸻ Deena, it seemed like an eternity before he

⸻ to pull any punches. You're in a tough ⸻ quietly. ''I hope you didn't come here ⸻ te solution.''

⸻ ' she lied. Had it been a wasted eve- ⸻ ile, she'd thought, maybe . . . She

⸻ He got up, walked around the ⸻ ''It probably won't be simple, ⸻ e about your husband. And ⸻ e. But I'm going to do ev-

⸻ ''Right now you're ⸻ ly, someone who is

'tied' or 'bound.' There are certain procedures, a specific schedule of events, that we have to follow to undo those ties."

"But I will have my *get?*"

He met her eyes. "I can't guarantee that. I've helped a number of women in your situation, but I don't have a perfect success record. Far from it. I've helped a few men, too."

"Men?" Deena frowned.

"The husband has to initiate the *get,* but the wife has to accept it. I know of women who have refused to accept the *get,* but that's not as common. But back to your case. One, I'm going to present it to the local *Beth Din,* the Jewish court of arbitration. The *beth din* will issue a summons ordering your husband to appear."

She shook her head. "Jake won't do it. Why should he?"

"I don't expect him to. Even religious men often ignore the summons. But we have to follow the process. The *beth din* will issue two more summonses. If Jake ignores the third one, the *beth din* will issue a contempt citation, a *seruv,* stating that he's refused to appear. The document will be publicized."

"But how will that help me?"

"It paves the way for community action. The rabbis can talk about the husband from the pulpit, restrict ritual honors, bar him from services. Jewish tradesmen can refuse to deal with him. The community can ostracize him. The works."

"Jake doesn't go to *shul,* Rabbi Markowitz. He isn't—"

He smiled. "I know. Buying kosher food isn't exactly a priority for him, is it? It's too bad he's not involved in the Jewish community. But there are other ways of persuasion. We can harass your husband with phone calls and pickets at his place of work, at his home. Everywhere."

"Why didn't Rabbi Brodin tell me any of this?" She felt a rush of anger against Brodin and the time he'd let her waste.

"He probably hopes the problem will resolve itself. It isn't easy dealing with an angry, sometimes vindictive husband, family members, friends—some of whom may be influential. It can get ugly. To be fair, though, most rabbis feel frustrated by the situation and sorry for the wife. And because they honestly don't see another solution, they encourage her to give the husband whatever he wants in exchange for the *get.*" Rabbi Markowitz shook his head. "To me, that's encouraging blackmail. And I think it's only going to perpetuate the problem. That's why we're trying to do something about it."

We? "You make it sound as though there's an organization that handles this."

"There is, in New York. They really get the community involved, and they've been successful in many cases. We're trying to follow their example here in Los Angeles. Ideally, of course, national Jewish organizations would come out with edicts banning these husbands from any involvement in Jewish affairs. That would take the pressure off the individual rabbi. So far, though, that hasn't happened."

"And you're personally going to walk in a picket line in front of Jake's office?" Deena looked at him.

"If that's what it takes. I know a lot of people who'll join me. Men *and* women. This isn't just your problem, you know. This issue is an embarrassment to Judaism, a perversion of the law. The *get* was intended to protect the wife, to make sure that if her husband divorced her, he would honor the provisions of the *ketubah*, the marriage document."

"Right now I don't feel very protected." She hesitated. "To be honest, I'm having a difficult time dealing with this on a philosophical level. I mean, I've always loved Judaism because it's so concerned with human rights, with justice, with kindness. How can the same Torah that commands special protection and compassion for widows and orphans and strangers, that even forbids us to take birds out of their nest while their mother is present, that—" She stopped and shook her head. "This just doesn't make sense to me."

"It's not the law that's at fault," Markowitz said gently. "It's unscrupulous men like your husband who circumvent the intention of the law and use the *get* for revenge or blackmail. Sometimes both. We have to put a stop to this. But we have to do it within the framework of the law."

"But you don't know Jake. He's very stubborn, Rabbi Markowitz. What if he stands up to all this pressure?"

"There are other ways," he said quietly. "Under certain circumstances a *beth din* could administer physical punishment—lashes—to someone like Jake. Today, in Israel, he'd be imprisoned until he gave you the *get.*"

"But—"

"But this isn't Israel. You're right. And a *beth din* doesn't have authority here, and the Torah commands us to follow the laws of the country where we live." He paused. "Nevertheless . . ."

"Oh." The word was half-whisper, half-exclamation. She

pictured Jake forced to his knees, his arms yanked behind him, his once handsome face battered, his lips caked and bleeding. The idea sickened and excited her. "But isn't it dangerous?" she managed.

"I doubt that it will come to that. But yes, it's dangerous. Harassment is dangerous, too. I've had threatening calls from husbands, from other rabbis. I've had lots of calls from the police." He shrugged.

"Have you ever . . . ?"

"Been in jail? No, but I've come close, and I figure it'll probably happen one day. My wife isn't thrilled about it, but she understands that this is something I have to do." His eyes were dark and pensive.

"But let's not get ahead of ourselves," he said briskly. "If your husband is sensible, he'll realize that it's to his advantage to give you your *get*. We can make life pretty miserable for him without resorting to extremes. Let me get started with the *beth din*. Unfortunately, they're not usually quick to take action. And I'm going to put you in touch with a support group of *agunot*. You'll find it helpful talking to women who understand exactly what you're going through."

"I don't know." The thought of revealing her intimate life to strangers made her uncomfortable.

"I insist; you'll thank me. The leader is Faye Rudman. Here's her phone number." He returned to his seat, scribbled a number on the bottom of the note-covered pad, tore the fragment unevenly, and handed it to Deena.

She glanced at the paper and put it into her purse. "How long has Mrs. Rudman been waiting for her *get?*"

He hesitated. "Her case is unusual. Her husband is in a mental institution. If he's not legally competent, he can't legally give her a *get*. She's been an *agunah* for eleven years." His voice was heavy with sadness.

Eleven years! "So what can you do for her?"

"Very little, I'm afraid. She'll have to wait until he's sane enough to be judged competent, even for a short while. A day, an hour. Or until he dies." Markowitz shook his head.

"That's horrible!" she whispered.

"It is. But Faye is amazing. You'll see when you meet her. And please, do yourself a favor. Don't compare yourself to her. Jake is not insane, and you won't have to wait until he's dead to remarry."

"Who knows, right?" The thought chilled her. But for the first time in many months, she felt a glimmer of hope.

It was ten-thirty by the time Deena pulled into her driveway on Guthrie. The pale gray stucco house, wrapped in shadows except for the triangle of light at the front entrance, seemed lonely and uninviting, and much too large for a solitary occupant. Our dream home, she thought.

She turned off the ignition and sat in the sudden stillness, preoccupied with what Rabbi Markowitz had told her. When she left her car a few minutes later, she didn't notice the red Porsche down the street or the figure who sat in it, watching her as she made her way up the brick path to the front door.

2

"DO ME A FAVOR," MAX NOVICK CAUTIONED HIS DAUGHTER as soon as she arrived to spend the Sabbath with them. Max and Pearl lived across town from Deena on Fuller Avenue, in the heart of the densely populated Orthodox Jewish community, in a white two-story home with a Spanish tile roof and black wrought-iron accents. "Don't mention Jake or the *get* in front of your mother. She gets too upset."

"I won't bring it up." Deena stepped on tiptoe to kiss his balding, gingery-gray head. "But what if she asks?"

"Tell her everything is coming along. Tell her this Rabbi Markowitz works miracles. I don't care what you have to say." He examined her critically. "You look pale, too skinny. Have something to eat. An egg. Toast, maybe."

"I just had lunch."

"Juice, then. Fresh. I just made some for your mother." He left the octagonal, beige marble–floored entry hall and headed for the kitchen.

Deena smiled. For as long as she could remember, her father had been a Jewish mother. She placed her overnight bag at the foot of the staircase and joined him. The kitchen— white lacquered cabinets and white ceramic tiles on the counters and floor—was spotless and permeated with the familiar aroma of all her favorite foods. "Where *is* Mom?"

"Resting. She cooked for *Shabbas* in the morning, then went to lie down." He handed Deena a glass of juice. "Every morning, every afternoon, she rests, but still she's tired." He sighed. "Her blood pressure is high again, did I tell you? The new pills, they didn't make a big difference." His eyes looked weary behind the gold-toned bifocals.

"What else is wrong? You sound worried."

"You saw her hand, the shaking? Now her left eye is twitching all the time, just like Mrs. Sobel's, and it's half-closed." Mrs. Sobel was one of the patients in the convalescent home Max owned.

Deena frowned. "But what did Dr. Melner say? Could it be an allergy?"

"Melner!" Max shook his head in exasperation. "He says it's just nerves."

"Can't he prescribe a tranquilizer?"

"He did. Valium. Big deal." He took Deena's empty glass, rinsed it, and put it on the drainboard. "So now she carries around a bottle of pills, 'in case of an emergency,' she says. But she doesn't take any. She's afraid she'll get used to them."

"What do you think we should do?" Deena asked.

"Do?" Max shrugged. "What's to do? Melner is talking maybe a whole work-up. You know what's going to make her better? You'll get your divorce, she'll be a new person."

Deena winced, as though he had slapped her. "It's not up to me, Daddy. Don't make me feel worse than I do."

"I'm sorry, I'm sorry." Max placed both hands on her cheeks, pulled her to him, kissed her forehead. "Believe me, I know it's not your fault, Deena. I'm just so worried."

But it *was* her fault, she told herself as she was unpacking in the pink and mauve bedroom of her youth. They'd warned her, hadn't they? Sandy, Alan, her parents—her father more than her mother; Pearl was always hesitant to make Deena unhappy. But Deena had glossed over inconsistencies with a romantic varnish, had shrugged off their opposition and accepted as genuine Jake's flirtation with her and with Orthodoxy. For every argument, she'd been fortified with an answer:

Jake was too old for Deena, Sandy and Alan had told her, too aware of his good looks, too slick, too experienced. He'd been living with someone until he started dating her. Didn't she see how different they were, that she was out of her league?

He's a changed person, Deena had told them. And Ann Douglas is out of his life, a part of his past.

Jake was unstable, mercurial, easily bored, Alan had pointed out—he'd started law school, switched after a year to an MBA program, then dropped out and gone into real estate. Didn't that give her pause about their relationship?

People take time to find themselves, Deena had countered. And Jake has been a successful real estate broker with the same firm for several years. His partner Ben swears by him.

And what about religion? they'd all demanded like a mournful Greek chorus. How could she consider marrying someone who didn't share her commitment to Orthodoxy and the life-style it entailed?

But he's becoming religious again, she'd insisted, and triumphantly reported her proof: Jake was thinking of keeping kosher. Jake had bought a yarmulke. And then, a milestone: Jake had gone to *shul*.

Her parents had been in the den when she told them. Her mother had been sitting on the brown and gold tweed couch; she'd looked up from her knitting and smiled; her father, stretched out on the black leather recliner, his ankles crossed, hadn't moved his eyes from the television screen.

"Daddy, did you hear me?"

"I heard."

"I thought you'd be interested."

"I'm overwhelmed. Jake Vogler went to *shul*. I'll call the *L.A. Times* and the *B'nai Brith Messenger.*"

"Max." The knitting needles clicked in gentle protest.

"Better yet, I'll call 'Eyewitness News': 'Jew goes to synagogue—film at eleven.' "

"He told me he really enjoyed the prayers. He's thinking about going again next week."

"And next week you'll tell me he ate gefilte fish and liked that, too. That doesn't make him religious."

"He's trying, Daddy. Can't you see that?"

"A suit, you try. You don't like the way it fits, you give it back. Religion, you don't try—one day yes, one day no. With religion, you are or you're not."

"But it takes time, Daddy. It doesn't happen overnight.

He's coming back to it. A lot of people nowadays are doing that, becoming religious, and they're sincere, committed.''

"Who says not? I know many people like that, and they could show me a thing or two about being Jewish. I respect them with my whole heart. I think it's wonderful. But I talked to Jake more than once, Deena.'' He shook his head. ''Believe me, this is not a man who wants to be religious. This is a man who is trying to impress a religious girl. It's a mistake for you. It's a mistake for him.''

"You don't know him. Why don't you give him a chan[ce]?" She looked at her mother.

"Talk to her, Max,'' Pearl said quietly.

Max sighed. He shut off the television and m[otioned] Deena on the couch, took her hands in his.

"Your mother and I came to this countr[y when] we were in our twenties. We survived Hit[ler's mir]acle.'' He paused, remembering. ''We [had nothing,] no hopes, no future. But we struggl[ed, and] we made it.''

"I know, Daddy.''

He put a finger on her li[ps.] "For many years, we tried to [have a baby. No prob]lems.'' He looked at P[earl.] "When we gave up hoping, [you came. And now] we thank God ever[y day. So if Jake wants] to be religious [he should] believe in it t[o]

"Of cour[se]

"So w[hat kind of a man is] not rel[igious and suddenly wants to] chan[ge]
ch[
be[

"[
not the
heart.''

But of cou[rse,]
later, against a[ll his advice,]
she had walked d[own the aisle]
lightly supporting [his arm under the]
flower-decked *chuppah*,

[The overlapping torn fragment reads:]

lucky
to be
parents
and hop[e]
appointe[d]
but the wo[rld]
Maybe [
her father's
announced th[
"Why, Dee[na]
Deena hadn[
Jake, hadn't wa[nted]
had hope, before [
want to be religio[us,]
father's words, wor[
But the words ha[d]
simply. "You need he[lp.]
her.'' "I have a lawyer,[
Max had nodded. "[
right away, before he de[
heard of that happening. [
the husband blackmails the [
"Jake isn't like that, Dad[dy,"]
"Right,'' Deena said alou[d]
on the overnight bag. No prob[lem]

and Ida, Jake's mother, Deena had circled Jake seven times, then stopped by his side to face Rabbi Brodin.

To Deena, the ceremony had passed with shutterlike speed in a succession of photographic frames. The intonation of the blessings. Pearl raising Deena's veil so that she could sip from the goblet of wine. Jake reciting the wedding vow in Hebrew—"Behold, thou art consecrated to me with this ring according to the ritual of Moses and Israel"—and placing the simple, polished gold band on the index finger of her right hand. The reading of the *ketubah,* the marriage contract, which was then handed to her. The chanting of seven benedictions, followed by another sip of wine. And finally, the muffled shattering of glass as Jake stomped on the wrapped goblet that someone had quickly placed beneath his foot.

"Mazel tov!" everyone had exclaimed excitedly. Good

there had been no good luck. Jake Vogler had proved neither the right man nor wonderful. And Deena, her only child, the repository of all their love and trust e, had ached with the knowledge that she had dis- them. Her father still hadn't said, "I told you so," rds hovered in the air like clouds heavy with rain. ot. Maybe the words were only in her head, not Max had sat, stone-faced and silent, when she'd at she was divorcing Jake.

na?" Pearl had cried. "You were so happy." t told her parents about her problems with ted to worry them. But that was when she she found out about Annie. "He doesn't us." She had tensed, waiting to hear her ds he was entitled to say.

dn't come. "I'm sorry," Max had said elp?"

Brenda DiSalvo. Alan recommended

Make sure you take care of the *get* ides to give you a hard time. I've A friendly separation, then boom, wife into giving up everything." y; there won't be a problem." now as she snapped the clasps em at all. She sighed. Despite what Rabbi Markowitz had told her, she would probably be married to Jake forever.

Suddenly, she saw herself with Jake in the bridal suite after the ceremony, examining the *ketubah*. Before the ceremony, Jake and two witnesses had signed the marriage document that a caligrapher had handwritten in Aramaic on an intricately illuminated background.

"You know what's missing tonight?" Jake said suddenly. "The part where we swear to love each other till death do us part."

Deena shook her head. "That's not in the Jewish ceremony."

"I know, but I kind of like it. Let's do it."

"Jake, I don't think it's right." She frowned.

"Is there a law against it?"

"Not that I know of, but it sounds ominous, doesn't it?"

"Come on, Deen. Do it for me. I'll go first." He cleared his throat. "I, Jake, take you, Deena, to be my lawful wedded wife, for richer, for poorer—how'm I doing?"

"Fine, I guess." She felt uneasy.

"Okay. For richer, for poorer, in sickness and in health, to have and to hold, till death do us part. Your turn."

". . . till death do us part," Deena echoed somberly.

Despite Max's warning, Deena was shocked when she saw her mother. Pearl looked wan and listless, unnaturally thin in a royal-blue velour robe—worse, somehow, than the week before. Her hair seemed more faded, too, as if the medium brown tint had given up trying to cover the invading gray. It was difficult for Deena to remember the cheerful, robust, energetic, slightly overweight woman her mother had been a year ago.

Mother and daughter lit the Sabbath candles Max had arranged on an oblong silver tray on the dining room table. For Deena, the lighting of the candles always ushered in a special, inviolable serenity, but tonight their magic was dimmed. All during the Friday night meal she tried not to notice Pearl's twitching eye or the now-pronounced tremor in her left hand.

On Saturday, it was Pearl who brought up the *get*. They'd been discussing Deena's summer job as a paralegal for Alan's law firm and Pearl had related some neighborhood gossip. Ethel Pollison went to Arizona to be with her daughter when she gave birth; Selma Lewitt was putting in a Poggenpohl kitchen because Harriet Kantor was bragging about hers. Natalie Brookman was getting a divorce, Pearl said, and stopped in mid-sentence. She paled, looked quickly at Deena, then averted her eyes.

Max frowned. He tried to signal Deena with his eyebrows, but she was able to satisfy her mother with vague half-answers and noncommittal "soons"—maybe because it was what she wanted to hear. A few minutes later, Pearl excused herself and went upstairs to take a nap. Max looked at Deena and shook his head. *See what I mean?* he said without words.

On Saturday afternoon, Deena walked the two blocks from Fuller Avenue to Vista, where Alan and Sandy lived. From infancy, Deena and Sandy Krantz (née Rosenberg) had been best friends and led parallel lives with parallel expectations. They'd attended the same Jewish parochial schools, used the same sadistic Bedford Drive orthodontist, and developed a special closeness that had lasted even after Sandy had married Alan.

Once Deena and Jake became engaged, Sandy and Alan had accepted Jake and tried to include him in their circle of friends. The four had gone out several times, once with another couple, but Jake hadn't encouraged the relationship.

"I'd rather be alone with you," he invariably told Deena.

At first, she'd been flattered, but after a while she'd found his possessiveness troubling. And when she and Jake separated, and she found herself alone in the house most of the time, she realized that with the exception of Sandy and Alan and one or two fellow law students, she had few people her age to call. In subordinating her needs to Jake's, she'd drifted away from most of her friends, and now she felt awkward about making those first phone calls. There would undoubtedly be questions, spoken or unspoken, about Jake.

She would have liked to blame Jake for her loneliness, too, but she knew that wasn't fair. She could have insisted that they go out with other people. She could have maintained the friendships on her own; she could pick up the phone and make the calls that would reinstate them. It was easy to fall into the trap of self-pity, far more difficult to climb out.

She'd been indulging in self-pity for quite some time, she realized, encouraged by the sympathy of everyone around her. At work Alan had overlooked more than a few mistakes because he knew she was preoccupied, under stress. But she hated depending on his generosity. And she didn't like the person she'd become—glum, enervated, distracted—hated the suppressed sighs she sensed when she entered a room. "Poor Deena. Her husband cheated on her. He won't give her a *get.*"

Well, in a month she'd start her second year of law school, and her professors wouldn't be that understanding or generous. Last semester, she hadn't distinguished herself in any of her courses and had come perilously close to failing the one on contracts. For a while, even though she'd been determined since tenth grade to become a lawyer, she'd toyed with the idea of taking a temporary leave from school until everything was settled, back to normal. But she could hear her parents' distress and disappointment. "All your plans, Deena! All your dreams."

More guilt.

And she *wanted* to be a lawyer, dammit! And she knew it wasn't a good idea to disrupt her plans, to put her life on hold. That would be playing into Jake's hands, giving him another measure of control. She hadn't asked Rabbi Markowitz, but she knew he'd agree. Get on with your life, he'd told her before she'd left his home that night. Keep busy. Don't sit around waiting.

Michael had told her the same thing. She wondered whether she should have told Rabbi Markowitz about Michael. Better not. He'd disapprove. According to Jewish law, she was married and had no business dating. That's why she hadn't told her parents about Michael, either. Only Sandy and Alan knew.

Deena had met Michael two years ago, when she'd been dating Jake. Sandy had invited her to dinner one night, and Michael had been there—Alan's friend, a psychologist. Tall, attractive, wavy brown hair, hazel eyes. And wearing a crocheted yarmulke. At first, Deena had been annoyed by Sandy and Alan's blatant attempt to draw her away from Jake. But the dinner had been pleasant, and she'd been taken with Michael's quiet good humor and intelligent, witty conversation. When he called her several days later, though, and asked her out, she told him she was seeing someone.

A year and a half later, Michael had recognized her in a Hughes supermarket—aisle three, near the ice cream, they often recalled, laughing. (Deena was an ice cream-aholic.) When he'd learned that she and Jake had divorced, he'd asked her out. Again, she'd said no. I don't have my *get,* she'd explained, but he'd persisted. Finally, she'd agreed. She'd grown tired of wearing loneliness like a shroud.

That had been months ago. Now she couldn't imagine her life without Michael in it. She loved being with him, careening clumsily on roller skates along the crowded sidewalks in Venice, mingling with a knowledgeable and visibly affluent clientele in the relatively new art galleries along La Brea, going out to dinner or a movie, or just relaxing in her den.

It didn't take much prodding to get Michael to discuss his work. He talked animatedly about his patients with a blend of humor and compassion that Deena found compelling. And unlike Jake, he was clearly attached to his family. He spoke often about his father, an accountant, who was involved in helping resettle Russian-Jewish immigrants in Los Angeles; of his mother, who had just been honored for twenty years as a preschool administrator in a private school near their home in North Hollywood. He'd shown her pictures of them and of his sisters, Rachel and Naomi, had pointed with brotherly pride to the freckled adolescent faces they'd presented to the camera. Deena couldn't help comparing Michael's attitude toward family with Jake's. "I love being an only child," Jake had told her more than once. "I'm not good at sharing."

She should have paid more attention.

Alan was taking a nap when Deena arrived at the house; Sandy, a petite blond with short, curly hair and wide blue eyes, was entertaining twenty-month-old Jonathan. The two friends sat in the den, where Jonathan was busy alternately making a pyramid of alphabet blocks and knocking it down.

'You're so skinny," Sandy commented.

Deena groaned. "Not you, too! My father already gave me three lectures this weekend. I'm fine, really."

"I'm just jealous. I guess you noticed I put on weight."

"Not really." She *had* noticed. Sandy's face looked fuller, too.

"So anything new from Rabbi Markowitz?" Sandy asked.

"Not yet. It's too early." Ten days had passed since Deena had met with him. Each time she called, he told her that the *beth din* was still reviewing her case. "I'm trying to be optimistic. And patient."

"How's Michael?"

"Michael? He's fine, I guess."

"Just fine?" Sandy smiled. "You're grinning. You do that whenever you talk about him, you know."

"Really?" Deena's smile widened.

"Yeah."

"Michael is better than fine." Deena laughed. "A whole lot better. Too bad I didn't take your advice two years ago. What about you? What's new?"

"Oh, nothing. I'm busy with Jonathan and fixing up the house. You know, the same old thing." She leaned over to hand Jonathan a block that had tumbled near her.

"He's adorable. I'll bet you wouldn't mind another one like him." Deena glanced at her again, then looked away.

"What is it?" Sandy asked suddenly.

"Nothing. I just thought . . . Never mind." Deena reached over to the coffee table and took a cookie.

"I'm beginning to show, right?" Sandy sounded embarrassed. "Actually, I'm in my fourth month. I guess I'll put on maternity clothes soon."

"You and Alan must be thrilled. That's wonderful news, Sandy." Deena smiled. It *was* wonderful, but her smile felt stiff. She hoped her voice didn't betray the twinge of envy that stabbed her.

"Alan didn't say anything because I asked him not to. I wanted to tell you myself. I was waiting for the right time." She avoided Deena's eyes.

Like the delivery room? "You don't have to explain."

"No, I want to. The thing is, I felt a little uncomfortable. You have so many problems right now. I don't know . . ." She turned to Jonathan, who had toddled over to her, and busied herself with adjusting the straps on his Oshkosh overalls.

"I'm really happy for you, Sandy."

"I know you are." Sandy moved over and hugged her. "It was stupid and thoughtless of me. I'm sorry, Deen. I should give you more credit."

"Poor Deena."

It was sad to think that Sandy had worried about Deena's reaction to her pregnancy, as if she were too fragile to handle someone else's good news. It was annoying, too. Deena was tired of having to convince everyone that she was all right, of having to tiptoe gingerly around the minefield of her parents' emotions. Suddenly, she thought about the support group Rabbi Markowitz had mentioned. Women like her. In limbo, like her. Women who would understand how she felt, with whom she could be herself—angry, bewildered, depressed, bitchy. The slip of paper with the group leader's number was still in Deena's purse. Maybe she would call.

An hour after sunset, three stars signaled the end of the Sabbath, and a little later, Max came home from *shul.* Deena held a special braided candle while over a wine-filled silver goblet, Max recited the *Havdalah,* the prayer that officially separates the Sabbath from the rest of the week.

"*Gut voch,*" Max began in his deep baritone, and led them in the Yiddish song that followed the *Havdalah,* a song Deena had always loved. "*Gut voch, a mazeldicke voch.*" May it be a good week, a week that brings *mazel,* luck. Pearl's voice had quavered, but she had sung all the words.

Afterward, Deena packed her bag and kissed her parents goodbye. "Take care of yourself, Mom," she said with a lightness she didn't feel, clinging to her more than she usually did.

Back in her house, Deena dialed Michael's number, but no one was home. She was disappointed, but they hadn't made any plans. She'd been undecided about whether she would spend Saturday night with her parents. She unpacked her overnight bag, looked through her mail. There was nothing of interest, except for a statement from Brenda DiSalvo's office. She flinched when she saw how much she owed her attorney. And there was no end in sight to the negotiations.

Deena was about to get undressed when the doorbell rang. She went to the entry hall and turned on the porch light.

"Pizza delivery for Deena Vogler."

She looked through the privacy window, then opened the door, laughing. "How'd you know I'd be home, Michael?" Just seeing him made her feel suddenly, irrationally happy.

"We psychologists have our ways." He followed her into the kitchen and placed the pizza box and a videocassette on the oak breakfast-room table. "Actually, I didn't know. I figured if you weren't home, I'd have a slice and freeze the rest. I got mushrooms and olives, by the way. Your favorite."

"I'll get some plates." Moving toward the kitchen cabinet, she brushed against him. Accidentally? she wondered. And then she was in his arms, and he was kissing her, lightly at first, then more intensely, slowly.

"I missed you," he whispered. His voice was hoarse.

"I can tell." They both laughed awkwardly. She felt pleasantly achy and flushed. She ran her finger along his nose, across his chin, rubbed her lips against his. "I missed you too, Michael," she said softly. "I'm glad you're here."

They kissed again, then he released her with a sigh. "Maybe this isn't such a good idea, being alone."

"Probably not," she agreed, reluctantly leaving his arms. They'd had this conversation before, would have it again, she knew, locked in a cycle of desire, frustration, and guilt.

After their third date, she'd invited Michael in for coffee. He'd been next to her on the black leather den couch, amusing her with some wonderfully silly story, and in the sudden silky silence that followed their laughter, it had seemed so natural when they moved closer and kissed. It had been strange, after Jake, to feel someone else's mouth on hers, someone else's hands arousing her, as though from a long sleep. Strange, but definitely nice. She had missed touching, being touched.

"I'm sorry," Michael had said suddenly, pulling away. "We shouldn't be doing this. Technically, you're still married."

"I know." For a brief, wonderful moment, she'd let herself forget.

Since then, each time they met, there was the renewed tension, at once exciting and unsettling. And each time they kissed—and it was increasingly hard not to—there was the disturbing awareness that they were treading on dangerous, illicit ground.

"We should eat the pizza before it gets too cold," Deena said now. She took out plates and glasses from the oak cabinet.

"I hope you haven't seen this yet." He picked up the video cassette. *"No Way Out?* With Kevin Costner?"

"How appropriate." She grimaced. "The story of my life."

"Don't start," Michael warned with mock gruffness. "I want this to be a stress-free night. We're not going to mention Jake or the *get*. We're just going to sublimate our desires and indulge in an orgy of great food, okay?"

"Okay." Deena laughed, thinking again how lucky she was to have Michael. And then, as always, her buoyancy was punctured by the knowledge that she was deceiving her parents by seeing him. It wasn't right, she knew, but was it so terribly wrong?

* * *

They had finished half the pizza and were sharing a quart of Monster Cookies ice cream when the doorbell rang.

"It's so late," Deena said. "Who could that be?" She switched off the video with the controller and got up.

"You have ice cream on your chin." Michael took a napkin and wiped it off, then walked with her to the front door.

The bell sounded with an impatient succession of rings.

"Who is it?" Deena asked.

"Who do you think it is? It's your father! How long do I have to stand out here before you answer the bell?"

She looked at Michael anxiously. He returned to the den.

"The door's stuck. Just a minute." She straightened her skirt, tried to smooth her tousled hair, then undid the deadbolt and chain and opened the door halfway.

"Finally," Max grumbled.

She had a terrible thought. "Is something wrong with Mom?"

"No. Are you going to let me in, or does the whole neighborhood have to hear our conversation?"

"I'm sorry. I'm so surprised to see you." She moved out of the doorway but stayed in the hall.

"You forgot your wallet on your dresser. I knew you'd worry when you looked for it; you can't drive without it." He placed her dark brown wallet in her outstretched hand.

"Thanks." What now?

"You're welcome." He smiled but made no move to leave.

"I guess you'd better get back to Mom. She's all alone."

"Your mother's all right. Seeing you did her a world of good. She's involved in an old movie. Some romantic junk. How about a cup of coffee for your old father?"

"Sure," she answered quickly. "Let's go into the breakfast room. I have some cake in the freezer."

"It's almost eleven. I'll turn on the news, see what happened while I was at *shul* today." He headed for the den.

"I have a television in the kitchen," she called to his retreating back, but it was too late. She followed him into the den. Michael was standing awkwardly with one shoe on, the other dangling guiltily from his right hand.

"I'm Michael Benton." He switched the shoe to his left hand and extended the right one.

"Max Novick." He took in Michael's yarmulke, ignored his hand, and looked at Deena with concentrated brows.

"Michael is a friend, Daddy. He knows Alan from UCLA."

"Very nice," Max said.

Michael put on his shoe. "I guess I'll be going. Good night, Mr. Novick. It was a pleasure meeting you."

Max nodded curtly. Deena walked Michael to the door.

"Call me after your father leaves," he whispered.

"If I'm still alive." She shut the door and returned to the den. "It's not what you think, Daddy."

"You're a married woman alone in a house with a man. That's what I think." Max sat on the edge of the couch, his shoulders hunched, his elbows on his knees.

Deena sat next to him. "We're just friends. Good friends."

He shook his head. "It's not right, Deena. Even if you're 'just friends.' " He accented the last two words with sarcasm.

"I have a divorce."

Max sat upright. "It's nothing. A piece of paper from a judge. Big deal. In the eyes of God, you're still married."

"I don't feel married."

Max looked at her. "Feelings don't count. If we did everything according to feelings, where would our religion be? You have no *get;* you're still Jake's wife. Period."

"And how long will I have to put up with this?"

Max put his hand on hers. "Nothing is forever. You have to wait. Rabbi Markowitz said he's going to help you."

"Maybe he won't be able to. He told me about a woman who's been waiting for eleven years. I couldn't live like that, Daddy. I don't think the Torah wants me to!"

"You think I'm happy you're going through this? Every day I curse that *mamzer* for ruining your life! If I could kill him, I would!" His eyes blazed.

"Daddy! Don't talk like that." Her protest was automatic, a startled response to his undisguised hate and the violence she sensed beneath it. But her protest was only half-sincere. For a fleeting moment she contemplated Jake dead, out of her life. It was an exhilarating, tantalizing thought, but an impossible one. Jake wasn't a problem she could wish away, a bug she could exterminate.

"So what should I do?" Max demanded, his hands outstretched. "Tell me what to do, I'll do it! I told you already to give up the house, the business." After the wedding, Jake, in a flamboyant gesture, had insisted on giving Deena half of his share in the realty firm. "Give him everything. I'll help you. This thing is killing your mother. You saw her."

At first, Max had told Deena not to give into Jake's property demands. "Not ten cents more I would give him!" he'd exploded. "To *shul* he doesn't go, but when it comes to a *get,* he's an expert on Jewish law." Time and Pearl's failing health had softened his stand.

"I don't know," Deena said now. "My lawyer wants me to go back to offering fifty-fifty."

"Your lawyer doesn't need a *get.*"

"But why should I give him everything, Daddy? It isn't fair! Rabbi Markowitz doesn't think so, either."

"We're not talking about *fair. Fair* has nothing to do with it. Jake has us over a barrel, and he knows it."

"I think we should still wait. We can always give in."

"You want to wait? Fine. But don't invite your boyfriend over to the house until you have your *get.* Promise me."

"I can't, Daddy. It would be a lie. Right now he's the only thing that's keeping me sane. Try to understand."

"It's wrong, Deena. Completely wrong! Can't you see that?" He sat for a moment, brooding. "He's religious?"

She nodded. "So is his family."

"He knows you don't have a *get?* And it doesn't matter? So how religious is he? Maybe he'll take advantage of you. Maybe he figures you were . . . married already, so it doesn't matter." Max looked embarrassed.

"Michael's not like that, Daddy. He would never consider anything . . . you know . . . like that." Sleeping together would be considered adultery, and the consequences were frighteningly clear: They would both be cast off from the Jewish people forever. She hesitated. "Michael wants to marry me."

"So fast?" Max's eyebrows rose.

"I know. But he says he's sure." Deena smiled. "He's a psychologist, did I mention that? I guess he should know his feelings. Alan thinks the world of him. Sandy does, too."

"And what about you?" Max studied his daughter's face. "You want to marry him?"

"I care about him very much. He's very bright and fun to be with. He makes me feel special. And we think the same way about so many things. But with the way things are . . ."

"And this person—"

"Michael."

"This Michael, he's willing to wait?"

"He says he is."

"For how long, though?" Max wondered aloud. "For how long?"

3

"COME IN," THE SMILING, DARK-HAIRED WOMAN WELCOMED Deena. "I'm Miriam Kalinsky. Faye told me you were coming."

Deena had still been hesitant about contacting the support group, but Michael had encouraged her. Faye Rudman, too, had urged her to attend the next meeting when Deena had finally called her.

"We meet on alternate Tuesdays at eight-thirty, unless someone calls a crisis session; this week we're meeting at Miriam's." She had given Deena the address of the four-unit apartment building on Orange Grove in the Beverly-Fairfax area, within walking distance of Deena's parents' home.

Deena followed Miriam through a narrow hall into a small living room and smiled self-consciously at the women seated on the gold brocade sofa and matching chairs. A slender blonde in a gray linen dress stood up and came toward Deena.

"I'm Faye." She had a low, slightly husky voice. "You must be Deena. I'm so happy you decided to come."

She introduced Deena to the other women: Elaine Presser, a strikingly attractive brunette who sat nervously swinging her right leg, Susan Bergman, a ponytailed, sloe-eyed blond who looked barely out of her teens, and Magda Feroukhim, an overweight woman with ordinary looks who seemed ill-at-ease.

"A few others come occasionally," Faye told Deena. "Sadly, the membership is growing, and who knows how many *agunot* in Los Angeles are unaware that the group exists?"

"Worse than that," Miriam added, "how many Jewish

women remarry without a *get,* not realizing or caring that they're committing adultery? And what about the children they may have later on?'' She shook her head.

"It's awful,'' Susan agreed. "They'd be bastards, Rabbi Markowitz said. They could never marry Jews. Imagine having that on your conscience.''

"Let's not depress Deena right away,'' Faye said, smiling. "She'll be sorry she came.''

"What exactly do you do at these meetings?'' Deena asked.

"Basically, we—''

"We compare horror stories,'' Elaine interrupted. She rummaged in her purse for a cigarette and lighter. "Frankly, I think it would be much more therapeutic if we put up a dart board and pretended we were aiming at our spouses. I'd aim right for Kenny's heart, if he had one.'' She lit the cigarette, noticed Deena's dismay. "Does this bother you?''

She hesitated. "Kind of.''

"No problem.'' Elaine took an ashtray from the coffee table and walked to the archway of the living room.

Faye smiled apologetically. "We've given up trying to get Elaine to stop smoking.''

"Actually, I'm quitting. This is my last pack.'' Elaine noticed Faye's expression. "No, it really is. Too bad, though, 'cause it's the only thing that calms my nerves. That and thinking about killing Kenny.''

"Have you been coming here a long time?'' Deena asked her.

"Too long. Seventeen months. Susan's been with us about ten months—right, Susan?—and Miriam joined a year before I did. This is Magda's third session. Faye's the veteran. She organized the group with Rabbi Markowitz four years ago.''

"He's wonderful, isn't he?'' Susan said to Deena. "So dynamic, so caring. He's really doing something to help us.''

"Are you all members of his congregation?''

"Faye is,'' Susan said. "I belong to a Conservative temple, but I heard about him through a friend.''

"So did I,'' Miriam said.

"Miriam is our *rebezzin,*'' Elaine said. "She's the most religious member we have. She never lets her hair down— probably because she's wearing a wig!'' She laughed.

"Stop it, Elaine,'' Faye warned sharply.

Many married Orthodox women followed the Bible's commandment to cover their hair. Deena had noticed immediately that although it was a warm night, Miriam was wearing a high-necked dress with sleeves well past her elbows, for modesty.

"My parents belong to a modern Orthodox synagogue," Elaine continued blithely, "but I rarely attend services. Actually, they're pushing me to have a *get*. It's not important to me, but they sure know how to lay on the guilt. I'm basically a three-days-a-year Jew: two days of Rosh Hashanah and Yom Kippur. Although I don't see that praying has helped any of us."

"Don't say that," Miriam said. "God hears our prayers."

"Come on, Miriam! He hasn't been listening to yours, has he?" Elaine addressed Deena. "Her husband was abusing her for years, whenever he was in the mood for a little home entertainment, insulting her in public, giving her a friendly slap now and then. To hear him tell it, he's the injured party."

"He won't give you a *get?*" Deena asked Miriam.

"Only if I give up the children. I'll never do that. Never." She bit her lip. Her eyes were bright with tears.

Elaine laughed. "Let him have them for a few weeks, Miriam; he'll change his tune. Kenny fought like crazy for shared custody and won. Now he hardly sees the kids, especially since he has his new wife. He does me a favor when he takes them for a day."

"He's married?" Deena was shocked.

"Sure. Why the hell not? He has his civil divorce."

"So why won't he give you your *get?*"

"Why should he? He has everything he wants. He's holding out for every penny I don't have!" She ground her cigarette viciously in the ashtray and returned to the couch.

"So is my husband," Magda said. Her voice was barely audible. "He wants a cash settlement for the *get.*" She sighed.

"Just like me," Susan remarked. "Barry wants $150,000."

"Except that your family can afford it, honey," Elaine told Susan. "Magda's parents would have to go into hock to come up with the kind of money her husband wants."

Susan colored. "It's not my fault that my family is wealthy. And my dad isn't running to meet Barry's demands."

"Yeah, but that's his choice. Magda's doesn't have one."

"That's not the point," Susan insisted. "You sound just like Rabbi Otterman. 'Give Barry the money,' he told me.

'Pretend you gave it to charity. It's worth peace of mind.'
But it's not charity. It's blackmail!''

"You're right," Faye said.

Elaine shrugged.

"How long were you married?" Deena asked Susan.

"Six months. Barry was interested in . . . uh . . . sexual
experimentation. I wasn't. What about you?"

"You don't have to say anything tonight if you're not
ready," Faye said quickly. "There's no rush."

Deena hesitated. "No. It's okay." Without looking at anyone in particular, she began talking in a low, halting voice.
At first she tried to gauge the other women's reactions to what
she was saying; gradually, though, she found her initial awkwardness disappearing. It was easier, she realized with some
surprise, to talk to these women whom she'd met less than
an hour ago than to people whom she'd known for years.

The four women listened with rapt attention, making no
attempts to fill the pauses in Deena's narrative. Miriam and
Magda sighed occasionally; Faye nodded in silent understanding; Elaine kept time with the rhythmic swinging of her
leg, which stopped only when Deena told them about Jake's
affair.

"Kenny was cheating on me, too," Elaine said quietly.
"With my best friend, as a matter of fact."

"Is that who he married?" Deena asked.

"You got it. Nice and neat, right?" Elaine's smile was
painful to see. "Your Jake sounds like a charmer, just like
Kenny. Good-looking, huh? Sexy?"

Deena nodded. "But we had a lot in common, too." Why
was she defending herself again?

Elaine raised an eyebrow. "Yeah, right." She grinned.
"Listen, honey, I've been there. I was taken in by good looks,
too, and look where it got me. They're all bastards, you know
that? For my money, they can all go to hell."

"Elaine, calm down," Miriam said.

"Why? That's why we're here, isn't it? To express our
feelings? Well, I'm angry, dammit. You are, too, but you just
don't want to admit it.''

"Don't tell me how I feel."

"I'm angry," Faye admitted. "I just don't know where to
direct my anger. My husband can't give me a *get*, even if he
wanted to," she told Deena.

"Rabbi Markowitz told me about it. You seem so calm."

"I wasn't calm eleven years ago." She smiled wryly. "I ranted at my in-laws, my rabbi, parents, friends. I blamed everyone, probably because I didn't know whom to blame."

"What happened, exactly?"

"Alex had a complete breakdown, lost touch with reality. Oh, I knew after the first year that he needed professional help. He was always suspicious—constantly accused me of cheating on him, of keeping him from being a success by undermining his confidence. I finally convinced him to see a psychiatrist by threatening to leave him unless he did."

"What did the doctor say?"

"That Alex was disturbed and his condition would probably deteriorate. He was right. Alex accused me of poisoning his food so I could be with my 'lover.' He wouldn't eat anything I prepared unless I tasted it first in front of him. He opened my mail. He had the phone tapped. He started sleeping in the spare room, locking the door so I couldn't come in during the night. It was horrible and pathetic."

"But why did you stay with him? I'm sorry," Deena said quickly. "I didn't mean—"

"It sounds so clear now, right?" Faye shook her head. "My in-laws convinced me that under a doctor's care, Alex would improve. They said only a heartless woman would leave a sick husband. I felt guilty—after all, it wasn't something he was doing intentionally. So I stayed. And by the time I decided I couldn't take any more, it was too late. Alex tried to kill himself, and his parents had to commit him. That's when I found out he couldn't legally give me the *get.*"

No one spoke.

"You're wonderful," Miriam said, breaking the silence. "You're an inspiration to all of us. I admire your courage."

"I'm no saint, Miriam. My faith hasn't survived intact the way yours has. Most of the time, I'm just resigned."

"Well, I have no intention of waiting eleven years," Elaine said. "And I won't give in to Kenny's demands. Hell, I can't afford to. I can barely pay my bills as it is."

"You have no choice," Miriam said. "None of us do."

"Maybe you don't, Miriam, but I'm giving this thing two more months, tops. I'm sorry I waited this long. If the rabbis don't get Kenny to cooperate, and I meet someone who wants to marry me, well, then, to hell with the *get.*"

"You don't mean that!" Miriam exclaimed. "You'd be cut off from the Jewish people for eternity."

"I sure as hell do meant it! I've been waiting till now only because the *get* is so important to my parents. But it's my life, dammit, and I'm not going to waste it because of some religious law! If the rabbis want me to stay pure, why the hell don't they do something to help me?"

"They're trying, Elaine," Miriam said.

"Why don't they just change the damn law?"

"You know that's impossible," Faye said. "We've been over this so many times. Only a *beth din* greater in number and in stature than the *Sanhedrin* of the Second Temple—the Jewish Supreme Court—can do that."

Elaine grunted. "I don't care about the past, Faye. I'm concerned about my future. Two more months, and then—"

"But aren't you afraid of the consequences?" Deena asked. "I know I am."

"Listen, you've just started this waiting game, honey. Why don't you sit around for a year and see how you feel?"

Deena flushed. "I'm sorry. It's none of my business."

"Don't apologize," Faye said. "We have to be honest with each other, or there's no point in meeting. Right, Elaine?"

"Right, right. Forget what I said, Deena. Anyway, who knows? Maybe your husband will have a change of heart."

"There's always hope," Miriam insisted. "Sometimes it's hard for us to understand God's ways, but we can't give up."

Elaine rolled her eyes dramatically. "Why don't you tell that to Faye, Miriam. Maybe in another eleven years she'll be able to marry. With her luck, though, Alex will live till the proverbial hundred and twenty. Unless she gives Nature a little push."

"Don't talk like that!" Miriam said. "Faye is upset, but she certainly doesn't want Alex dead."

"Come off it, Miriam!" Elaine said. "Are you saying you never wished Mordechai dead? Not even for a second?"

"It's wrong." She shook her head. "It's a sin."

"It's human. I think about it all the time. And I don't use a dart board. I use a gun." Elaine lifted her right hand, aimed at the wall. "Bam! Bam! Bam! He's gone."

"I do it in one shot," Susan said. "Right in his chest."

Elaine looked thoughtful. "I could do it in one shot, but I like three. One from me, one from each of the kids."

"This is fantasy hour," Faye said to Deena. She sounded uncomfortable. "We're really very civilized."

"Fantasizing is healthy, Faye," Elaine said. "Any shrink will tell you that. Magda, it's your turn."

Magda smiled but shook her head.

"Come on, Magda. Get out your aggressions. You won't be hurting anyone. Try it."

"Sometimes . . . sometimes, I use my hands, around Yossif's neck." Her tone was matter-of-fact as she pantomimed. "Other times, I have him hanging from a rope."

"That's good!" Elaine said. "I think—"

"A car crash." The words were a whisper.

Everyone turned to stare at Miriam.

"Mordechai is in the car—alone, of course. It's late at night, and there are no other cars on the road. He's driving down a mountain, and suddenly, the brakes fail, and he drives off a cliff." Her eyes looked somewhere in the distance.

Elaine started to say something, but stopped.

Susan asked, "Faye, do you ever think about Alex dying?"

"All the time," she admitted. "The first few years, my imagination was more ghoulish." She smiled. "Now I just pretend that I get a phone call from the hospital telling me that Alex died in his sleep. Not that it's going to happen."

"Well, if you need a little help, Faye, just let me know," Elaine said. "I mean, what's a support group for, right?" She grinned.

"It sounds depressing," Michael told Deena later that night. He'd come over after Deena had returned from the meeting. "Maybe I shouldn't have encouraged you to go."

"It was and it wasn't. All the women have grim stories, but they *are* surviving. And there have been a few successes. Rabbi Markowitz was right, you know. It *does* help to talk to people who really understand what you're going through."

"Meaning that I don't?" He looked troubled.

"Of course you do, Michael. You've been wonderful." She kissed him. "But you can't know what it means to be manipulated like this, to be under someone's control. It's demeaning, infuriating. Sometimes, when I don't see any end in sight, it's terrifying."

"I'm not in your shoes; I know that. But I'm as impatient as you are. If you had your *get,* we could talk about a future together. Right now it's pointless."

"Michael, you know I'm not ready to make a commitment. I'm attracted to you. I love being with you. But I can't trust my feelings. Look what happened the last time I did! I intend to think carefully before I marry again—if I ever can. And one thing is certain—I'd have a prenuptial agreement with a liquidated damages clause.''

''You're worried about money?'' He sounded puzzled.

She shook her head. ''It's not about money, Michael. It's to prevent this whole *get* situation. Rabbi Markowitz told me about it. Basically, if either spouse refuses to end the marriage according to Jewish law, the victimized spouse gets monetary damages because she—or he—can't enter into a new marriage, which could be financially advantageous. It could be hundreds of dollars a day, until the situation is resolved.''

''Is that legal?''

''Rabbi Markowitz said it's been upheld by civil courts. He won't perform a wedding unless the bride and groom sign this agreement.''

''Not very romantic, is it? Thinking about divorce at the wedding?''

''That's what I said to Rabbi Markowitz. But he pointed out that my situation isn't exactly romantic.''

''Not exactly,'' Michael agreed. ''So okay, we'll sign this prenuptial agreement. I have no problem with that.''

''I told you, Michael. I want to go slowly.''

''I hear you. As a psychologist, I'd have to say that your caution is well-advised.'' He smiled. ''But as a man who's interested in spending the rest of his life with you, well, I'm not exactly happy.''

''Even if I do decide we're right for each other, by the time I have my *get*, we'll be eligible for Social Security.''

''Then I guess I'll have to speed things along.''

''Michael! I don't want you talking to Jake! If he knew we were dating—''

''Okay. You're probably right. But I'm not going to let Jake ruin our lives. I'll think of something.''

She kissed Michael good night and was halfway to her bedroom when she heard the doorbell ring.

''What did you forget this time?'' she asked with amused disapproval as she opened the door. Last time it had been car keys.

Two men were standing under the glare of the porch light. One of them, wearing steel-rimmed glasses, faced her; the other looked casually around him and fixed his eyes on a spot down the street. Deena had never seen them before.

"Yes?" A faint hint of menace clung like fine lint to their expensive-looking suits. Instinctively, she wanted to shut the door.

"We'd like to speak to Mr. Vogler." The one with the glasses spoke with a quiet, even tone.

"Mr. Vogler doesn't live here anymore." Who *were* these men? She started to close the door, but he stopped it with his foot.

"Is that right? Well, where exactly does he live?"

"Please leave."

"Hey, Ed," he said to his companion, "the lady's shy." He moved closer to Deena. "You can tell us. We're his friends."

"I don't know where he lives. Why—why don't you call him tomorrow at his office?"

He smiled. "Now that would be a fine idea, Mrs. Vogler, but we've been trying him there for weeks. Wouldn't you know it? He's never around. Isn't that right, Ed?"

Ed smiled lazily without answering.

"I want you to leave," Deena repeated, more firmly this time. "This has nothing to do with me. We're divorced."

"Oh, yeah? Well, I bet the divorce wasn't his idea." He eyed her appreciatively. "If I were married to a pretty thing like you, I wouldn't let you get away. Getting a little lonely, Mrs. Vogler? I can help you pass the time." He reached for her cheek.

She flinched. "Get out! I'll call the police!" It was an idle threat, she realized. He would certainly stop her before she reached the phone. And then he'd be in the house. She felt fear twisting inside her stomach.

He laughed. "Not in the mood tonight, huh? Maybe another time. Tell you what you can do for me—just as a favor, of course. Tell your ex-husband that James Murdoch doesn't appreciate having his messages unanswered. It annoys him, you know what I mean? And it really isn't a good idea to get Mr. Murdoch annoyed. Will you tell him that for me, Mrs. Vogler?"

Murdoch! She hadn't thought about the steely-eyed business magnate in over a year. The Prince of Darkness, Jake had always called him. "I'll try to reach my ex-husband," she managed to whisper.

"Good girl. Well, it's been a pleasure, Mrs. Vogler. Come on, Ed. The lady has to get her beauty sleep." He turned to

Deena. "Tell your ex to get in touch, Mrs. Vogler. And tell him not to take too long. And by the way—I wouldn't open the door to strangers if I were you. You never know what could happen. Nighty-night."

Suddenly, he removed his foot from the threshold. Deena heard him laugh as she shoved the door shut and turned the deadbolt with trembling hands. She leaned against the closed door for a minute, breathing heavily, trying not to cry. When she was calmer, she searched through her purse for the card Jake had given her when he'd moved into an apartment. She dialed the number written on the card.

"Hello?"

"Jake, it's Deena. I—"

"No kidding! Yours is the last voice I expected to hear tonight—or, for that matter, any night."

"I have to talk to you."

"Let me guess: You thought it over and decided you can't live without me. Fatal attraction, right?"

"Jake, be serious. Murdoch sent some men here. They scared me half to death!"

"What are you talking about?"

"He didn't know you'd moved out. He's furious because you're not returning his calls. What's going on, Jake? I have a right to know!"

"It's nothing to worry about."

"You didn't see these men! They hinted that if you don't get in touch with Murdoch immediately, something will happen to you."

"Calm down. You don't know what's involved. I do. Murdoch's upset because his money's been tied up so long."

"Isn't that shopping mall done yet? It's been about two years since you started the project, hasn't it?"

"A little over that. But that syndication deal was cursed from the start. Remember all those construction delays? Rotten weather, poor foundation, delayed permits, increased costs down the line—we had one problem after another. But I convinced Murdoch that the mall was going to make him a fortune."

"So?"

"So now, just when all the problems seem to be ironed out—this new general contractor is really on the ball—Murdoch wants out. He's willing to take a loss on the money spent in preconstruction, but he wants to sell his shares. His lawyer wants us to prepare all the books for an audit.''

"What's wrong with that? Just do it and be rid of him.''

"Ben feels—and I guess he makes sense—that we won't be able to sell the rest of the shares as easily if Murdoch pulls out. His name carries a lot of weight.''

"But how can you stop him?''

"We can't. Ben wants to stall until we sell the rest of the shares to cover the increased costs. I have no idea how long that will take. We could find some interested party tomorrow, or it could take a few weeks. Longer, maybe. That's why I haven't been returning Murdoch's calls.''

"You can't avoid him, Jake. He's not stupid. And he won't sit around waiting. Why don't you explain everything to him the way you did to me? Maybe he'll be understanding.''

"Murdoch? Are you kidding?'' He laughed.

Jake was right, she admitted to herself. James Murdoch's reputation for ruthlessness was well-known. From the first time Deena had met him when she was working for Kasden and Vogler, Realtors, she'd been unnerved by his imperiousness and icy demeanor.

"But you can't stall him forever, Jake.''

"I know. Listen, I'm not thrilled about getting all the shit from Murdoch. Unfortunately, as far as he's concerned, I'm responsible, not Ben.''

"I think he means business, Jake. Call him.''

"Do I detect a note of concern in your voice, Deena?''

"I'm concerned about my safety. I don't want another visit from Murdoch's men!''

"Murdoch is my problem, not yours. They probably won't bother you again.''

" 'Probably' isn't good enough. When will you call him?''

"Not yet.''

"Why not?''

"Look, don't tell me how to run my business, okay, Deena? I've managed without your help till now. By the way, how are you? Enjoying the single life?''

"I'm hanging up, Jake. Good night.'' She shouldn't have warned Jake about Murdoch's men, she decided. She should have driven them over to Jake's apartment. And watched.

"Just don't have *too* good a time, Deena. Remember, you're still a married woman. I wouldn't want you to have any cardinal sins on your conscience.''

Even after she slammed the phone down, his smug laughter echoed in her ears. Some day he would pay for what he was doing to her. And she would relish every moment.

Later, as she was trying to fall asleep, she thought about Elaine and Magda and Susan and Faye, each with her own death script. Even Miriam had one.

Pick a fantasy. Any fantasy.

Deena lay back and closed her eyes.

4

A FAMILIAR WHITE CADILLAC WAS PARKED IN FRONT OF Deena's house when she pulled into her driveway after work. What was Ben doing here? she wondered as she took her briefcase and got out of her car.

In a minute, Ben was at her side. "You look great, Deena. Just great!" He beamed and hugged her tightly.

She thought again how much she liked Jake's partner.

"He's a character," her father had told her before she began working at Kasden and Vogler, Realtors. "Always joking. His mother was a patient in the home. A lovely woman, she should rest in peace. I've had business dealings with him, and always he's a gentleman. A *mensch*. But he's a character."

Max Novick had been right about Ben Kasden, too.

Ben was in his late forties, short—about five-foot-seven—had tufts of graying brown hair in sparse fringes around protruding ears, and had a large, bulbous, red-veined nose that dominated a cherubic face. He was almost completely round, and from the first time Deena had met him two years ago, whenever she saw him, she thought of Humpty Dumpty.

"So no smile?" Ben asked now. "No kiss? Aren't you glad to see me?"

"Of course. I'm sorry." She hugged him quickly. "You just surprised me, Ben. Let's go inside."

It had been almost a year since she'd seen Ben. When she'd

been married to Jake, she'd stopped at the Century City realty firm offices all the time. The visits had stopped with the breakup of the marriage. At first, Ben had called frequently—"How are you, Deena?" "Anything I can do for you, Deena?" His concern and affection had been genuine, but Deena had sensed his awkwardness and hadn't been surprised or hurt when the phone calls tapered off. After all, Ben was Jake's partner and friend, had been both long before he met Deena.

Ben followed her into the living room and sat on the peach cotton brocade couch. It was a wedding gift from Jake's parents, and aside from a travertine-based glass coffee table, it was the only furniture in the room.

"So let me look at you," Ben said.

"Is anything wrong, Ben?" She sat next to him.

"What could be wrong? I just miss seeing your pretty face. So how are you doing, Deena? Considering everything, I mean." His tone was suddenly hushed, somber. He drummed his fingers on his knees and glanced around the room.

"I'm okay." Poor Ben. He looked so uncomfortable. Had Jake sent him here? she wondered suddenly. And if so, for what reason? To convince Deena to reconcile? To negotiate a settlement? "Ben, what's up? I can see it in your face. Something *is* wrong, isn't it?"

"Not exactly *wrong.*" He drew out the word. "I have a little problem I hope you can help me with. No big deal."

So it wasn't Jake. Relief coursed through her. "If I can help you, I will."

"Terrific! The thing is, your lawyer called today. She wants to look at the books. She took me by surprise, Deena. I thought you were giving up your interest in the business."

"That was before, when I thought Jake would be reasonable. A lot has happened since then. I can't go into it."

"Well, I hope you know what you're doing." He laughed. "I told you before, this business can be a headache. Sometimes I think I should get out of it myself."

"I don't necessarily want to be an active partner, Ben. But my lawyer says we have to assess what my share is worth."

"Fine, fine. No problem. You're entitled. The thing is, we're terribly busy right now—thank God, right?—and I don't have time to go over all the entries with an accountant."

"I don't think it's a big project, Ben. A good accountant can figure everything out without much help from you."

"It's not just that." He paused. "It's Murdoch."

"Murdoch!" Deena shuddered. Almost two weeks had passed, but she still had nightmares about the visit from his men.

"I'm sorry," he said quickly. "You must hate hearing his name. Jake told me what happened. Deena, I feel terrible you had to go through that! You know, you should get an alarm or something, living alone the way you do. Not that I think you have to worry about another visit from Murdoch. But still."

"I already took care of it."

"I hope you got hot screens. That way, you can open the windows without triggering the alarm. That's what we have."

"I didn't get an alarm, Ben. I have a gun."

"A gun?" He stared at her. "You could get hurt, Deena. Your dad knows about this?"

"It's his gun. After what happened, he thought I should have one. But don't worry; I'm going to take lessons. I don't want to panic and shoot myself in the leg." She smiled.

"I should hope not! So where are you going to keep it, on the coffee table? It'll make a hell of a conversation piece, I'll give you that." He laughed.

"Actually, it's in my nightstand. Anyway, enough about that. You didn't come to talk about guns."

"No kidding! So where were we?" He frowned.

"Murdoch?"

"Yeah, Murdoch. How could I forget? Anyway, he's been popping into the office—I never know when he'll be there. And I don't want him to start wondering about the firm because some guy is poking around the books."

"Ben, there's no way to avoid an audit. You know that."

"Who said anything about avoiding it? I thought you could postpone it for three, four months. The pressure will be off by then, and the Murdoch problem should be solved one way or another. Jake convinced him to give us through November to sell the syndication shares on our own."

"It's okay with me, but you'll have to call my lawyer. Tell her I won't object if she postpones the audit."

"Actually, I did call. She agreed to wait two months, till the end of October." He paused. "But that's not long enough. I thought you could convince her, Deena. I don't really want to discuss my business with her. I'd rather keep it just between us—you know, friend to friend." He smiled.

"I can't tell her how to do her job, Ben. She wouldn't listen anyway. She's *very* independent." Why was Ben so worried about an audit—was there something he wasn't telling her? Immediately, she felt guilty at the thought. She had never known Ben to be anything less than honest.

"But you're the client, right? Why should she object to waiting a few months? You don't have a court date, do you?"

"No, not as far as I know. But she may see an angle I don't. I'm sorry, Ben; I'll have to leave the decision to her. I hope you're not upset."

"No, no. Don't worry. I told you, it's no big deal."

There was an awkward silence.

"How's Ruthie?" Deena said. "Still spending your life savings?"

Ruth Kasden's expensive taste had been a constant joke among Ben, Jake, and Deena. "She signs credit cards in her sleep," Jake had told Deena. "I met her at a slave auction," Ben had said. "I was the slave." But Deena knew that behind the joking, Ben loved his wife very much.

"Ruthie? She's okay." He sounded distant. "By the way, I have some papers for you to sign, some quarterly tax stuff. I forgot to bring them. I'll stop by in a couple of days; that way, you . . . uh . . . don't have to come to the office."

She squeezed his hand. "That's thoughtful of you, Ben. And I'd love to see you again."

"Right." He stood up. "Well, I'll say good night, then. I hope everything works out for you, Deena."

She waited at the door while he maneuvered himself onto the front seat of the Cadillac. She waved goodbye, but he didn't notice. Deena closed the door and sighed. Ben had always been kind to her; she hated to disappoint him now.

To Deena, time seemed to be passing with deliberate slowness. The *beth din* had finally reviewed her case and issued the first summons, but she knew that was only a start. Be patient, Rabbi Markowitz kept telling her, and she was trying her best. School had started, and she was grateful for the routine of classes and the seemingly endless homework. They gave her life a façade of normalcy and occupied her hours, keeping her from staring at the phone all day, waiting for it to ring with good news.

She had finally made some phone calls and reestablished contact with some of her friends. She'd started playing tennis again, too. And she'd attended two more sessions with the group, one at Susan's house, another at Magda's. Talking was therapeutic, and she enjoyed getting to know the other women, but each time, she came away more saddened than cheered, discouraged by the bleakness not only of her situation but that of her new friends.

And then, finally, there *was* good news: The *beth din* had issued a *seruv* and declared Jake "one who refuses to listen."

"Normally, they wait about thirty days between each summons," Reuben Markowitz explained, "but in this case they issued all three within two weeks. You have no idea how lucky you are."

"That's terrific! How did you get them to do it?"

"Apparently, Jake made it clear that he has no intention of appearing before the *beth din* or giving you the *get*. He did you a favor, Deena. Now we can take community action."

"I'll send him a thank-you note." But she was excited. "So what do we do first?"

"I organized a picket for tomorrow morning in front of Jake's realty offices. And we're sending out letters to the community. But you have to be realistic, Deena," he cautioned. "Don't expect Jake to call tomorrow night and beg you to accept the *get*. By the way, I saw Jake."

"When?" She was startled.

"A few days ago. I waited around his apartment until he came home. At first he wouldn't talk to me, but I convinced him he had nothing to lose."

"Was he difficult?"

"Not at all. He was very smooth, extremely polite. I can see how people can find him charming. But he's adamant about not giving you the *get*. The bottom line is that he's angry with what he sees as your betrayal."

"He's crazy!"

"You'd better hope not! Just kidding," he added hastily. "He's obsessed with the idea of punishing you. I'm hoping that with time and a little persuasion—friendly or not so friendly, that's up to him—he'll come around. He turned down your father's offer, you know."

"What offer?" She frowned. "What are you talking about?"

"I'm sorry." Markowitz sounded uncomfortable. "I assumed you knew. Your father came to me. He wanted me to approach Jake on his behalf. He didn't think he could handle it himself.''

"Handle what?"

"He wants to offer Jake a cash settlement for the *get*.''

"Oh, God!" She closed her eyes.

"He's determined to help you. He's extremely worried about you and how this situation is affecting your mother. That's why I'm so pleased that the *beth din* is taking an aggressive stand.''

She tensed. "What did Jake say?"

"He told me to tell your father that the *get* wasn't for sale, not at any price. He seemed to enjoy the idea that your father had come begging to him, so to speak.''

"I can imagine. Did you tell my father what Jake said?"

"No. I told him Jake's thinking it over. Frankly, I'm concerned about your father. He's under tremendous pressure, and I don't want to dash his hopes. That might make him feel more desperate than he already does.''

She felt a throbbing pain at her temples. "What are you trying to tell me?"

He hesitated. "Nothing specific. But when you talk to him, if you can't be optimistic, try to play down your negative feelings. And try not to increase his hostility toward Jake.''

That night, she lay awake in bed for hours. All she could think about was her father's desperation and her mother's deteriorating condition. Both her fault.

In the morning she called Brenda DiSalvo.

"Tell Jake I'll waive all my rights in exchange for the *get*,'' Deena told the attorney. "Give him everything. The business, the house, the furniture. The damn dishes.''

"You are completely out of your mind! You don't know what the hell you're doing! My fees are thousands of dollars, and don't expect me to feel sorry and return one damn cent!''

"I'm sorry. I know how hard you've worked to get me a decent settlement, Brenda. I know you don't understand. I can hardly believe I'm doing this! But I don't see any options. Will you take care of it right away?"

"Deena, come on.'' Her tone was softer. "Don't do this. You're playing right into Jake's hands, can't you see that?"

"I just want to get this over with, Brenda. The money isn't worth it. Or the house. None of it is.'' Not at the expense of her parents' welfare.

"Just be a little patient. He'll come around.''

"My mind is made up. Please call Jake's lawyer."

Brenda sighed. "It's your funeral, Deena."

"You did the right thing," Michael assured her at dinner several nights later. He had taken her out to an expensive restaurant to lift her spirits. "At least now you know I don't love you for your money."

"Very funny," Deena said glumly. "I feel raped."

"In a few years this won't mean much. What's important is that Jake will give you the *get*, and we can get married."

"I haven't said yes yet."

"You can't shoot a guy for being optimistic, can you?"

A smile lit up Deena's face, then disappeared. She was rigid with tension.

"What is it?" Michael asked. "You look so strange." He swiveled around, followed the direction of her gaze. He turned back. "Jake?"

She nodded, unable to speak. A few moments later, Jake stood at their table, grinning malevolently.

"How romantic! Aren't you going to introduce me, Deena?"

"Ignore him," Deena said quietly to Michael.

"Is this the steady, or one of a string of charmers?"

She noticed with embarrassment that nearby diners had stopped talking and were listening intently to Jake.

"You're making a nuisance of yourself," Michael said. "Why don't you leave before there's any trouble?"

"Cool guy, huh? Must be the yarmulke that gives you that edge. Is that what turns you on, Deena? A skullcap? Maybe I should have worn it to bed. You might have performed better."

"You're a poor excuse for an adult, Vogler. You need professional help."

"Oh, yeah? Are you an expert or something?"

"As a matter of fact, I'm a psychologist. If you like, I can recommend someone."

"And get a kickback, no doubt."

"Hardly. Just think of it as a community service. Right now you're a menace to everyone, especially yourself."

"Very fancy analysis. Do you know you're playing doctor with a married woman? Did little Deena tell you that? Or maybe you like getting it on with married women, is that it?"

Michael moved his chair back and stood across the table from Jake. "Listen, Vogler—"

"Michael, please!" Deena pulled his arm.

"Yeah, Michael, please!" Jake mimicked in falsetto. "Shrinks aren't supposed to lose their cool."

With a visible effort, Michael controlled himself. "You're right. I'm going to call the maitre d'."

"Pretty classy. 'I'm going to call the maitre d'.' Where'd you pick up that line? In some Audrey Hepburn movie? Well, I hate to break it to you, but you're no Cary Grant. You want to call the maitre d'? I'll give you something to complain about. This one is for messing around with my wife!"

He lunged across the table and launched his fist toward Michael's face. Deena screamed. Michael ducked, but the blow glanced his cheek. Jake slid over the table, dragging the cloth and everything on it with him as he landed on the floor.

There was the sound of shattering china and glassware. A waiter hurried away. Deena heard a solitary gasp, then waves of exclamations and a crescendo of murmurs. *This isn't happening,* she told herself. She was trembling, her face bleached of color.

"Get your purse," Michael told her quietly. His cheek was red and beginning to swell.

Jake stood up and brushed himself off. He was grinning.

The waiter had returned with another man wearing a three-piece suit and an anxious expression. The manager, Deena decided.

"I'm terribly sorry about this," the man told Michael. "Let me have someone get some ice for your face."

"Forget it," Michael said. "We'd like to leave now. I'll take care of the bill at the front."

"Leaving so soon?" Jake said.

The manager frowned at Jake, then turned to Michael. "There's no charge for tonight, sir. I hope you'll come back and allow us to make amends." To Deena, he said, "Of course, we'll cover the cost of cleaning your dress."

She looked down. The green silk was splattered with sauce and pasta. She hadn't even noticed.

The manager glanced at Jake. "I'll have to ask you to step into my office to discuss the damages."

"No problem. It was worth it." He grinned at Michael.

"It's only round one." He turned to Deena. "And I'm like a cat, honey. I have nine lives."

"Not if I can help it," Michael informed him calmly.

The ringing of the phone woke her up. Deena turned on the light on her nightstand and saw the time: one A.M. She was annoyed, then suddenly alarmed. What if something was wrong with Pearl?

She grabbed the receiver. "Hello?"

No answer. But someone was on the line. She could hear heavy breathing. "Who is this?"

"Just a friend, Mrs. Vogler," the voice whispered.

"Tell me who this is, or I'm hanging up!"

"Don't you remember me, Mrs. Vogler? I remember you."

Murdoch's man? But why? "What do you want? I told you last time; I have nothing to do with my ex-husband."

"I know. That's what he said, too. I thought you might be bored, or lonely. *Are* you lonely, Mrs. Vogler?"

"Please leave me alone!" She wanted to hang up, but some horrible fascination was keeping her glued to the phone.

"Are you wearing anything? I kind of picture you in bed, in something black and sexy and very, very sheer. Maybe I could come over right now, keep you company. Would you like that, Mrs. Vogler?"

"I have a gun! If you come near me, I'll use it!" She touched her nightstand to reassure herself of the gun's presence.

"I'm hurt, Mrs. Vogler. Really hurt. And here I was just trying to be friendly. Your ex-husband thought it was a good idea. He warned me that you might be shy at first."

"I don't believe you!"

He laughed. "I guess you don't believe I'm that bad, huh?"

It was Jake! "You bastard! You scared me half to death!"

"I just wanted you to see what it feels like to be harassed, honey The picket your rabbi organized? The letters? It's not going to work, Deena."

"What letters?"

"The ones you and your cronies mailed out, discussing our situation. My mother got one. So did a lot of her friends. She called me up a few hours ago, hysterical."

"Didn't they spell your name right? I'm *so* sorry."

"Don't involve her in this, Deena. It's between the two of us. And tell Max to stop his goddamn interference! He calls every day, sometimes more than once. At the office, at home. He even called a couple of clients, told them not to do business with me. Can you believe that?''

''Pretty soon everyone's going to know the truth about you, Jake. If Ben's smart, he'll get rid of you.''

''Ben thinks your father's nuts. I'm warning you: If Max doesn't lay off, I'll file a complaint. I'll tell the police he's harassing me, causing me loss of income.''

''Fine. Don't forget to tell them you're blackmailing me.''

''You think I'm kidding, don't you? I swear I'll have them put him in a cell! You can take kosher food along when you visit him. Maybe they'll put your boyfriend in an adjoining cell, if he gives me any trouble. Everybody in the restaurant heard him threaten me.''

''You're crazy, you know that, Jake? You should be committed.''

''So your boyfriend told me. Is he there right now, Deena, in my bed? Is he tracing Rorschachs all over your tingling body, peeling away the many layers of your consciousness, probing the mysteries of your mind? Or is that what he calls it in psychological terms?''

She slammed the receiver down. Less than a minute later, the phone started to ring again. She picked up the receiver and replaced it quickly, disconnecting the call. Then she lifted the receiver and left it off the hook. After a minute of shrill, staccato beeps, there was blessed silence.

5

''AM I TOO EARLY?'' DEENA ASKED WHEN SHE ARRIVED AT Faye's house for the group meeting. ''I was a little restless tonight. I couldn't wait to get out of the house.''

And away from the phone. Jake had started calling her almost every night. Deena had asked Pacific Bell for a new, unlisted phone number, but there had been a series of delays. All compliments of Jake.

"You're right on time," Faye smiled. "The others should be here soon." She led Deena down a center hall to a family room. "Make yourself comfortable. I'll be right back."

Looking around the room, Deena was immediately struck with the canvases that filled the ecru walls. There was an occasional still life, but most of the works—some charcoal drawings, some watercolors—clearly belonged to a sepia-toned study of women performing various Jewish rituals. The faces were gaunt, the sculpted planes elongated with suffering, the staring eyes haunted with an inexpressible pain. The mouths, mere slashes, gave the impression of forced silence.

"These paintings are so poignant," Deena said when Faye returned, carrying a tray with fresh fruit. "Are they all by the same artist?" She examined the signature on one of the canvases. "These are yours?" Deena was awed.

"Do you like them?" Faye placed the tray next to the other refreshments on the glass table in front of a beige leather sectional sofa. "Maybe someday I'll paint lighter scenes, with pinks and sea greens and amethysts instead of these gloomy ochers and burgundies." She sounded wistful.

"They're wonderful, Faye. I wish I had that kind of talent. Have you thought of having a gallery show your work?"

"No." She shook her head vigorously. "This is too personal. I don't often have company, so not too many people have seen my work. But I'm glad you like it."

Deena sat on the sofa and poured Seven-Up into a cup.

Faye sat next to her. "How are your law school classes going? Are they interesting?"

"They're okay. I'm taking labor law, securities. A course in family law, too, which is pretty funny, I guess." Deena smiled. "It's better than last year. There's a saying about law school—the first year they scare you to death; the second year they work you to death; the third year they bore you to death." She smiled again. "I'm certainly not bored."

"I don't think I could do it." Faye shook her head.

"Actually, I love it. And not just because it keeps me from thinking about Jake." She stared at the bubbles in the plastic cup, then looked at Faye. "Do you think about it all the time? The *get,* I mean. I do. I even dream about it."

Sleep sometimes allowed Deena to forget, if only for a few hours. But sleep was a terrible tease, lulling her into a hazy realm of tranquillity; then morning, a grim-faced warden, slapped her awake. It was that first, piercing instant of remembering that she found so unbearable. The rest of the day, it receded into a dull, steady ache.

Faye smiled. "It's not something I can forget. But I try to keep busy. The painting helps. And I do volunteer work with children at Cedars-Sinai four times a week. My in-laws have been very generous with their guilt money." There was a touch of bitterness beneath the amusement in her light laugh. "I love the kids; they're so special. I just wish I had my own. Over the years, I've thought about adopting, but agencies don't look favorably on single parents, and my mother and in-laws discouraged me."

It isn't too late, Deena wanted to say; but she couldn't. Even if Faye got her *get* tomorrow, she was probably too old to conceive.

"How old do you think I am?" Faye asked suddenly.

It was as if Faye had read her thoughts. Deena raised the cup to her face to mask her blush. "I have no idea."

"I'm thirty-nine. But I look older, don't I?"

"Not really." But it was true. Faye looked closer to fifty. Her fair skin was etched with a network of lines around thin lips and faded blue eyes, and her whole being, unnaturally thin, seemed sapped of energy.

"You're being kind. Unfortunately, the mirror isn't." She sighed. "I had a miscarriage, you know, a year after we were married. Alex accused me of having an abortion because I knew that paternity tests would show that the baby wasn't his." She looked at Deena. "You know the worst thing? I was relieved when I miscarried. I kept thinking what a miserable life the baby would have. Now I'm sorry. At least I'd have somebody to love."

The doorbell rang.

"Saved by the bell." Faye smiled. "I'm sorry, Deena. I didn't mean to put a damper on the evening." She left the room and returned with Magda, Miriam, Elaine, and Susan.

"Deena!" Elaine said. "We were just talking about you."

"We met Jake," Susan explained quickly.

"Where?" Deena exclaimed. "In front of Faye's house?" Was he following her everywhere?

"What would he be doing here?" Elaine looked at Deena strangely. "Susan and I were having lunch at that new fish restaurant on Pico a few days ago. He was there."

"But how did you know it was Jake?" Deena asked her.

"I heard him being paged. Then I watched to see who

answered the page. By the way, Deena, Jake's even better-looking than you described him. Too bad he's such a shit. Sorry, Miriam!'' She shrugged an apology. ''Anyway, I couldn't resist going over and telling him what I thought of him. It felt good, almost like I was telling Kenny off.''

''Was he angry?'' Faye asked.

Elaine grinned. ''You could say that. He described in graphic terms what I could do with my opinion. I told him it was refreshing to see a blackmailer with such a refined vocabulary. He got nasty. I got nastier. I figured we have to help each other out, right?''

''All for one and one for all?'' Susan smiled.

''Right. The *get* busters.'' Elaine laughed, then suddenly frowned. ''I hope I didn't make things worse, Deena.''

''I doubt that things could get worse.'' Careful not to look at Miriam, she explained about Michael and described the confrontation in the restaurant.

''A boyfriend, huh?'' Elaine said. ''Naughty, naughty, Deena. So is he as sexy as Jake?''

''Elaine, come on.'' Faye shook her head.

''I was just teasing. Deena knows that.''

''Michael's a psychologist?'' Miriam asked. ''So now that he's met Jake, what's his professional opinion?''

''Professional?'' Deena grimaced. ''Lately, when the subject of Jake comes up, Michael is barely rational. Anyway, now Jake is harassing me with late-night phone calls, and he isn't returning my lawyer's calls.'' She sighed. ''I was so excited when Rabbi Markowitz told me that the *beth din* was on my side, that we could start taking action. Now I wonder if the picket was a mistake. I think it backfired.''

''It's not a mistake!'' Miriam insisted. ''Deena, that's *terrific* progress! It took a year before the *beth din* would even issue Mordechai the first summons! As far as what happened at the restaurant, it just shows that Jake's rattled. Don't you think so, Faye?''

''Yes, yes I do.''

''Miriam's right,'' Susan said. ''Concentrate on the positive. Take it one step at a time. You'll see; it'll work out. You just have to be patient.''

''Aren't you Miss Optimist tonight,'' Elaine remarked.

''Well . . .'' A smile played around Susan's lips.

''Well, what?''

''As a matter of fact, I have some good news, too. The

thing is—'' She stopped. "The thing is, Barry and I agreed on a settlement. He's giving me my *get*.''

"That's wonderful!'' Faye said. "Absolutely wonderful!'' She went to Susan and hugged her. Magda and Miriam did the same.

Elaine stared at Susan. "You didn't say a thing at lunch.''

"It just happened today. I figured I'd see you tonight.''

Deena hesitated—she didn't know Susan well—then went over, too. "You must be thrilled!'' She kissed Susan's cheek.

"I hope it happens for all of you soon.'' Susan grinned. "God, I'm so relieved that it's over!''

"I'm so happy for you,'' Miriam said. "We *all* are.'' She looked pointedly at Elaine, who hadn't left the couch.

Elaine was searching through her purse. "Shit!'' she muttered. "You don't have a cigarette, do you Faye?''

"No. Anyway, you quit, remember?''

"You're not my mother,'' Elaine snapped.

"What's bothering you, Elaine?'' Susan asked.

"Nothing.'' Her right leg swung rapidly back and forth. "I thought you'd be happy for me.''

"I am. Very happy. See?'' Her smile was exaggerated. "I'm delighted, Susan. In fact, I think we should throw you a *get* party. How about it, girls?''

"Stop it, Elaine,'' Faye warned quietly.

"We could use green as the theme color—for all the dollars that Susan's daddy is paying to save his little girl.''

"Shut up!'' Faye ordered.

"Why should I? You're all pretending to be thrilled, but you're all just as jealous as I am! You just don't have the guts to admit it!''

Miriam said, "Well, I *am* happy for Susan. I think it's encouraging for all of us. I really do.''

"Yeah, real encouraging! I've been in this mess almost twice as long as Susan has, and I'm not getting anywhere!''

"That's not my fault!'' Susan said quickly.

"I didn't say it was. Don't put words in my mouth.''

"But that's your implication. You're always talking about my father's money, making me sound like a spoiled princess.''

"If the shoe fits.''

"That's nasty, Elaine. I don't appreciate it.''

Miriam said, "Faye isn't reacting the way you are. She's been an *agunah* for eleven years.''

"Leave me alone, will you? You're such a goody-goody, Miriam, always so damn righteous. I'll bet you don't believe half the things you say! It's just some line you've memorized because you can't face reality."

"Elaine, I *am* happy for Susan. That doesn't mean I don't want the same happiness for myself. If I don't feel bitter, it's because my faith in God is strong. And if that bothers you— well, that's your problem. I'm not going to apologize for who I am or what I believe."

"Well, I don't have that faith. So what am *I* supposed to do?" She stood up. "I'm going home. I've had enough *support* for one night."

Faye said, "Leaving isn't the answer, Elaine. You have to work things out."

"I don't see the point. Everyone's against me."

"Come on," Faye urged. "Come on, Elaine," she repeated when Elaine made no move to sit down.

Elaine hesitated. "Fine," she said, and sat down and stared at the fireplace.

To Deena, the uncomfortable silence seemed endless, but no one made a move to interrupt it.

"Look, Susan," Elaine finally said. "I'm sorry I hurt your feelings, but I was just saying what everyone is thinking. I'm jealous, okay? I admit it."

Am I jealous? Deena wondered. It was an uncomfortable thought, one that she didn't want to deal with right now.

"I can understand that." Susan nodded. "I guess I would be, too. Maybe I didn't break the news too tactfully."

Elaine shook her head. "It isn't your fault. I know that." She sighed. "It's just that Kenny is being such a bastard, you know? I wish I had the money to pay him off. But I don't. And I wish I were younger. But I'm not. And I am so damn tired of waiting!" Her eyes filled with tears.

"I don't blame you, Elaine."

"I just took it out on you. I'm sorry. I really am."

"It'll happen for you, too, Elaine," Miriam said. "It will. Just hang in there, okay? Rosh Hashanah is next week. It's a new year. Hopefully, it'll bring good news for all of us."

Elaine shrugged.

"The *get* busters, right?" Susan said.

"Yeah, right." Elaine's tone was glum, but she smiled.

* * *

For Deena, the beginning of the Jewish new year had always been a solemn holiday, a time of serious introspection and self-evaluation. Her present situation made it almost grim.

At *shul,* Pearl sat alongside her, her face marked with an unhealthy pallor, and except for her mouth, which formed the familiar, ancient Hebrew words she was following in her prayer book, she was almost motionless. Her breathing was labored. Every now and then, when the wheezing became more pronounced, she used an inhalator that she kept in a bag at her feet.

"The doctor thinks it's asthma," Max told Deena. "Stress." Was that anger or pain in his voice? Both, she decided.

On Rosh Hashanah and on Yom Kippur, ten days later, Deena chanted with the congregation, asking God for a myriad of blessings: good health, especially for Pearl; peace of mind for her parents; freedom for herself—really one wish, wasn't it, since the three were inextricably intertwined? She wondered what Miriam and Faye and Magda and Elaine and all the nameless *agunot* all over the world were thinking. Did they voice the same prayers, year after year? Or did there come a point when they stopped asking?

When Yom Kippur was over, Deena broke her fast with her parents. Stay tonight, they urged, but she decided to go home. Maybe Michael would come over. She longed to see him. It had been difficult being apart during the holidays, but he'd attended services with his parents in the Valley.

Once home, she was hungry again, but there was little to eat. A few apples, half a cucumber, a bruised tomato, and the browning remains of an iceberg lettuce rattled in the bin; an almost empty carton of nonfat milk was holding a lonely vigil on the tempered glass upper shelf. Her refrigerator, she decided, was a metaphor for her life: bare and desolate.

She was debating whether to go to the market when the doorbell rang. Michael! she thought happily and hurried to the front door, but it was Joe Vogelanter, Jake's father.

Now what? she wondered, flushed with alternating rushes of surprise, wariness, and discomfort. But she opened the door and invited her former father-in-law into the living room. Be calm, she told herself. Don't let him upset you.

"You must be surprised to see me, Deena."

"Yes, I am." She hadn't seen him since the divorce was final. "Why don't you sit down, D—"

"Call me Joe. It's simpler." He smiled awkwardly, still standing. "I won't stay long. Ida thinks I went back to *shul.* I said I forgot my *tallis.* I don't want her to know about this."

"Please. Sit down." She sat stiffly on the couch, acutely aware that it was a wedding present from her in-laws.

He chose the other end. "You look fine. Pretty like always."

"Thank you." He looked older, she thought, shrunken somehow. She felt a flash of pity, then thought about her mother. Let Jake worry about his parents.

"You're managing all right?"

She nodded.

"You're not afraid, living alone? It's a big house."

"I'm fine." Where were his questions leading? Was he going to suggest that she take Jake back? Or maybe Jake had sent him to convince her to sell the house.

"I noticed outside the street lamp isn't so bright. Maybe bars would be a good idea. Or an alarm. It's a nice neighborhood, but nowadays, with so much crime . . ." His voice trailed off.

"Thanks so much for your concern." Her childlike satisfaction at the color that suddenly suffused his face was replaced by guilt. He isn't the enemy, she reminded herself. He's a seventy-three-year old retired grocery store owner who was always kind to you.

He studied his knuckles. "You're angry; you have a right. Today was Yom Kippur. I came to ask you to forgive me, Deena. All day I'm sitting in *shul,* fasting and praying, and it's no good. My lips are saying words, but my thoughts—" He looked at Deena. "All day, I'm thinking about you. Do you believe me?"

She nodded.

"I wanted to come before, but I didn't know what to say. And Ida—" He stopped. "I feel terrible about what happened. Terrible. Such hopes I had! The day I met you, I said, 'Jake is a lucky guy.' " He shook his head. "I love you like a daughter, Deena. I wanted—"

"How can you say you love me and let him blackmail me! How, Joe?"

He winced at the anger in her voice. "You think I didn't try to talk sense into Jake? 'Give her the *get,* Jake!' I said. 'How can you do this to Deena?' Again and again I talked to him, but he won't listen."

She waited.

"And Ida." He sighed. "Jake is everything to her. He convinced her he's doing the right thing. 'Deena will change her mind, Joe,' she told me. 'Sure they have problems, but why should they rush into divorce? Deena will come back.' "

"That's not going to happen."

"I know. You think I don't know? He had gold, and he threw it away."

"Can't you talk to her, Joe? Can't you show her there's no point to this? Maybe she can get him to cooperate."

"I tried fifteen, twenty times. I tried again last night. I told her we shouldn't have anything to do with Jake until he gives you the *get*." He shook his head. "She won't listen. And I'm not the bravest man in the world, God should forgive me. I can't go on fighting with her, even though I know I should."

What did he want her to say? 'It's okay, Joe; I understand, Joe'? Well, it wasn't, and she wasn't about to pretend that it was just to alleviate his guilt.

"I'll try again, Deena. But I'm not hopeful. Ida hears what she wants to hear."

"Did she hear that my mother is sick? That she's having a nervous breakdown because of Jake? Did she hear that my father is going crazy with worry? Why don't you tell her that, Joe!"

"I don't know what to say. What can I say? Jake is ruining your life, and we're not doing a thing to stop him." He started to cry and buried his face in his hands.

"Don't. Please don't." In spite of her anger, she felt pity. She leaned over and touched his shoulder. "I know it's hard, being in the middle. He's your son."

He took a handkerchief from his jacket pocket and wiped his eyes. "You're being kind. I don't deserve it." He rose slowly, replaced the handkerchief. "Well, I'd better be going. Ida will be suspicious."

She walked with him to the front door.

He stood in the doorway. "When Jake wasn't religious, I was upset, embarrassed, worried he would marry a girl who wasn't Jewish. But this? I'm ashamed of him, ashamed of myself because I'm here, asking you to understand, instead of helping you."

On an impulse, he drew Deena toward him. She stood, stiff in his awkward embrace, but didn't push him away.

"I'm sorry," he whispered tenderly. "So sorry. Not that it helps, I know. You need action, not words, right?"

He walked out of the circle of light into the enveloping darkness.

This time, the group was meeting at Deena's house. She shopped for groceries, tried to remember what the women liked, bought too much of everything. After she pulled into the driveway, she took out the bags, lined them up near the side entrance, and locked the car. With her keys in one hand, she picked up a bag and walked to the side door.

It was unlocked.

She stood rooted to the spot, not knowing whether to risk going in or run to a neighbor to phone the police. She listened for unusual sounds but heard none; she decided she was being silly. It was entirely possible that she'd left the door unlocked on her way out in the morning. Lately, she'd been forgetful about many things.

But she opened the door warily, ready to run at the slightest sign of an intruder. She walked stealthily through the house, and although she found nothing missing, she had the uneasy feeling that someone had been in her home. Had she left her bedroom lamp on? She didn't think so; then again, maybe she had. As the afternoon wore on, she calmed down, and by early evening she'd made up her mind to forget the entire incident. *It was nerves*, she realized. *Just nerves.*

Since the living room sofa provided the only seating, Deena brought in folding chairs from the hall closet and placed them in a semicircle facing the couch. She set out the refreshments on the coffee table. An assortment of cookies; a platter with strawberries and sliced melon, pineapple, and kiwi; soda and Perrier—*I guess that's enough*, she thought.

The doorbell rang at eight-ten. Someone was early. Maybe it was Faye. She and Deena had become close during the past few weeks. It was strange, Deena thought on her way to the door. Faye was fifteen years older than she was, but Deena felt more comfortable talking to her than she did with anyone else she knew. Except Michael. But that was different.

It was Jake, she saw through the privacy window.

"What do you want?" she asked through the closed door.

"My lawyer showed me your new offer a while ago. I want to come in and talk to you about it."

"There's nothing to talk about. You've won. Just tell your

lawyer to contact mine. As soon as you give me the *get*, I'll sign the settlement papers."

"I want to talk to you first. In person."

"I don't think that's a good idea."

"Forget it, then. No settlement." He started to leave.

"Why is everything a game to you?" she demanded.

He stopped. "It's not a game. But I'm not going to talk about it through a door. It's up to you."

Bastard, she thought. She opened the door. He walked past her into the living room and made himself comfortable on the couch.

"Having a party?" He poured himself some soda.

She didn't answer.

"The place looks good, Deena. A hell of a lot better than my furnished apartment."

"You're getting everything you want, Jake."

He took a cookie, tasted it. "Home-baked, huh? Miss American housewife. So how's the psychologist?"

"You said you wanted to discuss the settlement. Let's stick to that." Don't rise to his bait, she told herself.

"I knew for a long time that you were going out with someone. I used to drive by the house in the evenings to see if you were in. I followed you to the restaurant, you know."

"Nothing you do surprises me, Jake."

"Even so," he continued as if he hadn't heard her, "it was a shock seeing you, with another guy. It blew me away. I guess I overreacted in the restaurant, huh?"

"If that's an apology, I accept. Let's just get on with it, Jake. I want to end this once and for all."

He looked up at her and smiled. "Okay. Let's do that."

She sat on a folding chair facing him. "Did you look at the offer? I've waived my rights to everything—the house, the business, the furniture. All I want is my *get.*"

"I've been thinking about your offer for a few weeks, you know. It really puzzled me."

"Why? I thought you'd be thrilled."

"Well, that's just it. I asked myself, 'Why is Deena giving up everything all of a sudden?' Good question, right?"

"Because this is wearing me down, Jake. My parents are a wreck; I'm a wreck."

"So then I asked myself, why is she in such a rush?" His voice was tinged with amusement. "I thought about it, and I thought about your boyfriend, and I figured it out. You don't give a shit about the house or anything because you plan to get married the minute I give you that *get,* don't you?''

"That's not true. I'm not engaged."

"Let's not quibble about words, Deena. I've seen you lots of times. Dining together. Grocery shopping together. Real cozy. What else are you doing together, huh, Deena? I'll bet it's not something they taught you in Hebrew school."

"It's none of your—" She stopped. "Jake, I don't want to fight. You've won. Just take the money and everything else and let's both get on with our lives."

"You know what else I wondered? I wondered how long you've known this guy. I mean, could you have known him months ago? Maybe even a year ago? Maybe you've been playing me for a fool. Miss holier-than-thou Deena, a married woman, screwing around."

"You're wrong. And we never went out before the civil divorce was final."

"Right." His voice was heavy with sarcasm.

"It's true!"

"Makes no difference. If he wasn't in the picture, you would've given me another chance. I know it." He nodded his head emphatically.

She stood up. "Get out, Jake. Right now."

"Look, I'm willing to forget all about this guy, Deena. We'll start even. We both made the same mistakes, right?"

"I'll call the police, Jake. I mean it!"

"God, I've missed you, Deena." Suddenly, he was standing next to her. He grabbed her and pushed her onto the couch. His mouth was on hers, hard, determined, his hands exploring her body with familiar insistence.

She shoved hard against his chest and freed a corner of her bruised mouth. "Stop it!"

"Come on, Deena," he whispered. "Don't pretend. I know you've been thinking about me, wanting me the way I want you."

She pounded on his chest. With one hand, he pinioned her arms above her head. With the other, he yanked her blouse out of her skirt and started fumbling with the buttons.

"You love me, don't you, Deena? Say you still love me!"

"Jake, stop! You don't know what you're doing!"

"For the first time in months, I know exactly what I'm doing. We belong together. You're just too stubborn to admit it. But you can't deny this." In seconds, her blouse was open, her breasts exposed. "I get crazy when I think someone else has been touching you like this!"

"I hate you!"

He forced her mouth open. She bit his tongue.

"Shit!" He looked at her, surprised. "You little bitch! Saving it for the boyfriend, huh? How about just one, then, for old times' sake?" He grinned. "Something to remember me by. What's the big deal, anyway? You're still my wife."

She tried freeing her arms, kicking him. His hand was an iron clamp; her legs were paralyzed by his weight. And then she was outside herself, watching in incredulous horror as he forced her skirt up around her waist.

The doorbell rang.

"Help!" Her cry escaped as a hoarse, indecipherable croak. "Help!" she screamed again as loudly as she could.

Jake stopped, startled. Deena wrenched her arms free and smacked him hard across the face. Her ring left an angry red scratch across his cheek. His lip was bleeding. Sobbing, clutching her blouse together, she edged off the couch and ran to open the door. It was Faye.

"The others are—oh my God, what happened?" She put her arm around Deena, who was crying and shaking uncontrollably.

Miriam, Magda, Susan, and Elaine came in together, laughing. Their laughter froze as they took in Deena's appearance.

"You monster!" Faye's voice was shaking. "Get out of here right now!"

Jake was standing in the archway to the living room. He glanced at Faye dismissively, then wiped his lip with the back of his hand and stared at the blood in disbelief. "You'll be sorry you did that, Deena."

Elaine said, "I think we should call the police."

Jake glared at her. "Well, if it isn't the bitch from the restaurant. Stay the hell out of my business, you got that?" He turned to Deena. "This isn't the end of it, Deena. I'll be back. And you can forget about the *get,* lady, 'cause there's no way in hell I'll ever give it to you."

"I wish you were dead," Deena whispered. "I really do!"

"Well, wish away, sweetheart, 'cause that's the only way you'll ever be free—over my dead body."

"Don't push me, Jake."

"What are you going to do, Deena, kill me?" He laughed as he shoved his way past the women and out the door.

6

THE RED PORSCHE PULLED UP IN THE DRIVEWAY OF THE house on South Sherbourne.

It was eleven on Sunday and unseasonably warm for the last days of October. Two toddlers were maneuvering their tricycles furiously up and down a series of steep driveways, and up the block a little girl played a desultory game of solitaire hopscotch. The street was sleepy, empty of traffic.

The car door opened and Jake emerged, swinging his long legs onto the ground. He smoothed his gray linen trousers, reached into the car for the jacket he'd carefully folded over the back of the passenger seat, and put it on. From the trunk he removed a black lizard-skin attaché case, a navy-blue athletic tote bag, and the Sunday edition of the *L.A. Times*.

As he made his way up the path to the front door, he noticed with irritation that the gardener had been overzealous in shaving the lawn; rough, bald patches pocked the complexion of the brittle, yellowing grass. The now-scraggly petunias in the bordered flower bed had lost their trumpetlike splendor. Bowed, listing, they waited for the cold metal of a shovel to uproot them and make them fodder for the snails.

The house was stifling and permeated with the stale, musty odor of vacancy. In the breakfast nook, Jake placed his paraphernalia on the pebbled Formica dinette table, removed his jacket, and draped it over the back of one of the chairs. He found the thermostat in the hall and turned on the air-conditioning to sixty degrees. The unit throbbed with a surge of power, then settled into a steady hum. He would adjust the temperature later, when the house was cool.

Some realtors hated open houses. Ben, for one. But Jake had always looked at them as a challenge. He enjoyed keeping score, seeing how many of the casual passersby he could entice into thinking about the property more seriously. There was an art to selling houses, and he'd mastered it.

Walking from room to room, Jake checked with an experienced eye to see that everything was in order. He'd arranged to have a domestic come the previous day to vacuum and do some light cleaning, but there were details that needed attention. With spinsterly precision, he aligned the chairs around the dining room table, plumped up the pillows on the living room sofa. On the coffee table, he arranged the current issues of *National Geographic, Newsweek,* and *L.A. Magazine* that he'd retrieved from his attaché case. From the blue tote he took a footed camel-toned ceramic bowl with miniature soaps and three fringed white guest towels, appliqued with satin shells. He placed these in the main bathroom.

Satisfied, he walked through the house again and misted each room with a mild, lemon-scented air freshener (this was also from the tote—he liked to think of it as his bag of magic tricks). He smiled, congratulating himself on having remembered the towels and the room deodorizer. It was a nice touch.

The freezer was working, and Jake was pleased to see that the woman had remembered to fill the ice cube trays. He found a glass in the cupboard, rinsed it thoroughly, put in a few loosened ice cubes, and filled the glass with Diet Pepsi (he'd brought a six-pack with him). While he waited for the soda to chill, he took a clipboard, some pens, and a stack of offset photos of the house and put them on the dining room table.

It was eleven-thirty. Jake went outside to his car, removed two pennants from the trunk, and drove them firmly into the ground on either side of the paved walkway. Back in the house, he sat down at the dinette table with his drink and opened the Sunday paper. He flipped quickly through the "Calendar" section, looked at the sports page, and then studied the real estate pages, circling several promising properties with a marker.

At eleven-fifty, he neatly reassembled the paper, got up, adjusted the knot of his silk tie, put on his jacket, and moved into the dining room. When the doorbell rang and the first visitors entered, he was ready.

By four-thirty, Jake had acquired the signatures and phone numbers of about thirty-five people. Many, he knew, were probably curious neighborhood residents who had come to unveil the mysteries of the home to which they had never been invited. They poked through bedroom closets, opened kitchen drawers and medicine cabinets, ran their hands over sofas and chairs, looking for clues that would explain the owners who were no longer there. Even with curious neighbors, Jake was always courteous, charming. You never knew—they could tell relatives, friends. Everyone was a potential lead.

He had sensed real interest in three couples, and with these he had spent more time, drawing attention to the best features of the house—the beautiful hardwood floors hidden under the somewhat dingy rust carpeting in the living and dining rooms; the graceful French windows; the high, arched ceilings with their exquisitely detailed moldings.

The rooms, he pointed out, were conveniently arranged (no, he admitted, not tremendous, but larger than average for a house in this area, with plenty of wall space), and offered so many possibilities for someone with imagination. There was central air-conditioning, relatively new copper plumbing (he would check to see when it had been installed, if they wanted; no, really, it was no bother). Best of all, the owner was willing to carry a second mortgage. He had already moved into a new home, and (but this was confidential) he was anxious to sell. The house, Jake felt, would not be on the market long.

Yes, *do* think about it, by all means. It's never a good idea to rush into anything. He had said the same thing to the pleasant young couple who had just left. Had they seemed interested? Yes, quite candidly; yes, they had. It *was* a lovely home, wasn't it?

By five-fifteen Jake decided that he had seen his last visitor for the day. He loosened his tie, went outside, and removed the pennants, leaving gaping wounds in the ground. He stored the pennants in his trunk.

Back in the house, he replaced the clipboard, pens, and depleted stack of photos in his attaché case. He was in the bathroom at the end of the long hall, collecting the soap dish and towels, when he heard footsteps tapping softly on the uncarpeted floor of the entry.

He was instantly annoyed, but he quickly returned the items to their former positions and automatically erased his frown. He exited the bathroom, an affable smile of welcome firmly in place, and stopped short.

''What the hell do you want?''

7

"I WARNED YOU," JAKE SAID QUIETLY. HE STOOD, LEANING over the bed. "I told you I'd be back. You tried to get rid of me, but it didn't work."

Deena struggled to open her eyes, heavy with sleep, then stared. It was impossible! He couldn't be here, in her house, in her bedroom!

"Get out!" she warned, trying to sound firm, to restrain the panic from her voice. She pulled the blanket tight against her. "Get out right now or I'll call the police." She reached for the phone on her nightstand. "I mean it, Jake!"

He grabbed her hand and forced it down. In an instant, he had torn the blanket away and was on top of her, pinning her thrashing body to the bed with manic strength, silencing her screams with his mouth. She began pounding on his chest. With one hand, he pinioned her arms above her head.

"You love me, don't you, Deena?" he whispered, his mouth still on hers. "Say you love me! We can still make it work."

"I hate you!" she cried. "I hate you!"

"You're still my wife, remember? According to your precious Jewish law, until I give you a *get*, we're still legally married. And I'll never give it to you, Deena. Never."

He forced her nightgown around her waist and started to undo his belt. She tugged her left hand free. He was concentrating on his pants and didn't notice. She groped for the phone cord and pulled it toward her until the receiver was in her hand. Then she brought it crashing down on his head.

He grunted. The blow had stunned him, but she couldn't be sure. She hit him again. With both hands now free, she started pounding on his chest, pounding and pounding, she heard the thuds, but he wouldn't stop, wouldn't go away. He just lay there, a dead weight, grinning at her, and she had no choice, she had to pound again and again and again . . .

She woke up with a start, bathed in sweat, her heart hammering wildly, and realized that the pounding was real, coming from the front of the house. She looked at her nightstand. The receiver was off the hook, just as she'd left it before she'd gone to bed. She'd been doing that since the calls had started.

Stumbling from the bed, she quickly found a robe in the closet, slipped it on, and hurried barefoot to the front door.

"Who is it?" she demanded angrily. If it was Jake, she would kill him. She really would.

"It's the police, ma'am. Would you mind opening up?"

She turned on the porch light and looked through the peephole at two men. One was tall and lanky, with a young, mustachioed face. The other, an older-looking black, was tall but had a paunch. Neither one was uniformed. She hesitated.

"Can I see some identification, please?"

"Of course." The older man held his ID up to the privacy window.

Deena studied it, then opened the door and stepped aside to let both men enter. For a moment, the three stood awkwardly in the entry hall.

"Can we come in, Mrs. Vogler?" the black officer asked.

"Of course. I'm sorry." They followed her into the living room and lowered themselves onto the sofa. She sat on one of the folding chairs she had set up for the group. Somehow, she hadn't gotten around to putting them away.

The black officer spoke. "Mrs. Vogler, I'm Detective Lewis. This is Detective Moran."

They were staring at her. She knew she must look a mess, tried to smooth her tangled hair, but gave up.

"I'm sorry." She tried a smile. "You just woke me up from a deep sleep. Were you waiting long?"

"We tried the bell first, ma'am," Moran said. "We knew you were home because your line was busy for quite a while."

"The bell gets stuck sometimes and doesn't work. The phone must have been off the hook." For the last three weeks, she wanted to add. "What can I do for you, officers?"

They shifted uncomfortably.

"Is something wrong?" she asked, suddenly alarmed.

"It's about your husband, ma'am," Lewis said quietly.

"Ex-husband." So Jake had done it! He had actually filed a complaint against Max. "Look, my father didn't mean any harm. He's upset about my situation, and he's trying to protect me."

They looked at each other strangely, but she didn't notice.

"But I don't understand why you've come to me about this. And at this hour. Have you spoken to my father yet?"

"Ma'am," Lewis began.

"He'll explain everything." She had a sudden thought. "Unless he filed a complaint against me too? Is that it? Is that why you're here?" She should have figured that out; Jake would enjoy humiliating her like this: "Are you going to arrest me?" She laughed harshly.

"Ma'am, I'm sorry to have to tell you that your husband— ex-husband—is dead. I'm really sorry, ma'am."

She stared at them. "May I see your identification again, please," she whispered.

They pulled out their wallets and showed her the official pictures that matched their faces. Deena examined the photos closely, then returned them.

"For a minute I thought he hired you to play a sick joke. You know—trick-or-treat?" It was Halloween. "That would be just like him." She laughed nervously. "You're telling me the truth? He's dead?" Was it over? Really over?

Their silence was confirmation.

She tried to keep her face expressionless, hoped she had successfully smothered the note of excitement and relief that had leaped automatically into her voice. "But why did you come here? We're divorced."

"This was the address on his license," Lewis said. He seemed to be doing most of the talking.

"But he doesn't live here anymore; he hasn't lived here for over a year." I am not involved!

"I guess he never reported his change of address to the DMV. Is there a next of kin we should notify, ma'am?"

She nodded. "His parents, Ida and Joe Vogelanter. Jake shortened his last name to Vogler," she added.

"Could you tell us how to reach them, please?"

She told him. "When . . . when did he die?"

"We don't have exact information yet; the coroner will have to do an autopsy first. The body was found tonight, but it would appear that he's been dead several days."

"Was it a gun?"

"Ma'am?"

"You said he was killed. Was it with a gun?"

Lewis looked at her for a moment. "Yes, it was."

"Where was it? At his apartment?" She didn't know why

she was so curious about the details. Maybe because it didn't seem real.

"No, ma'am. In a house on Sherbourne." He told her the address. "Does that sound familiar to you?"

She shook her head. Both men rose simultaneously.

"Well, ma'am, I think we'll be going," Lewis said. "We'll probably have to speak to you again within the next day or so."

She followed them to the door. "Do I have to identify him?"

"No, ma'am," Lewis said. "Usually, it's next of kin."

Deena stood in the cold entry, staring vacantly at the door she had closed on the backs of the two officers. Shivering slightly, she walked on surprisingly steady feet to the kitchen and turned on the light. She filled the chrome kettle, set it down on the gas burner, and waited in front of the stove for the water to come to a boil.

Dead, she said to herself. Jake is dead. Somehow, it still didn't seem real, and she said it again, out loud, letting the flat, heavy sounds explode in the silence. "Jake is dead."

Suddenly, she didn't quite know how she felt, how she should feel, but then the kettle was whistling shrilly, demanding her attention, and she knew she wasn't crying—why should she cry?—knew that the moisture on her cheeks was only the vapor escaping from the kettle she'd just quieted. But still . . .

She filled a cup with the steaming water, selected a jasmine teabag and a packet of Sweet 'N Low, and sat down at the breakfast room table.

Should I call my parents? she wondered. No, definitely not. It was almost one A.M., she noted; the ringing of the phone alone would frighten Max and Pearl to death, she thought, and cringed immediately at the irony of her expression. Michael? Faye? Alan? Brenda? But what would she say—"Jake is dead; I'm free! Come celebrate"? That sounded horribly crass, and it wasn't even totally true.

It wasn't totally untrue, either. She was feeling light-headed (probably shock, she realized), but she had to admit it was wonderful knowing that Jake would no longer be intimidating her, harassing her, controlling her. In the last few months, she'd come to hate everything about him—his arrogant self-assurance, his obsessive need to manipulate her, his grinning malevolence. She wondered fleetingly whether he had grinned at Death, too.

But although she had violently willed him out of her life, had wished him dead to his face and meant it, now that she was confronted with the reality of his death, she couldn't help but feel a sharp twinge of sadness for the man who had been her lover and friend (strange, but she hardly remembered him like that; it seemed a lifetime ago), and, until a day or two ago, somebody's son.

Deena had never come in close contact with death before. Her grandparents had all been victims of the Holocaust, and although Max and Pearl had made her painfully aware of the atrocities of Nazi Germany, they had never given her details of their parents' deaths, having none to give her. There had been no funerals in Max's family as far as Deena could remember. He was the only member of his immediate family who had survived the war, and although there were some distant cousins in Canada, he hadn't heard from them in years. And when Pearl's older sister had died fifteen years ago in Chicago, Deena had been a child and now had only the vaguest, second-hand recollections of the events surrounding her death.

And murder? That was something she read about avidly in mystery novels, encountered with dread on the front page of the *L.A. Times* and on the eleven o'clock news, a fiction she watched unfolding behind the protective twenty-six-inch barrier of her television screen. And now it had invaded her house in the form of two officers who told her that her ex-husband was dead.

Funny how she'd known the Jake had been killed with a gun. Now she wondered why she had leaped to that assumption. Why not a car crash? That was more probable, wasn't it? But the officer had said "killed," and she'd automatically pictured a gun. Because of Murdoch and his threats? She hadn't asked about the wound, and the policemen hadn't offered any information. She hoped it wasn't on his face. She shuddered at the gruesome image that flashed across her mind.

The tea was cold. She got up, dumped the contents of the cup into the sink, and rinsed the stains from cup and sink. She wondered whether there had been a lot of blood.

In the bedroom, she removed her robe and slipped under the quilt onto the cooled sheets. She lay on her left side, her head propped on her bent arm, and noticed the receiver, still off the hook. Sighing, she replaced it. She knew with ironic certainty that some time tomorrow morning Mrs. Perris at the phone company would call to tell her that they'd solved her problem. Now that it didn't matter anymore.

She rolled onto her back and folded the pillow beneath her head. Had Jake surprised a burglar—was that what happened? Had he tried to play the hero instead of giving him his wallet? Maybe they'd never find out. As far as the house on Sherbourne, why had he been there? A girlfriend? A client? Ben might know. The police would follow up on it. She was sure they would be efficient.

She tried her side again—the right one, this time—and as she drifted off to sleep, she hoped anxiously that she wouldn't dream about Jake's death. But she was comforted by the thought that with Jake dead, the nightmare that had come to haunt her with merciless repetition, that forced her to relive, again and again, Jake's manic attack, wouldn't disturb her sleep tonight.

Or ever again.

8

AT TWO-THIRTY IN THE MORNING, THERE WAS ONLY A SKELeton shift at the homicide section of the LAPD Wilshire Division on Venice Boulevard. A policewoman sat at the front desk, answering the phone that rang sporadically; two officers were huddled in quiet conversation in a corner near a water cooler; and another was writing a report.

Detective Sam Ryker walked into the squad room, made his way around his taupe metal desk, and settled his large, six-foot frame into a tan vinyl upholstered swivel chair.

Ryker was pleasant-looking—not handsome, exactly—with a weathered face, a square jaw, and a nose that sat slightly off-center between small, hazel eyes hooded by heavy lids. He hadn't shaved since six o'clock the previous morning, and the hint of stubble gave his face a bluish cast; he was exhausted and felt older than his forty-six years. He rubbed his tired, red-rimmed eyes with his knuckles, raked his fingers through wavy brown hair that still showed no hint of thinning, and clasped them behind his head. After yawning expansively, he sighed, then grimaced. He took a bottle of Tums from the bottom right drawer, selected two pastel-orange tablets, and crunched them quickly, impatient for relief.

From an inner pocket of his gray tweed jacket, he removed a green spiral notebook and flipped through it until he found the pages he wanted. He was still reading with forced concentration when George Lewis and Tom Moran arrived. They sat down heavily on two wooden chairs in front of the detective's desk.

"Where've you guys been?" Ryker asked. "I didn't think it would take this long to talk to the victim's wife."

"Ex-wife," Lewis told him. "That's the hitch. They've been divorced six months. Anyway, she gave us the name and address of his parents—Joe and Ida Vogelanter; Vogler shortened his last name, she said—and we just came back from breaking the news to them. Older people, both in their seventies, I'd guess. They took it pretty bad." He shook his head sympathetically.

"Who wouldn't?" Ryker said. "It's rough hearing something like that—you don't expect to outlive your kid." He thought about Becky and Kelley, his two teenage daughters, and was intensely thankful that they were safely asleep in their beds.

"Yeah, seems he's an only child, too," Lewis added. "The mother was hysterical—I thought she was going to faint. The father was more together—he was trying to calm her down, but he wasn't too successful. When we left, he was calling the family doctor to come give her a sedative."

"Actually, he seemed a little too controlled," Moran said. "Not that he wasn't upset. And he said something strange, too."

"I think he was in shock," Lewis said.

"What do you mean, 'strange'?" Ryker asked.

"Well," Moran said, "as soon as George told them we found their son's body, the mother starts screaming, but the father, he just stands there and mumbles some words. I couldn't really figure out what he was saying—I think he was talking Hebrew; he was wearing one of those skullcaps."

"What did it sound like?"

"I wrote it down." Moran checked his notes. "It's something like *Brook dine a mess.*"

"What the hell does that mean? Never mind. Probably some ritual saying. Hank Stollman's Jewish, isn't he? Ask him about it, Tom. If he doesn't know, have him ask a rabbi."

"Right."

"I'll pay the parents a visit tomorrow. And I think I'll take Stollman along with me. He may pick up something I might miss. I'm hoping they'll be able to give me the names of some people who might've had it in for their son."

"It wasn't robbery?" Lewis asked Ryker.

"Could be. Too early to say. The killer took cash but left a nice eelskin wallet with MasterCard, American Express, and a few charge cards to some fancy department stores. His watch is missing—that's clear from the impression on his hand. No indication that anything else was taken. His car keys were in his pocket—they fit the Porsche in the driveway."

"I wouldn't mind driving that home!" Moran sighed.

"You couldn't afford the upkeep," Ryker told him. "Anyway, if it was a robber, why didn't he take the credit cards?"

"Maybe he panicked," Lewis said. "He took the watch, started looking through the wallet, thought he heard someone, and ran."

"Unlikely." Ryker shook his head. "Then why didn't he just take the whole wallet? That would've taken less time, and he could've used those cards or sold them. Another thing. Why didn't the robber take the victim's keys and go to his residence? He knew from his driver's license where he lived."

"Where he *used* to live," Moran said.

"Oh? Well, the robber didn't know that. He threw away a perfect opportunity to empty the place."

"So if it wasn't robbery, then what?" Moran asked.

"I'm not ruling it out," Ryker said. "It's an option, but we have to check out Vogler's background, his business associations, his private life—everything."

"Did you find out who lives in the house?" Lewis asked. "Assuming, of course, Vogler doesn't own it. It's furnished, but it doesn't have a lived-in look, know what I mean? Everything's too perfect, nothing out of place."

Ryker said, "The neighbor to the left, Raymond Frisch, gave me the facts. The owners are Mr. and Mrs. Louis Pomerantz, but they moved to the Valley a few weeks ago. Frisch says the house has been up for sale for about three months.''

''I didn't notice a sign,'' Lewis said.

''There wasn't one. Maybe the owners didn't want one. By the way, the victim's business card says he's with Kasden and Vogler, Realtors. If their firm is handling the sale of the property, that would explain why Vogler was there.''

He swiveled abruptly toward Lewis. ''George, call his partner and find out if he knows what Vogler was doing in that house, when he saw him last. The whole routine. And get the new address and phone number for Pomerantz. They could've met Vogler at the house and had a confrontation. Also, ask the partner if Vogler made any enemies recently—some client who's unhappy because he sold him a lemon with a leaky roof and a rotting foundation.''

''I'll get on it first thing in the morning,'' Lewis promised. ''Did they find the murder weapon?''

Ryker shook his head. ''I'm sending a team in the morning to check a two-mile radius around the crime scene, but I'm not hopeful. The suspect must've taken it with him. From the prelim, the M.E. says the weapon was probably a small-caliber gun fired from close range. There was powder residue all over the guy's neck. Lots of blood, too. A godawful mess. The bullet apparently entered his neck and traveled up to his brain.''

''Do we have an approximate time of death?'' Moran asked.

''Are you kidding? You were in there. The place is a goddamn icebox! The heat broke Sunday night, but someone turned the air-conditioning down to sixty degrees. The medical investigator almost had a fit when he came in.'' He grinned, then frowned. ''Frankly, I don't blame him. This throws all the normal figures about body temperatures out of whack. We'll have to talk to all the neighbors, see if they remember the last time they saw Vogler enter the house.''

''What about Frisch?'' Lewis asked.

''He's pretty sure he saw the Porsche in the driveway since Sunday, but he doesn't know whether it was driven in the meantime. His wife can't be sure, either. They both work. We'll have to talk to the other neighbors during the next two days.''

Moran said, ''It's going to be a bitch to figure this one out.

By the way, about those kids who found the body? You want me to follow up on that?''

''Not necessary. I spoke to the officers who responded to the call, then to the kids and the parents. The facts are pretty straightforward. They were out trick-or-treating.''

''Some treat, huh?'' Moran grimacéd.

''Yeah,'' Ryker agreed. ''Anyway, the older boy figured he'd explore the house—thought it would be a real gas. The little one stayed in the entry the whole time—claims he didn't want to go in to begin with—until he heard his brother screaming. At first he thought the brother was pulling a fast one—Halloween stuff. By the time he realized it wasn't make-believe and ran to the end of the house, the older kid was trying to reach the bathroom. He didn't quite make it. Puked all over the hall carpet.'' He wrinkled his nose in disgust.

''Poor kid,'' Lewis clucked. ''Pretty shook up, huh?''

''Yup. Especially since we didn't let him keep a knife he picked up in the kitchen for a souvenir. His mother wasn't thrilled about that, either, I'll tell you, This is one Halloween those boys'll never forget! But there's no point in talking to them again. And the parents certainly have no idea who Vogler is. I showed them his driver's license—nothing.''

Lewis said, ''Speaking of Vogler's driver's license, he never filed a change of address. That's why we went to his ex-wife's house.''

''Where does he live now?''

Lewis checked his notes and repeated the address the Vogelanters had given him.

Ryker said, ''If it's an apartment building, we'll have to talk to the other tenants, the landlord or manager. Whatever. Tom, why don't you tackle that.''

''Done.''

A yellow light on the phone started flashing.

Ryker picked up the receiver. ''Homicide, Detective Ryker speaking.'' He talked for a few minutes, hung up, and scribbled a phone number and a few notes on a pad on his desk.

''That was the Vogelanters' rabbi. Name of Pearlstein. He wanted to know if there was any way to avoid an autopsy. Seems the family *is* Jewish, very religious, and performing an autopsy is forbidden. I told him there's no way in a violent death to get around it. He seemed to accept it; I think he knew what the answer would be, but I guess he promised the parents he'd give it a try. He also asked when we plan to release the body. The family wants to have the funeral as quickly as possible. Another law, the rabbi said. I told him it could take a couple of days before the autopsy would take place, depending on how backlogged the schedule is, but I promised I'd try to push Kanata to do the autopsy some time this morning.

"Good luck." Lewis grinned. "Kanata doesn't like to be pushed."

"Yeah, but he owes me one."

"Hey," Moran said, "you could've asked the rabbi about those Hebrew words Vogelanter was saying."

"You're right. I forgot. No problem; I'll be speaking to him again. Anyway, what about the ex-wife? A wasted trip, huh?"

Lewis said, "Not exactly. I was saving that for last. Something funny's going on, I think. First of all, she indicated that there was some trouble between her father and her ex. Wait a minute—I'll get my notes." He thumbed through his notepad until he found the page he wanted and read aloud.

"Interesting." Ryker's eyes narrowed.

"Also, I never said her ex was killed. I'm positive I said *dead.*"

"You did," Moran seconded.

"But she asked me right away if he was *killed* with a gun. Her word. That was before I told her anything about where the body was found. For all she knew, he could've been the victim of a hit-and-run accident or a heart attack."

"How'd she seem?"

"Nervous. Kept fidgeting with her hair, stuff like that."

"Pretty hair," Moran added. "Long. Auburn, I think they call it. Terrific green eyes. She's a looker. Tall, slim, even in her robe. I couldn't tell much about her figure, though."

"Guess you'll have to live with the suspense," Ryker said.

Moran grinned. "She was a little out of it. Said we woke her up from a deep sleep. But then, once she believed us, she seemed pretty unemotional."

"Believed you?"

"At first she thought her ex-husband was pulling a prank."

"Some prank. How'd you read her? Is she happy he's dead?"

Moran considered for a moment. "Not necessarily. But she wasn't torn up about it, either."

Lewis nodded in assent.

"Asked questions about the murder like she was talking about a stranger," Moran continued.

"Shock?"

"I think so." He nodded. "Yeah. Maybe that accounts for her conversation. It was a little weird."

"Good work, both of you. I'll see her tomorrow, too. I wonder what Vogler and his ex-father-in-law were battling about. Whatever it is, she seems to be involved in it." He yawned. "Okay. Get some sleep and I'll see you in the morning."

"What about you, Sam?" Lewis asked. "You look beat."

"I think I'll call Kanata and go home. I'll be back by 7. If Kanata cooperates, he should be starting the autopsy then, and as soon as he extracts the bullet, I can send it off to ballistics. I didn't notice any exit wounds, so I'm assuming it's still in the head. I'll get Zeke to rush it through. And maybe we'll have some information from SID about prints." SID is the Scientific Investigation Division of the LAPD. "I'm not optimistic, though. The older kid must've touched just about every goddamn surface in the house." He sighed.

"If something's there, you'll find it," Lewis assured him.

"Damn right I will."

Three and a half hours of sleep hadn't been nearly enough, but Ryker was accustomed to functioning on less. The stinging needles of the shower helped, too, and he felt almost awake when he came into the squad room at six-forty on Wednesday morning.

He hung his tan wool jacket around the back of his chair, sat down, and examined the material occupying his in tray.

Rabbi Pearlstein had left a message marked "Urgent." Ryker returned his call, assured him that the autopsy would take place that morning, and that, barring unforeseen difficulties, the body would be released some time that day. After he hung up, he realized with chagrin that he'd once again forgotten to get the Hebrew words translated.

The autopsy revealed no surprises. Jake Vogler was a white male Caucasian in his early thirties, five feet, eleven inches tall, weighing 162 pounds. He had no surgical scars, and aside from the fact that a bullet had prematurely ended his life, he had been a remarkably healthy specimen of the human race.

Death, Dr. Kanata observed, had been quick. Entering at

the neck, the bullet had punctured the esophagus and severed the carotid artery; that accounted for the gruesome pool of blood. Then, traveling at an upward angle of thirty-eight degrees, it had ricocheted off the jawbone, pierced through the tongue and upper palate, and injured the optic nerve. As a result, there were pronounced black and blue bruises around the victim's eyes. The bullet had wreaked considerable damage as it played a deadly game of ping-pong through the brain.

Powder residue was observed on the neck, face, and hands.

"A struggle with the assailant?" Ryker asked.

"It certainly looks like it," Dr. Kanata told him. "And since there's no sign of the murder weapon, I think we can rule out suicide, don't you?"

The bullet, flattened by its progress through the victim's head, had finally lodged near the top of the skull. Ryker had it sent to ballistics to determine the caliber of the gun.

"I'm sending up the contents of the stomach to the lab," Kanata said. "You should have an analysis within a day or so."

The time of death was uncertain. Decomposition of the body had not yet begun, but because of the air-conditioning, no standard formula could be applied. Ryker would have to talk to the victim's family and acquaintances to reconstruct a schedule of his activities during the past few days.

By the time Ryker returned to his office, it was nine-forty.

Lewis had left for a nine-thirty appointment with Kasden. Moran was checking out Vogler's residence. He had also told Hank Stollman to make himself available.

Ryker called the Vogelanters and arranged to go over within the hour. When he tried the phone book listing for Mrs. Jake Vogler on Guthrie, a recording told him that the number had been changed but offered no new number; directory assistance informed him that there was no new listing.

After identifying himself to a Mr. Hurley in the business office of Pacific Bell, Ryker obtained the new, unlisted phone number.

"Incidentally, when did Mrs. Vogler request an unlisted number?" he asked just as he was about to hang up.

"I'd have to look up her account. I know it was recently. You should talk with Mrs. Perris. She dealt with Mrs. Vogler. I do know that Mrs. Vogler called here more than once about getting her number changed. Apparently, there was a problem.''

"Can I speak to Mrs. Perris now?''

"I'm afraid not. She's out with the flu. She'll probably be back in a day or so. Shall I have her call you?''

"Please.'' He left his name and phone number.

"Should I say it's urgent police business?''

"Just ask her to call. Thanks.''

When Ryker called the new phone number, no one answered.

Hank Stollman's curly head popped into view. "You wanted me?''

"Yeah. Tom filled you in?''

"Uh-huh.'' He took a seat and stretched his legs.

"Are you working on anything now?''

"Just finishing some paperwork on that girl who O.D.'d on heroin. The roommate gave us the name of her supplier. We picked him up yesterday.''

"Okay. I want you to come with me when I talk to Vogler's parents. Do you know any Hebrew?''

"Not much. I haven't been to a synagogue in years; even when I did go as a kid, I usually faked it. Tom said you wanted a translation. Sorry. Should I call a local rabbi?''

"No. The Vogelanters' rabbi called me last night, about the autopsy. I'll check this out with him.''

"Okay. When do you want to go?''

"In about fifteen minutes. I'm waiting to hear from ballistics. And I wonder if SID has turned up anything.''

"Want me to check?''

"No. I'll take care of it. But I'd like you to call the Department of Water and Power. Ask them to check their meters for the house where the body was found and tell us when there was a noticeble surge in electric power, like you'd get if you turned on an air-conditioning system.'' He gave him the address.

"Okay.'' Stollman rose and walked over to his desk.

Ryker called ballistics, but Zeke didn't have any answers.

"Give me an hour; I'll try to fit you in,'' Zeke promised. "We've been swamped the last two days.''

Ryker didn't learn anything new from SID. There were prints all over the house, but most of them belonged to the deceased and to Christopher Borden, the boy who had discovered the body. There were some other prints, as yet unidentified.

"We have a leather attaché case and an athletic tote; both apparently belonged to the deceased," the crime lab technician told him on the phone.

"Anything interesting in them?"

"A lot of stuff. Lafferty from your division's here picking something up. I'll send it all over with him."

A half-hour later Ryker smiled with amusement when he glanced at the contents of the tote, especially the aerosol can of room deodorizer. He rubbed his hands over the embossed surface of the attaché case; it looked and felt expensive. He was examining the contents of the case when Stollman returned.

"I spoke to a meter reader at the DWP. They can check the meters and tell us how much electricity is being used per hour, but they can't tell exactly when the air-conditioning went on."

"No problem. I think we can figure out more or less when he got to the house. Look at these." He handed Stollman some offset photos of the crime site. "At least now we know that Vogler was there on Sunday—handling an open house."

"Are you certain it was Sunday?"

"Pretty sure. That's when realtors usually hold open houses. But we'll verify that with his partner. Sunday was a hot day. Vogler probably turned on the air-conditioning when he was setting up. But why would he turn it on to sixty degrees?"

"Maybe he had to cool off the house first. And with the doors being constantly opened and closed—and you're right, it was a hell of a hot day—maybe he decided to leave it low so that everyone would feel comfortable."

"Maybe. Let me double-check to see whose prints are on the thermostat." He made a call, spoke with someone in charge, and hung up. "Vogler's prints, superimposed on someone else's. Maybe the homeowners'. We'll have to get their prints, too."

"What else did you get?"

"A copy of the *Times*. Vogler made notations in the real estate section. Looks like he wasn't interested in any of the properties—he wrote 'NO GET' all over the margin, underlined the word several times. Here." He showed the paper to Stollman.

"What's 'REC'?" Stollman asked.

"What?"

"He wrote 'REC' with a question mark after it." He pointed to the paper.

"I don't know. Receipt? Record? Probably nothing."

"What's this?" Stollman pointed to a paper on Ryker's desk.

"A list of people who came to the open house. The last one signed in at four-forty P.M., so we can assume Vogler was alive at least till what—five? That's when open houses usually end. We'll have to interview all these people, find out if they saw anything. Maybe they heard Vogler fighting with someone."

"The good thing is we have names, addresses, and phone numbers for all of them."

"All except one. Too bad the murderer didn't sign in, too."

9

AT SIX FORTY-FIVE ON WEDNESDAY MORNING, THE FIRST faint notes of the music alarm began to nudge Deena from a deep sleep, and by the time the tune, building with a subtle yet persistent crescendo, reached its preset volume, she was awake. She knew she should get up, shower, dress, get the ritual of rising behind her. Her first class wasn't until nine, but she'd planned to put in a load of laundry before she left the house and drop off her black patent pumps at Nick's Shoe Repair on Pico. Now, wrapped in the insulating warmth of her down quilt, she was reluctant to abandon the comfort of her bed for plans that suddenly struck her as somewhat ambitious.

Tomorrow, she decided. Yawning lazily, she reset the alarm for seven-thirty. She indulged in a slow, feline stretch, her feet arched, toes curled; then, folding her knees halfway to her chest, she resumed a semi-fetal position and tried to recapture the elusive strains of sleep.

With a start, she bolted to an upright position.

How, she wondered with amazement tinged with guilt, could she have forgotten about last night? How could she have slept so soundly after learning that Jake had been killed? Maybe it wasn't true. Maybe she was remembering another dream. But even as she jumped out of bed and hurried to the kitchen, shivering in the frigid early morning air, even before she found the mute testimony of the cup and saucer sitting on the drainboard, the shriveled teabag resting nearby in its porcelain holder, she knew this was no dream, that the bullet that had killed Jake was real, not some angry missile directed by her imagination.

She glanced at the oven clock: six fifty-six. She picked up the receiver. The dial tone sounded unnaturally loud. Michael first, she decided. No one answered, but his recorder was on. She waited obediently for the beep. She knew he often went to early morning services at a *shul* near his apartment.

"Michael," she began, then stopped. Somehow, it seemed crass to relegate Jake's death to a message on a recording device. "Michael, it's Deena. Can you—I have to see you. Today. I'll be back from my classes by four-thirty. Please come over."

Max would be at the convalescent home by now, going over reports from night nurses, checking on the residents. She would speak to him later. And she certainly didn't want to tell Pearl without her father around. She had no idea how her mother would react. Relieved for Deena's sake, of course. For all of them. But she'd loved Jake once, had envisioned him as the father of her grandchildren. What would the news of his death do to the delicate fabric of her already frayed nerves?

Deena went back to the bedroom. She smoothed her quilt, took off her nightgown, folded it, and placed it under the pillow. She decided not to bother with the bedspread.

She supposed she should call Ben; he'd want to know; Jake was—*had been*—not only a partner, but a friend. The police, though, would certainly contact Ben as soon as possible to discuss Jake's whereabouts during the past few days. She would rather have them be the bearers of grim news.

Coming out of the shower, she grabbed the terry towel she had readied and rubbed herself vigorously dry. The mirror that occupied an entire bathroom wall had disappeared behind a filmy veil of steam, and she had disappeared with it. Jake's ex-wife. Gone. She wasn't his widow, either. As she mechanically brushed her teeth and then expertly jiggled the blow dryer around her head, allowing jets of warm air to play with her hair, she watched her body—a body that had been intimately and, yes, pleasurably entwined with someone now dead—come slowly into focus. First her hips and waist; then her breasts, shoulders, the slender column of her neck. Finally, her face, framed by still moist coppery tendrils. She examined herself critically.

She looked the same.

She should notify Brenda, she thought as she tossed laundry into the washing machine. Carefully, she measured detergent and softener into the dispensers. She had no idea how Jake's death would affect the property settlement. Not that it mattered, really. She didn't give a damn about the money. The most important thing was that she was free, that she no longer felt like a rat frantically running around in a maze where every path led to a dead end.

Was it terrible if she felt a kernel of joy—no, admit it, more than a kernel, much more—even though her freedom had come on the wings of death?

Probably. A lot of people would think so.

But she had done nothing wrong. And if, by some cruel twist of fate, Jake had died at the hands of a desperate criminal (because that's what probably happened, she reasoned; that's the only logical explanation for what happened), that didn't make her less entitled to shut the door on the painful past and begin a new life, did it? With Michael, if that's what they both wanted.

Faye would understand. Deena would call her later, ask her to tell the others. She smiled when she thought of the circle of support she knew they would build around her. Even, she thought wryly, Elaine.

By the time Deena was ready to leave, her textbooks waiting in a sturdy canvas tote on the floor near the side door, it was nine-twenty. Although the sun had been out for some time, an opaque mist clung to the windows of her blue Honda. Rummaging through her purse, Deena found two Kleenex and used them to wipe the rear and side windows, leaving the glass panes blotchy and dotted with tissue residue. Once inside the car, she turned on the ignition and activated the windshield wipers to clear the front window. She watched enviously as the rubber blades efficiently erased the film in two swift marches across the field of tinted glass.

Almost one hour later, she was still in her car, her eyes fixed on the hypnotic motion of the wipers as they relentlessly moved back and forth, back and forth, back and forth. She didn't know how long she'd been sitting there. Or how long her phone had been ringing so insistently. By the time she reached the extension in the kitchen, the ringing had stopped.

"Still no answer," Ryker told Stollman. "I've been trying the ex-Mrs. Vogler for a half-hour, but damned if she hasn't gone out."

"So? What's the big deal?"

"So nothing. But I wonder where she is. Even if he was an ex, I would've thought she'd be shaken up a bit. No matter. I'll catch her some time today. Let's go see Vogler's parents."

"What about George and Tom?"

"George is meeting with the partner. Tom's checking out Vogler's place, talking with the neighbors. They'll meet us here around twelve-thirty, and we'll compare notes."

They found the apartment on Curson easily but had a more difficult time locating a parking spot. The closest vacancy was half a block away. Ryker pulled up in front of a hydrant.

"No choice," he muttered.

"Right." Stollman nodded, smiling.

Joe Vogelanter opened the door without asking to check their identification and invited them into the living room. He was wearing slippers. His eyes were red and puffy.

"My wife is resting," he told them. "Maybe it's enough if I answer your questions? The doctor gave her a shot last night, and for this morning, pills."

"I'm afraid we'll have to speak to Mrs. Vogelanter, too," Ryker said. "We'll try to make this short. Just a few questions. Unless you'd like us to come back later today."

"No, no. Later will not be better." He left to get her.

The room was small and overfurnished with two large sofas and matching ottomans, a glass coffee table with an ornate gilded base, a vinyl recliner, and a brown spinet piano. The piano and fireplace were crowded with framed photos. Some of Vogelanter, his son, and a white-haired woman, presumably the mother. One of Vogler with his former bride. A dozen or so of Vogler alone, tracing his life from infancy through adulthood.

Vogelanter returned with the woman in the photos. "My wife, Ida." He helped her onto the sofa and sat next to her. "Please, sit," he told the detectives.

Joe fixed his eyes on a spot somewhere above Ryker's head; Ida's face was buried in a handkerchief that she kept wadded up under her nose. Her sniffles punctuated the silence.

Ryker spoke. "Your rabbi explained the urgency of your situation, and I want to assure you we've been working as quickly as possible. The medical examiner tells me the department will be releasing your son's body by around four this afternoon, so you can make the necessary arrangements."

"Thank you," Joe whispered hoarsely.

Ida sat, hugging herself, rocking her upper torso.

"I know what a terrible time this is for you. And to have us come here and ask you questions about your son—well, that doesn't make things easier. But if we have any hope of catching the person who murdered your son—"

"Aaah!" A keening moan escaped from Ida's lips, then subsided into subdued whimpers.

"If we want to catch this person," Ryker continued softly, "we have to gather as much information as we can. We need leads, Mr. and Mrs. Vogelanter. Right now we have nothing."

Joe nodded.

"Can you tell us the last time you saw your son?"

"Saw him?" Joe pondered. "I think it was maybe ten days ago. That's right, isn't it, Ida?"

She stared without answering.

"He spent the last days of *Succos* with us. A Jewish holiday," Joe explained.

"You haven't seen him since then?"

Joe shook his head. "He's a very busy man, Officer. But he calls all the time."

"When was the—"

"Not one week in his whole life did he ever forget to call me before *Shabbas!*" Ida's eyes were brimming with fresh tears.

Ryker waited, but she had apparently finished. "When was the last time you spoke to him, Mr. Vogelanter?"

Joe looked at Ida.

"Saturday night," Ida said. "He called Saturday night, asked how I was."

"Did he tell you anything about his plans for the week?"

"Not really. He had so many business deals, my Jackie. Always running."

Jackie? Probably a childhood name, Ryker decided. "Did your son mention anything more to you, Mr. Vogelanter?"

"No."

"And you didn't think it was odd that you didn't hear from him since Saturday night?"

"He doesn't have to call every day, Officer," Ida said. "To check in like a little boy. He's a grown man!"

She had slipped unconsciously into the present tense. Most people did, Ryker knew from experience. "Did you know he was conducting an open house on Sunday?"

"He's always showing houses," Joe said. "He's a broker."

"But did you know which property he was showing Sunday?"

"I don't think he mentioned it," Joe said.

"Of course he did," Ida said. She turned to Ryker. "Jackie always told us where we could reach him. Just in case. I remember I asked him if the place had air-conditioning—such a hot weekend it was, even Saturday we left on the unit in our bedroom all night long. Who cares about the cost?" She turned back to Joe. "I told you. You don't remember?" she demanded.

"I guess not. What's the difference?"

"The difference?" she asked sadly. "No difference. You didn't talk to him, so you don't remember," she said pointedly. "But you're right; it wouldn't make a difference."

There was some friction here, Ryker saw. Had the father and son quarreled? "Mr. and Mrs. Vogelanter, I want you to think about my next question carefully. Do you know anyone who was angry with your son? Someone who may have wished him harm?"

"Everybody loved Jackie," Ida said firmly. "Everybody. But I don't understand. It wasn't a robber? I thought, when you said he was killed, that it must have been a robber."

"We're not sure what the motive was, but we have to check everything, even if it sounds remote." He saw her puzzled face. "A far shot," he explained. "Something that may seem unlikely."

She nodded.

"Anyone at all?" Ryker repeated. No one answered. "What about his partner, Ben Kasden? Did they get along well?"

"Ben? He and Jackie were like this." She hooked her index fingers. "Like brothers. Ben gave him a start, but he knew how much business Jackie brought in. Ben always told me that the best day in his life was the day Jackie came into the firm."

"And the worst day, when he married Ruthie," Joe added, with a shadow of a smile.

"What was that?"

"Just a joke. He's always joking about his wife, what a big spender she is. But my wife is right. Jake and Ben got along fine."

"They never quarreled about commissions, stuff like that? I mean, it would be normal for partners to disagree."

"Jake never mentioned anything," Joe said. "But why are you asking us all these questions about Ben? You can't think he could be mixed up in Jake's death! That's crazy!"

"We don't think anything right now, Mr. Vogelanter. But we have to get a complete picture." He checked his notebook. "What about your ex-daughter-in-law?" he asked casually. "Was she on good terms with your son after their divorce?"

Joe placed his hand on Ida's knee. "Deena is a wonderful girl, Officer. We love her like a daughter. Of course, we were sad when they decided to divorce, but what could we do? They knew their own minds."

"How long were they married?"

"A little over a year," Joe said.

"Did you know they were having problems?"

"Not really. Maybe they didn't want to worry us."

"And her parents—what's the name again?"

"Novick. Max and Pearl Novick. Fine people. Wonderful people."

"Did they get along well with your son?"

"They always treated him well. Always."

"I see. Was it a friendly divorce?"

Joe shrugged. "Divorce is divorce."

Ryker looked at Ida, sitting tight-lipped. She avoided his gaze. He made a point of checking his watch.

"Mr. Vogelanter, I wonder if could ask a favor. I'd like

Detective Stollman to call the precinct to see if I received any important messages. Could you show him to a phone, please?''

Joe looked at him uncertainly, then got up and escorted Stollman into the kitchen.

"Mrs. Vogelanter?" Ryker leaned toward her. "It's funny. Here I am, almost forty-seven, but when something bothers me, I still like to talk it over with my mother. I wonder if maybe your son wasn't like that. Maybe he was having problems with his ex-wife, something he thought only you would understand.''

"No, not really." She looked around uncomfortably, then studied her tightly clasped hands.

"Maybe she was nagging him about money, and he didn't want to worry your husband about it. Something like that.''

"Money? No," she shook her head, "I don't think they were fighting about money. The lawyers are taking care of everything. But Jackie didn't worry about money.''

"Was there something else, though, that you think I should know? Something that may not seem important but is bothering you?'' There *was* something. The ex-wife had practically thrown it in their faces last night, but what the hell was it?

"I don't—'' She craned her head toward the kitchen and stopped short when she saw Joe and the detective coming back.

"Any messages?'' Ryker asked Stollman.

"Nothing that won't wait.''

"Before we go, would it be all right with you if we took your fingerprints?'' Ryker asked the Vogelanters.

"Fingerprints?'' Joe exclaimed. *"Our* fingerprints?''

Ida gaped at the detectives; her face a curious mix of indignation and incredulity.

"It's just routine procedure," Ryker assured them. "We'll be taking prints of everyone who knew your son. We need your prints so we can rule them out if we find them in his apartment. If the killer knew your son, he may have visited him sometime where he lived.''

"I see," Joe said quietly. "If you have to, you have to. Ida?'' He turned to her.

She shrugged. "If it will help.''

Stollman brought up a print kit from the car. After he had

taken a full set from Ida and Joe, he handed them treated towelettes to remove the ink.

Ryker got up. "By the way, Mr. and Mrs. Vogelanter, do you know if your son owned a gun?"

"Yes, he did," Joe said. "One time, he *was* mugged when he was showing a property. After that he bought a gun. But I don't think he always took it with him. Just if he was going into a bad neighborhood, or somewhere very late at night. You know."

"Do you know what caliber gun he bought? What size?"

Joe shook his head.

"Do you own a gun, Mr. Vogelanter?"

"No. I hate guns. Jake bought it for protection, he said. But always, if there is a gun, somebody is getting killed."

No one, lease of all Detective Sam Ryker, could argue with that.

10

DETECTIVE GEORGE LEWIS SAT PATIENTLY ON THE TAUPE leather sofa in the outer office of Kasden and Vogler, Realtors, thumbing through an issue of *Architectural Digest*.

Where the hell do they get the money for these places? he wondered. He and his wife had bought a modest three-bedroom house four years ago and were struggling with the mortgage payments. Their entire house, he calculated, could fit into the living room of the palatial home featured in the magazine.

"Mr. Kasden will see you now," the receptionist said.

"Thank you, ma'am."

"Come in!" a booming voice answered Lewis's knock.

Lewis entered and immediately suppressed a smile. Kasden was a comical figure, a ball-like man bouncing across the room.

"Ben Kasden." He pumped Lewis's hand. "What can I do for you? My secretary said it was important police busi-

ness. Not arresting me for false termite reports, are you?"
He smiled.

"Not exactly, sir. It's about your partner, Jake Vogler."

"Oh, Lord! What's he done now? Sold the business in a
poker game? I warned him that he'd get us both into trouble!" He laughed nervously as he walked around the desk to
his chair.

"Mr. Kasden, I'm sorry to have to tell you that Mr. Vogler
is dead. His body was found last night in a house on Sherbourne." He told him the address.

Ben Kasden stared at the detective, blinked rapidly, then
sagged into his chair like a limp rag doll. He didn't try to
hide the tears that coursed down his cheeks.

"Mr. Kasden, I know this is terribly upsetting, but there
are a number of questions I have to ask. We need your help."

"I don't—what—how can I help you?" He found a handkerchief in his jacket and roughly blotted his face.

"I'd like you to confirm a few facts, if you would."

Kasden silently signaled for him to proceed.

"Now the house where Mr. Vogler's body was found is
listed with your company, is that right, sir?"

Kasden nodded. "Jake—Jake got the listing, worked damn
hard to get it, too. My God! I just can't believe this! How
could this have happened?"

"We're trying to find out. When did you last see him?"

"That would be Friday."

"You didn't see him on Sunday?"

"No. I knew he was doing an open house on that property,
but I didn't see him, no."

"Did you speak to him after the open house?"

"Not personally, but I did get a message from him at the
office on Monday."

Lewis tried to sound casual. "When was that?"

"Some time in the afternoon. Around two, I think. I didn't
speak with him. Someone called to say Jake had gone out of
town unexpectedly for a few days."

"Is that unusual?"

"It happens once in a while. I handle his appointments
myself, or if I'm busy, I have one of the salesmen help out."

"Did you recognize the caller's voice?"

"No." He frowned. "It was a strange voice, come to think
of it. Muffled. I had a hard time understanding the message."

"Would your receptionist possibly be able to identify it?"

"She didn't hear it. She was on a coffee break when the call came in. I picked it up myself."

"I see. You weren't bothered by this call until now?"

"No. Why would I be?"

"Mr. Kasden, were there any clients who were upset with Mr. Vogler, or even with the firm?"

Kasden sat upright. "What're you saying? Do you mean Jake was killed by someone he knew? Is that what you're telling me?"

"We have to look into all the possibilities, sir."

"But *Jake?*" He shook his head in disbelief. "Detective, let me tell you something. Jake was a hell of a nice guy. One in a million. To me, he was the greatest. So when you suggest he may have been killed by someone he knew, I have to tell you it's ridiculous."

"Mr. Kasden, from my experience, few people go through life without offending someone. And I doubt that your partner, as wonderful as he must have been, was any different. There must have been *some* people who didn't like him."

Kasden picked up a pen, twirled it between his fingers. "In business, especially a business like this, there are always clients who like to complain, who feel they got the short end of the stick. But that doesn't mean a guy who finds out the plumbing is faulty takes a gun and shoots the broker who sold him the house! Come on, Detective! If that were the case, I'd get the hell out of this business tomorrow!"

"*Were* there any clients that he argued with?"

"Sure. One or two."

"Can you be more specific?"

Kasden put down the pen. "Look, I don't want you harassing our clients. That wouldn't do wonders for the business. And I doubt it would lead you anywhere."

"Mr. Kasden, I assure you that our inquiries will be discreet. And the information you give us could be vital."

"I know, I know," he said unhappily. "Okay. There was a couple just two months ago, name of Ferkins. Buyers. They had their attorney write a formal complaint to the office, claimed Jake had knowledge of serious structural damage to the property they bought but didn't inform them about it."

"Okay." Lewis finished some notes. "Anyone else?"

"Let me think." He pinched the bridge of his nose. "A guy named Pratt—Prather, that's it. He gave us an exclusive listing. He insisted Jake hadn't shown him all the offers, said

Jake had pushed the offer Prather finally accepted because Jake was anxious to sell the prospective buyer's property."

"And?"

"And nothing. Jake said he showed him all the offers; I saw them, too. Everything was kosher. Prather's a jerk."

"And that was the end of it?"

"Not exactly. Prather threatened to report Jake to the Real Estate Commissioner. Get his license revoked. Big talker!"

Lewis waited patiently.

"I just remembered. Four months ago, Jake got a listing for a Hancock Park property that belonged to a guy named Dyson. Alexander Dyson. A mansion—over thirty rooms. Eight bedrooms, twelve baths, maid's quarters that make my master bedroom suite look like a hut in Tijuana, a kitchen you could bowl in. Tennis court, indoor and outdoor pools, two-story guest house, topiary gardens—you know, the kind where they prune the bushes to look like lions and seals? Me, if I want lions and seals, I go to the zoo. Which is never.

"Anyway, the property listed for $2.5 million. A steal, right?" Kasden grinned. "With the commission on that, Jake would be sitting pretty. He worked his tail off, let me tell you. And he found a few prospective buyers."

"So what happened?"

"Dyson turned them all down. Which is his prerogative. But a month after our exclusive ended, Jake heard that Dyson sold the property by himself, and when he checked into it, he learned that the buyer was one of the people Jake had walked through the house. Which means Jake was entitled to the commission, even though the listing contract had expired."

"Did he get his commission?"

Kasden grinned. "You better believe it! Dyson was madder'n hell, but Jake was ready to take him to court."

"Interesting."

"It's a fascinating business, Detective. You meet all kinds of people. Men and women. That reminds me—Jake had a run-in with this realtor, Laura Brackwood. She claims he stole several of her listings. Threatened to sue him."

"Did he? Steal the listings, I mean?"

Kasden shrugged. "Jake swore he didn't; I believed him. End of chapter. Look, Detective, this kind of thing goes with the territory. It's a cutthroat business, everybody knocking on doors to get exclusive listings. This Brackwood woman's probably sore because Jake beat her on a few choice deals.''

''Was Mr. Vogler worried about this realtor?''

''Jake? Are you kidding?'' He laughed. ''He *never* worried. That was part of his charm. Listen, he got into a few sticky situations, but he always came out okay. Lady Luck was definitely on his side. Until now,'' he added soberly. ''God, I can't believe he's dead!'' He hesitated. ''And of course, there's Murdoch.'' He grimaced.

''Who?''

''James Murdoch. You never heard of him? He's a multi-millionaire; name's in the paper all the time. He's into oil, commodities, real estate—anything that makes money. I don't know how I could've forgotten about him. Wishful thinking, I guess.'' Kasden smiled weakly.

''What exactly was the problem there?''

''Where should I start?'' Kasden groaned. ''There were problems with the deal from the beginning. I think it was jinxed.'' He gave the detective a summary of the project, the construction delays, and Murdoch's decision to sell his shares. ''In another month, the whole mess should be resolved. We have investors lined up who are seriously interested in buying Murdoch's shares. I can't wait for this thing to be over!''

''So you and Mr. Vogler managed this project together?''

''No way. Jake handled Murdoch. To tell you the truth, I worried all along that we were getting in over our heads. Jake wasn't worried, though. The confidence of youth, right?''

Lewis smiled.

''And he was excited about the potential profit, too. Hell, so was I! Who wouldn't be? But it wasn't just the money. It was a real challenge to Jake, handling someone big like Murdoch.'' He hesitated. ''I think he was surprised Murdoch didn't take to him. That never happened to him before. And then, well, they had some pretty heated arguments, and Murdoch made Jake nervous, he and those goons who work for him. They're like guys from some B-movie, know what I mean? I think they practice looking sinister first thing in the morning after they brush their teeth, just to make sure they haven't lost their touch.''

''Did they threaten him physically?''

''Not in so many words. But Jake wasn't happy. They scared Deena, too. Jake's ex-wife.'' He told the detectives what had happened. ''I thought they were just talking big, though.'' He looked at Lewis, his eyes forming a silent question.

Lewis ignored it. "Mr. Kasden, you've been very helpful. Just a few more questions, and we'll be through for now. Although I'd appreciate it if you'd give me the exact names, addresses, and phone numbers for the people we've discussed.''

"No problem, Detective.'' He buzzed the receptionist, gave her instructions over the phone, and turned to Lewis. "Miss Battaglia will have a typed list for you in a few minutes.''

"Thanks. Mr. Kasden, do you know if Mr. Vogler had a will?''

"I know he did. I advised him to get one when he got married. I don't know the details. You'd have to check with his attorney. Marvin Cooper. His office is nearby. Ask Miss Battaglia for his number and address on the way out.''

"Thanks again.'' Lewis rose. "I'd like to take a look at Mr. Vogler's office now. By the way, for purposes of elimination, we'd like to have your fingerprints. I'd appreciate it if you came in within the next few days, at your convenience. I'm assuming that you've been in your late partner's apartment.''

"Yeah, I've been there more than once. I'm going to be a celebrity, huh?'' He laughed nervously. "What if you find out that I'm a fugitive from justice? My wife doesn't know.''

Lewis smiled. Kasden escorted him to Jake's office.

"Well, I guess I'll leave you here, as long as you promise not to plant anything incriminating.''

"Maybe next time.''

Vogler's office revealed very little. One drawer of the rosewood desk contained a grooming kit in soft black kid leather, a lint brush, some Halston aftershave, two small vials of Binaca mouth freshener. From another, Lewis pulled a chain of paper clips and replaced it next to a stapler and some 3M Post It notepads. There were several files stacked neatly on his desk; Lewis picked them up, along with the appointment calendar, and walked back into Kasden's office. Kasden was just sitting, slumped in his chair.

"I'd like to take these. I'll sign for them, of course. And I'll need the files for the clients we talked about today.''

"What's that?'' Kasden looked up. "Oh. Well. That may be a problem. I mean, I'll have to check through Jake's calendar, see what appointments he scheduled for the next few weeks. You can see what I mean. And the files, too. Could you come back, say in a few days, give me a chance to go through all this?''

"Tell you what. I'll take these and the other files, have them Xeroxed at the station, and return them to you tomorrow.''

Kasden shook his head. "Gee, I'd like to cooperate, but I can't let you take the files. What if one of Jake's clients calls up before tomorrow for some information? It's business, you understand? Look, take the calendar if you want. I'll just Xerox the pages for the next few days.''

Lewis handed Kasden the calendar and the files. Kasden left the office. A few minutes later he was back.

"Sorry it took so long. The machine was cold. Here you go.'' He handed Lewis the calendar. "Listen, come back any time if you want to look at those files. Today, even. And I promise I'll release them in a few days. I want to do everything I can to help you find Jake's killer. I mean that.''

"I know you do, Mr. Kasden. I'll bring this calendar back in a few days at the latest.''

"No problem, no problem at all.'' He walked Lewis into the reception room and picked up a piece of paper from the desk.

"Judy—Miss Battaglia—must've taken a coffee break. Drinks a lot of coffee, that girl!'' He grinned. "Here are the names and numbers you asked for.'' He handed the list to Lewis.

"The lawyer?'' Lewis reminded him.

"Right. Sorry.'' He placed the list on the desk, flipped through the Rolodex cards, found the one he wanted, and added Marvin Cooper's address and phone number to the typed list.

Suddenly, he looked up. "I just realized I'll have to tell Judy that Jake is dead.'' He sounded shaken. "She'll be crushed, totally crushed. She was crazy about him. Everybody was.''

Everybody, Lewis thought in the elevator on his way down to the lobby, except four or five people Kasden happened to think of without too much difficulty.

And maybe there were others.

11

"THAT'S ALL OF IT?" RYKER ASKED. HE'D LISTENED WITH-out commenting while Lewis had repeated his discussion with Ben Kasden, had nodded once or twice with interest.

"Yeah. I'll write up my notes now, if you want."

"No rush. Finish your lunch first." He pointed to Lewis's half-finished turkey sandwich. Ryker, Stollman, Lewis, and Moran had ordered from a nearby deli, and Ryker's desk was littered with mostly empty wrinkled sheets of wax paper—still strongly perfumed with pastrami, corned beef, and pickles—and with two large cardboard cartons of potato salad and cole slaw.

"Looks like Vogler wasn't as popular as Mama thought," Moran commented.

"Who knows?" Lewis said. "From what Kasden said, it's that kind of business. And I can't see a client running off to kill Vogler because of a disagreement. There are courts for that."

Moran said, "Remember that case two months ago, where a guy offed his brother-in-law over $350? People don't always act rationally. If they did, you and I would be out of jobs."

Lewis shrugged, concentrated on his sandwich.

"So what do you make of that call on Monday?" Ryker asked. He'd finished his pastrami sandwich, contemplated taking another spoonful of the cole slaw, but decided against it.

"Obviously, the killer called," Stollman said. "The way I see it, Vogler was killed on Sunday after the open house. The killer called Monday to throw us off about the time of death."

"And maybe," Moran added, "he has an alibi all set up for Monday, but nothing concrete for Sunday."

"Maybe," Ryker agreed. "But we don't know when Vogler was killed."

"Sunday," Stollman insisted. "Why would he be in the house on Monday?"

Ryker said, "One, the owners arranged to meet him there. Two, he was showing a couple through the house. Three, he forgot something when he was there on Sunday. There are lots of possibilities, Hank, but for what it's worth, I happen to agree with you. I think Vogler was killed Sunday. But for now, we'll have to get alibis from everyone concerned covering a time period from about five P.M. Sunday through Tuesday morning. That air-conditioning really screwed things up royally."

"What about the caller?" Stollman asked Lewis. "Kasden has no idea who it was? Man or woman?"

"None. He said the voice was muffled. What about the murder weapon? Any news on that?"

Ryker said, "Smith and Wesson .22. From the damage inflicted by the bullet, that's what Kanata guessed. With a more powerful gun, the bullet would probably have gone clear through the skull."

"Not too hard for someone to get hold of one," Moran said.

"Vogler had a gun," Ryker said. "His parents don't know what kind, but we'll run a check on the registration. Tom, did you check out his apartment yet?"

"The crime unit's there now. I figured I'd go back this afternoon after they're done. The place is going to be sealed."

"Fine. Did you talk to any of his neighbors?"

"He lives on the third floor in a high-security building on Elm between Wilshire and Olympic. Lots of neighbors; we'll have to talk to all of them. I talked to the doorman. He says he last saw Vogler returning from an early Sunday morning jog."

"He didn't see him that night?" Ryker asked.

"This guy's shift is from six A.M. to two P.M. I'll catch the second shift when I go check out the apartment. The third guy doesn't start till ten."

Ryker said, "So what've we got? A dead guy, no weapon, no identifiable prints as of yet. No witnesses, no apparent motive. Your average homicide case, right, guys?" His grin turned into a grimace. He shouldn't have eaten the pastrami.

"What's next?" Lewis asked.

"I think you should go with Tom to Vogler's apartment and talk to the neighbors. Then, if you have time, contact the owners of the Sherbourne property—wait a minute, I have the name.'' He checked his notebook. ''Here it is. Pomerantz.'' He dictated the phone listing and address. ''Got it, George?''

''Yeah.''

''We also have to contact everyone who was at the open house and the neighbors. Who knows? Maybe we'll get a break. We'll split up the list, start with the neighbors first. Hank?''

''Sure. I'll try to get to some of the names on the list, too.''

Lewis handed Ryker the paper. ''Sam, here's a list of the people Kasden told me about. And the name of Vogler's lawyer.''

''I'll call him today. I guess we should find out how much he was worth. Although since the parents are probably going to get the whole bundle, I don't think money was the motive.''

''And this is Vogler's appointment calendar. Kasden said we could come and look at any files we need, said he can't part with them 'cause he may need them. We could get a subpoena, but I don't see the point. He seems to want to cooperate, and I can't blame him for being nervous about letting his files out of the office.'' He placed the calendar on the desk.

''What about the receptionist? You said she wasn't in when the phone call came, but she may have heard something important that Kasden doesn't know about. Did you talk to her?''

''She was on a coffee break when I finished with Kasden. I'll talk to her when I return the calendar.''

''Great. I'll look at this when I get back. The body's going to be released some time today, so I guess the funeral will be tomorrow. I plan to be there.''

''Want me to go with you?'' Stollman asked.

''Yeah. Your Hebrew may be rusty, but you may pick up on something I won't notice. I was going to call that rabbi about that Hebrew phrase, but since I'll be seeing him tomorrow, it can wait. Right now I think it's time I paid a call to the ex-Mrs. Vogler. And then, maybe to her father. I'm curious about that problem she referred to the other night.'' He checked his watch. It was one-thirty. ''Let's meet here at four to compare notes.''

Ryker rose, leaned over, and started clearing the desk from lunch. The other detectives followed suit.

"A real looker, the ex-wife," Moran said, winking. "You'd better take one of us along as a chaperone."

"I'll have to take my chances. Hazards of the job, and all that." He grinned, opened his desk drawer, and shook three Tums into his palm. "Protection—in case I'm overpowered." He popped the tablets into his mouth.

Deena woke with a start and looked at the clock on her nightstand: one-thirty-five. The morning seemed to have slipped away. She had sat in the kitchen for a while and then had drifted into her bedroom. She'd slipped off her shoes, climbed, fully clothed, into her bed, and buried herself under the quilt.

She thought about the classes she'd missed; she'd have to contact a classmate for the notes. She felt groggy and a little nauseated. Her head was throbbing dully, the pain radiating to her eyes. Slowly, she got out of bed, wobbled into the bathroom, and took two Extra-Strength Excedrin tablets.

She looked a mess. Her face, still creased from sleep, was streaked with splotches of black mascara. Her hair was tangled, her clothes wrinkled. She splashed cold water on her face, erased the mascara with a cotton ball soaked in makeup remover, wet a washcloth and squeezed it almost dry. Back in bed, the wash-cloth resting on her eyes, cool and comforting, blocking out the light, she waited for her headache to recede.

When the doorbell rang, she groaned, reluctantly removed the compress, and got out of bed. She put on her shoes, tried to smooth out her skirt, and made her way to the front door.

"It's Alan, Deena."

"Alan?" she echoed, surprised. She let him in quickly.

He hugged her tightly. "I came as soon as I could. Reuben Markowitz called. He heard about Jake."

"Reuben? How?"

The last time Deena had spoken to Rabbi Markowitz, he'd asked her to call him by his first name. "By now we're friends, not just collaborators," he'd insisted when she'd balked. "Let me worry about proprieties."

Alan said, "Rabbi Pearlstein told him. Your phone's been busy all morning. I was terribly worried."

"It's probably off the hook. Habit, I guess." She hadn't even noticed.

He took in her appearance. "Are you all right?"

"I guess. I feel a little strange, like I'm not really here."
They went into the den and sat down on the couch.

"How are your parents taking it?"

"I haven't told them yet. I haven't told anyone. I picked
up the phone a few times, but I just don't have the energy to
talk to anyone. The police were here, you know."

"When?"

"Last night. They thought Jake still lived here. Ironic,
isn't it? I thought they came because he filed a complaint."

He frowned. "Did you tell them that?"

"I don't think so. I don't really remember what I said. Do
you know he was killed? Shot, I mean." She shuddered.

"Yes. Rabbi Pearlstein's trying to get the body released.
They have no idea who did it?" He looked at her carefully.

"Probably a burglar, I guess. They didn't say. But what
else could it be?"

"Don't worry about it. Listen, I have a client coming soon,
but Sandy's coming over later. Is there anything I can do
before I leave? Do you want me to call someone?"

"I left a message on Michael's machine and asked him to
come over when he gets home. I'll call my parents a little
later. I want to tell my dad first; my mother will probably
get hysterical." She looked at him. "It's so awful, isn't it?"

"It's a shock, all right."

"I feel so confused. I hated Jake for what he was doing to
me, but now that he's really dead . . ."

"Don't think about it. It's over. You have to—"

The doorbell rang. She looked toward the front door.

"Go see who it is," Alan said. "I'll call the office and
tell them I'm on my way back."

"Okay. Check the phone in my bedroom. I don't remember if I put the receiver back on the hook." She pointed the
way.

Maybe it's Reuben, she thought as she walked to the entry,
but the face she saw in the peephole was totally unfamiliar.

"Detective Sam Ryker, LAPD. I'd like to talk with you
about the death of your ex-husband."

"All right." She opened the door and invited him in with
a graciousness she didn't feel.

"Is there somewhere we can talk comfortably? This may
take a while." Even though she looked disheveled and a little
pale, Moran was right. She was a good-looking woman.

"Of course." She was about to lead him into the living room when Alan came down the hall and joined them.

"Detective Sam Ryker." He gave Alan his hand.

"Alan Krantz. I'm a friend of Mrs. Vogler, Detective." He turned to Deena. "I just found out that my client's going to be delayed, so I can stay a while longer."

"You don't have to, really."

"It's no problem." He smiled at Deena reassuringly.

She looked at him curiously and went into the living room. The two men followed. Alan sat next to Deena on the couch; Ryker took a chair facing them.

"Sorry about the mix-up last night, Mrs. Vogler, but I'm sure you can see how it happened."

"I understand."

"You've probably had some time to think about this, and I wonder if you've come up with any ideas that might help us."

"Ideas?"

"Names of people who might have been on especially bad terms with your husband."

"Are you saying Jake was killed by someone he knew?" She leaned forward.

"It's a definite possibility."

"I see. I don't really know much about my ex-husband's business dealings, Detective. I suggest you talk to his partner. I can give you his number."

"We've talked to Mr. Kasden. He's helping us out on that end." He pulled a paper out of his inner pocket and handed it to her. "Are you familiar with any of these names?"

She took the paper and studied it, looked blank until she came toward the end of the list. She looked up quickly. "James Murdoch. He was very upset with Jake. Did Mr. Kasden tell you what happened? To me, I mean?"

"Yes. Can you tell it to me in your own words?" Ryker listened carefully while Deena spoke. Then he said, "Murdoch's men didn't harm you?"

"It was more suggestion, but I was very frightened. And they were looking for Jake, not me. They made it clear that if Jake didn't take care of the situation, he'd be sorry."

"Did you interpret that as a physical threat?"

"I think so, yes. They sounded very serious."

"Did you tell your ex-husband about this?"

"I called him as soon as they left. He was upset, but he said he could handle it."

"Do you know if they contacted him again? Threatened him?"

"I have no idea, Detective. They never bothered me again, though, thank goodness."

"Okay. We'll check into Mr. Murdoch and his men. Do you recognize any other names on this list?"

She glanced at the rest of the list. "Just this one. Marvin Cooper. He was Jake's lawyer."

"You've had some dealings with him?"

"Only through my attorney. Mr. Cooper was representing Jake in our divorce."

"How long have you been divorced, Mrs. Vogler?"

"Almost six months. The divorce became official on May 19th. We separated six months before that."

"Were you still on friendly terms?"

She pushed her hair behind her ear. "Is this relevant, Detective?"

"I'm just trying to get a picture of your ex-husband, Mrs. Vogler. It helps to get the entire background."

She looked at Alan. He nodded encouragement.

"We weren't on great terms, but we talked when we had to."

"When did you last see him?"

"A little over two weeks ago."

"Was that the last time you talked to him?"

"Yes." *"I'll never give you the* get, *Deena."*

"And what did you talk about, if I may ask?"

"Just details of the divorce." *"I wish you were dead, Jake."*

"I'm a little confused, Mrs. Vogler. I thought you said it was final."

"It is, but the property division hasn't been settled."

"I see. Isn't that unusual?"

"Not at all, Detective," Alan interjected. "I happen to be an attorney, and I've handled several divorce cases. It's not atypical for a couple to dissolve the marriage before the property is divided. The term is 'bifurcation.' "

"Thanks. I didn't know that." Ryker smiled easily and turned to Deena. "How long were you married, Mrs. Vogler?"

"A little over a year."

"Children?"

"No."

"Who wanted the divorce?"

"Do I have to answer? I really think it's my business."

"You don't have to, no. But I'd appreciate your cooperation. It may sound strange, but if I can get a better idea of the personality of the victim, sometimes I can get a handle on the killer."

"I don't see where you're going with this, Detective, but Jake and I separated because we weren't suited to each other."

"Irreconcilable differences, huh?"

"Yes. Exactly."

"Okay. So the divorce was final, but you were having problems dividing the property. Like this house, for instance?"

"Detective, I think you've asked Mrs. Vogler enough about her personal life. It has absolutely no bearing on Mr. Vogler's death, and it's upsetting her to talk about it."

Ryker looked at Alan. "Are you here as her attorney, Mr. Krantz? I thought you said you were her friend."

"As her friend and an attorney, I intend to protect her rights."

"No problem. I just have a few more questions." He took out his notebook, made a point of looking at it. "Mrs. Vogler, when my men came last night, you alluded to some difficulty between your ex-husband and your father. Can you explain that?"

"I don't remember that." Oh, God! What had she done? They would misconstrue everything; she knew they would.

"According to the officer's notes, you said, 'My father didn't mean any harm; he was trying to protect me.' " He looked up. "And then you asked the officers if they were going to arrest you." He closed his notebook. "I'm sure you have an explanation that will clear this up for me." He smiled at her.

"Deena, you don't have to answer that. Detective, I'm not Mrs. Vogler's attorney, but until she gets one, I'm going to advise her not to answer any more questions without an attorney present unless she feels completely comfortable doing so."

"I have to be honest, Mrs. Vogler. Your comments *do* sound suspicious. I can probably get a judge to sign an arrest warrant, if that's what it takes to get some answers." Which wasn't technically true.

"Why don't you do that, Detective," Alan said coldly.

Their eyes locked for a moment.

"Mrs. Vogler, this is a routine question we're going to ask everyone who knew your ex-husband. Where were you between five P.M. on Sunday, October 29th, and Tuesday, October 31st?"

Alan nodded his approval.

"I'd have to think."

"Take your time." Ryker smiled in encouragement.

"I didn't do anything special on Sunday. Cleaned the house. Did some homework. A lot of homework, actually. I'm a law student," she explained.

"What about Sunday evening?"

"I didn't leave the house all day. I talked to some friends on the phone, watched television, that kind of stuff."

"Did anyone come over?"

"No. Not on Sunday. On Monday and Tuesday I went to classes." She thought for a moment. "I shopped for groceries on Monday, and I went to a self-defense class." She'd signed up for the course after Jake had tried to rape her, but she wasn't about to volunteer that to Ryker.

Ryker jotted notes in a spiral notebook. "Mrs. Vogler, could you give me your parents' phone number and address?"

She hesitated.

"I can find it out anyway, Mrs. Vogler, and I *do* have to speak with them. I think you can see that."

She gave him the information in flat monosyllables.

"If you think of anything, let me know." He handed her his card and got up. Deena and Alan followed him to the front door.

"One last thing for now, Mrs. Vogler. We know that your ex-husband owned a gun. Do you happen to know what kind?"

She shook her head. "I have no idea. I didn't even know he had one. He must've bought it after we separated."

"By the way, do you own a gun?"

"Yes, I do. I felt I needed one after the incident with Murdoch's men. I felt very unprotected, living alone."

"What kind is it?"

"A .22-caliber. It's registered, by the way."

"May I see the gun, please, Mrs. Vogler."

"Certainly. It's in my nightstand. I'll get it."

She left the two men standing in the entry and walked quickly to her bedroom. She opened the small drawer in her nightstand and reached in for the gun.

It wasn't there.

Confused more than alarmed, she searched through the nightstand, pulling out stationery boxes, old magazines, some scarves, several paperback novels she had intended to read.

Nothing.

Could she have misplaced it? She tried to think clearly, tried to visualize the last time she had held it. She knew she had checked to see that it was in place when Jake had started making the phone calls. Not that she'd ever really believed she'd have to protect herself with it against him. But she'd felt more secure, touching the cold metal, knowing she could reach it in an instant.

She walked back slowly to the waiting men.

"I can't find it right now." She looked at Ryker steadily.

"Would you like to check again? I can wait."

"I thought it was in my nightstand. I probably put it somewhere else, but at the moment I can't think where."

"How many people know that you have a gun?"

"I don't know. My family. My friends. It wasn't a secret."

"And do people know where you kept it?"

"I suppose so."

"When was the last time you saw it?"

She thought for a moment. "About two weeks ago, I think. I can't be sure."

"Well, I think it would be a good idea if you went over the whole house carefully. And please call me if you find it."

After Ryker left, Alan turned to Deena. "Do you want me to help you look for the gun now?"

"There's no point. I always kept it in my nightstand."

"You couldn't have misplaced it? Put it somewhere and not remembered? You've been under a lot of strain lately."

She shook her head. "I don't think so."

"Then who on earth could have taken it?"

"I don't know." She was shaken to the core. Until this minute, she'd thought of Jake's killer as some nameless, cloaked figure stalking helpless victims. It had never entered her mind that it could be someone she knew. But now her gun was missing. Someone had taken it from her home.

"It could be anyone," she said dully. "Anyone at all."

12

"WE FOUND THE GUN," MORAN ANNOUNCED. HE SLOUCHED down onto a chair and tossed a clear plastic bag containing a dark blue revolver onto Ryker's desk. "It was in Vogler's apartment. Not hard to find. He kept it in a hall closet in plain view."

Ryker studied the gun. "A .38? That lets Vogler's gun out of the running. I sure as hell would like to know what happened to his ex-wife's gun." He told Moran about the missing gun.

"No shit. You think she's lying?"

"Who knows? Without a warrant, I couldn't check. And even if I could have gotten a warrant—which is highly unlikely—by the time I got back to the house, she could've dumped the gun."

"You don't look worried."

"I'm not. I called headquarters from the car, ordered a tail put on her, and waited until he showed up. If she leaves the house and tries to dispose of the gun, we'll know it."

"But if she's lying, why'd she admit she had the gun?"

"Because she's not stupid. She told me herself it's registered. She probably figured we'd find out about it sooner or later. This way, she's volunteering the truth."

"Truth about what?" Lewis asked as he walked over.

Ryker explained. "What else did you find at Vogler's?"

"He's a classy guy, Vogler," Lewis said as he sat down. "Custom shirts, monogrammed cuffs, nice jewelry—gold cuff links, a dress watch. Expensive, but not gaudy."

"Anything interesting?"

"Nothing unusual. Athletic gear—some weights, racquetball equipment, books on body building. From the pictures around the place, he was a good-looking guy.''

"Before he was dead,'' Moran said. "A bullet doesn't do much for a guy's overall appearance.''

"What about personal effects? Letters?''

"We took a bunch of stuff from his desk,'' Lewis said. "Most of it looked like business correspondence, a lot of it from his lawyer. We'll sort through it after SID checks everything. There were also a few pictures of the ex-wife around the house. Looks like he never got over her, huh?''

"I don't know about that,'' Moran said. "He wasn't letting the grass grow under his feet. I found some condoms in the bathroom. Or maybe he was just being a good Boy Scout— 'Be Prepared'—isn't that their motto?'' He grinned.

"You're just jealous, Moran,'' Lewis told him. "Vogler's better looking dead than you are alive.''

They all laughed.

"What did you learn from the ex-wife, Sam?'' Lewis asked.

"Now that's interesting.'' He repeated the conversation.

"You pulling her in for questioning?'' Moran asked.

"Not yet. I can always do it later. First, I'm going to talk to her parents.''

"Funny that the lawyer friend was there,'' Moran commented.

"Isn't it, though?'' Ryker grinned. "A little too much of a coincidence, don't you think?''

"But it could be just that,'' Lewis argued. "Coincidence.''

Ryker said, "Yeah, but we have to consider the other side, that she called him because he's a lawyer and she needed his advice. You know your problem, George? You're too soft. I saw right away that you liked this Vogler woman from the minute you met her.''

"You're right. There's something about her that strikes me as real. Even though she did make those statements about her father. I think she's just trying to protect him.''

"From what?'' Moran asked. "We have no idea.''

Ryker said, "Something's definitely going on, something we should know about. She was nervous; this Krantz guy, the lawyer, was nervous. Okay. Next. What about the doorman?''

Lewis said, "I spoke to him. He hasn't seen Vogler since

last Saturday, and he was on duty every afternoon, including Sunday and Monday. Except Friday. That's his day off.''

''The neighbors?'' Ryker asked.

Lewis said, ''I spoke to one woman on his floor. She lives three doors away. An older woman, hard of hearing. Stays home most of the time and watches TV. She knew Vogler, though, said he was always very polite, helped her with her groceries whenever he saw her, opened the door. Always smiling. 'A charming young gentleman,' she called him.''

Moran said, ''Most of the neighbors aren't home yet. We'll go back, speak to the other doorman while we're there.''

''Where's Hank? He should be back by now,'' Lewis said.

Ryker said, ''He called in a half hour ago. His battery died, and he's waiting for the auto club to send someone out. He's going back to talk to some more neighbors. He also checked out four names on the open house sign-up sheet. Nobody saw anything or heard anything unusual. So what's new?'' He sighed.

''You find out about the funeral?'' Lewis asked.

''Tomorrow, ten A.M., in a chapel at a cemetery in Downey. I've never been to a religious Jewish funeral before, have you?''

Both men shook their heads.

''Anyway, Hank's coming with me, so he'll clue me in if I do anything wrong.''

''Did you look at Vogler's calendar yet?'' Lewis asked. ''Kasden Xeroxed some pages, but I want to get it back to him.''

''I forgot all about it.'' Ryker looked on the desk, then remembered he'd stored the calendar in a drawer. He took it out and flipped through the pages to November.

There were staggered appointments for the first few days of November, and on the page marked Friday the 3rd, Vogler had drawn heavy circles around the date. The second week was lighter—only two appointments, one on Tuesday, the other on Friday. The rest of the month and all of December were blank.

Ryker thumbed backward through October. On Tuesday, the 31st, Vogler had scheduled a morning meeting, lunch, and two afternoon appointments. On Monday, he'd planned to meet with Murdoch from early in the morning.

''Nothing special except for this appointment with Murdoch. He penciled in a large block of time—all day, it looks like. What's this squiggle? I can't make it out." He turned the calendar toward Lewis and Moran and pointed to some letters.

Moran leaned over. "Looks like CPR. Why would he want to study CPR during business hours?"

"Not CPR," Lewis said, "CPA."

Moran said, "Some handwriting. Almost as bad as a doctor's!"

"Murdoch and his accountant?" Ryker mused. "Interesting."

"You want me to ask Kasden about it?" Lewis asked.

"Not yet. I want to think about it first." Ryker continued flipping pages backward, pausing now and then. "What's this?"

"What?" both detectives echoed.

"There's a page missing. Monday, October 23rd on one side, Tuesday, the 24th, on the other."

"What's the big deal?" Moran said. "Maybe he wrote some notes down on it and didn't feel like copying them over."

"What's wrong?" Lewis asked Ryker.

"Maybe nothing. I guess I have a suspicious mind. Did the partner give you a hard time about taking this with you?"

"No. He was concerned about the files. He just took the calendar, Xeroxed some pages, and gave it to me."

"You watched him Xerox the pages?"

"Not exactly." Lewis sounded unhappy. "The Xerox machine was in another room. Kasden took the calendar with him."

"How long was he gone?"

"A few minutes. I'm not sure. It didn't seem that long."

"I think I'll give this to the lab boys and see if they can raise the letters on the following page."

"I'm sorry, Sam. It was careless of me."

"Don't worry, George," Ryker said quickly, seeing the detective's face. "It probably isn't important. You know me— I just don't like loose ends. Look, it's almost five. Why don't the two of you head back to Vogler's apartment, see if you can find some neighbors home so we can crack this case wide open."

"What about you?" Moran asked. "Staying in the office?"

"Nope. I'm off to see Mr. and Mrs. Max Novick. The ex-wife's parents."

"Happy hunting," Moran told him.

"You need a lawyer, Deena," Alan said.

"I haven't done anything wrong!"

"That's beside the point. From what I can see, Ryker is going to uncover all this business about Jake and the *get*. Too many people know about it to keep it hidden."

"Then why didn't you want me to answer his questions?"

"Because I want you to think carefully before you say anything. This is serious. We're talking about a murder case."

"Can't you be my lawyer? You've handled criminal cases."

"It's not a good idea. We're friends. You're better off getting someone who's not emotionally involved the way I am."

"I don't know anyone else. Aside from Brenda, that is."

"Brenda doesn't do criminal law. I'll try to get someone."

"Alan, please. Think about taking me on as a client. I'd feel a lot more comfortable about the whole thing."

"I'll think about it. You'd better call your father, tell him what's happened. Prepare him for a visit from the police. Tell him not to say anything until he's talked with a lawyer."

"You're right." She sighed. "I'm not thinking straight. I can't stop worrying about the gun."

"I wish I could say you have nothing to worry about. Don't be surprised if Ryker comes back with a search warrant."

"Why? Don't you think he believes me?"

"Deena." He shook his head. "You're so naive. Put yourself in Ryker's position. A man is killed with a gun—I'm assuming it's a .22-caliber, or why the interest in yours?—and his ex-wife's gun suddenly and conveniently disappears."

"Ryker thinks I killed him?" She was aghast.

"It's a possibility that has to have occurred to him. Either that, or you gave the gun to someone who did. Or, if you're telling the truth, someone who knows you well enough to be in your house took the gun and did it."

"But we don't know that Jake was killed with my gun! It could all be just one horrible coincidence."

"It could. The problem is that without your gun, we can't prove it wasn't used to kill Jake. If we had your gun, the police could run ballistic tests to prove that the bullet that killed Jake didn't come from your gun."

"I see what you mean."

"But then again, and I hope to God this isn't the case, it could be the murder weapon. You do see that, don't you?"

"I don't believe that someone I know killed Jake. I *can't* believe it."

"So where's the gun?"

Deena didn't answer.

"It's horrible to think that you may know the killer, but you know it's a possibility. I don't want to frighten you, but you have to see how serious this is."

"I do. Thanks for everything, Alan. I'm going to call my father as soon as you leave."

"Do that." He kissed her on the forehead. "I'll call you later in the day. Do you want Sandy to come over?"

"I'm not sure. I wouldn't be very good company."

"I'll tell her to call you, and then you can decide. She'll understand, either way. Take care of yourself."

When Deena called Max at the convalescent home, Janice Brenner, his assistant manager, answered the phone.

"Hi, Janice. Is my dad there? I have to talk to him."

"Sorry, honey, but you just missed him."

"Did he leave for the day?" It was a little after three.

"Well, I know he had an appointment at the bank. There was some error in his checking account that's been annoying him for weeks, and he finally decided to take care of it in person."

"Is he coming back to the home?" She certainly didn't want to page Max at the bank, even if she knew which one it was.

"I don't think so. He mentioned meeting your mother and taking her shopping. A new dress, I think he said, to cheer her up. How are you, Deena? I never get to talk to you anymore, much less see you."

"I'm fine, Janice." Jake is dead, my gun is missing, and I have to get hold of my father before he gets himself into serious trouble. Just fine. "How about you?"

She was anxious to get off the phone but didn't want to hurt Janice's feelings. Janice had been with Max since Deena was in elementary school and had always taken an interest in everything Deena did. Max and Pearl considered her a member of the family.

"Pretty good, thanks. A little lonely now that Sarah's back

East in college. Lou and I are going to surprise her and send her a plane ticket so she can come home for Thanksgiving.''

"That sounds great. Janice, I have to reach my dad. If he calls in, would you ask him to call me, please?''

"Is something wrong?''

"Nothing serious, but I do have to talk to him.''

"Okay. You know, he's been tense the last few days, more than usual. Sometimes I really worry about him. And your mom. I know things are rough. Any time you want to talk, I'm here.''

"I know. I appreciate that. Anyway, I'd better get off the phone. My dad may be trying to call me.''

Deena hung up and quickly dialed her parents' number, hoping to reach Pearl before she left the house. After twenty rings, she admitted defeat. She would try again a little later. With any luck, she would get to Max before Detective Ryker did.

She spent the next hour looking for the gun. Maybe she *had* moved it from the nightstand, had forgotten all about doing so; she tried to imagine where she would have put it. She rummaged through drawers in her bedroom, in her kitchen, through several closets. She took apart the den couch (could she have tucked it under a cushion?), went back into the bedroom and looked under the beds, behind the nightstand.

If the gun was in the house, it was invisible.

She was sitting on the reassembled couch in the den, watching the four o'clock news, the receiver in her hand. Ten minutes ago, she'd been excited by a busy signal when she dialed her parents' number, but when she redialed, no one answered. Somebody else had obviously been trying to reach them at the same time. She'd dialed again a few minutes later and decided to let the phone ring indefinitely until her parents came home.

With the steady ringing of the receiver sounding in her ear, Deena didn't even hear the front doorbell. But she did hear the shorter, more strident sound of the bell at the side door. She hung up the receiver and went to the door.

It was Michael. She opened the door to let him in.

"You sounded so strange on the answering—''

"Michael!'' She buried her head on his chest and sobbed.

He held her tightly, stroking her hair, until her crying subsided. "What happened?''

"Michael, it's Jake." She felt his sudden tension.

"What about him?"

"He's dead, Michael," she whispered. "Jake is dead."

"When did it happen?"

"The police came here last night." They went into the den, and she told him about their visit. "And a Detective Ryker came today to ask me more questions. Luckily, Alan was here."

"What do you mean, 'luckily'?"

"The detective was asking a lot of questions about the divorce, and Alan advised me not to answer them. I don't think I would've had the nerve to refuse on my own."

"I'm glad Alan was here. You must've been terrified."

"It was horrible, Michael. You have no idea."

"You know something? This is just like Jake. The bastard can't even die without causing trouble!"

"Michael!" She was shocked by his anger.

"What do you want me to do, Deena? Shed a few tears? I'm not going to pretend I'm sorry he's dead. He wasn't exactly a prime specimen of humanity. And I can't believe you're feeling sorry for him, not after everything he put you through."

"But he was murdered! Doesn't that make it different?"

"As far as I'm concerned—oh, forget it. I guess I'm just upset that you had to deal with the police."

"Michael, I made a terrible mistake. When the police came, I thought Jake had filed a complaint. I don't remember exactly what I said, but apparently, I let them know there was a major problem between my father and Jake."

He stared at her. "How could you do that!"

"I don't know. It was late at night; I was flustered. How did I know Jake had been killed?"

"But why would you volunteer something like that? You practically handed the police a motive for Jake's murder!"

"Why are you yelling at me? The last thing I need right now is for you to tell me how stupid I was!"

"I'm sorry; you're right. It's just that I'm so worried about you, Deena." He drew her to him, but she pulled away. "What else did this Ryker ask you?"

"A lot of things. Whether I knew anyone who hated Jake. That's kind of funny, isn't it? When I last saw him, talked to him. And before you ask, I didn't mention the phone calls."

"I said I was sorry, Deena. I overreacted. Go on."

"He asked where I was from Sunday at five through Tuesday."

"They don't know the exact time of death?" he asked.

"I don't know. Maybe they don't want to pinpoint it."

"What did you tell him?"

"The truth, of course. That I was home most of the time."

"Great." He shook his head in exasperation.

"Well, what did you want me to do, Michael? I didn't know I'd need an alibi! If I had, I would've planned a party from Sunday through Tuesday, invited a few reliable witnesses."

"Calm down, Deena. Obviously, I'm upset with the situation, not with you."

"Well, I wish you'd be more supportive. You've been acting strange since you got here. What would you say if Ryker asked you for an alibi, Michael? Can you account for every minute?"

"Of course not."

"It's too bad you had to cancel our date Sunday. If you hadn't, we'd both have an alibi for at least one of the days."

"I *did* want to come over Monday night. You said you were too tired."

"I know. But we'd planned on Sunday. You still haven't told me what happened." She waited.

"I did tell you; maybe you weren't listening. I was with a patient. It was an emergency. I don't understand all this. You weren't upset Sunday when I told you I couldn't make it."

"I've just been thinking about it more. You've never canceled a date before."

"I never had to. I told you; it was an emergency. I was fearful about my patient's safety."

"I just find it very strange, that's all."

"What is this, Deena? Are you checking my alibi?"

"No. I'm sorry. Forget it. I'm just a little edgy."

"Okay. So what does your father think about all this?"

"Oh, no!" She grabbed the receiver, dialed quickly, and slammed it down. "Now it's busy! I've been trying to reach my parents all afternoon to warn them that Ryker plans to question them. First they weren't in, and now someone's on the line!"

"Try again in a few minutes. I want to hear more about what happened with the police. Did they search your house?"

"Why would they do that?"

"I have no idea. I don't know police procedure. I just wondered."

"What would they be looking for, Michael? Another body?"

"Why are you so annoyed?"

"Because you're asking stupid questions, and instead of calming me down, you're making me more nervous."

"Tell me why you're so upset, Deena."

She looked at him impatiently.

"No, come on. I know you're shaken by Jake's death, and you're worried about Ryker talking to your father. But I sense that there's something else."

"Isn't that enough? If Ryker finds out about the *get*—and Alan says he will—we'll all be investigated. Me, my father, my mother. You, too." She looked at him. "Does that bother you?"

He shrugged. "I'm not wild about having the police poke into my life, but I have nothing to hide."

"Are you sure?"

"What's that supposed to mean?"

"You figure it out."

"Maybe I should leave, come back when you're rational."

"Maybe you should!"

He got up from the couch and headed for the door, then turned around and came back. "This is silly. I want to be here with you, to comfort you, to do whatever the hell you need. I know I've been behaving like an ass. Let's start over."

"Okay."

He sat down next to her, took her hands. "Tell me what's wrong. What's really wrong."

"It's my gun." She studied his eyes. "It's missing."

"How do you know?"

"Ryker asked if I owned a gun. When I said yes, he asked to see it. I looked in my nightstand, but it wasn't there."

"Maybe you misplaced it, Deena."

"I know I didn't. But I searched the entire house anyway, just in case I was wrong. It's gone."

"Okay. So you think your gun could be the murder weapon."

She pulled her hands away. "I didn't say that."

"Well, why else would you be concerned? And what's really bothering you," he said slowly, "is that someone you know took the gun. That's it, isn't it?"

She nodded.

"It could be just a coincidence, couldn't it?"

"I hope so." She felt miserable.

"But you're skeptical; I don't blame you. So who's on the list?"

"I don't want to do this." She started to get up.

He pulled her down. "You have to do this. If nothing else, you'll put your mind at ease. Who knows you have a gun?"

"My parents, of course. It's my dad's gun. I told you that." She looked at him but he didn't notice.

"Right. I remember. Who else?"

"My support group. They all know about it, I think." She thought for a moment. "Reuben Markowitz. He thought it was a good idea, actually. Alan and Sandy."

"That's it? Think!"

"I'm trying. Brenda knows, but she's never been here. And there's Berta. She comes to clean every other week. I told her about the gun because I was worried she might come across it and hurt herself."

"When was she at the house last?"

"Last Thursday."

"No mysterious strangers, huh? And not a butler in the group."

"This isn't funny, Michael."

"I'm sorry. It's a nervous reaction. This whole thing's impossible. I can't believe we're wondering whether decent, caring people—including a rabbi, for God's sake!—could be involved in murder! There has to be another explanation."

"Like what?"

"I don't know. Some factor we don't know about."

"Anyway, that's it. I can't think of anyone else."

"You left out someone."

"Who?"

"Me." He smiled.

She didn't respond.

"This is where you're supposed to say, 'Not you, Michael. I could never suspect you.'" His sober stare belied his casual tone. "Deena?"

"I just wish you hadn't known about it."

"You think I took the gun?"

"No. I don't think you did. But I can't stop thinking that you could have. It would be so much simpler if I could just erase your name from the list."

"I didn't take the gun, Deena. I didn't kill Jake. Why on earth would I want to kill him?"

"Because you love me and he tried to rape me. Because you knew how terrified I was of what he would do next. Because he was never going to give me a *get*, and without a *get* we have no future. Those are pretty good reasons for hating someone."

"But not for killing him, Deena. There's a big difference. Do you really think I would've taken his life in cold blood!"

"No. Of course not. But I have to be honest. The thought flashed through my mind, especially when I remembered about our canceled date. You admitted you weren't unhappy he was dead," she reminded him. "And you were asking such strange questions."

"So that's why you were grilling me?"

She nodded. "I know you couldn't have done it. I know it logically and emotionally. But Ryker doesn't. He can make out a case against you. Or against my dad. Or against me."

"You?"

"Don't pretend the thought never crossed your mind. I had the gun. And I have the perfect motive—Jake was ruining my life. You could always have married someone else."

"Deena, stop torturing yourself. I know you didn't kill Jake. The police will find the guilty party. You'll see."

"Under the circumstances, that's· not such a cheering thought."

Ryker stood on the porch waiting for someone to answer the door. Nice house, he thought, taking in the balconies on the second story. He wondered whether the Novicks ever used them. Finally, he heard footsteps, then a woman's tentative "Yes?"

"Mrs. Novick? Detective Sam Ryker, LAPD." He pressed his badge against the security window on the front door.

After a hesitation, the door opened and revealed a frail woman in her late sixties with faded brown hair. "What can I do for you?" she asked. Her voice and being exuded tiredness.

"Who is it, Pearl?" a man called.

She glanced at Ryker, turned to answer, but stopped as a tall man with thinning gray-red hair joined her. Definitely Deena Vogler's father, Ryker decided.

Max Novick looked questioningly at his wife.

"He's a detective, Max." She seemed uncertain what to say.

"Sam Ryker." He stretched out his hand.

"Max Novick." He shook Ryker's hand. "There's a problem?"

"Not exactly. But I do have to talk to you and your wife." He stood, waiting, but Max made no move. "May I come in?"

"Yes. Of course." He led the way past the entry hall to the living room, waited until Ryker seated himself on a wing chair, then settled Pearl on the couch and sat next to her.

The room was an attractive study in peach and gray—definitely a decorator's touch, Ryker thought. A portrait of Deena Vogler hung on one wall. A larger picture had been there before, Ryker noted. The moiré wallpaper around the frame was noticeably lighter. A photo of the bride and the groom?

"Mr. and Mrs. Novick, I know this is going to come as a shock to you, but your ex-son-in-law, Jake Vogler—"

"Deena!" Pearl gasped. She clutched her throat. "Something happened to Deena?"

Max put his hand on her shoulder. "Pearl, let him talk."

"Mrs. Novick, your daughter is fine. I spoke to her this morning. The fact is, though, that Mr. Vogler is dead."

"Oh, my God!" Pearl cried. "Oh, my God!"

"What happened, Detective?" Max asked quietly.

"He was killed, Mr. Novick. We're not exactly sure when, but we found his body Tuesday night."

"Terrible," Max said solemnly. "You said you spoke to my daughter?"

"Yes. We're speaking to everyone who knew Mr. Vogler, trying to get as much information as possible. You understand."

He nodded. "Of course."

"What I'd like to do is ask you both a few questions."

"Fine." Max nodded again.

"Mrs. Novick, when did you last see Mr. Vogler?"

"A long time ago. Almost a year, I think. Right, Max?" Her voice was raspy, her breathing labored.

"Right. Just before Deena and Jake separated."

"And you haven't seen him since then?" Ryker asked.

"No." She sounded surprised. "There was no reason."

The phone rang. Pearl rose. "Excuse me a minute?"

"No problem." Ryker smiled at her as she left the room. "Mr. Novick, did you see Mr. Vogler recently?"

"As a matter of fact, yes." He met the detective's eyes. "We discussed some personal business."

"Can you tell me what it was about?"

"I'd rather not say, Detective. It has nothing to do with Jake's death."

"You're probably right, but you never know what piece of information can help."

"Believe me, if I thought it would help, I'd tell you." He smiled.

"When did you see him? The last time, I mean."

"The last time I spoke to him," Max said carefully, "was about a week ago. At his apartment."

"Was it a friendly meeting?"

Max's eyebrows rose.

"Let me be honest with you, Mr. Novick. We understand there was some bad feeling between you and your ex-son-in-law."

Max shrugged. "Tell me, Detective, you're surprised to hear that ex-in-laws don't get along? We had some differences, that's true. Nothing we couldn't work out."

"Differences about what?"

"If you have to know, the property settlement. My wife and I gave the children most of the downpayment for the house. I felt that Deena owned a larger interest in the house. Jake disagreed. I went to talk to him about it."

"When I spoke with Mrs. Vogelanter, she didn't seem to think there were any problems about the division of property."

"Could be Jake didn't tell her. I knew about it."

"Weren't the lawyers handling the settlement? Mrs. Vogelanter seemed to think so."

"Lawyers sometimes make things more complicated, Detective Ryker. I thought I could help work things out more quickly."

"And did you?"

"Frankly, no. Jake was very stubborn. But I tried."

"And that's all you talked about?"

"More or less."

"Did you argue, Mr. Novick?"

"I gave my opinion; he gave his. Some people might call it arguing." He shrugged.

"You didn't strike him?"

"Never!"

Ryker took out his notebook and turned the pages until he found the one he wanted. "Your daughter said, 'My father didn't mean any harm; he was just trying to protect me.' And then she asked my officers whether he—meaning Mr. Vogler—had filed a complaint against her, too. What did she mean by that?"

"When did she say that?"

"When she was informed of Mr. Vogler's death."

"I don't know what she could have meant, Detective. She was probably confused. The shock, and everything."

"How were you trying to protect her, Mr. Novick?"

"I told you. I was trying to work out the property settlement for her. Jake may have been angry that I mixed in. Maybe he called her up, yelled at her about it, threatened to file a complaint. Who knows? I get a little excited sometimes."

Pearl returned and quietly took her place next to Max. "It was Deena," she told Max. "I told her we'll call back."

"And that was the last time you saw him, Mr. Novick?"

Max nodded. "That was the last time we spoke."

"Where were you from Sunday, October 29th, through Tuesday morning, October 31st?"

"Am I a suspect, Detective?" Max smiled grimly.

"We'll be asking the same question to everyone who knew Mr. Vogler. It's just routine."

"Most of the time, I was home or at work. I own a convalescent home, Detective. My wife used to help, but she hasn't been well lately, so she stays home most of the time."

"I'm sorry to hear that, Mrs. Novick. Nothing serious, I hope."

"Asthma, they think." She smiled self-consciously.

"Mr. Novick, can you be more specific, please? Were you home Sunday evening?"

"I had to go to the home to see one of the patients. She was causing a disturbance. That was about four, I think."

"When did you get back?"

"Six? Six-thirty? Some time around there. I had a meeting with the family of another resident."

"Mrs. Novick, can you help your husband remember?"

"I'm not sure. Six-thirty, I think. Not later, because I know we finished supper and then watched 'Sixty Minutes' at seven. We watch it every week.''

"And what about you, Mrs. Novick? Were you home all day?''

"All day. I don't have so much energy, you see.''

"And after that? Did either of you go out?''

"I went to the market,'' Max said. "We needed milk, eggs, some fruit.''

"How long were you gone?''

"How long does it take to buy a few apples? I'm not so picky. Twenty, twenty-five minutes. A half-hour, tops.''

"He was hardly gone, Detective.''

"And Monday?''

Max said, "Monday morning, I left for work at seven-thirty, like usual, and spent the whole day there. Tuesday, too.''

"Did someone see you there all the time?''

"Everybody saw me. My assistant manager can tell you that. We worked together all day.''

"Could you give me his name, please? Just a routine check.''

"*Her* name. Janice Brenner. You can reach her at the home in the morning, or, if you think it's an emergency, I can give you her home number.'' The sarcasm was mild but clearly there.

"Tomorrow's fine. One final question, for now. Did you know your daughter had a gun?''

"Of course I knew. It's my gun. I gave it to her.''

"Why did she need a gun?''

"She's all alone in the house. No alarm, no bars. Also, she had a problem with one of Jake's client's. She asked me if she should buy a gun; I told her to borrow mine.''

"I see. You didn't by any chance borrow it back recently?''

"Why would I do that?''

"I don't know. But the gun's missing.''

"I'm sure it's going to show up, Detective. Deena probably just misplaced it.''

"Probably. By the way, we need your fingerprints, just for purposes of elimination. Since you were at Mr. Vogler's apartment, you may have touched something, and we'd like to identify as many prints as we can. You can come to the station during the next few days, at your convenience.''

"I'm a very busy man, Detective."

"It won't take long. Of course, I can't force you to do it, but it would look suspicious if you refused."

"Fine." Max's voice was cold. "My wife, too?"

"If she's been at Vogler's apartment. We're not singling you out for special treatment, Mr. Novick. This is—"

"I know. Just routine, right, Detective?"

"You got it." Ryker smiled. "Just routine."

13

"DEENA?"

She knew from the darkened room that she'd fallen asleep after all. Michael was leaning over her.

"I didn't know if I should wake you. Rabbi Markowitz is here. So is Faye. Should I tell them you're resting?"

"No. I'm getting up." She sat up gingerly, but her headache seemed to have disappeared. "Did my dad call?"

"A little while ago. I told him you wanted to talk to him, but he said not to wake you. He's coming over with your mother. A lot of people called. I wrote down all the names."

"Thanks. What time is it?"

"Seven-thirty. You slept for two hours; you obviously needed it. I'll tell them you're coming; go freshen up."

For the second time that day, Deena regretted having slept in her clothes. She contemplated changing into something less wrinkled but decided she didn't really care how she looked.

When she entered the den, Reuben approached her. "I wanted to come in the afternoon, but your line was busy; I thought you might be resting. I just came back from *shul*. How do you feel?"

"A little groggy, but otherwise okay. I'm glad you came. Where's Faye?" she asked Michael.

"In the kitchen. She's fixing something for you to eat."

"I'm not really hungry."

"You look awful," Reuben said.

"Thanks." She smiled.

"Rabbis have to tell the truth. Look, no one's going to force you to eat, but you don't get extra points for starving."

"I know; you're right. Maybe some toast or something." She started for the kitchen, stopped, and looked hesitantly at Michael. This was the first time the two men had met, and Deena felt uneasy about leaving them alone. Reuben had been openly critical when she'd told him about Michael.

"I can sympathize with your loneliness and frustration," he had told her, "but legally, you're married. Don't expect me to sanction what you're doing."

She'd been disappointed but had respected his honesty. Both had been careful to avoid talking about Michael.

"Go ahead," Michael told her. "We'll be fine."

Faye was slicing a tomato when she heard Deena enter the kitchen. She looked up, startled. "Ouch!"

"What happened?"

"I cut myself. It's nothing." She licked the blood off her finger. "I'm a little nervous. This thing has thrown me." She walked over to Deena and hugged her tightly. The two women looked at each other without speaking.

"I'm making you a tuna sandwich. I wanted to make something more substantial, but I don't know which utensils are meat and which are dairy." She went back to the counter and finished slicing the tomato.

"Aren't you going to have something?" Deena asked.

"I ate before I came." She brought the finished sandwich to Deena and made her sit at the breakfast room table. "I'm not going to ask how you feel. I'm sure everyone's asking that; besides, you probably don't know."

"You're right. I'm pretty confused."

"When you feel like talking, we'll talk. I wish I had known sooner; I would've come over. Reuben reached me just before he left *shul.*"

"That's okay. I've been sort of floating through the day. And Michael's been here for a few hours."

"I thought I'd stay with you tonight, if that's okay."

"I'd like that." She smiled weakly.

"Fine. Eat your sandwich." She busied herself with clearing away the food and utensils.

The doorbell rang. Deena started to get up.

"I'll get it," Michael called from the den.

"Finish," Faye said. "Whoever it is won't mind waiting."

Deena took two bites and shook her head. "I can't."

She found her parents in the den. "Daddy, you already met Michael. Mom, this is Michael Benton." She noticed Pearl's quizzical expression. "A friend. This is Faye Rudman; I know I've mentioned her to you several times. And this is Rabbi Markowitz." How odd, Deena thought, to be performing introductions as though they'd all assembled for a party.

Reuben extended his hand to Max. "Mr. Novick, I'm sorry we have to meet again under these circumstances."

Max shrugged, shook his hand.

Deena motioned her parents to the couch and sat next to them. Faye looked at her uncertainly. "Stay," Deena told her. She turned to Michael. "Would you mind getting some folding chairs from the living room?"

"No problem." He left quickly.

"You look so pale!" Pearl smoothed Deena's cheek. "Sandy called. She wanted to come, but the baby has a cold. She said she'll see you tomorrow."

"Did you talk to the police yet, Deena?" Faye asked.

"A detective was here today."

Michael returned with two chairs. Faye sat near him.

"Do they have any idea who killed Jake?" Reuben asked. "Rabbi Pearlstein didn't say much. Was it a burglary?"

"I don't know. They're checking out all the possibilities. They asked a lot of questions about my marriage."

"You didn't mention the *get*, did you?" Faye asked.

"No. But Alan says they'll find out about it. He thinks I should get a lawyer."

"Why?" Faye asked.

Deena told them about the gun. There was a heavy silence. Reuben said, "Obviously, you misplaced it."

"I can't find it anywhere."

"Do you want me to help you look?" Faye asked.

"Later. Faye is sleeping over," Deena told her parents.

"A good idea," Max said. "You shouldn't be alone." He turned to Reuben. "Did Rabbi Pearlstein tell you anything about the funeral?"

"Ten A.M. tomorrow at the Home of Eternal Rest in Downey. The services will be at the chapel there."

"Deena, Mommy and I will pick you up at nine."

"What are you talking about?"

"I'm talking about the funeral. We'll all go together."

"I have no intention of going to the funeral."

Max frowned. "You have to go. How can you not go?"

"Listen to Daddy," Pearl said. She patted Deena's hand. "He knows what's right."

She stared at Max. "Daddy, you hated Jake. *I* hated him! Why should we go to his funeral? His parents wouldn't want us there. It would be completely hypocritical."

"I don't know from 'hypocritical.' All I know is we should go. Period." He turned to Reuben. "You're a rabbi. Tell her."

Michael said, "Mr. Novick, I don't want to interfere, but if Deena doesn't want to go, maybe she shouldn't. She's under a great deal of stress."

Max glared at him.

Deena looked at Reuben for help.

"This is complicated," Reuben said uncomfortably. "I have to check some sources for a definitive answer."

"Talk plain," Max told him. "Tell her she has to go."

Reuben said, "Deena, if you can honestly say you never had a moment of happiness with Jake, I'd say you're justified in not going. But I don't think you can say that, can you?"

Deena didn't answer.

"And if you *were* happy for a while, then you might want to show your respect and go. But please understand that I'm not telling you that you *have* to go."

"This is an answer?" Max turned to Deena. "How will it look if you don't go?"

Deena laughed shrilly. "How will it look? I don't give a damn how it looks or what people think!"

"Deena!" Pearl implored. "Calm down."

"And what about the police?" Max demanded. "Do you care what *they* think?"

"What do you mean?"

"You think he's not going to be there tomorrow, the detective? He's not going to find it strange that a woman won't even come to her ex-husband's funeral?"

Deena was quiet. "I didn't think about that."

"Well, start thinking!"

Michael said, "Your father's right, Deena. Ryker will be suspicious."

"Thank you, mister psychologist!" Max turned to Deena. "So. It's settled? You're going?"

"I guess." Did she have a choice?

"Deena," Faye said, "it won't be that bad. Your family will be there with you. I'll come too, if you want."

Deena nodded. "Please."

Reuben said, "I'll ask Rabbi Pearlstein to arrange for you to sit in a separate section. Deena, I'm sure there are things you want to discuss privately with your family. But before I go, I want to make sure you don't have any questions about the laws of sitting *shivah.*" He was referring to the seven days of mourning that the family of the deceased has to observe.

"*Shivah?*" Deena was startled. "Why would that concern me?"

"I thought you understood, Deena. Technically, you were Jake's wife when he died. That makes you his widow. I'm afraid that all the rules of mourning apply to you."

She stared at him. "You can't be serious."

"I understand how upset you must be, but it's the law. You have to sit *shivah* for seven days, and keep a less rigid period of mourning for thirty days."

"But we weren't living together. Doesn't that change things?"

Reuben shook his head. "I'm sorry. The Torah obviously can't dictate emotions. But you're still obligated to show respect for the deceased family member."

"Reuben, this doesn't make sense! I'm supposed to sit for seven days and let people console me for the death of a man who was making my life a living hell?"

"I wish there was a way around this. Look, this is obviously a shock for you, and I know it's not going to be easy. But once the thirty days are over, you can forget all about this and start a new life. Try to concentrate on that."

"Wonderful. In the meantime, Jake is laughing his head off!"

"Deena, don't talk like that," Pearl said. "It's not right."

"Well, it's true, isn't it? He's managing to harass me even from the grave."

Michael and Reuben left together. Faye busied herself in the kitchen, leaving Deena alone with her parents.

Max put his arm around Deena's shoulder. "Deena, I'm sorry I lost my temper, but you have to be careful. This Ryker is asking a lot of questions, and he's suspicious about the gun.''

"I know. I tried to call you, to warn you he was coming, but first you were out, and then your line was busy. I made a terrible mistake, Daddy. I told the police—''

"I know what you said. Don't worry about it. I'm sure I explained everything. Tell me, did Ryker ask you for an alibi?''

She nodded. "For Sunday and Monday. I told him I was home all the time, except for school and a self-defense class.''

"You said you were home by yourself?" He sounded troubled.

"What else could I say?''

"Nothing. You're right. Oh, well, don't worry. You'll see. Everything will be fine.'' He kissed her forehead.

"You think so?''

"I know it. Haven't I always taken care of you? Trust me.''

After questioning Max and Pearl Novick, Ryker went home to have a quick supper with his family. His wife Linda had prepared broiled lambchops, his favorite, but he couldn't really enjoy the meal. He was chewing without tasting, his mind back at the precinct, wondering whether Hank had learned anything.

Linda noticed Sam's preoccupation but didn't say anything. She was used to his silences when he was in the middle of a case and had long ago accepted the fact that he didn't like to discuss his work. He made up for it in so many ways.

"Supper was delicious,'' he said on his way out the door.

"How would you know?'' She kissed him warmly. "Late night?''

"I hope not. Wait up for me?'' He put his arm around her waist and drew her close.

She smiled. "You can count on it.''

Ryker found Stollman in the squad room, waiting for him.

"Did you learn anything from the neighbors?''

"Not really. I talked with a few people who live across the street. They didn't notice anything unusual, and everyone says the same thing. They're pretty sure the Porsche was in the driveway since Sunday, but no one can swear to it.''

"Figures. What about the next-door neighbor? Not Frisch, the other one.''

"Her name is Pearson. Muriel Pearson. She's a widow. A

neighbor two houses away told me Mrs. Pearson left Tuesday to visit her daughter in San Jose for a few days. I left a note in her mailbox asking her to contact us as soon as she gets back.''

"Okay. The funeral's at ten, by the way." Ryker told him the name of the cemetery. "I've never been to an Orthodox funeral. Is there anything I should take with me? I don't want to stick out."

"I'm sure they'll provide skullcaps. I sure as hell hope so—I don't have one. Anything you want done tonight?''

"Not really. Tom and George are talking to Vogler's neighbors. And Tom's going to see the night doorman."

"George called while you were out, Sam. He tried reaching the owners of the Sherbourne house. The housekeeper answered. Seems that Mr. and Mrs. Pomerantz have been on a cruise to the Bahamas since last week. They'll be back next week.''

"Did George check it out?"

"Uh-huh. The housekeeper gave him the name of the travel agency. He called and confirmed that they left as scheduled."

"Well, that's good news. We can forget about them."

"So what's with the ex-wife? Did you speak to her?''

Ryker filled him in on the meetings with Deena and with her parents. "The father's a shrewd guy. Not very forthcoming, but then again, why should he be? If his daughter's divorce had nothing to do with the murder, why would he want to rake up all that dirt again? And as far as not being excited about having his prints taken, I can't really blame him."

"So you think there's no connection?"

"Not so fast." Ryker smiled. "There's still the comment the daughter made to Tom and George. Novick made some half-assed attempt to explain it, but I don't buy it. Then again, it may have nothing to do with the murder. Maybe Novick thinks it's none of our business. Or maybe he's worried we'll be suspicious if we find out there was bad blood between him and Vogler. In the long run, though, he'd be better off telling me what happened. I'll find out anyway.

"And there's still the missing gun." He explained the situation. "And from what the ex-Mrs. Vogler told me, she practically put an ad in the *L.A. Times,* telling the world she owned one. Actually, she borrowed it from her father.''

"Back to the father, huh?"

"Looks like it. Probably just a coincidence, though."

"You really think so?"

Ryker shrugged. "Who knows? It's not as though Novick stands to inherit Vogler's fortune. Shit! I just realized I forgot to call Vogler's lawyer. Oh, well, I'll do it tomorrow."

" 'Tomorrow, and tomorrow and tomorrow.' "

"*Macbeth,* right?" Ryker smiled. It had been one of his favorites in high school.

"That, or *Gone with the Wind.* I always mix them up."

"Leave it for tomorrow," Deena told Faye.

After Max and Pearl had left, Faye had removed several sheets from the linen closet and started placing them over the mirrors in the house. Jewish law dictated that all mirrors in the house of a mourner be covered during *shivah.*

"I can do it by myself," Faye said. "I really don't mind."

"No. Really. I'd rather do it tomorrow. Where's your bag?"

"I didn't bring one. I stuffed a nightgown and a toothbrush into my purse. I figured I'd go home in the morning and change before I left for the funeral. Are you hungry?"

Deena shook her head.

"Tea, then? I'll join you."

"That sounds good," Deena admitted. They went into the kitchen. Deena sat at the table while Faye prepared tea.

"You know what's funny?" Deena said. "Earlier today, I was sad about what happened to Jake. I mean, there was no love lost between us, but it didn't have to end this way. If Jake and I had been divorced according to Jewish law, I probably would've gone to the funeral."

Faye brought two cups to the table and sat down.

"But then," Deena continued, "everyone started telling me I *have* to go to the funeral, and Reuben said I *have* to sit *shivah.* I felt trapped, you know? Pushed into a situation against my will. The whole thing is so crazy, isn't it, Faye? I mean, Jake tried to rape me!"

"It doesn't make much sense." Faye stirred her tea. "But you don't have a choice, about the *shivah,* anyway. As far as the funeral goes, I think your father's right. You have to avoid looking suspicious or drawing attention to yourself."

"No kidding! Especially with my gun missing."

"I'm sure it's just a horrible coincidence. You'll see; the police will find that Jake was murdered by a burglar."

"But where's *my* gun? I can't remember the last time I saw

it.'' She'd liked knowing it was there, but had avoided looking at it, holding it.

Faye thought for a moment. ''Well, the night Jake attacked you, you said how glad you were that you had a gun in the house. Did you check to see that it was there?''

''I don't think so. I just assumed it was.''

''So that doesn't help.'' Faye's eyes looked troubled over the rim of the teacup. ''It *is* strange. Have there been any burglaries in your area recently?''

Deena shook her head. ''Michael and I spent the afternoon trying to figure out who knew about the gun and had access to it.'' She hesitated. ''Do you want to hear something awful? For a moment, I even suspected Michael of having taken it.''

''Michael?'' Faye put down her cup. ''Why?''

''Because he was acting strange, and he canceled a date Sunday night. He's never done that. But I know it's ridiculous. Michael's so even-tempered; he could never kill anyone.''

''Look, Deena. We *all* knew you had a gun; you never kept it a secret. I could've taken it. For that matter, so could anyone in the group or anyone who's been here. But if you start thinking like that, you'll drive yourself crazy.''

Hours later, after tossing restlessly for a while, Faye had finally fallen asleep, but Deena, wide awake, was reading an overdue library book when she suddenly remembered.

''Faye?'' she whispered excitedly. She nudged her gently.

''What?'' she mumbled.

''Faye, I just remembered something!''

Faye propped herself up on one elbow. ''What is it?''

''Remember when the group met at my house? Well, when I came home from the market that day, I thought someone had been in the house. I don't know how I could've forgotten!''

She sat up. ''Was anything missing?''

''Not that I could see.''

''Then how do you know?''

''First of all, the door was open. And I just had the feeling that something had been disturbed. Don't you see? If someone was in the house, he might've taken the gun!''

''But how would he know where it was?''

''I don't know. You're right.'' She sounded disheartened.

''Although,'' Faye said slowly, ''a burglar would naturally look in a person's nightstand, wouldn't he? That's where people often keep jewelry and other important things. You have to call the police, Deena. This could be very important.''

''I will, in the morning. But I think I'll call Michael now. He'll be as relieved as I am to hear this. It makes sense out of everything. I'm sorry I woke you.''

''I'm glad you did.'' She yawned. ''Get some sleep.''

Deena was disappointed by Michael's lukewarm reaction. ''What's wrong? I thought you'd be relieved.''

''Look, if nothing was missing, how do you know you didn't leave the door open yourself? Maybe you're just reaching for answers, Deena, because you don't want to deal with your fears. Have you thought about that possibility?''

''Thanks a lot. And if you're implying that I'm imagining this just to set my mind at ease, you're wrong. I *know* someone was here.''

''Then why didn't you remember it till now? And why didn't you mention it to anyone?''

''Forget it, okay, Michael? I wish for once you'd stop being so damn analytical! You don't have to search for motivation and hidden meanings behind everything a person does. I forgot about it, that's all. It's perfectly natural.''

''Can we talk about this tomorrow, Deena? It's one A.M.''

''This is important. Can't you admit there's something to this?''

''Look, I just don't want you to get your hopes up. I don't think Ryker's going to be convinced.''

Deena set her alarm for eight, but at six-fifteen she was up, impatient to call the detective. Careful not to wake Faye, she slipped out of bed and washed up in the bathroom.

She would call at seven, she decided. In the meantime, she finished draping the mirrors, using masking tape to secure the sheets to the walls. She left the bathroom mirror for later. She would cover it after she and Faye finished getting dressed.

At six fifty-eight, Deena called the precinct from the den, but Ryker wasn't in yet. She left her name and phone number and told the operator it was important.

She was in the shower when she heard the phone ring. Abruptly shutting the faucets, she pushed open the shower door, grabbed a towel, and ran, dripping, into the bedroom.

''You just missed Ryker,'' Faye told her sleepily.

''I'm sorry he woke you. I should've showered later.''

''It's no big deal. I should get up, anyway.''

Sitting on the edge of her bed, Deena dialed Ryker's number and was connected with him immediately.

"What can I do for you, Mrs. Vogler? The message said it was important."

"It is. I think I know what might have happened to the gun." She told him what had happened.

"I see. Did you report this incident to the police?"

"No. There was no point. Nothing was missing. Nothing that I was aware of," she corrected herself quickly.

"And you didn't check to see if the gun was still there?"

"No. It didn't enter my mind. But the more I think about it, the more I feel that's what happened. Someone broke into my house and took the gun." She waited to hear his reaction.

"Well, this is all very interesting. Unfortunately, Mrs. Vogler—and I hope you don't take this the wrong way—all we have is your recollection about the incident. You say nothing valuable is missing—no jewelry, silver, anything like that?"

"No. But I don't really have any important jewelry in the house. I keep everything expensive in a safe deposit box at my bank. Maybe the person was looking for drugs or something and then found the gun. Isn't that a possibility?"

"Maybe. Anyway, there's nothing I can do to verify this or follow up on it. But I'll keep it in mind. And thanks for calling. I appreciate your cooperation. I'll be in touch."

"He doesn't believe me," Deena told Faye dejectedly after she hung up. "Michael was right, dammit. Ryker thinks I'm making this up to protect myself and everyone I know."

"Did he say that?"

"No, but I could hear it in his voice."

"You know, just because Ryker doesn't believe you doesn't mean anything. He's trained to be skeptical, and you don't have any evidence to show him, just a theory. The important thing is that *you* know what probably happened. Now you can stop looking at everyone you know and wondering who took the gun."

"I guess." She didn't sound convinced, even to herself.

14

"WHAT DID THE VOGLER WOMAN WANT?" LEWIS ASKED. HE and Moran had approached Ryker's desk while he was on the phone.

"You won't believe this. Seems she 'just remembered' that someone *probably* broke into her house last week."

"Did she report it to the police?" Lewis asked.

"No. She didn't think it was important at the time because—get this—nothing was missing. So now I'm supposed to believe that this *probable* robber *probably* stole her gun."

"But it doesn't mean that her gun is the murder weapon," Lewis said. "Maybe she's just trying to get us off her back."

"Could be," Ryker agreed. "I'm not running out and getting a warrant for her arrest. But she could be involved, trying to protect herself or covering for someone else. Like maybe her father?" He told them about his conversation with Max.

"You had a cop tailing her, didn't you?" Moran asked. "Did he see her leave with a strange, brown parcel, by any chance?"

"Nope. According to Lou Jeffreys—he's the one I talked to—Mrs. Vogler didn't leave her home at all. And the guy who took over for Jeffreys at night said the same thing. Jeffreys did say she had quite a bit of company in the evening."

"So?" Lewis asked. "It's normal, under the circumstances."

"I didn't say it wasn't. Anyway, there was an older couple—her parents, I figure—two men, and a woman. The woman spent the night. One of the men—young, goodlooking—came in the afternoon and stayed late. Jeffreys got his license number."

"Want me to check it out?" Moran offered.

"No rush. What did you learn from the doorman, Tom?"

"Basically what we thought, but now we have confirmation. He swears Vogler didn't return to his apartment Sunday night. The doorman was in the main lobby all night—he has a little battery-operated television to keep him from dying of boredom—and there's no way he would've missed Vogler.''

"Okay. Vogler didn't sleep at the crime scene—we didn't find a change of clothes, and I can't see the killer taking a pair of pajamas. So we'll assume he was killed late Sunday afternoon. Maybe we'll get corroboration of the time element from the neighbor. Hank learned she's out of town.''

"Did Hank give you my message about the Pomerantz couple?'' Lewis asked.

Ryker nodded. "Write it up, though. I want it on record.''

"Fine. I also talked to the guy who lives next door to Vogler. He told me Vogler had quite a few male visitors over the past few weeks, doing a hell of a lot of shouting.''

Moran said, "What does he do, sit all day with a stethoscope against the wall?''

"He's a graduate student, working on his Ph.D. Spends a lot of time in his apartment working on his doctoral thesis, so naturally, he's been a little annoyed with Vogler.''

"Did he see any of these visitors?'' Moran asked.

"No. He doesn't have X-ray vision, you know. He did say that some of the voices sounded youngish, others much older.''

"How many voices were there?'' Ryker asked.

"He's not sure. He doesn't know if he heard the same voice on different occasions or a new one each time. Great, right?''

"Could he hear what they were arguing about?'' Ryker asked.

"No. But he said they were shouting so loud he could barely concentrate. One time—that was two weeks ago—he almost went to ask them to quiet down, but he lost his nerve.''

"Does he remember when these people showed up?''

Lewis took out his pad. "He can't remember details from two weeks ago, but after a while he decided to keep a log. He wanted documentation if he complained to the manager. The way this guy described it, Vogler should've installed a revolving door. Okay. On Tuesday night, someone came at eight-fifteen.''

"Old or young?'' Ryker asked.

"He can't say. This one wasn't as noisy, only stayed a short while. Vogler seemed to be doing most of the yelling.

Next, an older guy on Thursday night at nine-thirty. And Saturday night was like a convention. First an older voice at eight—he doesn't know if it was the same voice from Thursday or a new one—then, much later, the younger one—past one in the morning. Our guy was sleeping and the shouting woke him up.''

Moran said, ''Lucky for us our graduate student didn't have a hot date on the weekend.''

''What do you think, Sam?'' Lewis asked.

''Odds are the older guy—or one of them, if there are two—is Novick. He told me he visited Vogler last week, admitted he lost his temper. The others? Could be anybody.''

Moran said, ''Maybe he was dating some woman who's got another boyfriend on the side. The condoms, remember?''

''Did you ask the doorman about these people, George?''

''I asked the night doorman, but naturally, he wasn't on duty this past Saturday night. That would be too easy. I'll have to check with the guy who was, and with the day doorman.''

''Fine. Hank and I are leaving here around nine-fifteen for the funeral. I don't want to get there too early and be conspicuous, but I don't want to miss anything, either. Tom, check out the rest of the names on this open house list. Hank marked off the ones he questioned.''

''Okay.''

''George, after you contact the doormen, talk to Murdoch, find out what the hell's going on. His secretary keeps putting me off, so don't call. Just show up and insist on seeing him.''

''No problem. Anything else?''

''Yeah. See if you can contact the first two people on Kasden's list. It's here somewhere.'' He spotted it under a stack of papers. ''I'll give Hank the rest.''

''Sam, what about that calendar page? Anything from SID?''

''Not yet. They're swamped. But I told you not to worry, George. I'm sure they'll be able to figure it out.''

After Lewis and Moran left, Ryker got up, walked to a corner of the room, and picked up a box filled with Vogler's personal effects. He was about to start sifting through the contents. Instead, he picked up the phone and dialed.

Marvin Cooper's secretary politely informed Ryker that the

attorney wouldn't be in until later in the day. "He'll be in court all morning. Would you care to leave a message?"

"My name is Detective Ryker. I'm with the LAPD."

"What is this in reference to, may I ask?"

"I'll discuss it with Mr. Cooper. Please have him call."

The box proved uninteresting. Ryker sorted through some client files that Vogler had apparently kept at home, then opened one of a dozen or so large manila envelopes. Vogler, he admitted grudgingly, was damn organized. On the front of each envelope, he'd neatly printed the name of a major department store or credit card; the receipts inside were arranged in chronological order, each accompanied by the check with which Vogler had paid the bill. One envelope was marked "miscellaneous"—this one probably drove a methodical guy like Vogler crazy, Ryker thought with amusement.

Another envelope, a thick one, was marked "Cooper." The lawyer. Ryker opened some of the letters, read a few paragraphs. Most of the correspondence seemed to deal with a dispute between Vogler and his ex-wife regarding the distribution of their jointly held property. Mrs. Vogler, he noted, was a partner in Kasden and Vogler, Realtors. Interesting. He opened a few more letters but decided he'd talk to Cooper first. Hopefully, the lawyer would save him hours of reading.

Ryker was about to replace the contents in the envelope when he noticed something inside it. He drew out a white paper and unfolded it. For a minute he stared at it, puzzled, then grinned. He was still grinning when Stollman walked over.

"What's so funny?" he asked Ryker.

"Somebody obviously played a practical joke on Vogler. They made up a 'Wanted' poster with his face on it. Here. Take a look at this." He handed the paper to Stollman.

"Where do you get these printed up, Universal Studios?"

"I think so." He took back the paper from Stollman and scanned it. "This is interesting. I'm not so sure it's a gag."

"Why? What do you mean?"

"First of all, there's a notation here, probably from Vogler: 'Is this legal?' I guess he was going to ask his lawyer about it. And there are signatures, all belonging to rabbis."

"What does the letter say?"

"Give me a second." Ryker read quickly. "From what I can see, it's talking about Vogler not giving his wife a *get*.

What's a *get,* Hank? Something Jewish? I've never heard of it.''

"I don't know, Sam. I told you before, I haven't brushed up on my religion in years. But you can ask the rabbi today when you see him at the funeral.''

"Right.'' He checked his watch. "It's a quarter past eight. Listen, why don't we swing by Sherbourne on our way to the funeral and see if this Pearson woman is back.''

"And if she's not?''

"If she's not, we'll have time for coffee and a donut.''

"I vote for the donut. But we'd better be neat. It wouldn't look classy if we showed up at the funeral chapel with crumbs on our mouths. It's not couth.''

"What are you wearing to the funeral?'' Faye asked Deena. She was straightening the beds. Deena had just showered.

"Probably just a sweater and a skirt. I don't think it's black tie optional, do you? What difference does it make?'' She was surprised by the question. It was so unlike Faye.

"Of course it makes a difference, Deena. Some time during the service, you have to tear your garment. I think the rabbi usually makes an initial slit with a razor.''

"You're right. I wasn't thinking.'' She walked to her closet, rummaged quickly through a row of dresses, and chose a plain, beltless brown shift. "I've always hated this. Now I can get rid of it without feeling guilty.''

"What time did your father say he's picking you up?''

"Nine o'clock. That means he'll be here at five to. He's obsessive about punctuality.''

"You don't have much time, then. I'll change at home and see you at the chapel.''

"Isn't there a song like that? 'Going to the chapel and I'm gonna get married.' ''

Faye put her hand on Deena's shoulder. "Are you okay? If you want me to wait till your parents get here, just tell me.''

"I'm okay. I just feel a little weird. Should I wear makeup? Or should I opt for funereal? I mean, I wouldn't want to look too healthy, or too happy, God forbid. What about black circles under my eyes? Maybe I should bring an onion-scented handkerchief along with me so people can see the grieving, tearful widow. What do you think?''

"I think you're nervous as hell,'' Faye said gently.

"How'd you guess?" Deena's smile was grim.

At seven minutes to nine, Max was honking impatiently in the driveway. Deena was ready, but she purposely stayed in the house a minute longer. Just because, she told herself. When she got into the back of the car, she slammed the door. "I hate it when you honk like that, Daddy! It isn't even nine yet."

"I don't want to be late. I checked with Pearlstein. There's a procession leaving from his *shul* at nine-fifteen. It's easier if we follow it." He moved the gear into reverse, turned around to make sure the street was clear, and abruptly braked.

"What's wrong?" Pearl asked anxiously.

"Where's your scarf?" Max asked Deena. "In your purse?"

"No. I didn't bring one."

"A married woman can't go to a service without something on her head. It's just like going to *shul.*"

"If you tell me one more time that I'm a married woman, I won't go to the funeral. I mean it!"

"Go inside and get something. Not a hat; a scarf."

"All right, Max. Leave her alone."

Deena glared at him but did as he had instructed, returning a few minutes later with a lace mantilla in her hand.

"Very nice," Pearl said. Her own mantilla lay carefully folded on her lap.

They drove in silence to Rabbi Pearlstein's *shul.* They were early. Deena immediately spotted the shiny black hearse, watched curiously as some men carefully slid a simple wood coffin into the curtained back seat.

Jake.

A limousine was parked in front of the *shul.* She guessed that Ida and Joe were inside it. Within a few minutes, other cars had assembled, and, escorted by four motorcycle police who led the way through red traffic signals, the motorized entourage made its solemn pilgrimage to Downey.

Max entered a wide driveway leading to the chapel and parked a safe distance from the limousine carrying the Vogelanters. When they had disappeared past the wide doors of the chapel, Max got out of the car and helped Pearl out. Slowly, the three made their way along a paved walkway and climbed the four steps to the chapel entrance.

Deena was grateful to see that Reuben was already there, waiting inside the lobby. He came up to them quickly.

"There are two sections for family," he told Deena. "Do your parents want to sit with you or in the main room?"

"We'll come with you," Max said firmly to Deena.

They followed Reuben along a narrow corridor off the lobby that led to a small, rectangular room. Two short rows of upholstered seats faced a curtain that afforded total privacy. Max helped Pearl into a seat and sat down next to her.

Who's doing the service?" Max asked. "Rabbi Pearlstein?"

"He's the main rabbi, but I understand that Rabbi Brodin has asked to speak, too."

Deena groaned. "You've got to be kidding!"

"Jake *did* go to his *shul.*"

"Right. He was congregant of the year."

"Enough," Max told her quietly.

After Reuben had left, Deena sat down next to Max. Pearl had draped her mantilla over her head. Deena did the same. She listened to the sounds of people filling the chapel—the thudding of shoes muffled by carpeting, the squeaking of seats pushed down into position, the mournful murmurs of somber greetings. Finally, she heard first a tap and then a hesitant cough amplified over the static of the sound system.

In a lilting, almost sing-song Yiddish, a man who Deena assumed was Rabbi Pearlstein began his eulogy, and, almost like a Greek chorus, a strain of quiet sobbing immediately accompanied it. It was hard to remain impassive in the face of Ida's grief; Deena found herself grateful that they weren't sitting together, but at the same time filled with compassion for a mother's loss. Pearl had paled and was dabbing her eyes with a tissue that she had taken from her purse. Deena hadn't thought to bring one.

Having listened to her parents speak over the years, Deena understood conversational Yiddish, and although she couldn't translate some of the more flowery phrasing, she had no difficulty in understanding the rabbi's remarks or in accepting them. Jake *had* been a good son; Deena had no quarrel with that, and as Rabbi Pearlstein elaborated on that theme, illustrating how Jake had brought Ida and Joe much pride and joy, had always treated them with respect and consideration, she found herself nodding in agreement. And when Rabbi Pearlstein mournfully reminded the congregation that Jake was the Vogelanters' only son, taken from them in the prime of his life, what could Deena say? It was all true. And all terribly sad.

There was a brief silence. Then Rabbi Brodin began speaking. Deena had no difficulty recognizing his articulate, carefully modulated voice; she'd heard it often enough during the past months, urging her to be patient, to wait, even suggesting that she give Jake another chance. Hearing it now, Deena flinched, the feelings of pity that had coursed through her suddenly frozen. She listened stonily as he echoed Rabbi Pearlstein's comments, explaining his close relationship to Jake, how he had come to know him well over the past years. He seemed to be talking interminably, and Deena was only half-listening, wondering how long this would take, when the word "marriage" jolted her into wary attentiveness.

". . . took it very seriously," she heard him intone. "No one was more committed to making a marriage work, no one more persistent in the face of seemingly insurmountable obstacles."

Deena heard herself gasp, felt herself rise from her seat, prepared to escape from the room, from this insane man and his insane fabrications. Max forced her down, put his arm around her, and pulled her to him with rough tenderness.

"Don't listen," he commanded in a fierce whisper. "It's almost over."

"I share this with you, dear friends, because if you are here, then you know that his personal life was plagued with difficulty. He made mistakes; who among us has not? But Jake learned from his mistakes and was hopeful. Only last week, he reiterated that he would never give up reclaiming the woman he loved so desperately."

"Daddy, I can't!"

"One more minute, just one, Deena." He stroked her arm.

"And in the face of that goal, that determination, how much more cruel and tragic does his senseless, violent death appear! Jake Vogler was snatched away before he could realize his dream. Today, November 2nd, ironically just one day before what would have been his second wedding anniversary, we have gathered not to share in his joy and personal triumph but to pay our final respects. But I would like to think that had he lived, Jake Vogler would have been reunited with his beloved wife, that he would have built a family, raised children who would have perpetuated his name."

He was finished. After reciting a Hebrew verse of condolence, he left the lectern.

"All rise," the cantor intoned, and began chanting a memorial prayer for Jake.

Deena felt faint, weak-kneed, barely able to stand, and she was relieved when the cantor concluded and she could sit down. She heard someone announce the pallbearers and inform the gatherers that *shivah* would take place at the homes of Joe and Ida Vogelanter and Deena Vogler, and she had an urge to part the curtains and shout her protest. But then Reuben was there, his face ashen, his eyes burning with helpless fury.

"I'm so sorry! I could wring Brodin's neck! If I had known he would do this, I would never have let you come."

"I want to get out of here."

"You should come to the grave site. I know you're upset, but you may as well go through with the entire ceremony. Alan told me Detective Ryker is here."

"Where are Jake's parents?" Deena asked.

"They're exiting from their side. There's no way you can avoid seeing them at the grave site, but if we hurry, at least you won't have to walk there with them."

She nodded.

Quickly, Reuben ushered them out of the room through a side door. They walked with hurried steps along a narrow cemented path, past rows of granite slabs, etched with epitaphs in Hebrew and English, that marked the graves. After a few minutes they arrived at a tented area that shaded several metal chairs from the sun. About fifteen feet away a neatly prepared cavity marred the bright, emerald-green lawn. On either side of the grave was a tall mound of reddish-brown earth.

"Do you want to sit down?" Reuben asked.

"Not yet." She stood resolutely still, waiting.

First came the pallbearers—she recognized Ben, Rabbi Brodin, some people who looked vaguely familiar. They walked to the grave and carefully lowered the casket onto wide canvas straps attached to a pulley. They were closely followed by mourners, some walking singly, others in silent clusters of three or four. She noticed Judy Battaglia walking with Ruth Kasden, saw Ben join them, watched an attractive blonde approach Ben and talk to him. Deena thought she had met her someplace, wondered who she was; she would ask Ben later. Faye and the others were in the crowd; Deena welcomed their silent support. She looked for Michael but remembered they'd agreed he shouldn't come. It wouldn't do for the widow to bring a boyfriend to her husband's funeral.

And then she saw them, Ida and Joe, their heads bowed with grief. They were walking slowly with a middle-aged, gray-bearded man—Rabbi Pearlstein, she guessed—and with each approaching step, Deena felt a knot of anxiety and dread tighten within her. Max saw them too; instantly, he was at Deena's side, gripping her elbow so hard that she winced with pain.

Ida reached the tent a few steps ahead of Joe, lifted her eyes, and looked around as though she had difficulty focusing. But then she saw Deena, and for a long moment, their eyes met.

She's going to scream at me, Deena realized, and I will just die in front of all these people, but I won't be able to say a word. She is an old woman, a mother who has lost her son.

Max shifted slightly, trying to block Deena from Ida.

"Don't." She could easily have moved away, but didn't.

With a strangled sob, Ida threw herself at Deena, but instead of flailing at her with her fist, she hugged Deena to her and stood, rocking and weeping.

"So much he loved you!" she moaned. "So much. And you loved him too, Deena, I know you did. Tell me you loved him."

Hit me, Deena wanted to tell her former mother-in-law; hit me or spit at me, tell me that you hate me, that I was never good enough for your son, that I ruined his life.

"I loved him," Deena said, forcing the lie to her lips, telling herself that once upon a time it had even been true.

Gently, she pried Ida's arms away from her. Joe put his arms around Ida and helped her sit down, all the while careful to avoid Deena's eyes.

Deena was nauseated, trembling, and she realized with a sudden ironic appreciation that anyone looking at her would think she was the perfect widow, distraught, grief-stricken. Let them, she thought tiredly, and spotted Ryker in the crowd. His eyes suddenly met hers, and she stared at him, almost defiantly, until he looked away.

All heads had turned toward the grave. Deena turned with them. A cemetery worker had released the lever on the pulley, and the casket was making its slow descent into the damp ground. When the low hum of the machine stopped, two men swiftly removed the straps.

Rabbi Brodin stepped forward. With a shovel that was lying on the ground, he attacked the mound, lifted some clumps of earth, and dropped them onto the casket. The sound was hollow, eerie. Final. He repeated his action several times, then relinquished the shovel to the first in a line of men. Another line formed at the other side of the grave, where another shovel had been placed. Rabbi Pearlstein took his turn. Then Ben. Joe went up, and after one feeble shovelful, gave up.

Then Rabbi Pearlstein approached, a razor blade discreetly in his hand, and Deena watched, fascinated, horrified, as he made a neat cut on Joe's lapel and waited for Joe to tear his garment. Ida was next; she pointed to her collar. Then Deena. When the grave had been fully covered, Joe recited *Kaddish*, the mourner's prayer that the deceased's closest male relative recites daily for a year.

And it was over.

Standing with Stollman, a shiny acetate black yarmulke perched on his head, Ryker had carefully watched the entire ceremony. He waited in the background until the mourners had filed past the family and made their way toward their cars, until Rabbi Pearlstein had escorted the Vogelanters into the limousine, until it rolled smoothly out of the cemetery.

Rabbi Pearlstein had unlocked his car door and was about to open it when Ryker approached.

"Rabbi! We've spoken on the phone. Sam Ryker, LAPD."

Rabbi Pearlstein shook his hand. "What can I do for you, Detective?"

"I know this isn't a good time, Rabbi, but there are a couple of things I think you could help us with."

"Of course. But it has to be now? Here?"

"No. I can meet with you at your convenience. There *is* one thing you could answer for me now, if you don't mind."

Rabbi Pearlstein looked at him patiently, waiting.

"What exactly is a *get?*"

15

"A *GET?*" Rabbi Pearlstein asked.

"A *get,*" Ryker repeated.

"It's a religious divorce document, Detective."

"The reason I'm asking, Rabbi, is that I found this while I was looking through Mr. Vogler's personal effects." From an inner jacket pocket, Ryker withdrew the 'Wanted' poster and handed it to Rabbi Pearlstein. He watched him unfold the paper, noticed the consternation that flashed across his face.

"This is probably a prank." He returned the paper.

"I don't think so, Rabbi. Look at those signatures on the bottom. They're all names of rabbis."

"Who knows? Maybe that's part of the joke." He looked at his watch. "Detective, I wish I could help you, but I really don't have any information to give you. In any case, I have to get back to the city. Mrs. Jacobsen, a member of my *shul*—congregation—was operated on yesterday, and I promised I would spend some time with her. She's probably wondering where I am."

"Can we set up an appointment, then, Rabbi?"

"If you want, we can meet. But I don't think I can tell you much. I'm sorry." He pulled the car door open.

"Just one more thing, Rabbi Pearlstein. I wonder if you could translate something for me. It's Hebrew." He took out his notebook, read the phrase Moran had repeated to him.

Pearlstein looked bewildered. Then recognition dawned. *"Baruch dayan ha'emes.* That's what you mean, yes?"

"I guess so."

"Translated, this means, 'Blessed is God, the true judge.' In our religion, a person says this when he hears that someone has died. Is that it, Detective? Because I really must rush."

"Yeah. That's it. Thanks for the translation, Rabbi."

"Any time, Detective." He backed out of his parking space quickly before Ryker could change his mind.

Stollman was waiting in Ryker's car, doing a crossword puzzle. "What's a five-letter word for circumlocution?"

" 'Rabbi.' "

"What? Oh, I get it. He wouldn't tell you anything, huh?" He grinned. "You're still wearing the skullcap, by the way."

Ryker took it off, folded it along its original creases, and put it on the dashboard. "He had no problem telling me what a *get* is, but when I showed him the poster, he clammed up. Suddenly remembered he had to visit a sick congregant."

"So now what?"

"I think I'll ask the lawyer, Cooper. If Vogler asked him whether this poster was legal, he should know all about it. And I can always check out the rabbis who signed the paper."

"What about the translation?"

Ryker repeated what the rabbi had said. "It's traditional to say it when you hear someone's dead, but I'm kind of surprised a father would have the presence of mind to do that."

"Yeah, a guy would have to be pretty cool. Which means what? You don't think he killed his son, do you? I can't buy it. The old man looked like a ghost today. You saw him."

"Hank, the first thing they teach us at the academy is that most violent crimes are committed by family members. I haven't talked to the lawyer yet, but what if Vogler left everything to his parents—which he probably did—and the father couldn't wait? Or maybe they hated each other."

"It's possible. But he was damn upset today."

"Okay. So he was upset. Maybe he regrets what he did."

"Come on, Sam! Can you honestly see that old guy taking a gun to his own son?"

"So maybe he didn't kill him himself. Maybe he had someone do it for him and found out from Tom and George that the job was done. Or what if—and this is another possibility—what if he said that because he thought his son got what he deserved: 'Blessed is God, the true judge.' It could fit."

"A father happy that his son is dead?"

"Not *happy*, Hank. Just hearing that what he was afraid was going to happen finally happened."

"Maybe," Stollman said uncertainly. "Or maybe the guy's just very religious, sees everything as God's will."

They left the cemetery with Ryker driving and headed west on the Santa Monica Freeway. "By the way," Ryker said, "did anything strike you as odd at the funeral?"

"You mean when the old lady threw herself at Mrs. Vogler? I thought for a minute Mrs. Vogler was going to faint."

"I figured that was standard funeral fare—emotions all in high gear. But I didn't get why the ex-Mrs. Vogler was participating in the ceremony. I mean, I figured she'd attend, but I found out from a guy next to me that she sat in a family section during the eulogies. And then she was right up there, under the tent with Vogler's parents."

"It *is* kind of strange."

"Then again, maybe in Jewish law the ex-wife is still considered part of the family. Maybe that's what the other rabbi meant. What's his name again?"

Stollman checked his notes. "Brodin."

"Brodin. Right. Anyway, he made it sound like Vogler and his wife would get back together, did you get that? But when I talked to Mrs. Vogler, she didn't say anything like that."

"Interesting, huh?"

"Maybe. After lunch, why don't you check out the Pearson woman again, see if she's back. I'll call Cooper again. If he's available, I'll see him. And he'd better be available."

Ryker found several messages waiting for him on his desk. Marvin Cooper had called at twelve-ten. Ryker called him back. The secretary promptly connected him with the lawyer.

"Marvin Cooper here. How can I help you, Detective?" He sounded smooth, but wary.

"I'd like to see you today, if you can arrange it."

"When I called the number you left with my secretary, someone connected me with homicide. Was that a mistake?"

"I'm afraid not. The fact is, one of your clients has been murdered. Jake Vogler. I'm in charge of the investigation."

"Jake!"

"I'm afraid so. I'm kind of surprised you didn't know."

"I was out of town. I got back last night, spent the morning in court. I started going through my messages when I saw the one from you. God, I can't believe it! What happened?"

"Why don't we discuss it when I see you. Can you make some time for me today?"

"Of course. One minute." He checked his calendar. "Three o'clock?"

It was two now. "I'll be there."

Ryker got a cup of coffee from the machine in the squad room and returned to his desk. He was writing his impressions of the funeral, taking occasional sips from the still-hot coffee, when his phone rang.

He picked up the receiver. "Detective Ryker, LAPD."

"Detective, my name is Louise Perris. I called earlier. Didn't you get my message?"

Ryker looked quickly at the slips of paper on his desk. Cooper. Douglas. Kasden. There it was. Perris.

"I was just about to return your call, Mrs. Perris. I've been away from my desk all morning." For the life of him, he couldn't remember who the hell she was.

"I'm sorry I missed you when you called yesterday. Mr. Hurley said you sounded concerned. About Mrs. Vogler, that is."

Hurley? Ryker thought wildly. Hurley?

"Frankly, he often overdramatizes things, but I thought I should get in touch with you as soon as possible."

"Right. I appreciate it." He waited.

"I have Mrs. Vogler's file right in front of me, Detective. I checked to see when she requested that phone change."

Of course. Pacific Bell. "Mrs. Perris, Mr. Hurley mentioned that there was some difficulty in having Mrs. Vogler's number changed."

"Poor woman! I felt so bad that I couldn't expedite matters, but my hands were tied." She explained that Deena had requested an unlisted number; that Jake, under whose name the phone had been listed, had insisted on knowing the new number.

"There was nothing I could do. He had every right. And then, when Mrs. Vogler tried to set up service under her name, wouldn't you know it, her check was lost in the mail!"

"When was new service finally set up?"

"Let me see." She checked the file. "Her new check arrived on Friday, October 27th. But it came too late in the day to do anything with it. A new, unlisted number under Mrs. Vogler's name was assigned on Monday, October 30th."

"I see." A day after the murder?

"She was very, very agitated the last time I spoke to her. As a matter of fact, she was almost hysterical, yelling at me on the phone, demanding to know why everything was taking so long. But of course, I didn't take offense. I understood that she wasn't angry with me. She did sound so desperate, though.''

She paused. Ryker was careful not to interrupt.

"But I guess they still haven't resolved their differences, then. If you're calling me, that is.'' It was more of a question than a statement. "I assume he's still harassing her, making those late-night phone calls. Despicable, really. Isn't there anything you can do to help her?''

"Actually, Mrs. Perris, the phone calls have stopped.''

"Oh, really? Well, I'm certainly relieved to hear that. But if that's the case, then why . . . ?''

"Mr. Vogler is dead, Mrs. Perris. He was murdered.''

"Oh, my.''

Oh, my, indeed. After informing a subdued Mrs. Perris that it might be necessary for her to come into the station and sign a report, Ryker hung up, finished writing some notes, and looked at his watch. Time to meet the lawyer.

The offices of Cooper and Lichstein, Attorneys at Law, were located on the eighth floor of a concrete and glass office building on Century Park East. Not far, Ryker noted, from the firm of Kasden and Vogler. He wondered whether Cooper was Kasden's lawyer, too.

Ryker was five minutes early, but as soon as he identified himself to the secretary, she jumped up and escorted him to Cooper's office. She was a nervous-looking woman, not unattractive, whose unnatural tan and bottle-lightened blond hair did nothing to camouflage the telltale lines of middle age that had worked themselves into her face. Ryker noticed her slim figure, guessed that she worked out several times a week at a health club to maintain it. He stood straighter, sucked in his belly, then gave up.

"Detective Ryker.'' Cooper had come around his desk, hand extended. "Please. Make yourself comfortable.'' He indicated two leather chairs in front of his large, mahogany desk.

Ryker glanced appreciatively around the attorney's office. The hunter-green carpeting was nubby; the walls were painted a light café au lait. Three of the walls were lined with bookcases, framed diplomas, some photographs. Ryker noticed Cooper in one, shaking hands with the mayor. Not bad. The furniture—Cooper's desk, several chairs, a tweed loveseat and antique credenza against the unoccupied wall—

was large-scaled but not overbearing. The overall effect was of warmth, comfort, assurance. *Come tell me your problems, I can Help.*

Cooper was wearing a suit but had loosened his tie. He was somewhere in his forties, about five feet, nine inches tall. He had a pleasant face, light brown hair that he parted unnaturally low on his left side—to hide his receding hairline, Ryker noticed. Unconsciously, he smoothed his own hair.

"I still can't believe what you told me, Detective. I just talked to Jake last week! He was so alive, so vital!" He shook his head. "How did it happen? A robbery in his apartment?"

"He was found in the bedroom of a property he was apparently showing. We can't say at this point what the motive was. It could be robbery; it could be anything."

"How can I help you?"

"Mr. Cooper, I understand from Mr. Kasden that you were Mr. Vogler's attorney, and that you drew up a will for him."

"That's true. I handle quite a bit of the firm's business, as a matter of fact. But about the will . . ." He hesitated.

"If you're worried about confidentiality, I can get a court order to have you release the information. But to tell you the truth, I'd hate to do that. It's just a waste of time, and in the end, the results will be the same."

"I see your point. All right, then. Excuse me a moment." He got up, left the room, and came back with a manila folder. "What exactly did you want to know?"

"Just the usual stuff. Who inherits. What his assets are."

"As far as his assets, I don't have all that information. You'd have to talk to his accountant. I can give you his name." He looked through the file. "Here it is. Charles Gorman." He gave Ryker the phone number.

"What about the will? I assume his parents are the heirs."

"No. According to Mr. Vogler's last will, his wife inherits everything. Excuse me, his ex-wife."

"Isn't that odd?"

"Not really. This will was drawn up two years ago, just after Mr. Vogler was married. As a matter of fact, I urged him repeatedly to draft a new will, one that would reflect the change in his marital status, but he never got around to it."

"Is Mrs. Vogler aware that she's the sole heir?"

"I have no idea."

"I see. Mr. Cooper, there's something else I hope you can help me with." Ryker took out the 'Wanted' poster and handed it to him. "From the notation here—" he pointed to the top of the page—"I'm assuming Mr. Vogler contacted you about this."

Cooper coughed. "He did. He wasn't too happy about it, but I told him there was nothing we could do to stop it."

"I spoke to a rabbi today. He said this *get* the poster refers to is a religious divorce document. Is it a formality?"

"I don't know very much about it, Detective."

"Why would all these rabbis sign this letter? They're basically telling everyone to avoid Vogler like the plague until he gives his wife a *get*. Pretty heavy stuff, isn't it?"

"I guess."

"Were you handling the *get?*"

"A rabbi has to do that. It's a very technical procedure."

"So you do know something about it."

"Only that I'm not the person you want to talk to, Detective. You really should talk to a rabbi."

"I did. He wasn't very helpful." And neither are you.

"I wouldn't want to give you the wrong information. I'm hardly an expert on religious matters." He smiled.

"Why was Vogler opposed to giving his wife this *get?* Was it expensive, is that it?"

"No. Not that I know of."

"Help me out here, Mr. Cooper. We're talking about a murder investigation, not a probate. You know better than to withhold vital information."

"I just don't want to give you the wrong impression."

"About what?"

"And I'm not so sure my information is vital, as you put it. I doubt that it has anything to do with Jake's death, and I'd hate to send you off in the wrong direction."

"Why don't you let me be the judge of that, okay? Why didn't Vogler want to give her the *get?*" Ryker repeated.

Cooper smoothed his hair with the palm of his hand. "Okay. At first, he didn't even want the divorce. It was her idea."

"Why did she want a divorce?"

"That would be hearsay on my part, since I never even talked to her."

"You got me there, Counselor." Ryker grinned. "Go on."

"Then, Jake learned about this *get,* and he tried to use it as leverage to get a better settlement. You see, without a *get,* an Orthodox woman can't remarry."

"For how long?"

"There's no time limit. Forever, I guess."

"Can't a rabbi give her a dispensation?"

"It doesn't work like that. From what I understand, the only person who can give the *get* is the husband."

"I guess you know a lot more about this than you thought, huh, Counselor?"

Cooper smiled, clearly embarrassed.

"So what was Mr. Vogler doing? Practicing a little blackmail? Shame, shame, Mr. Cooper. Didn't you tell him that wasn't ethical?"

"To tell you the truth, I was sick about the way the whole thing was going. I kept telling Jake to be reasonable, but it was like talking to a wall."

"So he wanted everything, is that it?"

"I'm not sure."

"Did he or didn't he ask for all the joint property?"

"He did, but I don't think that's what he really wanted. If you want to know the truth, Detective, I think he just wanted to make things so difficult that his wife would drop the divorce action."

"But she didn't."

"No. They were officially divorced on May 19th of this year. The property settlement was still being disputed."

"Did they ever resolve it?"

"Not really. In September, Mrs. Vogler's attorney—Brenda DiSalvo—called to tell me her client was going to waive all her rights to any community property. DiSalvo was steaming, and I didn't blame her. A couple of weeks later, DiSalvo called and said we were back to square one. Her client was going to fight for half, or more."

"What happened?"

Cooper shrugged. "I have no idea. I asked Jake, but he told me to mind my own business."

"I see." He looked at the paper again. "The date on this letter is September. If Vogler was refusing to give her the *get* to make her change her mind about the divorce, why was he still refusing to give it after their divorce was final?"

"I'm not sure. He was upset, I guess."

"About the divorce? It wasn't exactly unexpected."

"He was a very stubborn man, Detective. I don't think he believed for one minute that she would go through with it."

"But when she did, it became revenge. Is that it?"

"Please don't put words into my mouth. We never discussed it. I'm his lawyer, not his shrink."

"Was there someone else? For Mrs. Vogler, I mean?"

"Not that I know of." He shifted uneasily on his chair.

"Come on, Cooper. I'll find out one way or the other."

"Jake thought so," Cooper admitted unhappily. "But it could've been his imagination. He wasn't himself the past few weeks."

"So let me get this straight. According to civil law, Mrs. Vogler was out of her marriage. But according to Jewish law, she was as married as the day they exchanged their vows."

Cooper nodded.

That explained the funeral. It all made sense. Ryker rose, shook hands with Cooper, and headed for the door.

Cooper stopped him midway. "Detective, I don't want you to get the wrong idea. These are all nice people. I'd feel terrible if you started asking them a lot of questions based on our discussion. The fact is that in time, Jake would have given Deena the *get*. I'm sure of it. Sooner or later, she would've been out of her marriage, even according to Jewish law."

"Looks like somebody decided to make it sooner, doesn't it, Counselor?"

16

ON THE WAY BACK TO THE STATION, RYKER HAD PLENTY OF time to think about what Cooper had told him. He had taken Olympic Boulevard out of Century City, hoping to avoid the four o'clock traffic, but first there had been a disabled vehicle at Roxbury Drive, and at Doheny, three city maintenance crews and their trucks had blocked off most of the intersection. He had heard somewhere that in Switzerland, most road repairs were done late at night. When there was little traffic, if any. As he sat in his car, inching along the newly created serpentine lane formed by tangerine cones, he wondered why no one had tried it here. Too practical, he decided.

By the time he reached the precinct, it was almost five o'clock. Only Lewis was back. Ryker found him in the squad room, filling a cup of water from the cooler.

"Headache," Lewis explained. He swallowed two aspirin tablets and followed Ryker to his desk.

"Tom or Hank call in?" He loosened his tie as he sat down.

"I don't know. I just got in myself." He sat down and massaged his temples. "It's the damn smog."

Ryker shook his head sympathetically. "You up to filling me in? If not, I have a couple of calls I can make."

"No. I'm okay. Where should I start?"

"Did you talk to the doorman?"

"Yeah. His name is Alfred—he has the shift from two P.M. till ten. He remembers that Vogler had an unusual number of visitors the last few weeks, was kind of surprised by it."

"Does he remember any names?"

"Better than that." Lewis smiled. "He knew two of them by sight. Vogler's old man and his ex-father-in-law."

"I figured on Novick. When was he there?"

"Alfred can't be sure, thinks it was Thursday. He says Vogler didn't want him to let the guy up, but Novick started making a scene in the lobby—apparently, Vogler could hear it over the intercom—so he gave in. Want to hear what Vogler told Alfred?" Lewis was grinning now, his headache temporarily forgotten. "He told him to frisk Novick before he let him up."

"And Alfred didn't remember any of this when Tom spoke to him yesterday? How does he explain that?"

"He thought Vogler was joking, said that's a typical example of his humor. He still thinks Vogler was just kidding around, but he figured he'd better tell me everything."

"What about the father? When was he there?"

"Early Saturday evening. Alfred says he didn't stay long."

"Anything else?"

"He knows there were at least two other visitors during the two weeks, but he can't identify them. He did say one of them was a rabbi. That really narrows it down, doesn't it?"

"Maybe it does. We'll see. So what are we missing now?"

"The late Saturday night guy. His name is Jerome. Alfred gave me his number. I called him twice, but he wasn't in.

I'll call again later, and if he's still out, I'll check with him at the apartment building after ten.''

"If your head's still bothering you, I'll get someone else to take care of it.''

"Thanks. I'll be all right. You want to hear about Vogler's business connections next?''

"Anything interesting?''

"I'm not sure. I saw Murdoch first, like you told me to, but I'll save him for last. Okay. Ferkins, first name Andrew. Age thirty-seven. One of these types who reads a contract three times and asks fifty questions. He checked my ID for five minutes before he let me in. Anyway, he didn't deny he was mad at Vogler. Claims the deceased sold him the property knowing the foundation was shifting radically, that he got some fly-by-night termite company to do a phony inspection.''

"Didn't he arrange for an independent inspection?''

"Yeah. Vogler gave him the names of a few companies and he took one of them. Same thing with the termite company.''

"Why didn't he sue the realty firm?''

"He wanted to, but his lawyer said he didn't have a case.''

"Sounds like he might be a possibility, George.''

"Unfortunately, Ferkins has a solid alibi for the entire time in question. He and the wife were at a restaurant with five other couples, a birthday celebration. He gave me the names of the couples, of the restaurant. Didn't hesitate.''

"Too bad.''

"Yeah. It really is. He still hates Vogler. Didn't even pretend to be sad that the guy bought it.''

"Who's next?''

Lewis checked his notes. "Prather, Leslie J. and Marcia. Nice couple. Kind of shook up when I told them Vogler was dead. Originally, they were pissed because someone told them Vogler hadn't shown them all the offers. Turns out this someone was another broker who lost the listing to Vogler and was trying to make trouble. Vogler proved he handled everything properly, and they believed him. No alibi—supposedly home all day and through the evening, relaxing. But I think we can forget them.''

"Okay. Sounds like a dead end with those two. Hank's checking out the others. Maybe he'll come up with something. What about Murdoch? Did he tell you that he and

Vogler made up, that he was nominating him for membership in his country club?''

''Nope. He said Vogler was a skunk, Kasden was an asshole, and he was sorry he ever stepped into their office. Looked me straight in the eye and said Vogler got what he deserved.''

''Alibi?''

''Not really. But he didn't seem in the least worried. He and the missus were home, decided to make it an early evening. He had a few business appointments scheduled for Monday, wanted to get a good night's sleep.''

''You mean that meeting with Vogler and the CPA?''

''No. I asked him about that. According to Murdoch, Kasden's secretary canceled on Friday. Murdoch was really pissed. This wasn't the first time Vogler had pulled this.''

''But Vogler didn't cross out the appointment.''

''Right. Maybe he forgot to.''

''What was the problem with Vogler? Did Murdoch tell you?''

''Oh, yeah. He wasn't shy. The way he explained it, Vogler screwed up all the way down the line. Mishandled the preconstruction, let the project drag on. The bottom line is Murdoch was tired of having his money tied up for almost two years with no visible return. He wanted out. Vogler talked him into staying on until they could find some buyers to take over his shares. He gave them till the end of November. But his CPA was supposed to meet with Vogler to check the investment.''

''Interesting. What about his goons? Were they home, too, toasting marshmallows in front of the fire?''

''At first, Murdoch pretended he didn't know who I was talking about, but when I told him that according to both Kasden and Mrs. Vogler, they claimed to work for him, he admitted he used them for 'occasional' jobs that needed special attention. Names are Eddie Beauchamps and Tony Padrillo. Murdoch said they spent Saturday through Tuesday in Vegas. A little bonus for handling another 'problem' so well.''

''Any proof of that?''

''Murdoch said they stayed at Caesars Palace. I'll check it out.''

''Did you ask Murdoch why they spooked Mrs. Vogler?''

''He claimed that was an 'unfortunate mistake,' as he put

it. Said his boys sometimes let their loyalty carry them too far. But he said they'd never hurt anyone. You want me to run a make on them?''

"Not yet. First see if their alibi holds out."

"I'll take care of it right now." He got up. "I almost forgot to tell you. I checked with records to see if Vogler filed a complaint against his ex-father-in-law. He never did."

"I forgot all about that! Nice going, George."

Lewis smiled and went to his desk.

Ryker called SID. "How long are you going to keep me waiting on this calendar, Marty?" he asked the lab technician.

"I was just gonna call you, Ryker. Let me get the report."

While Ryker was waiting, he glanced at the morning messages still sitting on his desk. He picked up the top one. Douglas. Who the hell was Douglas?

"You got lucky." Marty was back. "We were able to make out the impressions. We also finished the analysis on the victim's stomach contents. Hope it doesn't ruin your breakfast, Ryker."

"I can handle it. Go ahead." He wrote quickly, using a shorthand he'd perfected over the years. "Thanks," he said when Marty had finished. "I really appreciate your rushing it."

"Yeah, sure. Consider it an early Christmas gift. I'll put a copy of the report in the mail. You should have it tomorrow."

The stomach contents showed nothing unusual—toast with grape marmalade, bits of eggs, hard cheese, pastry of some sort, coffee, and a carbonated cola. Probably Diet Pepsi. There had been a half-empty can on the counter (the kid had admitted to enjoying the other half) and more cans in the refrigerator.

The report on the missing calendar page was puzzling. Ryker sat for a moment, pensive, drumming his fingers on his desk, then looked at his other messages. Douglas first, he decided, before he forgot. He dialed the number, listened to six or seven rings, depressed the receiver button, and called Kasden's office. The secretary answered.

"Detective Ryker, LAPD."

"One minute, please." She sounded young, awed, more than a little nervous.

A few seconds later, Kasden came on the line. "Detective,

I'm glad you called. I was wondering if you found out any-thing about Jake's killer. You can't imagine how this has thrown me! I can't think about anything else. I'm even having nightmares.''

"As a matter of fact, Mr. Kasden. I'd like to come by your office tomorrow and talk to you in person."

"But I told your associate everything I know."

"I'm sure you did. We're following up on the information you gave us. But there are one or two little details I'd like to go over with you. What time would be convenient?"

"Tomorrow's pretty busy. Could we make it Monday?"

"Afraid not, Mr. Kasden. We need every lead we can get. The longer we wait, the colder the trail."

"I have an appointment at twelve-fifteen. I should be back by two. I'll have to juggle a few appointments." He sounded peeved.

"I appreciate it. See you at two."

Ryker was rereading the notes he'd transcribed from his shorthand when Moran walked over and slouched into a chair.

"I saw Hank pulling up," he told Ryker. "Where's George?"

"He must've stepped away from his desk for a minute. He's calling Vegas to check on the alibis for Murdoch's men." He told him about the visit with Murdoch.

"What were you reading when I came in?"

"I spoke to Marty at SID. They were able to make out what was on the missing calendar page." He gave Moran his report.

" 'Ben—REC.' What's REC?"

"I have no idea. But I'm sure I saw it somewhere else."

"Saw what?" Stollman asked, joining them.

Moran handed the paper to Stollman, who stood looking at it for a minute.

"You in a trance?" Moran asked.

"Just thinking. I'm trying to remember where I—I know! It was scribbled on that Sunday copy of the *L.A. Times* we found in Vogler's attaché. Where's Vogler's stuff?"

Ryker pointed to the attaché case, waited while Stollman hunted through it for the newspaper.

"Here it is." Stollman turned the paper over. "Bingo. It says 'REC' with a question mark after it."

Moran said, "So you found it in two places. We still don't know what it means."

"I can ask Kasden when I see him tomorrow," Ryker said. "That and a few other things."

"You think he tore out the page?" Stollman asked.

"It's a strong possibility. He had time enough to do it when he went into the other room to Xerox the pages he said he needed. And whatever Vogler's message meant, Kasden was obviously involved."

Lewis returned. "I spoke to the manager at Caesars Palace, Sam. Murdoch's men were very visible from Saturday through Monday night. Lost quite a bit at the tables, but didn't seem to mind. And they ordered drinks all night, so their signatures are available, if we want to check them."

"No point," Ryker said. "Sounds like a dead end. What did you find out about Vogler's clients, Hank?"

"Nothing. I spoke to Dyson, the one who tried to stiff Vogler out of his commission. He laughed when I asked him for an alibi, thought I was joking. He knew Vogler was entitled to the commission, but he thought he could get away with it. Once he lost, he made some noise for a while, but basically forgot all about it. Or so he claims."

"Does he have an alibi, though?" Ryker asked.

"Yeah. His married daughter's here with her two kids. He and his wife took everyone to Disneyland, stayed till closing time. The daughter backed up everything. So did the chauffeur."

"Limo?" Moran asked.

"Stretch. It was in the driveway, along with the Silver Cloud. Stop drooling, Moran; you're getting spots on your polyester tie." Stollman grinned.

"Is that it?" Ryker asked.

"I still have to get in touch with the realtor, Laura Brackwood. *Ms.* Brackwood—the secretary made it clear. She's been out in the field all day, won't be back until tomorrow."

"Tom?" Ryker prompted.

"Not much to report. I saw five people on the open house list. Most of them lived within a few blocks of the Sherbourne place. Probably nosy neighbors who wanted to get a look at it before it was sold. They didn't see or hear anything unusual. One couple—name of Plotkin—was interested. When I told them a guy was killed there, the wife almost fainted. The husband didn't seem to mind; asked me if I thought the price would go down. Human compassion—it warms the heart. Anyway, I should be able to finish the list tomorrow. I only have six names left.''

"Mrs. Pearson isn't home yet?'' Ryker asked Stollman. "Nope.''

"Who's Pearson?'' Lewis and Moran asked simultaneously.

Stollman told them. "I talked with the neighbor again. She thought Pearson would've been home by now. And I left a second note in her mailbox, just in case.''

Moran said, "Hey, Sam, how was the funeral? Did the bride wear black?''

"Funny you should ask.'' He filled them in on all the details of the funeral and his conversation with Cooper. "So that explains why Mrs. Vogler participated. According to Jewish law, she's Vogler's widow, not his ex-wife. Cute, huh?''

Moran whistled. "This puts a different light on everything. I mean, if Vogler wouldn't give her a religious divorce, and she couldn't marry without it, she had a motive for killing him. So did her old man. He must've been madder'n hell at Vogler for not letting his little girl off the hook.''

Lewis said, "Who can blame him? Vogler sounds like a real prize.''

"Maybe he wasn't the nicest guy around,'' Ryker said, "but that didn't give someone the right to kill him. Anyway, we don't know that Mrs. Vogler was in any rush to remarry. We don't even know if she had a boyfriend.''

"Vogler told Cooper she had one,'' Stollman reminded him.

"That's not fact. Cooper wasn't sure it was true. We'll have to check into it.''

Moran said, "And if she *does* have a boyfriend, then he has a motive, too. This is getting better every minute.''

"Just don't go rushing out with your handcuffs, okay, Tom?'' Lewis said. "I think you're jumping the gun here.''

"Mrs. Vogler's missing gun?'' Moran said. "Don't forget about that, George.''

"Okay,'' Ryker interrupted. "Hank, arrange to get prints from the ex-wife, her father, and Kasden. See if you can get them to come in before the weekend. Novick wasn't keen about it. If he balks, I'll see what I can do. I don't remember if I mentioned it to his daughter. Don't make a big deal out of it. Tell her it's just routine. And Kasden—''

Lewis said, "I told Kasden we need his prints, seeing that he's been at Vogler's apartment. He didn't make a fuss."

"Good. So that's about it. George, you look terrible. Why don't you go home. Someone else can handle the doorman."

"You don't mind? The aspirin didn't help much."

"I'll talk to the guy," Moran offered. "He knows me."

"Thanks. I owe you one."

Moran got up and waited while Lewis lifted himself tiredly from his chair. The two men left the room together.

"You have anything else for me to do right now, Sam?" Stollman asked. It was after six. "I told Penny I'd try to make it home early. It's my kid's birthday. She just turned three."

"No problem. Great age." It seemed like only yesterday that Becky and Kelley were toddlers. Now they were both in high school. "Enjoy the party."

A funeral in the morning and a birthday party at night. Life was strange. Ryker wondered suddenly about Deena Vogler, tried to picture her in the house on Guthrie. Was she mourning her not-quite-ex-husband—or bringing out the champagne?

17

THERE WASN'T MUCH SHE COULD DO TO OCCUPY HERSELF, Deena realized when she returned from the cemetery. According to Orthodox law, she was confined to her house during *shivah*. Watching television or listening to music was inappropriate. Max had suggested a nap, but she was too tense to sleep.

Before leaving the cemetery, Reuben had given her a book, *The Jewish Way in Death and Mourning*. Maybe it'll help you, he'd told her. She thumbed through the pages, then put it aside. She couldn't concentrate. No, that wasn't true. The truth was that she doubted that the book held anything of interest for her. Unless, of course, there was a chapter deal-

ing with laws applying to the wife of a deceased person who
had refused to grant her a divorce. Knowing that she was
being silly, that she was wallowing in bitterness and self-pity,
she opened the book again and studied the table of contents.
No, there was no listing for *agunah*. She hadn't thought there
would be.

She realized suddenly that she'd be missing an entire week
of classes. How would she ever make up the material? In a
panic, she picked up the phone to call the school but found
herself listening to the strident whine of the dial tone, unable
to recall the number. She'd written it down in the black
pocket-sized daily planner she kept in her purse; the purse
was on her dresser. She went into her bedroom, found the
number, and called the school. The line was busy. She tried
again; again, she heard a busy signal. She lay down on her
bed—just for a few minutes, she told herself.

She must have dozed off, because her alarm clock said
four-ten. Her mouth had an acrid taste. She could stay in bed
indefinitely with Camille-like languor, she thought, or eat
something. She got out of bed, walked into the bathroom to
wash her face, and stopped short. She'd forgotten about the
sheet-shrouded mirrors. They were in heavy mourning, even
if she wasn't.

After splashing her face with cool water, Deena brushed
her hair with automatic strokes and put on her dress. At least
I don't have to waste time putting on makeup or deciding
what to wear, she thought as she walked into the kitchen.
Sandy had come by after the funeral. She'd brought Deena a
tuna casserole for dinner and a few bagels and hard-boiled
eggs.

"I told your parents I'd bring this over. You're supposed
to eat the bagel and an egg for the first meal after the funeral—something round for the cycle of life, Alan said."

Deena took a water bagel and a hard-boiled egg, peeled
the egg, and placed both on a stoneware plate. She was about
to slice the bagel but stopped. If I cut it, she wondered, will
it still be considered round? And then she wondered why it
mattered, why the hell she was worrying about roundness,
and the cycle of life, why she was going through the motions
of mourning for a man she had come to hate.

This is stupid, she thought; everything is so damn stupid.
But she ate the bagel anyway, chewing dutifully, glumly swal-

lowing a dose of self-enforced piety with each dry mouthful.
I am such a good girl.

At six, Max and Pearl arrived at the side door. Pearl went
to Deena and kissed her. Max deposited several grocery bags
on the kitchen counter then handed Deena a newspaper.

"You left it on the front porch. I'm surprised it's still
there." He put his arm around her, kissed her. "You look
tired, Deena. You're all right?"

"I'm okay, Daddy. What about you?" He looked tense,
she thought.

"Fine. How should I be? I'll set up chairs in the living
room for when the people come."

"There are a few chairs there. The others are in the den."

While Max set up the chairs, Deena helped Pearl unpack
the groceries. When they were done, Pearl arranged a platter
with cake and cookies and filled a bowl with apples, tanger-
ines, and pears.

"The navels aren't good yet," she told Deena. "Some
fruit you should always have on the table. Which tablecloth
should we use?"

"I don't care. The white, I guess."

Deena found a simple linen cloth and spread it on the
dining room table. Pearl arranged the fruit bowl, the platter,
and some napkins.

"I brought you some dinner, Deena. Broiled chicken, a
baked potato. Should I warm it up?"

"I just ate a bagel. And an egg," Deena added, seeing
Pearl's expression. "Sandy sent over a tuna casserole."

"So eat the chicken first. Tomorrow it won't be fresh. The
casserole will last."

"Okay. I will. Later, though."

"Fine." Pearl nodded, satisfied. "Go into the living room,
so people shouldn't have to wait. I'll tell Daddy we're ready."

"Right." With the sofa and the extra chairs Max had set
up, there was sitting room for about twelve people. More
than enough under the circumstances. Who would be coming, anyway? Rabbi Pearlstein had announced that the Vogelanters would be sitting *shivah* at their home. Their relatives
and friends would be there, offering condolences; Jake's
friends (funny, but she couldn't think of any) would be doing
the same.

Deena was about to sit on a chair when Max stopped her.

"Wait," he ordered. He removed a sofa cushion and placed

it on the floor. "Sit here, Deena." He pointed to the spot where the cushion had been.

"You're right. I forgot." During *shivah,* a mourner doesn't use a regular seat. Deena knew that from having paid one or two condolence calls with her mother. She walked over to the sofa. The doorbell rang.

"You shouldn't answer the door," Max told her. "I'll go."

"What else shouldn't I do?" she snapped, and was immediately sorry. None of this was Max's fault. He was just trying to be helpful. "I'm sorry, Daddy," she said.

But he had already left the room, and when he came back, Michael was with him. Michael stood in the doorway and looked uncertainly at Deena. She smiled wanly.

"Come sit," she invited, patting the cushion next to her.

Max glanced at her reprovingly, started to say something, but changed his mind. The doorbell rang again and he left to answer it.

Michael sat next to Pearl. "How are you, Mrs. Novick?"

"Fine, thank you." She looked toward the archway, where Max was standing with Ben and Ruth Kasden.

Ben was clearly ill-at-ease, hands clasped behind his back, stealing glances at Deena, sighing audibly, uncertain of what to do. Ruth was more composed, but she had toned down her appearance for the somber occasion. Deena couldn't help feeling, though, that the woman had searched her wardrobe for the perfect condolence call ensemble before settling on the olive-green sweater, matching skirt, and pewter accessories.

Without any hesitancy, Ruth marched over to Deena and sat next to her on the couch. Ben followed his wife into the room and sat on the edge of a folding chair across from her.

"This is a nightmare," Ruth said in her nasal Brooklyn whine. She pronounced it *nightmeah.* "A horrible, horrible nightmare." She emphasized each syllable. "Ben and I were at Ida and Joe's, and somebody mentioned that you were sitting *shivah.* Who was that, Ben?" she asked, turning to him.

He shrugged helplessly.

"So right away I said, 'That Deena is amazing.' Didn't I say that, Ben?" She turned to him again.

He nodded.

"And of course, as soon as we left there, we came right here. I insisted. How are you doing? You look terrible, dear.

This must be brutal for you, absolutely brutal.'' She smoothed her expensively cut short blond hair and turned to Pearl. "You're Deena's mother? I'm Ruth Kasden." She extended a ringed hand.

"I'm sorry," Ben said quickly. "I forgot you never met Max and Pearl. I used to see them all the time when Mama was in their convalescent home."

"I know how you feel," Ruth continued to Pearl. "I'm a mother, too. With the divorce and everything, it must be pretty confusing, right?" She turned her attention to Michael. "Who are you?"

Michael was saved from answering by the sudden appearance of Sandy and Alan (Max had left the door unlocked—another custom during *shivah.*) Minutes later, Faye came in with Miriam, Susan, and Elaine. Ruth looked at Deena expectantly; Deena performed the introductions—she was the only one who could.

"Magda planned on coming, but something came up," Faye said. "She told me to tell you she'll try to stop by tomorrow. And Rabbi Markowitz will be here soon. I just spoke to him."

"Who's Rabbi Markowitz, dear?" Ruth asked Deena. "Is he one of the rabbis who spoke at the funeral today? I don't remember that name. Do you, Ben?" She didn't wait for an answer, turned to Pearl. "It was a lovely service, don't you think? I haven't heard Yiddish in such a long time, and that rabbi spoke very well, I thought . . .''

In a way, Deena thought as she listened to Ruth flit from one subject to another, it was a relief having her here. Her incessant chatter masked the absence of tearful remembrances, poignant silences, comforting assurances—everything that marks a condolence call. But then, this was a condolence call only in the most technical sense. Of everyone assembled, only Ruth and Ben would miss Jake. And maybe not even Ruth.

Ruth had stopped talking. Now she was getting up, smoothing her skirt, adjusting her belt. Ben, taking his cue, sprang to his feet.

"Deena, dear," Ruth said, "we have to leave. But I want you to know we're here for you if you need anything. I mean that, dear." She looked around the room. "So nice to have met you all." She turned to her husband. "Ben?" They exited, Ruth leading the way, leaving a cloud of perfume behind her.

As Ruth and Ben Kasden walked into the entrance hall, the door opened and a tall, bearded young man came in. Ruth stared at him.

"I'm Rabbi Markowitz."

"Ben Kasden. This is my wife, Ruth. Jake was my partner."

The men shook hands. Reuben walked into the living room. Ruth followed him with her eyes.

"Let's go," Ben told her. He escorted her out the door and shut it firmly behind them.

Ruth's departure had left a sudden, strange silence; there was a note of suppressed laughter in the air; Deena was sure of it. Sandy had quickly filled the void, talking about Jonathan, asking the other women about their families. Alan was sitting near Michael, and the two were talking quietly.

Reuben moved his chair closer to Deena. "How do you feel?"

"Okay. I slept a lot. Too much, I think. To tell you the truth, I was bored. I don't know what I'll do for the next six days. There's always television, I guess. Or a jigsaw puzzle. Maybe I'll find a five-thousand-piece one. That should keep me busy."

"About watching television, Deena—"

"Reuben, I don't want to hear it. I really don't."

"Deena, don't get upset," Pearl told her.

"I know you must hate all this," Reuben said, "and I can't blame you. But there are a lot of laws concerning *shivah*, and I know you'll want to do the right thing."

"The right thing? I always do the right thing."

I went to the funeral; I ate a round bagel; I am sitting on a cushionless seat; I will wear this awful, mutilated dress for as long as I have to. But I don't want to hear any more laws about mourning. Not one. If I want to watch television, I'll do it. And if I want to laugh, I'll do that too. And I don't want to feel guilty about it. But she knew she would.

"I just feel like a hypocrite doing this for Jake," Deena said.

"Do what makes you comfortable," Michael said quietly.

"But you're not doing it for Jake, Deena," Miriam said. "You're doing it for yourself."

"Oh, come on, Miriam," Elaine said. "Don't get started."

"Not now, Elaine," Faye said firmly.

"I agree with Deena," Elaine continued. "Frankly, if I were in her shoes, I wouldn't be sitting *shivah* at all."

"It's the law," Miriam said. "The laws don't change according to our emotions or whims."

"It's ridiculous! The truth is that Jake was a son of a bitch, that he was never going to give Deena her *get,* and she's better off than she was last week. I'd trade places with her like that!" She snapped her fingers and glared at Miriam, indifferent to the tension she'd introduced into the room.

Sandy and Alan exchanged embarrassed looks; the Novicks stared resolutely ahead. Faye and Susan were waiting for the tirade to end; they had heard Elaine before. Michael was watching Deena carefully, his face marked with concern.

"How can you talk like that!" Miriam whispered. "Especially here, now."

Elaine turned to Deena. "You're not sorry he's dead, are you, Deena? Is anyone?" She looked around the room.

"Elaine," Reuben said calmly, "the loss of a human life is always tragic. Deena recognizes that, and she's already agreed to sit *shivah.* Getting her upset all over again is pointless."

"She should never have been put in this situation in the first place! I hope you don't take this personally, but as a group, you rabbis have really screwed up."

"Elaine!" Miriam warned.

"No. She's right," Reuben said. "I can't argue with that. We're doing too little, too slowly."

"I need a cigarette," Elaine said suddenly. She picked up her purse, got up, and left the room.

"I thought she gave up smoking," Susan said.

"There's fruit in the dining room," Pearl offered hesitantly. "If anyone's interested."

No one was interested.

"We'd better be going," Sandy said. "Jonathan still has fever, and I don't want to leave him too long with the sitter." She walked over to Deena. "I'll call you tomorrow."

Deena nodded.

Alan came over. "Did you find the gun?" he whispered. She shook her head.

"I'll call you tomorrow from the office. Try not to worry." He patted her hand, stood up, and left with Sandy.

"You okay?" Michael asked.

She nodded.

"Deena," Reuben said, "one more comment and I promise I won't bring this up again."

"Okay," she said warily.

"Maybe it would help you get through the next week if you could try to see the tragedy in Jake's dying before he saw what a terrible mistake he was making. I mean, he'll never have the chance to make it right. That's terrible, isn't it?"

"I guess. Yes, it is. I don't know if it will help me, but I'll try to focus on that."

"As far as everything else goes, do what you think is right. I have confidence in you."

"That's not fair." She smiled ruefully. "Now I have to live up to that."

Elaine came back into the room, a little calmer. "Are you ready to leave?" she asked the other women.

Miriam and Susan were.

Faye looked uncertain. "Do you want me to spend the night?" she asked Deena. "I don't mind at all."

"No thanks. I'd like to be alone. I hope you understand."

"I'll stop by tomorrow." She left to get her sweater.

"Deena, I'm really sorry if I got you all riled up," Elaine said. "I probably should've kept my mouth shut."

"That's okay. Don't worry about it."

"I only wanted to help. I hope you believe me."

"Come on, Elaine," Susan said. "You're the one who wanted to leave."

"It's just—" She stopped. "Take care, Deena."

Miriam approached Deena hesitantly. "There's a special phrase that a person's supposed to say when he or she takes leave of a mourner—I'm sure you know it—but after what happened tonight, and with the way you feel about all this . . ."

"Do what you think is right, Miriam." She took her hand.

"There's a shorter version of the phrase," Reuben said. "I've always liked it better anyway." He was standing in front of Deena and addressed her. *"Tenachami.* May you be comforted."

"Tenachami," Miriam echoed.

"I have no problem with that," Deena told them. With the way things were going, she could use some comfort.

Michael stayed after everyone left (Max had fixed Deena with a long, disapproving look before Pearl ushered him out the side door), keeping Deena company as she ate the supper her mother had brought. To her surprise, she was ravenous. She told Michael all about the funeral, about Rabbi Brodin's eulogy.

"I should have been there for you!"

"You wouldn't have been able to do anything, Michael. Anyway, it's over. I'm glad you're here with me now."

"I wanted to come over earlier, but I had a full schedule, and my last patient stayed longer than usual."

"You don't have to explain, Michael. I know you're busy."

"I tried calling several times, you know. I figured you had the phone off the hook."

"I did. I wasn't really in the mood to talk."

When the doorbell rang, they looked at each other.

"I'll go," Michael said. "You finish eating. And anyway—"

"I know; 'I'm not supposed to.' " She smiled.

"Feeling better?"

"Yes. But only temporarily. Nothing's been resolved."

Ben Kasden looked startled and not at all pleased when Michael opened the door and let him in.

"Is Deena available?"

"She's in the kitchen. I'll get her." He left Ben in the hall and walked to the kitchen. "Ben Kasden," he told her.

"Ben?" She looked puzzled. "Tell him I'll be right there." She wiped her mouth and hurried into the living room. Ben was pacing in front of the fireplace.

"Is something wrong?"

Ben looked pointedly at Michael.

"I think I'll watch the news," Michael said, and left.

"I feel terrible bothering you at a time like this, with everything you're going through." He was avoiding her eyes. "Can we sit down?"

Deena assumed her former spot; Ben sat across from her.

"You know I've been having some problems with Murdoch."

Deena nodded.

"And you remember I told you your lawyer was on my back about an audit?" He sounded accusing. "Well, first she gave me till the end of October. But I persuaded her to give me another week. The accountant was supposed to come over yesterday, but of course, what with Jake getting killed and everything, I had to cancel.'' He looked at Deena to see if she understood.

She nodded again.

''Anyway, we agreed that the guy is going to come in on Tuesday, but I'll tell you the truth, it just won't work.''

''Why? What's the problem?''

''Listen.'' He leaned forward. ''I have a couple of big names serious about buying Murdoch's shares. Hell, you don't know what that would mean, getting Murdoch off my back!''

''You explained that to me last time, Ben. I still don't see why you're so concerned.''

''The thing is, Murdoch's accountant is also bugging me to see the books. He had an appointment set up with Jake, as a matter of fact, but Jake canceled it.''

''I don't see what you're getting at.''

''Deena, I need more time. I don't want to blow this deal, you understand. If Murdoch bows out before these guys buy his shares, the firm will be in big trouble. And I mean big.''

''But it's Murdoch's money that's on the line, isn't it, Ben? We just put the deal together.''

''Not exactly.'' He wiped his forehead again. ''See, Deena, real estate is pretty complicated. That's why I told you to give up your share in the business.''

''What's going on, Ben? Just tell me.''

''This is very hard for me, Deena.''

She waited.

''I built this business up from scratch. I worked hard, damn hard, getting listings, hustling my ass all over the damn city to get clients. And I was good.''

''I know. Jake always said you were the greatest salesman.''

''But somehow, no matter how much I took in, it was never enough. Ruthie likes nice things. Don't get me wrong— I do, too. And the more you buy, the more you want. It's an old story. Sometimes, I'm a little short of cash, so I pay a little more interest on the credit card. No big deal. In the end, who cares, right?

''Then Ruthie decided we needed a vacation home, and a fancy car, and we had to remodel the house here and in Palm Springs. I tell you, Deena, she has no idea how much things cost or where I can get the money to pay for everything. And I should have said no; I know that. What can I tell you? She's a spender, she's loud, she talks too much; but what the hell, I love her. And I know she loves me. I know that.''

"I'm sure she does, Ben," she reassured him, wishing he would get to the point.

"So here I am with all these bills and no money to pay them. And I figured the best way to make fast money is with stocks. Lots of people make fortunes playing the market. Why can't I do the same, right? But it didn't work out. Every goddamn company I invested in went down the drain. I'm a jinx.'' He smiled grimly. "What's worse, I bought on margin. You know what that is?''

"No.''

"When I bought the shares, I only gave a down payment. That's okay if the stock is going up. But when the stock goes down—and mine went way, way down—you have to pay everything.''

"I still don't understand what this has to do with me.''

"I'm coming to that. This is the part that's really hard for me, Deena, 'cause I love you like a daughter, and I don't want you to think badly of me. The thing is, I had to pay my margin calls on some stocks, and it involved a lot of money, money I didn't have. So I did something terrible." He took a deep breath. "I withdrew funds from the firm's trust accounts.''

"I know.''

"You know?" He looked startled.

"A few years ago, Jake told me about one time you did that. But he said you promised never to do it again.''

"Two years ago? Yeah, I remember. But that was for a couple of days, and it was a small amount.''

"That's not the point, Ben. It was still illegal.''

"I know that! You think I need you to tell me that? I'm sorry," he said quickly. "I have no right to get upset.''

"Go ahead.''

"I borrowed from several accounts, including Murdoch's.''

"Ben!''

"I know. It was crazy. But I didn't know what else to do. That's why I have to push off these audits. Do you see that? If they check the books, I'll go to jail. And I can't face that.''

"Ben, you can't postpone the audits indefinitely.''

"I don't need 'indefinitely.' All I need is a couple of weeks. A month, tops. See, I have a sure thing coming in soon—no, I know what you're thinking, but this is guaranteed. As soon as it comes through, I can put back the money into all the accounts, and no one ever has to know. That's it."

"I don't know what to say."

"Say what you think. You're angry?"

"Of course I'm angry! I'm furious! You embezzled funds; you put us all in jeopardy. This is insane, Ben!"

"I know. But what can I do, say I'm sorry? I'm sorry."

"That doesn't do anything."

"You hate me?"

"No, I don't hate you. But I'm disappointed in you, Ben. I really am. Even when Jake told me about that other time, I wasn't thrilled, but this . . . How could you do it?"

"I was desperate. You don't know what it feels like to be pressed against the wall."

"Yes, I do."

"That's different. You could've worked everything out eventually. I'm talking about going to jail, Deena, for God's sake, not getting a divorce."

She didn't answer.

"So can you help me? I need you to call your lawyer, tell her to cancel the audit. Now that Jake's dead, the whole picture's different anyway. We can work it any way you like. You can stay in, be a partner in this godforsaken mess, or I can buy you out."

"With what? Monopoly money?"

"I told you. I have a big deal coming through very soon. But we don't have to talk about that now. What do you say?"

"I don't know. You're asking me to do something illegal."

"No one will ever find out. There's no risk to you."

"I'm not as sure about it as you seem to be. Anyway, it's immoral. I can't see myself covering up something like that."

"You'll be sending me to jail, Deena. And for what? I made a mistake, sure, but in the end, no one's going to be hurt. I swear to you I'm going to put back every goddamn cent!"

"And if your 'sure thing' doesn't work out?"

"It will."

"I have to think about it. I can't give you an answer now."

"This can't wait, Deena. Why do you think I came here tonight, of all times?"

"What about Murdoch's accountant?" she asked suddenly. "What are you planning to tell him?"

"I told him the police need to see the books. It'll buy me some time to put the rest of the money back into that account. I already transferred some cash over the last few days into some other accounts. If I have to, I'll a get short-term private loan. If Murdoch finds out what I did . . ." His voice was shaky. "I don't even want to think about it. You've got to help me, Deena!"

"I understand what you're saying, Ben, but you'll have to give me a day or so at least."

"I can't—okay." He got up. "You'll call me?"

Michael was stunned when Deena repeated what Ben had told her. "I can't believe what you're saying." He shook his head.

"I can't believe it myself. Poor Ben! He's terrified."

"Poor Ben? What about you? He didn't worry much about your interests when he pulled this stunt."

"He didn't plan for this to happen. He got in over his head."

"So you're going to keep quiet about this, call Brenda and tell her to cancel the audit? If anyone finds out about this, you could be legally responsible, too, couldn't you?"

"It's called 'accessory after the fact,' I think. You're probably right. But what should I do? Let him go to jail?"

"I don't see that it's your problem. He got himself into this mess by himself, and you'd be crazy to let him pull you into it."

"You're right, but I can't turn him in, can I?"

"You know what puzzles me? Jake was a shrewd businessman, wasn't he? I don't understand how Ben did this under his nose."

"I don't know. He trusted him, I guess. Although there was one incident that *did* get Jake angry." She told him about it.

"What did Jake do when he found out?"

"Nothing, really. What could he do? He yelled at him, of course, made him promise not to do it again."

"Big deal. I'm surprised he didn't get more upset."

"Oh, you're wrong. He was very upset. He threatened Ben that he'd report him if he ever co-mingled funds again."

"Report him to whom?"

"Someone important."

"Like me?" He smiled.

"Not that important." She laughed. "No, someone in the industry who supervises ethics in real estate."

"You mean the Real Estate Commissioner?"

"I guess. That sounds right. But that was two years ago."

"So what? If Jake was that worried then, he'd be even more careful with Ben, more suspicious. Don't you see that?"

"So? What's your point?"

"I'm not sure I have one. Yet."

18

THERE WAS NO POINT TO SOME OF THE THINGS HE SAW, RY-ker thought. No point at all.

At three-thirty Friday morning, Ryker had been called to investigate the suspicious death of a four-year-old boy. He'd arrived at the second-floor apartment; had looked at the vacant-eyed, twenty-two-year-old mother who sat twisting the belt of her dingy, wrap-around robe; had listened impassively while she admitted that her boyfriend may have hit her son too hard "this time."

"It's the crying," she explained dully. "Larry can't take it 'cause he has to get up so early, you understand. He works in the flower market downtown. And Matthew's been so fussy the last three nights, what with his cold 'n everything." She wiped her nose with the back of her hand. "So tonight, when he started crying again, real loud, I saw Larry was mad, so I said I'd take care of it. But Larry, he said, 'No, I'll go,' and I figured if I argued, I'd only make him angrier." She paused.

"I thought he just gave him a smack, to kind of quiet him down, you know? It usually works. But when I got up later to go to the bathroom, I thought I'd check to see how Matthew was doing. Maybe he needed another blanket or something. And he was awful still. So I called 911 and they came out here, and they said he was dead. But I know Larry didn't mean to hurt him. He took him for a Slurpee at 7-Eleven last week.''

"Where is Larry?" Ryker asked.

"At his folks'. After he came back from Matthew's room, he told me he figured he'd better sleep there tonight, in case Matthew started crying again. So you see, he didn't even know he was dead.'' She looked at Ryker for confirmation.

"You'll have to come down to the station,'' he told her.

"But I didn't do nothing wrong! It was an accident. You can see that, can't you?''

At the least, it's child endangerment, you stupid bitch, he wanted to tell her. *If not murder.* But he said nothing, just waited while she got dressed, then put her in a squad car. "Where do Larry's folks live?''

In a flat voice, she gave him a nearby address.

"Stop by this place and pick up her boyfriend,'' Ryker instructed the officer who was driving. Then he walked back upstairs to wait for the coroner.

The body, pitifully small, was purpled with bruises. Ryker had seen others like it, but he'd never gotten used to it. He hoped he never would.

By the time he was ready to leave, it was six o'clock. It made no sense to go home. He stopped at a coffee shop for breakfast and two cups of passable coffee and waited while the sleepy waitress wrapped his apple turnover and slipped it into a bag.

It took him an hour to write up his notes. When he was finished, he reread them, made a few corrections, and set them aside. He called Linda, told her he'd see her that evening.

"Kiss the girls for me,'' he told her. *Keep them safe.*

"You'll see them when you get home.''

"I may be late, though.''

"Not too late, or I'll put out an APB.'' She yawned.

Grinning, he hung up. He clasped his hands in front and stretched his arms over his head. His calisthenics for the day.

At eight, Lewis called to say he had the flu. Five minutes later Stollman rang to say he was going directly to Laura Brackwood's office. "I tried reaching Novick about coming in to be printed, but he left for work. I'll try him there later. I haven't called the daughter yet, and I figured I'd reach Kasden after I finish with this Brackwood woman.''

"I'm seeing Kasden later. I'll take care of it. Something

else I'd like you to do." He told him about the dead boy and the fugitive boyfriend. "This Larry wasn't at his parents' house. See if you can get on his tail. I'll leave my notes in case I'm not here when you come in."

The message from Douglas was still on his desk. He'd tried calling Thursday. He tried again now. A woman answered.

"Detective Ryker, LAPD. I'm returning your call."

"Oh." She sounded uncertain.

"How can I help you, Miss Douglas?"

"Look, Detective. I'm not sure I want to get involved."

"You called me. Involved in what?"

"I'm a friend of Jake Vogler's." She paused. "I think there's something you should know." She agreed to come to Ryker's office at ten that morning.

When Moran entered the room, Ryker was slouched down in his chair, swiveling back and forth, his arms clasped behind his head, his eyes focused on the ceiling.

"Any answers up there?" Moran asked, straddling a chair.

"Not a one. Sometimes this job gets to me."

"What? Vogler?" He sounded surprised.

"Worse. A kid." He told Moran about it.

"They get the boyfriend?" he asked quietly.

"Nope. He packed a few things, asked his old man for some cash, and skipped. He wasn't about to stick around for a murder rap. We'll find him, though. We've got his picture, prints, license plate. He's bound to surface. Maybe he'll be too stupid to dump the car."

"You want me to pursue it?"

"Stick with the open house names. I'm putting Hank on it."

"Whatever you think. I spoke to the doorman, Sam. Jerome Oliver, aka Geraldo Olverano. A nice kid, ambitious. Doesn't plan on being a doorman forever. He remembers that Vogler had a visitor late Saturday night, but he doesn't know the name."

"What did he look like?"

"Average height, late twenties, good-looking. Jerome liked his jacket—preppy-looking, patches on the elbows."

"Would he recognize him?"

"He's not sure, but he said he'd be happy to look at some pictures. What do you think?"

"A Fuller Brush salesman? Who the hell knows?"

"Maybe it's Mrs. Vogler's boyfriend."

"We don't know yet that she has one."

"Oh, she has one." Moran grinned. "I'd put money on it."

After Moran left, Ryker tackled some paperwork he'd been neglecting, determined to make a respectable dent in it before the morning was over. More than an hour later he was still engrossed in transcribing notes, and he sensed rather than heard someone standing in front of him.

"Detective Ryker? I'm Ann Douglas."

She was very striking, Ryker decided, as he stood up to greet her. Tall; slim but not skinny; nice legs beneath a burgundy leather skirt that skimmed her knees; high cheekbones; large, almond-shaped brown eyes that looked straight at him. Her hair was brushed away from from her face and fell to her shoulders. It was streaked blond, the way his wife Linda had wanted to have hers done until she found out the upkeep was too steep. He knew she must be wearing makeup, but she had done a damn good job. Her sweater, he noticed, was the same shade as her skirt.

Her handshake was firm, confident.

"Please sit down."

She sat down gracefully, crossed her long legs. "Thank you for seeing me."

"That's what we're here for. I'm very interested in what you have to say, Miss Douglas. If it's all right, I'd like to tape this conversation. It's easier than taking notes."

A slight hesitation. "All right."

Ryker pulled out a small cassette player, checked to see that there was a blank tape in it, and turned it on. "What do you do for a living, Miss Douglas?"

"I'm an assistant buyer for an expensive line of women's clothing at a major department store."

He wondered whether she'd gotten a discount on the sweater and leather skirt. "You sounded nervous on the phone."

"I was. But I'm not anymore. Frankly, I can't afford to be. This is too important. Jake and I were very close."

He looked at her.

"We weren't living together, if that's what you want to know." Her eyes were steady, calm. "We *were* a few years ago. That was before he met Deena and married her." Her tone was cold. "During the past year we were sleeping together. Less often than I would have liked. Does that shock you, Detective?''

He smiled. "I appreciate your honesty."

"You could find out anyway, if you wanted to; several people knew about us. I'm not ashamed of our relationship, and I don't see the point in having you waste your time on that. Are you aware that Jake was being threatened?'' she asked suddenly.

"By whom?"

"Several people. Mostly Deena's father.''

"What kind of threats are you talking about?''

"Some of it was harassment; the others sounded serious.''

"Tell me about the harassment first. Who was involved?''

"A rabbi friend of Deena's organized it. Jake told me his name, but I don't remember it. You could find out, though.''

"Why were they harassing Mr. Vogler?''

"This is a little complicated.'' She recrossed her legs. "Okay. Jake and Deena had a civil divorce, but she wanted a religious divorce, too. Without it, she couldn't remarry.''

"And he wouldn't sign the paper?''

"He was very angry at Deena, at the way she just threw him out. Little miss perfect. He was going to sign it eventually.''

"Why *did* they get divorced?''

"Because she found out he was sleeping with me.'' She looked uncomfortable, but she met his eyes. "Look, Detective, obviously I'm not a saint, but Jake wouldn't have come to me if everything was fine at home. And if I hadn't welcomed him, someone else would have. He was a very attractive man. Sexy. Funny.'' Her eyes started tearing; she bit her bottom lip.

"You okay?'' He opened a drawer, pulled out a tissue from a box, and handed it to her.

She nodded. "Thanks. He should never have married her in the first place. She's Orthodox, did you know that? Jake is Jewish, but Orthodox?—that's so ridiculous!''

"Are you Jewish?''

"No. But that never bothered him. His parents probably wouldn't have been happy about us. But his mother adored him. She would have come around, eventually.''

"When Mr. Vogler met his wife, your relationship with him was already over, though?''

She nodded. "But we were very close. Even after he moved

out, we slept together once in a while. I thought he just needed time to think. But then he got serious about Deena.''

She was wrapped up in her narrative, eager to tell it; maybe no one had ever listened. Ryker was careful not to interrupt her.

''He was intrigued by her, you see. She played this prim virgin waiting for a Jewish knight, and he fell for it. She told him she wouldn't sleep with him until they were married, and she wouldn't marry him unless he was religious. Clever. So he convinced himself he was interested in being religious. I told him he was crazy, but he said I was just being jealous.''

''Were you?''

''Sure I was jealous! I loved him. It was his idea to stop living together; I couldn't very well force him to stay. He told me he wasn't ready for a commitment. And then he married Deena.'' Her tone was edged with bitter irony. ''But I knew it wouldn't work. And I wasn't really surprised when he called me a few months after they were married. It wasn't just sex, you know. We were really right together. We always were.''

''But he wouldn't give her a religious divorce. Didn't that bother you?''

''I told you. That was temporary. It was over between them.''

''The rabbi who spoke at the funeral made it sound as though Mr. Vogler wanted to work things out with his wife.''

''That's not true! You mean Brodin. Jake just told him that to get him off his back. I *know* Jake. He was playing a game.''

''What about the boyfriend?''

''What boyfriend?''

''I spoke to Mr. Vogler's lawyer. Apparently, Mr. Vogler told him there was a boyfriend, that he was upset about it.''

She was silent for a moment. ''Jake said Deena was seeing someone. It bothered him a little. But that was his male ego.''

''And that didn't worry you? The fact that he was jealous of his ex-wife? That he wouldn't give her a divorce?''

''He wasn't jealous!''

Ryker looked at her evenly.

''Okay. Maybe Jake was having a hard time getting over this. But not because he was in love with Deena. He just didn't like losing. But I knew everything would work out for us.''

''How long were you going to wait?''

''I don't know what you mean by that.''

"Nothing, really. Me, I don't even like to wait in line for a movie if there are more than five people ahead of me." He smiled. "I'm just surprised that an attractive woman like you would sit around waiting for someone indefinitely."

"When it comes to getting something I want, Detective, I can wait a long time. And Jake was worth waiting for. But I didn't come here to discuss my relationship with Jake."

"Let's get back to the harassment. Exactly what did this rabbi do?"

"First he pestered Jake with phone calls, trying to convince Jake to give Deena this religious divorce. Then he organized pickets in front of Jake's office in Century City."

"Was Mr. Vogler angry?"

"He wasn't thrilled. Then this rabbi started mailing letters all over the city with Jake's picture on it, like a 'Wanted' poster. Jake was furious. But it just made him more determined not to sign the paper. There were threats, too."

"From the rabbi?" Ryker was surprised.

"Anonymous calls. Jake couldn't recognize the voice."

"What kind of threats?"

"Vague stuff, really. The basic message was that if Jake knew what was good for him, he'd give Deena this divorce."

"What about the father? Did he personally harass Mr. Vogler?"

"Absolutely. He called up clients, told them Jake was refusing to give his wife a divorce. He told Ben—Jake's partner—to get rid of him. The man became unhinged. And then he threatened Jake."

"What do you mean?"

"He said he would kill Jake. Is that specific enough?"

"Mr. Vogler told you this?"

"I heard it myself. I was at Jake's apartment when Mr. Novick showed up. He didn't know I was there. I was in the bedroom, but the door was open and I heard everything."

"When was this?"

"Last Thursday night."

"What happened exactly, can you remember?"

"The doorman signaled on the house phone and told Jake Mr. Novick wanted to come up. Jake refused at first, but in the end he said okay. He asked me to wait in the bedroom until Novick left. The minute Jake opened the door, I could hear Novick yelling. 'You're ruining my daughter's life'—stuff like that."

"What did Mr. Vogler say?"

"He told Novick to butt out of his life. The yelling went on for a while. The neighbor started banging on the wall."

"When did he threaten to kill Mr. Vogler?"

"Just before he left. He said something like, 'If you touch my daughter again, if you make one more phone call, I'll kill you.' Then he said, 'I'll be doing the world a favor.' "

"Do you have any idea what Mr. Novick meant about touching his daughter or calling her?"

"No. I asked Jake, but he said Novick was just ranting."

"I see." He smiled at her. "This is very interesting. Do you usually have such a good memory, Miss Douglas?"

"I'm not sure I like your tone, Detective."

"I'm just impressed, that's all."

"How could I forget something like that?"

"When did you find out that Mr. Vogler was dead?"

"I called the office Wednesday. Judy—the receptionist—told me what had happened. She couldn't stop crying."

"But you didn't contact me until yesterday. If you thought Novick was responsible for Mr. Vogler's death, why didn't you call immediately?"

"At first I didn't make a connection. People make empty threats when they're angry. I've probably said something like that once or twice. But the more I thought about it, the more I realized Novick *could* have killed Jake. I just couldn't ignore it, could I?"

"When was the last time you saw Mr. Vogler?"

"Saturday night. We went to a movie and then had some drinks at a cocktail lounge. He dropped me off around twelve-thirty."

"Did you talk to him on Sunday?"

"No. I was out most of the morning, and I knew he was doing an open house and that he'd be busy till around six."

"Were you home?"

"I was home. Are you checking up on my alibi? I don't understand this, Detective. I came here voluntarily, to assist you, not to be cross-examined." Her eyes were angry.

"Of course not. But if you were home, and Mr. Vogler called you, it could help us fix the time of death."

"I see. Well, I was home all afternoon, and during the evening, too. But he didn't call."

"Were you surprised when you didn't hear from him?"

"Not at first. He didn't call me every day. I called the office Monday, and Judy said he'd gone out of town."

"He never mentioned he was going?"

"No. But he's impulsive. It didn't worry me. That was just like Jake." She seemed lost in thought.

"Is there anything you'd like to add?"

"No. That's it. What are you going to do about Novick?"

Ryker shut the tape recorder. "I'm going to follow up on the information you've given me. In the meantime, I'm going to have your statement typed up, and I'll call you when it's ready so that you can come in, read it over, and sign it."

"Fine." She got up to leave.

"Just one thing. Since you've been in Mr. Vogler's apartment, we'll need to get a set of your prints so that we can eliminate them from the prints we took. You understand."

"I suppose so. I've never had my fingerprints taken."

"It's a very simple procedure. I'll have someone do it now before you leave." He got up, walked over to a detective from burglary at a nearby desk, and arranged to have her take Ann Douglas to have her prints rolled.

Ryker watched Ann Douglas's graceful exit, then got his fourth cup of coffee for the day. He'd forgotten about the turnover. He unwrapped it and took a bite. The pastry was a little tough, the apple filling sour. Maybe it was him. He ate it anyway, washing it down with the hot liquid.

An hour and a half later, Ryker sighed, dropped his pen, and flexed his cramped fingers. It was twelve-ten. If he left now, he would have plenty of time to talk with Judy Battaglia before Ben Kasden returned from lunch.

19

THE YOUNG, DARK-HAIRED MAN SITTING AT THE RECEPTIONIST'S desk in the waiting room of Kasden and Vogler, Realtors, was simultaneously talking on the phone and rapidly punching numbers on a pocket-sized calculator when Ryker walked in.

"Let me get back to you with those figures," he said into the phone and hung up. He smiled at Ryker. "Can I help you?"

"I'd like to see Miss Battaglia. Is she out to lunch?" He tried to mask his disappointment.

"She is, but she'll be back in about fifteen minutes. I'm just filling in until she gets back. We've been a little short-handed lately. Maybe I can help you."

Ryker took out his wallet, showed the man his ID.

"Oh." His voice was subdued. "You're here about Jake. The whole thing is so awful." He got up quickly and adjusted his glasses. "I'm Gerry Kowalski. Did you want to see Ben? Because he *is* out to lunch, and I'm not sure when he'll be back."

"I have an appointment to see Mr. Kasden at two, but I thought I'd come by earlier and talk with Miss Battaglia. While I'm waiting, maybe I could get some information from you, too."

"Of course! I want to help, if I can. Although I don't think there's much I can tell you."

"Just office background, basically. Where can we talk?"

"I can't really leave the waiting room; someone might drop by. Why don't I just get a chair and we can talk right here." He brought a chair and placed it next to the desk.

"How long have you been working here?" Ryker asked.

"Three years. I trained with a big firm, but I wasn't happy there. Lots of internal fighting and back-stabbing. I heard about this outfit from a friend. I really like it here."

"It's just the three of you—aside from Miss Battaglia?"

"Five. There's Paul Kashanian—he's on his honeymoon—and Lynne Walters. She joined about a year ago."

"Things must be pretty hectic around here now."

"I'll say! First Paul left, so I had to take a lot of his appointments. Then Jake. God, I can't believe he's dead! And Ben said it happened in the Sherbourne house!" He shuddered.

"So who takes over when Miss Battaglia goes to lunch?"

"Ben. He's mostly in the office. Jake is—*was*—the field guy. Today Ben had something important to take care of, so he asked me to stay, and Judy said she'd only take a half hour."

"Meeting a big client, huh?" Ryker smiled.

"Actually, I heard him arranging to meet his broker. But he may have another appointment, too. Can I ask you something? Have you made any progress in finding Jake's killer?"

"We're following up on several leads. So when was the last time you saw Mr. Vogler?"

"Thursday, I think. I was in the office very early Friday morning just for an hour, but I left before Jake came in."

"What about Saturday?"

"Ben and Jake alternate Saturdays. That one was Ben's."

"Was Mr. Vogler in a good mood when you saw him?"

"So-so. I mean, he's been under a lot of stress, what with his divorce and everything. I was real sorry about that. I like Deena." He shrugged. "I guess it just didn't work out."

"Did Mr. Vogler talk about his marriage?"

"Not really. But you could see he was upset. And the Murdoch deal going sour didn't help things either." He looked at Ryker. "Do you know about that?"

Ryker nodded. "Was Mr. Kasden worried about Murdoch?"

"Everybody worried about Murdoch. I made it a point to be out of the office if I knew Murdoch was coming in." He laughed nervously. "But yeah, Ben was preoccupied. And remember, he was crazy about Jake. So if Jake was hurting, Ben would be, too."

"They got along well?"

"Like brothers. I mean, they had their disagreements and everything, but so do brothers, right?"

"Right. So what did they argue about?"

"I didn't say they *argued*." He sounded uncomfortable. "I said they disagreed sometimes. Anyway, it was no big deal."

The front door opened to the accompaniment of a soft bell.

"Judy's back," Kowalski announced. He sounded relieved.

Ryker stood up as the petite brunette entered the room. She was cute, he thought, with an elfin quality accentuated by saucerlike brown eyes and a tiny nose. She looked very young.

She glanced quizzically at Ryker.

"This is Detective Ryker," Kowalski said.

"Mr. Kasden isn't expecting you till two," she said.

"Actually, Miss Battaglia, I'd like to speak to you for a

few minutes.'' He turned to Kowalski. "Thanks for your time.''

"No problem.'' He got up quickly. "I have a one-thirty showing on Drexel. I don't want to be late. Judy, there were two calls. I left the messages on your desk.'' He headed for the door.

Ryker stopped him. "Mr. Kowalski. One thing before you go. I've been looking through some of Mr. Vogler's papers, and he keeps referring to 'REC'. Can you tell me what that means?'' Ryker had a theory; he wanted verification.

"REC? That would be the Real Estate Commissioner. Is that it?'' He sounded like a truant eager to make a quick exit from the principal's office.

"That's it.'' Exactly. "Thanks. Thanks again.''

Judy Battaglia had seated herself behind the barricade of her desk and was busy arranging papers and straightening files.

"Hectic day?'' Ryker asked, smiling genially.

"Very. I still have to reschedule some of Jake's—Mr. Vogler's—appointments. And one of our men is on his honeymoon. I only took a half-hour for lunch.''

"I won't take much of your time.''

She looked at him. "It isn't really the time. To tell you the truth, I'm a little nervous. I've never talked to a detective before. And I'm so upset about Jake. Every time I think about it, I feel like crying. He was wonderful.'' Her voice was husky with emotion.

"I'm sure he was. I don't want to upset you, but there are some points I hope you can clear up. It could be important.''

"Okay.'' She folded her hands on top of the desk and gave the detective her full attention.

"When was the last time you spoke to Mr. Vogler?''

"That would be Friday. He came into the office around ten, but he didn't stay long. He had several appointments.''

"Were you surprised when he didn't come in on Monday?''

"A little. Mr. Kasden didn't seem worried. Then someone called for Jake and said he wouldn't be in for a few days.''

"That wasn't unusual?''

"I guess it was. But Jake was full of surprises. That was one of the exciting things about him.''

"Didn't he have any appointments scheduled for Monday?''

"Just one. But that was canceled on Friday." She picked up some loose paper clips, opened a desk drawer, and put the clips into a small cardboard box.

"What about the open house that Mr. Vogler conducted last Sunday. Who knew about that?"

"We had an ad in the papers. We always do."

"I mean, who knew that Mr. Vogler would be there?"

"That's difficult to say. Everybody in the office, of course. And there were several calls about the property."

"But callers wouldn't necessarily ask who was doing the open house, would they?"

"Not usually. It's funny that you mention that, because several people wanted to know which realtor would be there. But I don't see—oh my God! Do you mean that one of the people who called was the killer? I thought it was a burglar!"

"We're checking all the possibilities. These people who called, were they men or women?"

"Both. I can't believe this!"

"Did you recognize any of the voices?"

She shook her head. Ryker thought she was about to cry.

"Miss Battaglia, you mentioned that you saw Mr. Vogler on Friday morning. Did he seem upset or worried?"

"Not more than usual. He was having some personal problems lately. I guess you know all about that." She looked at him.

Ryker nodded.

"But he was always friendly to me. I remember that before he left, he asked me how my courses were going. I started taking some classes at a real estate school. Jake encouraged me to do it. He said I had real potential."

"I gather you liked working for him."

"I loved it. He was great—always joking, always putting everybody at ease. I'm really going to miss him."

"Did you ever see him socially?"

"No." She seemed amused by the question. "He used to talk about taking me to Vegas for the weekend, but I knew he wasn't serious." She smiled wistfully. "It was just his way."

"What about Miss Douglas?"

"What about her?"

"What was Mr. Vogler's relationship with her?"

"She called here pretty often, and they went out to lunch once in a while, but I don't know what went on between them. As far as I know, he wanted to reconcile with his ex-wife.''

"Did he tell you that?''

"No. He didn't really discuss it, but I heard him talking to Mr. Kasden about it once or twice.''

"Did you ever meet Mr. Vogler's father-in-law?''

"He came to the office about a month ago. I don't remember the date. He didn't have an appointment, and Jake wasn't in. But he waited for almost an hour until Jake came.'' She stopped.

"And?''

"Jake said he didn't have time to talk to him, but Mr. Novick said he wouldn't leave until Jake *did* talk to him. In the end, Jake gave in. Mr. Novick didn't stay long.''

"It wasn't a friendly meeting?''

"I don't know. But Mr. Novick looked upset when he left.''

"Was that the only time Mr. Novick was here?''

She nodded. "But he called several times. As a matter of fact, two weeks ago Jake instructed me that whenever Mr. Novick called, I was to say that Jake wasn't in.''

"But you don't know why Jake didn't want to talk to him?''

"It wasn't really any of my business.''

"Could Mr. Novick have been one of the people who called about the open house last Sunday?''

She thought for a moment. "I really don't know. I mean, I might not have recognized his voice anyway, and if he had a cold or something . . .'' Her voice trailed off.

"Okay. Don't worry about it. Let's get back to last Friday. What did Mr. Vogler do while he was in the office?''

"Well, he had a short meeting with Mr. Kasden; then he went into his office for a while and made some phone calls. That's it. Oh, and he asked me if I'd received any calls.''

"Is that when he asked you to cancel his Monday meeting with Murdoch's accountant?''

"Yes.'' She began aligning some pencils so that the points were all facing the same way.

"According to Murdoch, that wasn't the first time Mr. Vogler canceled. You must've found it a little embarrassing to call this guy and cancel so many times.''

"I didn't enjoy it.''

"I don't suppose you know what the problem was. I mean, why didn't he just see this accountant and get it over with?''

"I really don't know. You'd have to ask Mr. Kasden."

"Who decided to cancel, Mr. Kasden or Mr. Vogler?"

"I believe they both agreed to cancel the meeting."

"So you heard them discussing the problem?"

She looked away, obviously flustered.

"Miss Battaglia, I know you feel a strong loyalty to the people you work for. I think that's great. But I'm investigating a murder. Now legally, I can't force you to answer my questions, but to tell you the truth, it won't look very good if you refuse to cooperate."

"This has nothing to do with Jake's death."

"You're probably right, but I'd like you to answer my questions anyway. What exactly was the problem?"

No response.

"Were Kasden and Vogler arguing about the meeting with the accountant? Is that it?"

"Yes." Her voice was almost inaudible.

"What were they arguing about?"

"Jake wanted to get the audit over with, and when Ben— Mr. Kasden—told him that the books weren't ready yet, he got really upset. You see, Jake was the one who was going to have to face Murdoch, and he wasn't very happy about it."

"Why weren't the books ready?"

"I have no idea. Really I don't." She met his eyes.

"So on Friday morning, when Mr. Kasden told Mr. Vogler that the meeting with the accountant would have to be postponed, Mr. Vogler was surprised?"

"Yes, and—"

"What were you going to say?"

She took a deep breath. "He told Mr. Kasden that this was the last time he was going to cover for him, that the next time Murdoch called, Mr. Kasden could explain." Her eyes were filled with guilt and fear and the faintest hint of excitement.

"You heard all this?"

She looked embarrassed. "They were both yelling pretty loud. I couldn't *not* hear. I don't want you to get the wrong impression, though, Detective. Mr. Kasden and Jake were very close. Since Jake's death, he hasn't been himself. Are you going to have to tell him that I told you all this?"

"I don't know. I'll try not to involve you, but I can't promise. But you did the right thing, Miss Battaglia."

"I guess. You didn't give me much of a choice, did you?"

"Not much." Ryker smiled. "But that's my job." He looked at his watch. It was one-forty. "Mind if I look in Mr. Vogler's office while I'm waiting for Mr. Kasden?"

"I suppose it's all right." She got up, waited for Ryker to follow her, walked to Jake's office, and opened the door.

Ryker had barely made his way around the large desk when he heard the doorbell and a voice which he took to be Kasden's.

"I need some coffee," the voice said. "Strong."

"Mr. Kasden—"

"Not now, Judy. Just get me the coffee."

By the time Ryker retraced his steps to the waiting room, Kasden had already marched across the room and into his office. Ryker walked to his doorway. The short, rotund man was facing the rear window, bouncing impatiently on the balls of his feet.

"Mr. Kasden?"

Kasden whirled around. "What the he—" He composed himself quickly. "What can I do for you?" He smiled tightly. His eyes darted past Ryker, looking for his receptionist and an explanation.

"Detective Ryker. We spoke on the phone." Ryker entered the room, hand extended. "How are you, sir?"

They met in front of Kasden's desk. The detective loomed over the smaller man. Kasden's palm, he noted, was clammy.

"You're early, aren't you, Detective? I'd hate to think you wasted your time sitting here when you could've been out protecting us citizens. I hope you haven't been waiting long."

"Not too long."

Judy came in carrying two stoneware mugs. "I thought you might like some coffee, Detective. I made it black, but I can get you some cream and sugar, if you like." She placed the mugs on the blotter on Kasden's desk.

"Black is fine," Ryker said. "Thanks."

She smiled nervously and left the room, clicking the door shut behind her.

"Nice girl," Kasden commented absently. "You talk to her?"

"A little. While I was waiting. I met your salesman, too."

"Gerry? He's a great guy. Great." He sat up straighter in his chair but he still looked dwarfed by the desk. "So what can I do for you, Detective?" He smiled.

Humpty Dumpty, Ryker thought, looking at the egg-shaped

man. "There are a few things I wanted to ask you, Mr. Kasden."

"What, more questions about unhappy clients? I told your partner when he was here that you'd be wasting your time."

"We've eliminated most of them. But I wanted to ask you a few more questions about Murdoch."

"Murdoch? You think he could really be involved in Jake's death? You know, Detective, you may be right. Even though he dresses in imported three-piece suits and has his hair styled—not cut, *styled*—the man is ruthless. The more I think about it, the more it seems possible." He nodded sagely.

"Actually, Mr. Murdoch has a solid alibi for the time in question. I was more interested in your firm's dealings with him. I was wondering, for instance, why your office canceled several appointments with his accountant."

"Who told you that?" His tone was sharp.

"Mr. Murdoch mentioned it to Detective Lewis."

"I don't see what this has to do with Jake's death."

"Maybe nothing; then again, it may be important." He sipped his coffee. Kasden, he noticed, hadn't touched his.

"See, I don't know if you'll understand this, Detective. It's a question of priorities. The reason we were putting off the Murdoch audit was because we were involved in a major audit with the accountant for Deena; that's Jake's ex-wife. Deena has a one-fourth interest in the business, and her lawyer wanted to find out what that share amounted to. I can't blame her for that, right? So until we were finished with Deena's accountant, we couldn't very well have some other guy poking around."

"Have you met with Mrs. Vogler's accountant? I didn't see an entry on Mr. Vogler's calendar. Did you handle it yourself?"

"We haven't actually scheduled an exact time yet. Things have been very hectic in general, and now with Jake dead, I don't see how I can handle an audit in the near future." He shook his head sadly. "The man was like a brother to me, Detective. You have no idea how hard this has hit me."

"I still don't understand why you had the audit with Mrs. Vogler's accountant pending so long."

"Listen, Detective, this is a realty firm. You know what they say in real estate? 'Time is of the essence.' You think I can afford to tie up days sitting with some guy who's going to wrinkle his nose every time he comes across a number he doesn't like? I'm in business to sell houses, Detective, not to hold some CPA's hand.''

Ryker smiled and jotted some notes. ''Roughly speaking, Mr. Kasden, what is Mrs. Vogler's share of the business worth?''

''I'm afraid I can't answer that. First of all, I have no idea. Second of all, I'd have to get Mrs. Vogler's permission before I disclosed anything like that. You understand.''

''What happens to Mr. Vogler's share?''

''Well, now, that's complicated. His share reverts to the partnership, but of course his heirs are entitled to the full assessed value of his share. That would be his parents, I guess.'' He looked questioningly at the detective.

Ryker smiled. ''Who handles the firm's books, Mr. Kasden?''

''Charles Gorman.''

''Isn't he Mr. Vogler's personal accountant, too?''

Kasden nodded.

Ryker made a mental note to contact the man; he'd forgotten to call him after his meeting with Cooper. ''There are a few things I wanted to ask you about Mr. Vogler's calendar.''

''You have the calendar. I gave it to the other detective.''

''Right. The thing is, we seem to be missing a page.''

''So what's the big deal? Jake probably tore out an old page to write some notes. I do it all the time. A fancy office, and I never seem to have any scratch paper around.''

''The good news is that we know what was on the page. You see, I don't like missing pages, so I asked SID—that's Scientific Investigation Division—to fool around with the other pages, and they were able to raise the impression on the following page. Amazing what they can do nowadays.''

''I'm impressed,'' he said dryly. ''Why are you telling me?''

''It seems the notation on the missing page was 'REC— Ben?' What do you make of that?''

''What *should* I make of that? 'REC' could mean anything. Maybe Jake wanted to ask me about some financial records. Or it could stand for 'receipt'—come to think of it, I seem to remember that Jake asked me if I'd seen a deposit receipt he misplaced somewhere. Yeah, that must be it.''

Ryker shook his head. ''I don't think so.''

''Why not? It makes perfect sense.''

''It would, but we found the same notation on some other

papers that belonged to Mr. Vogler. As a matter of fact, he scribbled it on the newspaper he was reading last Sunday. Almost like his subconscious speaking, you know what I mean? So to my mind, it must've been something important, something that was bothering him.''

''Well, then, I can't help you, Detective. I have no idea what he could have meant. I'm not a mind reader. I can't even tell when the interest rates are going up.'' He laughed.

''I thought about 'real estate commissioner.' Now that would make a lot of sense to me. It would really fit. The only thing is, why would he connect the Real Estate Commissioner with you? I couldn't figure it out.'' He smiled at Kasden. ''Kind of a puzzler, isn't it?''

''I don't see what you're getting at, Detective.''

Ryker put down his mug on the blotter and relaxed against the back of the chair. ''I think you do, Mr. Kasden. I think you know exactly what I'm talking about. As a matter of fact, I think you removed that page when you went to Xerox the calendar pages before you gave the calendar to Detective Lewis. I just don't know why.''

''You're crazy! You can't prove that!''

''No, I can't.''

''This is ridiculous!'' Kasden sputtered. ''A page is missing from a man's calendar and you act like I committed a federal crime! What the hell are you accusing me of, Ryker?''

''Did you take the calendar page, Mr. Kasden? If you *did* take it, now would be the best time to tell me all about it, clear the whole thing up. It's probably something unimportant, but I just don't like loose ends. That's just the way I am.''

Kasden shoved his chair back and stood up. ''Detective, this interview is over. I've been damn cooperative with your department, but I get the feeling I'm being railroaded here, and I don't like it one bit!''

''Suit yourself, Mr. Kasden. But I should tell you that I'll probably need to talk to you again.'' Ryker stood up. ''By the way, I almost forgot.'' He took a folded document from the inner pocket of his jacket and handed it to Kasden. ''I have a subpoena for your books. I'll be sending someone over in a few hours to pick them up, so please have them ready. We're also going to subpoena your firm's bank statements. Could you please give me the name of the bank and branch your firm deals with?''

"First Federal. The one on Camden and Wilshire." His voice was pinched with anger.

"And don't worry, Mr. Kasden—we'll find somebody competent to go over them who won't take up too much of your time." He smiled. "I just hope he doesn't find any erasures or strange entries. You know these accountant types—they're so picky, and they get upset with the slightest irregularities. Damn perfectionists.''

Kasden looked at the subpoena as though it were contaminated and glared at the detective.

At the doorway, Ryker turned to face Kasden. "Don't forget to come into the station and have someone take your prints, Mr. Kasden. Any time today or tomorrow will be fine. And thanks for the coffee. If you like, I'll ask Miss Battaglia to get you a refill. Yours must be completely cold by now.''

"Thank you, Detective. But I can take care of myself.''

"Glad to hear it," Ryker said. "See you around.''

20

DEENA LOOKED AT HER WATCH AGAIN. IT WAS TWELVE-thirty. Reuben had said she could interrupt *shivah* to prepare for the Sabbath an hour before candle-lighting time, but that was four hours away.

The day was dragging on with merciless tedium. She'd spent several hours poring over her text on securities law. When she couldn't concentrate any longer, she'd read the *Times* and worked one-third of the crossword puzzle before she gave up and tossed the paper onto the floor. Then she'd tried reading the best-seller Sandy had lent her. The critics called it "engrossing." It had barely held her attention.

She remembered her flip comment to Reuben about doing a jigsaw puzzle. Maybe it wasn't such a bad idea. She took a pattern cutting board, unfolded it, and placed it on the den floor. Michael had bought her a thousand-piece Springbok puzzle called "Super Sundae." She found it on the top shelf of the bookcase. Sitting cross-legged on the floor, she sifted through the irregular shapes, looking for the straight-edged pieces that would form the frame.

She couldn't stop thinking about Ben. His visit had unnerved her, and she resented him for having subjected her to a whole new arena of problems. Michael insisted that she had to protect herself from criminal involvement, and of course he was right. But how could she go to the police and tell them that her ex-husband's partner had embezzled funds from the company?

She found a corner piece, felt a surge of childlike pleasure.

And this idea of Michael's that Ben was somehow more involved than he'd admitted was preposterous. Really it was. The man had been foolish, greedy, but Michael had insinuated that there might be something far more devious attached to Ben's activities, some connection with Jake's death. And she couldn't believe that, couldn't reconcile a sinister, Machiavellian Ben with the kindly, jovial, almost fatherly figure she'd known for the past two years.

She'd been working for a while, assembling a scoop of pistachio ice cream, when she heard the front doorbell.

It was Faye.

"I thought you did volunteer work with the children at Cedars on Fridays," Deena told her after she invited her in.

"They're having a special program today, a puppet show about disabled kids. How are you doing?"

"Okay. Bored, really, if you want to know the truth."

"A jigsaw puzzle?" Faye asked when they entered the den. "Is there anything really wrong with it?"

"No. I guess not. I was just surprised, that's all."

Faye sat on the couch. Deena resumed her position on the floor. She looked at Faye. "Are you okay? You look so tired."

"I'm exhausted. I went to visit Alex today."

"Why?" Deena was startled.

"I'm not sure. This whole thing with Jake, I guess. Who knows? Anyway, it's been months since I've been there."

"And?"

"He wouldn't even talk to me. And when I tried to touch his hand—just to make contact, you know?—he flinched as if I wanted to hurt him. The nurses know his situation, but it was embarrassing and pathetic. I couldn't wait to leave.''

''You shouldn't have gone. What's the point?''

''No point,'' Faye agreed listlessly. ''Anyway, I came to invite you for *Shabbas*. What do you say?''

''I'm spending the weekend with my parents. Next time?''

''Sure.'' She picked up a chartreuse puzzle piece, handed it to Deena. ''I think this goes with what you're working on.''

''Thanks.'' She pressed the piece firmly into place. ''Ben Kasden came back last night.'' She told Faye about the visit.

''My God! What are you going to do, Deena?''

''Nothing yet. I have to give this some more thought. Michael practically suggested that I make a citizen's arrest.''

''Well, he doesn't have the same relationship with Ben that you do, Deena. And he's just looking out for your interests. Has that detective called you again?''

''A different one called. The police want me to come to the station and be fingerprinted. Supposedly, they want to eliminate my fingerprints from those they may find on anything that belonged to Jake.''

''You're not worried, are you?''

''Not about the prints. But I *am* worried about the gun.''

''I thought you decided it was stolen.''

''The mysterious burglar.'' She smiled. ''I think I was desperate for a solution. Detective Ryker wasn't impressed.''

''But it *could* have happened just that way.''

''It could have. But I'm not hopeful.''

''Then again, maybe it's still somewhere in the house. You can't know for sure that it isn't here, right?''

''I checked pretty thoroughly, but anything's possible.''

''Oh, well. Try not to worry about it.'' She smiled. ''Easy for me to say, right? So when are you going to the station?''

''I told the detective about *shivah*, that I couldn't leave the house until Wednesday. He said someone would come to take my prints today. VIP treatment. I should be flattered.''

''Wednesday will be here before you know it. Then you can put your life back together and forget any of this happened.''

''I don't see how. I can't just forget that Jake was murdered, Faye. It's not as if he died of a heart attack or something.''

''I guess you're right.'' She sighed. ''How *do* you feel?''

''The truth? I know it sounds awful, but basically I feel

relieved that Jake's out of my life. Of course, I feel terribly sorry for his parents, and sometimes I feel sad for him, that he had to die; other times—'' She hesitated.

"Other times what?"

"Other times, I think he deserved it for what he put me through. Lovely, right? I wonder what Reuben would say."

"Just don't blame yourself, Deena. None of this was your fault. You're not responsible for what happened to Jake."

"I hope not."

"What do you mean, you hope not?"

"Nothing, really." She hesitated. "Okay. This is assuming that Jake wasn't killed by a burglar, and that the murder weapon was my gun."

"Those are pretty large assumptions, Deena."

"Maybe. But let me finish. If my gun wasn't stolen, then it was taken by someone I know. And in that case, it's possible that whoever killed Jake did it because of me."

"You're kidding, right?"

"It makes perfect sense, Faye, as much sense as anything else. Think about it."

"So why are you telling me this? For all you know, I could be that someone."

"I thought about it." She grinned.

"Deena!"

"But you're too level-headed. And I can't see you shooting Jake just to help me out. Friendship goes just so far."

"I don't know if I should be flattered or insulted. I suppose I should be relieved that I have an alibi. I was with Alex's parents all Sunday—afternoon and evening."

"You're kidding! Do you see them often?"

"Too often." She sighed. "I'd been promising for a long time to go over some financial papers, and we decided a Sunday was best. Once I got there, they insisted that I stay for dinner. It was easier to stay than argue." She shrugged. "Thank God I won't have to go through that again soon. Anyway, so you've ruled me out. Who do you think did it—Reuben?"

"You're being sarcastic, Faye, because you don't want to admit that what I'm saying is possible. I considered Michael. I told you that. He still won't tell me where he was Sunday night. Some client, sure. That's very convenient."

"He can't tell you the client's name, Deena. That's privileged information."

"I guess. But he really hated Jake for what he did to me. And lately, he's been acting edgy around me."

"Maybe you're the one who's edgy. Isn't that possible?"

"That's probably what Michael would say. He'd call it 'projecting.' "

"Michael didn't do it, Deena. You know that."

"Well, somebody did! I know! Remember that Agatha Christie mystery? The one where a whole group of people conspire to kill this detestable guy? What was it called?" She frowned. *"Murder on the Orient Express.* That's it. Maybe all my friends banded together to eliminate Jake."

"This is stupid, Deena. Stop it."

"Or what about Elaine? Maybe she pretended she was shooting Kenny. Did you see how uptight she was last night? She looked like she was about to jump out of her skin. Sandy never liked Jake, and Alan was jealous of his hairline and his Porsche. That's motive enough for murder, don't you think?"

Faye grabbed her arm. "Deena, I don't like the way you're talking. You sound . . . I don't know, almost hysterical."

"I'm not hysterical. Hysteria is a sign of overreacting. I have good reason to be afraid."

"What is it, Deena? What are you afraid of?"

"My father." She shut her eyes. "God, I don't know if it's worse thinking it or saying it! He had a strong motive. He thought Jake ruined my life, first by marrying me, then by refusing to give me the *get.* "

"But Deena—"

"And he blamed Jake for my mother's condition! I did too. He knew about the phone calls, and about the attempted rape— I could kick myself for that! And of course, he knew about the gun. It was his, after all."

"You really think he could've killed Jake?"

"I'm praying he didn't. And if he did," she said evenly, "if he did, then I pray he doesn't get caught."

"Look, everything you've said is speculation. And even if the police suspect your father, which they probably won't, they won't have any evidence."

"But my gun—"

"A missing gun isn't proof of anything. They need solid evidence. A witness who saw your father at the scene of the murder, something like that. Believe me, you have nothing to worry about. I think it was a random killing, a burglar who knew the house was vacant. And the police may never solve it.''

"I'd hate that, Faye. It would always be over our heads."

"You'd learn to live with it. You'd have to." She looked at her watch. "I didn't realize how late it is. I still haven't shopped for *Shabbas,* and I have one or two errands to take care of, some things to return, if I ever find the receipt." She sighed. "The problem is, I don't feel like doing anything. This visit to Alex has upset me." She got up.

"Thanks for coming, Faye. It helped to talk."

"You'll see; it'll be all right." She kissed Deena. "I'll talk to you tomorrow night. Don't get up; I'll let myself out."

After Faye left, Deena continued working on the puzzle. There was something comforting about handling and arranging the pieces, some elemental satisfaction in dealing with tangibles, with absolutes. A piece either fit or it didn't. There was no nebulous middle ground to perplex and torment her, no shady hinterland of "what ifs."

When the phone rang, she was amazed to see that it was almost three. She got up stiffly and made her way to the phone.

"You told them, didn't you!"

"Who is this?" she asked.

"How could you do that to me, Deena? I begged you to help me! And you said you'd think about it. But obviously, you didn't waste any time running to the police, did you?"

She sighed. "Ben, I didn't talk to anyone."

"Then why was that detective here ten minutes ago asking me so many questions about the audit, huh? Tell me that!"

"Ben, I promise I didn't tell him anything."

"Then how did he know?"

"Maybe he's just guessing."

"He knows, Deena; he knows! And he has a subpoena for the books and for my bank statements. I'm finished!"

"I don't know what to tell you, Ben. I'm sorry; I really am. But I didn't say anything."

"What's the difference?" he said dully. "It's over. I'll be in jail for God knows how long. What should I do?"

"I don't know, Ben. I think you should get a good lawyer."

"Yeah, sure. A lot of good that's going to do!"

* * *

"And you should have seen Kasden's face when I handed him the subpoena," Ryker told Stollman and Moran, grinning.

"Not a happy guy, huh?" Moran said. "So you want me to pick up the books?"

"Yeah, but call the bank first and make sure the statements are ready. That way, you'll only have to make one trip. It's the First Federal on Camden and Wilshire. The manager's expecting you."

"So what do you think this calendar business means?"

"I think Vogler was toying with the idea of contacting the Real Estate Commissioner about Ben."

"But why should he do that?" Stollman asked. "The guy was his partner."

"He'd do it to save his own ass. I have a hunch our Mr. Kasden was playing around with money the firm was holding. He was damn evasive about the audit. And if something illegal *was* going on, and someone reported the firm to the commissioner, Vogler would've had a hard time proving he wasn't involved."

"And Kasden knew that Vogler was upset?" Moran asked.

"The receptionist confirmed that," Ryker said.

"So that gives him a motive for killing Vogler, doesn't it, Sam?" Moran asked. "If Vogler was going to rat on him, Kasden could've lost his license. Maybe gone to jail."

"Wasn't it Kasden who took the call Monday about Vogler's being out of town? Maybe he made that up," Stollman said.

"It's a definite possibility," Ryker agreed. "But we're getting ahead of ourselves. Let's get the books and see what they show. I could be all wrong. What happened with the other names on the open house, Tom? Any luck?"

"I struck out with the first couple. They didn't see anything. And according to the neighbors, the Futrells—they're the last name I have to check—went away for a few days."

"Seems like everyone's on vacation except us," Stollman said. "I checked with Mrs. Pearson's neighbor again, Sam. Mrs. Pearson called and told her she'll be coming back tomorrow."

"Fine."

"And I met Laura Brackwood. A real good-looker, by the way. She admitted she had no love for Vogler. Matter of fact, she told me he made a pass at her—a chauvinist pig, she called him. But she has an alibi. She was conducting her own open house on a Hancock Park property and then went directly to meet some friends for dinner. She gave me names and phone numbers. I'll check everything out."

"What about the prints from Novick and his daughter?" Ryker asked. "Kasden should be coming in today or tomorrow."

"I spoke to Mrs. Vogler. She can't leave her house right now for religious reasons." He explained about *shivah*. "I figured I'll take a print kit and go to her house."

"Good idea," Ryker said. "What about her father?"

"I'm not sure," Stollman said. "He's not exactly jumping at the idea, claims he's very busy today."

"Tomorrow, then."

"Tomorrow is his Sabbath—he can't drive. He said he'll come in, but I wasn't able to pin him down to a specific time. Why are you so interested in him?" Stollman asked. "Do you really think he's involved?"

Ryker told them about his meeting with Ann Douglas. "She seems to think now that he was serious about the threat."

"Maybe he was just blowing off steam," Moran said. "People say crazy things when they're angry."

"I know," Ryker agreed. "But we have to check it out."

"What about the Douglas woman herself?" Stollman asked. "Did you consider that *she* could've killed Vogler?"

"What do you mean?" Moran asked.

"Yeah, I did," Ryker said. "I was wondering if you'd see it, too. She told me she and Vogler were getting back together. According to her, he was going to give his ex-wife her religious divorce after he made her sweat a while longer. But what it that's not true? What if Vogler told her that he wanted to reconcile with his wife, and that even if she didn't take him back, there was no place for Douglas in his future?"

"So she kills him?" Moran looked skeptical.

Stollman said, "Come on, Tom. 'Hell hath no fury . . .' and all that crap. It's trite, but it could happen. Hell, it *does* happen, all the time. So we need her prints, too."

"I took care of it when she was here," Ryker said.

Moran said, "But why would she come in and tell you all this incriminating stuff?"

"One, she may not have realized how it would sound to someone else. Two, maybe she's playing it smart. She knows I'll find out about all this, so she figures she'll be the one to tell me. That way she scores points and looks innocent. *And* she points me in Novick's direction.''

"And the murder weapon?" Moran asked.

"Either she had her own gun, or—and this is stretching, I'll admit it—she stole the Vogler woman's gun. She could be the 'burglar' Mrs. Vogler suddenly remembered."

"How would she know that Mrs. Vogler had a gun?" Moran said.

"You've got me there. Unless Vogler knew about the gun and mentioned it in passing to the Douglas woman."

Moran said, "But how would Vogler know about it?"

"Maybe Mrs. Vogler warned him about it after he started making the phone calls."

"What phone calls?" Stollman asked.

Ryker frowned. "I thought I told you guys about that." He described his conversation with Mrs. Perris from Pacific Bell. "According to her, Mrs. Vogler sounded frantic."

Moran said, "But that brings us right back to Mrs. Vogler and her father. And the boyfriend, too, whoever he is."

Ryker said, "Probably the guy Lou Jeffreys saw at Mrs. Vogler's house all evening. Tom, we have his license plate number; why don't you get his name and address from DMV and talk to him. I know you're itching to do it."

"Go ahead and laugh, Sam." Moran grinned and stood up.

"By the way," Ryker said, "do you guys mind coming in this weekend for a couple of hours? I thought we'd get a head start on the books. I really think we're on to something."

"Okay by me," Moran said. "I have nothing planned."

"I could use the overtime," Stollman said.

"Great. I appreciate it. By the way, Hank, I'd like you to call the Vogelanters. Ask them to come to the station and check their son's personal effects, see if anything's missing. Jewelry, stuff like that. Offer to pick them up."

"Okay. But today's out, and tomorrow is the Sabbath. And they probably can't leave their house, not until the mourning period is over."

"Okay. It's a long shot, anyway. In the meantime ask them if they can describe Vogler's missing watch. If we get a decent description, we can give it out to the fences."

"I'll call them now." He went to his desk.

Moran left for the bank. Ryker scanned his notes from his meeting with Marvin Cooper. There it was. Charles Gorman,

CPA. He dialed the number, introduced himself to a pleasant-sounding secretary, and waited patiently until she connected him with Gorman. Ryker introduced himself.

"Mr. Gorman, we're investigating the death of one of your clients, Mr. Jake Vogler."

"I just heard. Terrible thing," he sighed. "Terrible."

"We'd like to take a look at Mr. Vogler's personal papers and also at the books for Kasden and Vogler, Realtors. We'll have a subpoena for those records, of course."

"I see. Well, then if you have a subpoena, I don't see any problem. Is Mr. Kasden aware of this?"

Ryker grinned. "Yes, he is. There's something else, Mr. Gorman. I spoke to Mr. Vogler's attorney, and he said you'd be the right one to talk to about Mr. Vogler's estate."

"That's correct. I was his investment counselor."

"I'd like to set up an appointment to discuss the estate."

"It's a little late for today. Would Monday be all right?"

"I'll tell you the truth, Mr. Gorman, ordinarily Monday would be fine, but I'm kind of anxious to get a picture of Mr. Vogler's financial status. It might be relevant to his murder."

"I see. What about tomorrow, then? Ten-thirty?"

"That would be fine. I appreciate it. I wonder if you can tell me if we're talking about unusually large sums of money."

"Frankly, I'm reluctant to discuss this on the phone."

"I understand that. But it could be important."

He hesitated. "I can tell you that Mr. Vogler was comfortable, and that he had several major investments."

"I see. Anything more specific?"

"There's the insurance. He had a substantial personal term policy."

"Do you know who the beneficiary is?"

"If I remember correctly, it was his wife. His ex-wife, that is. But he probably changed that after the divorce."

Probably not, Ryker thought. "Is that it?"

"There *was* one more policy," Gorman told him.

Ryker listened and jotted down some notes. "Where would I find these policies? They weren't in his apartment."

"He probably kept them in a safe deposit box at his bank, Detective. That's what I would do."

After Ryker hung up, he checked again through the box holding Vogler's papers. The policies weren't there, but he did find a savings account passbook. According to the last entry, Jake Vogler had $28,972.26. Not bad. Ryker called information, got the number for the bank, dialed, and asked to be connected with the manager.

"What can I do for you, Detective?" she asked guardedly.

Ryker explained the situation. "I'd like to find out whether Mr. Vogler kept a safe deposit box at your bank."

"I'm afraid I can't give you that information without a court order, Detective."

"I realize that. How late will you be open?"

"Until six tonight."

"I guess it'll have to be tomorrow, then."

"Don't forget to bring the key."

Ryker hadn't noticed a key, but then again, he hadn't really looked for one. "What if I don't have one?"

"Then you'll have to bring a locksmith to break the lock." Her voice hinted at disapproval.

Ryker went back to the box and searched through it. No key. He walked over to Stollman's desk.

"I'm on my way to Mrs. Vogler's," Stollman said. "I spoke to the Vogelanters. They have to check with their rabbi to see if they can come in before Wednesday."

"Hank, I'm looking for a key to a safe deposit box Vogler had." He told him about his conversation with Gorman. "It's not in the box. Can you go back to Vogler's apartment and look for it? I'd hate to have to take a locksmith along tomorrow."

"No problem. I'll go there right after I get the prints."

Ryker made a call and arranged for a subpoena for the safe deposit box and another one for the accountant's records. If he had a nickel for every subpoena. . . .

There was one more thing he had to do, and then, as far as he could see, he could go home and surprise Linda. He called information for the home number of Rabbi Brodin and dialed.

"Hello?"

"Rabbi Brodin, my name is Detective Ryker. I'm investigating Mr. Vogler's death. By the way, I heard you speak at his funeral. A very moving eulogy, if I may say so, Rabbi."

"Thank you, Detective."

"The reason I'm calling, Rabbi, is that I need some information about this *get* issue. We already know what it is, and that Mr. Vogler was refusing to give it to his wife, so you don't have to worry about betraying confidences."

"I see. Then what exactly do you want from me?"

"The thing is, Rabbi Brodin, we're also aware that some people in the community were trying to pressure Mr. Vogler into giving his wife the divorce, and I was hoping you could direct me to the person in charge of that effort."

"Frankly, Detective, this entire situation was mishandled shamefully. Given time, I believe that Jake and Deena would have reached a mutual accord—possibly a reconciliation. I realize I'm in the minority on that opinion. But are you suggesting this had something to do with Jake's death? I can't believe that!"

"Not necessarily. It's helpful, though, to get the victim's complete background, to try to understand his frame of mind at the time he was killed. You understand."

"Still, I don't feel comfortable giving you someone's name. I think you can understand my position."

"I do, Rabbi. Believe me, I do. And I certainly don't want to compromise you in any way. I have a letter that was circulated about Mr. Vogler and his refusal to give the divorce. It's signed by several rabbis. I *could* call them, one by one, until I find the man I'm looking for, but frankly, I'd be wasting a lot of precious time in the process."

"Of course. Well, then, I suppose you should talk to Rabbi Markowitz. Reuben Markowitz." He said the name disdainfully. "He precipitated much of the problem, I can tell you, he and that support group of his. I'll give you his number."

Ryker thanked the rabbi, depressed the receiver button, and immediately dialed Markowitz's number.

"I'd be happy to meet with you, Detective," Reuben Markowitz said after Ryker introduced himself. "Today's impossible, though, and so is tomorrow. What about tomorrow evening, my home at eight-thirty? My calendar is free."

Mine isn't, Ryker thought. Linda would be just thrilled; they had planned on catching a movie. "That's fine, Rabbi. Eight-thirty it is. Have a nice Sabbath," he added before he hung up.

Detective Stollman had taken Deena's fingerprints and left. She packed a few items into a small bag—some underwear, deodorant, a hairbrush—and put on a green cotton sweater and skirt. After the Sabbath, she would have to change back into her mourning dress. She secured the windows and was about to leave by the side door when she heard the front doorbell.

"Delivery for Deena Volger." The messenger was a lanky, jean-clad young man with long hair and a bored expression on his pimply face.

"Just a second." She got a dollar from her purse, returned to the entry hall, and opened the door.

The man handed her a flowering plant, its base wrapped in metallic paper and decorated with a large red bow.

"Who is this from?" She was surprised. No one she knew would send her flowers today, not during *shivah*.

"Beats me."

She fumbled with the small envelope attached to a spear embedded in the plant and finally drew out the card.

Happy anniversary, Deena. Hope you're smiling, 'cause I sure as hell am!

> *Jake.*

She stared at the note. This couldn't be! Someone must be trying to torment her—but who? Or was Jake harassing her from the grave? She shivered.

"Got a real romantic touch, this guy. Betcha ya don't know what this plant's called, right?"

"What?" She'd barely heard him. "No. No, I don't." She looked at the cluster of small blue flowers, then at the young man.

"Forget-me-nots. Cool, ain't it?" He put his hand out for his tip and left without thanking her, whistling as he strolled down the walkway.

21

"WHAT ARE YOU SMILING ABOUT?" RYKER ASKED STOLLMAN on Saturday morning. He could see the curly-headed detective's wide grin as he made his way toward Ryker's desk.

Stollman pulled a tiny manila envelope from his pocket and dangled it in front of Ryker. "The key." He tossed it into Ryker's outstretched hand.

"Where was it?"

"In a tall, black chest, under a stack of sweaters. Great sweaters, by the way. The man had good taste. What time are you going to the bank?"

"As soon as I get the subpoena." He glanced at his watch. It was nine-fifteen. "It should be ready now. The thing is, I'm not sure Vogler kept a safe deposit box at this bank, but without the subpoena, the bank won't tell me a damn thing. If it's not there, I'll call his parents; they may know where he kept it."

"Maybe you'll be lucky first time around."

"Here's hoping. I want to get the papers before I meet with Vogler's accountant. I had a ten-thirty appointment, but I postponed it to eleven. Did you get Mrs. Vogler's prints?"

"Sure. She was a little nervous, but very cooperative. I dropped them off yesterday at SID. Where's Tom?"

"Checking out the boyfriend." Ryker stood up and put on his jacket. "I'll be back around twelve, twelve-thirty." He started for the exit.

"You have a hacksaw with you?"

Ryker stopped. "What?"

"You forgot the key, Detective." Stollman grinned and ducked quickly as Ryker feinted with a left to his shoulder.

After scrutinizing the subpoena, Ms. Billingham, the bank manager, went to check the records. A few minutes later, she returned and confirmed (almost unhappily, Ryker felt) that

Jake Vogler had maintained a safe deposit box at that bank location.

With almost funereal solemnity, she ushered the detective into a heavily protected room, inserted a key into a box, and waited until he produced its mate. The ceremony completed, she slid the elongated box out of its compartment, reluctantly handed it to Ryker, and indicated a small cubicle where he could examine its contents in privacy.

All the papers were there. Ryker had brought along a manila envelope, and he slipped the contents of the box into it. Exiting the cubicle, he signaled to Ms. Billingham that he was ready and watched as she returned the box to its slot.

"Thanks for your assistance."

She nodded curtly.

A hacksaw, he decided, would have been more satisfying.

The meeting with Charles Gorman didn't reveal anything surprising. Jake Vogler had been speculating to the tune of approximately $38,000, mostly in commodity futures and options. He also had $15,000 in municipal bonds and several real estate investments, including the Murdoch deal.

"Not to mention the house on Guthrie," Gorman said. "Even with today's tough market, homes in Beverlywood are getting top dollar. It's probably worth about $600,000. And then, of course, there's the insurance. But I assume you have the policies?"

Ryker nodded. He thanked Gorman for his time and left.

Stollman was leaning against his desk, talking to another detective, when Ryker entered the squad room. "How'd it go?"

"Piece of cake. Anything up?" He took off his jacket.

"Yeah. Good news. The Arizona police caught up with that Larry creature. They spotted his car; the dumb shit's probably wondering how they got on to him. Anyway, they're holding him until we send someone to get him. So what was in the box?"

Ryker told him. They were still discussing Vogler's assets and were unaware of the elderly woman approaching them with careful steps until she stood in front of them. She was wearing a gray dress, belted at the waist, with a tiny pink rosebud design and white lace at the collar and cuffs; slender ankles encased in heavy stockings disappeared into sensible black laced shoes. Her hair, silvery with a bluish cast, framed her face in a cap of soft curls; her papery skin was almost translucent, revealing a fine network of capillaries. Faded blue eyes looked at them inquisitively.

"Can I help you, ma'am?" Ryker asked. She smelled of talcum powder and lilac. He thought of his grandmother.

"Is one of you gentlemen Detective Stollman?" Her voice was reedy and slipped from high notes to low notes and back, like a diva trying unsuccessfully to find her perfect range.

"I'm Detective Stollman." He jumped up from his chair and made his way around the desk. "How can I help you?"

"I'm Muriel Pearson. I believe you left several messages for me? I only got back this morning, you see, but Betty—she's my neighbor—told me what happened to poor Mr. Vogler, and I thought I should come here as soon as I could. I haven't even unpacked my things yet, although I did open one or two windows, just to get rid of the musty smell, don't you know."

"I see. Mrs. Pearson, my name is Detective Ryker. Detective Stollman and I are working on this case together. Why don't we go over to my desk, and then we can talk comfortably."

Ryker escorted her to his desk, helped her into a chair, and sat down. Stollman pulled up a chair next to her.

"I *did* want to say how terribly sorry I was to hear about Mr. Vogler. He was ever so nice."

"You knew him?" Stollman asked, surprised.

"Why, of course! He was at the Pomerantz house so many Sundays doing the open houses, and I used to take him a pot of herb tea and a slice of fresh apple pie, or some cinnamon twists, just to break the tedium. He was so appreciative, and he always complimented me on my baking. He said he would have to get my recipes for his mother. Of course, I didn't bother him if he had visitors. My kitchen faces the Pomerantz house, you see; I can see their front door from my window."

"Did you go over this past Sunday?" Ryker asked.

"Well, no. I wanted to, but I had so much to do before my visit to Jane and the children, and I was baking oatmeal cookies and some ginger snaps for them. Jane's my daughter. My only child. She and Donald met here through a mutual friend nine years ago. They had a church wedding, and I prepared a buffet reception in my yard. It was all quite lovely. And they found the cutest two-bedroom apartment, not too far from my house. But then five years ago Donald got this wonderful offer to be an associate professor of economics at the university in San Jose, and they couldn't really pass it up.

"I told Jane that. I knew she was worried about leaving me alone, especially with Henry gone. He passed away just about a year before that—very sudden, it was. The doctors said it was his heart. But I told her, 'Jane,' I said, 'you can't be worrying about me. You've got to think of your husband and your family. I've got good neighbors and friends, and I know we'll be seeing each other real often.' And we have. They come for Thanksgiving and Christmas and Easter, and I visit as often as I can. And last summer they sent Joey and Ellie, those dears, to spend a week. They were a joy." She smiled, reminiscing.

"Mrs. Pearson," Ryker said, "did you happen to see Mr. Vogler leave the house after the open house?"

"No, I'm quite sure he didn't, at least not in the early evening. His car was in the driveway from late morning through the evening, and when I woke up in the morning, too. As a matter of fact, I wondered why he had left his car there, you know. I even mentioned it to Genevieve."

"Genevieve?" Ryker asked.

"My companion." She smiled. "We have grown very fond of each other over the years. I don't know what I would do without her."

"But you didn't see him leave?"

"No. And it is so sad to think that I'll never see him again." She sighed.

"Mrs. Pearson, I'd like you to think carefully. Did you notice anyone going into the house after five?"

"Well, yes, I did."

Ryker tried to control his excitement. "What time was it?"

She cocked her head to one side. "Well, now, I can't say whether anyone came from around four-thirty to around five-thirty, because I was in and out of my bedroom then—it's on the other side of the house—packing a few sweaters and skirts and one or two dresses. I always like to pack each item in some tissue paper; it keeps the clothes from wrinkling. I read that in a woman's magazine, and it really does work."

"When did you see someone entering the house?"

"At five-forty. I was about to eat a light supper with Genevieve when I noticed someone walking up the path to the Pomerantz front door; I thought it was late for a buyer to be coming. We always eat promptly at five-forty-five. We have both found it better for our digestion if we eat at a set time, early in the evening."

"Can you describe this person?"

"It was a man. He was wearing a gray suit that reminded me of one Henry used to wear. I gave it to the Good Friends after he died, and it was still in excellent condition."

"Was he tall or short?"

She thought for a moment. "Not terribly tall, I don't think. But I'm not a good judge of heights, Detective."

"Could you see his hair color?"

"I'm afraid not. He was wearing a hat, which was surprising, of course, considering the heat."

"Were you able to see his face?"

"For the briefest moment. He was looking around him, you see; I thought he wasn't sure he had the right address, but then he pushed the door open and walked right in. I have always thought these open houses are somewhat unsafe, what with leaving the doors open so that anyone can come right in. But I suppose it wouldn't be practical to have the realtor jumping back and forth to answer the bell."

"Mrs. Pearson, do you think you'd be able to identify this man if we showed you some pictures?" Ryker asked.

"Quite honestly, I'm not sure, Detective. I want so to help you out, but I'm afraid I just don't know. It happened so quickly. But I could certainly try."

"How long was this man in the house, do you know?"

"Not long. About ten minutes. I must admit I was a little curious, so I kept an eye out for his departure," she confessed with obvious embarrassment. "Genevieve was curious, too."

"Did you hear or see anything while he was there?"

"Nothing strange, if that's what you mean. As I remember, it was an unusually hot day, and I had my air-conditioning on and my windows closed, so I couldn't really hear anything. I don't really like air-conditioning; neither does Genevieve. It's so artificial, and I have found that it dries the skin, don't you? But when it's that hot, I don't see that there's much choice. I turned mine off around seven o'clock, because the heat had broken. But Mr. Vogler left the unit on in the Pomerantz house all night, and it was still running in the morning. My windows were open then, you see, and I could hear the unit working during the night when I went to the lavatory." She coughed delicately. "I *did* see the lights go on in one of the back bedrooms—it faces my sewing room—when this man was in the house, but it went out soon afterward."

"Did Mr. Vogler escort the man out?"

"No, he didn't. Detective, do you really think this man is the one who killed Mr. Vogler?" Her agitation was clear.

"It's very possible, Mrs. Pearson. That's why what you're telling us is so important."

"I wish I had more to tell you; truly, I do."

"You mentioned your companion, Genevieve. She didn't stay in your home while you were visiting your daughter?"

"No. She would have been too lonely. She stayed with some friends. That is our usual arrangement when I go to visit Jane. I don't think Genevieve minds."

"Is it possible that she saw something you might not have noticed? Could she have gotten a better look at this man?"

"Well, she was right with me in the kitchen when he entered the house, keeping me company while I fixed our plates, but I rather doubt that she can be of any help."

"Could you ask her to call us? Just in case."

"Well, I don't see how she could do that." She looked at them uncertainly. "Genevieve is a cat."

Stollman erupted in a violent paroxysm of coughing. Ryker, struggling to control his twitching facial muscles, pursed his lips. "I see. Well, Mrs. Pearson, you've been extremely helpful, and we appreciate your coming here today."

"I haven't done anything, really. And it's too late to help poor, dear Mr. Vogler. I *do* hope you find who killed him."

"We will. Don't you worry. In the meantime, if you remember anything else, please contact us immediately. And if you don't mind, we will stop by with some pictures to show you, just in case you can identify the man you saw."

She nodded her head. "That would be fine." She stood up, shook their hands, and made her slow exit from the room.

Ryker and Stollman stared at each other. "A cat?" they cried in unison, and groaned with laughter.

In retrospect, Deena decided, she shouldn't have gone to her parents for *Shabbas*. There had been a definite current of tension, primarily between father and daughter. Pearl seemed more or less oblivious to the problem; maybe she didn't want to know there was one. But throughout the weekend, Deena found herself stealing surreptitious glances at Max only to meet his eyes boring into her own. *Is he worried about what I'm thinking?* she wondered. Pearl went upstairs for an afternoon nap, but Deena didn't have the courage to confront him, and once, when it seemed as though *he* wanted to initiate a serious conversation, she pleaded a headache and insisted she wanted to take a walk by herself to clear her head.

The fresh air was exhilarating. She hadn't realized how much she'd missed it since being restricted to the house. She ought to take in huge gulps, she thought; she ought to store them, and the image of the unbounded, graceful, tree-lined street that ran up into the Hollywood Hills, against the remaining days of *shivah.* This weekend, after all, was only a reprieve. Mourning was forbidden on the Sabbath, but with the conclusion of *Havdalah,* the separation between the Sabbath and the rest of the week, she would return to her house and to her confinement, to draped mirrors and cushionless seats. Like Cinderella at the stroke of midnight, she thought. But Cinderella had a fairy godmother working overtime to help make all her problems magically disappear. Not that fairy godmothers could help Deena now. They were experts at dealing with bitchy stepmothers and poisoned apples and Wicked Witches of the West. She doubted that they had much sway over homicide detectives.

She left immediately after *Havdalah.* Her parents kissed and hugged her and promised they'd see her the next day. Max's embrace seemed a little intense, she thought. Was it her imagination, or did he seem relieved to see her go? Or was it her relief that vibrated like a discordant chord in the air between them? She couldn't tell.

The kitchen phone was ringing as she entered through her side door. It was Michael. Could he come over? Why not? she said listlessly into the phone. Why the hell not?

After changing back into her mourning dress, Deena went to check the mail slot in the living room and passed the broken shards of the ornamental cachepot that had housed the plant. They were scattered all over the entry hall, where she'd angrily hurled the plant onto the tiled floor. Some had bounced into the dining room.

She'd called the florist on Friday and learned that there was no one trying to spook her, except maybe Jake. He'd ordered the flowers a week ago. *Bastard,* she thought again; *controlling bastard.* She kicked a large fragment viciously and sent it skittering across the floor.

She'd resumed work on the puzzle when she heard the front doorbell. Stepping carefully around the debris, she walked toward the front door and let Michael in.

"What's this?" He looked at the shards on the tile floor.

"The remains of an anniversary gift, from Jake. I think he's haunting me. 'The Twilight Zone.' " Her laugh was hollow.

In the den, sitting on the floor, she told him about the flowers. "I smashed it. It wasn't very mature, I know that. But I can't tell you how good it felt! I'll clean it up tomorrow morning. I don't feel like dealing with it right now."

"Deena—"

"Michael, I don't want to hear one word that sounds even remotely analytical. Not one psychological insight, okay?"

"I was going to say it must have been horrible for you."

"Oh."

"And," he admitted, grinning sheepishly, "I guess I *did* have one or two psychological insights."

She punched him playfully. He pulled her close, was about to kiss her. "It's probably not the right time, huh?"

"Probably." She sighed. "Want to help me work my puzzle?"

"Not really. How about backgammon?"

"Okay. The set's in the entry hall closet."

He left to get the set; a few minutes later, he entered the den. She was still on the floor, working the puzzle.

"What took you so long?" she asked. She looked up and saw his empty hands. "Where's the set?"

"Come with me."

She got up quickly and followed him to the hall and the open closet. The backgammon set was on the floor. He pointed to the shelf above the hangers. Staring at her was the snubnosed barrel of her gun. She reached out to take it.

He grabbed her hand. "Don't touch it!"

"Why not? It's my gun. I'm going to call Detective Ryker."

"How did it get here?"

"I must've put it there. I thought I checked every place, but obviously I didn't look carefully enough. Michael, don't you see how wonderful this is?"

"I have to think this through. Come into the den."

"But Michael—"

"Just come with me. And leave the gun. We have to talk."

She sat on the floor with her head resting against the couch; he joined her.

"When did you look in that closet?" Michael asked.

"I checked there after Detective Ryker left—actually, after Alan left."

"But you didn't find it."

"No, but then again, Michael, I was distraught. I don't know if I was thinking clearly or searching all that well. I thought I was, but obviously, I didn't do a thorough job."

"But you were so sure you never took it out of your nightstand."

"I guess I was wrong." She turned to him. "And you know, it really makes sense that I would've put it there. If I went to the door, I'd have it right there, in case I needed it."

"But you never remembered doing that. Never. And it was behind the backgammon set. How accessible is that?"

"I don't see why you're being so difficult! The gun is here, and you should be as relieved as I am!"

"Why?"

"Because," she said with exaggerated patience, "it means that no one took my gun. Why can't you see that?"

"It doesn't mean that at all, Deena. All it means is that someone returned it."

"You're wrong! I know you're wrong."

"Maybe I am. But then again, you could be, too. What if it's the murder weapon?"

"It's not. It's not because it never left this house."

"I hope you're right." He sounded skeptical. "Just for argument's sake, who do you think could've returned the gun?"

"I don't want to do this! For the first time in days, I don't feel frightened, and you want to ruin it for me! I'm not going to let you do it, Michael. I'm not!"

"You're so desperate to find a solution that you're willing to overlook some unpleasant possibilities."

She got up. "I'm calling Detective Ryker." She dialed the number she'd written down several days ago on a notepad near the phone, talked for a few minutes, and hung up.

"He's not there. But the detective I talked to is going to find him and give him my message. I told him it was urgent."

Michael shrugged. They waited without speaking. Deena's hand was hovering over the receiver, and she grabbed it quickly when the phone rang.

"Mrs. Vogler? Detective Ryker. I got a message that you called. The officer said it was urgent."

"It is. I found my gun, Detective. It was in the entry hall closet. I thought you'd want to know right away."

Interesting. "Please don't touch it, Mrs. Vogler. I'll come by this evening to pick it up."

"But that's not necessary, Detective Ryker. Don't you see? The gun was here all the time. I'm terribly sorry for the misunderstanding. I feel so foolish."

"I'd still like to pick up the gun, Mrs. Vogler. Just to make sure. That way, we can eliminate it as the murder weapon and you can rest easy. Have you touched it?"

"No. Michael told me—" She stopped. "I didn't think it would be a good idea."

"Good. Well, I'm a little late for an appointment as it is, Mrs. Vogler, but I should be there within a few hours. Before eleven, at the latest. Is that all right?"

She hesitated.

"Mrs. Vogler, if you're not involved in your ex-husband's death, I don't see why you wouldn't want to have me check out your gun. But you don't *have* to give me the gun voluntarily. If you don't, I'll have to get a search warrant, and that means I'll have to bother some crusty old judge who's going to chew off my tail for bothering him on a weekend. But in the end, Mrs. Vogler, he'll sign the warrant, and I'll get the gun."

"Fine." She hung up and turned to Michael. "He's coming here tonight to pick up the gun."

"I'm sorry. I know you're disappointed."

"Actually, maybe he's right; maybe it *is* for the best. When they test my gun, they'll see that it's not the one that killed Jake. You'll see, Michael."

"I guess you're right." He looked away from the anxious hopefulness in her eyes.

22

"SORRY I'M LATE, RABBI. SOMETHING CAME UP."

They were sitting in a book-lined study off a narrow living room. Markowitz was very young, and not at all what Ryker had expected. He was wearing casual black cotton slacks, a gray Adidas sweatshirt, and running shoes. The only rabbinical thing about him was his black suede yarmulke and beard.

"My job is pretty stationary, so I jog whenever I can." He had noticed Ryker's curious glance. He pushed some Tinker Toys to the side of his already cluttered desk, almost toppling a lucite framed photo of a pretty, smiling, jean-skirted young woman wearing a colorful print scarf that covered most of her blond hair. He caught it just in time and adjusted it.

"My wife, Alisa," he said, smiling more at the photo than at Ryker. "So what can I do for you, Detective?"

"I'll be blunt, Rabbi. I've spoken to several people, and I know all about the *get* problem Mrs. Vogler was having."

"I'll be equally blunt. So what do you want with me?"

"Information. I'm trying to get a clear picture of Mr. Vogler's background. Exactly why did the marriage fall apart?"

"It really *was* a case of irreconcilable differences. But the differences were primarily religious. I know that sounds strange in today's world. But Deena has always been committed to Orthodox Judaism; Jake tried it for a while and found it too rigid." He explained their situation.

"I understand that you organized a community protest against Mr. Vogler to pressure him into giving this *get.*"

He nodded. "It was the right thing to do, morally and legally. If Jake were alive and still refused to give Deena her *get*, we would have continued pressuring him."

"You said 'legally,' Rabbi Markowitz. What do you mean?"

Reuben explained the Torah view on divorce and the options available to someone like Deena. "Of course, we're careful to obey civil law."

"What if Vogler had filed a harassment suit against you?"

He smiled. "Then I would have faced the consequences."

"And if that meant sitting in jail?"

"The idea doesn't thrill me, but it would be worth it if Jake, or someone like Jake, would give his wife a *get.*"

"Because she can't marry without it, right?"

"Exactly."

"What about living with someone without getting married?"

Reuben shook his head. "Under Orthodox law, without a *get,* that's still considered adultery. The consequences are severe. Eternal excommunication. And any children of that union would be considered outcasts."

"Heavy stuff. So you organized pickets, stuff like that?"

"Exactly. We asked rabbis in the community to address the problem in their sermons."

"And you sent letters. I saw one. Not exactly subtle."

Reuben smiled. "We were trying to make Jake realize that life would be more pleasant if he gave Deena the *get.*"

"What about phone calls?"

"Phone calls?"

"We understand from a reliable source that Mr. Vogler received threatening phone calls. Did you make those calls, Rabbi, or arrange to have them made?"

"I have no knowledge of those calls, Detective Ryker. I *did* meet with Jake personally several times at his apartment."

"Did you argue?"

"Not that I recall. He seemed intent on convincing me that none of this was getting to him."

"Were you at his apartment the week before he was killed?"

"Yes, I was. During the week."

So that was one mystery visitor. "And that was just another visit of the same nature? To try to convince Vogler to give his wife this *get?*"

"More or less, yes." Markowitz looked uncomfortable.

"Were you aware that Mr. Vogler was harassing his exwife with late-night phone calls?"

"You know about that? Actually, that's why I went to Jake's apartment that night. I begged him to stop the calls."

"What did he say?"

"He told me two could play the same game."

"So how far were *you* willing to take this game, Rabbi?"

"I'm not sure what you mean."

"What about physical violence? Would you consider that?"

"The Torah frowns on physical violence, Detective, except in unusual circumstances," Markowitz said carefully. "And as I said, we're careful not to violate the laws of this country. Anyway, I'm sure Jake would have come around eventually."

"Are you? That's funny. From everything I've been hearing, I don't think he was about to sign that *get* for some time."

"You have no way of knowing that, Detective."

"True. But you still haven't really answered my question, Rabbi. How far were you willing to go to help Mrs. Vogler?"

Markowitz looked at him, his eyebrows raised in mock surprise. "Are you asking me whether I killed Jake, Detective? I didn't. When was he killed, may I ask?"

"On Sunday, between four and eight."

"Every Sunday, between three and five, I lead a study group at my synagogue. After the session, the members stay through *Minchah,* late afternoon services, and *Maariv,* evening services. So you see, Detective, I have a roomful of witnesses. I'll be happy to give you their names and phone numbers."

"I'd appreciate that. Just a formality, you understand, but we can't play favorites. What about Mrs. Vogler?"

"What about her?"

"She must have felt desperate, right?"

"Deena was extremely frustrated, Detective Ryker, but there is no way on earth she would have killed Jake."

"Not even with the phone calls he was making? She must've been frightened. Maybe they pushed her over the edge."

"Not even then. It's just not in her nature."

"Why, because she's Jewish? I don't mean to be rude, Rabbi, but I don't buy that line. Under extreme circumstances anyone—I don't care what race or religion he belongs to—can be driven to homicide. Even nice, law-abiding citizens, Rabbi."

"That isn't what I meant, Detective. We could debate that point another time, if you like. It's just that I know Deena; she simply isn't capable of violence."

"Did you know she had a gun?"

"Yes, I did." He paused. "Under the circumstances, I thought it was a good idea."

"Why? Just because Vogler wouldn't give her a divorce? Or was it because of the phone calls? Or maybe he was bothering her in some other way—is that it?"

"I didn't say that, Detective. You're making unfounded assumptions. I can't tell you anything about that."

Can't or won't? "Did you know she's interested in another man? That must have made her more anxious to get this *get*."

'You'll have to ask her about that, Detective."

"I plan to. What about her father? Is he capable of violence?"

"I don't know Mr. Novick well. I've only talked to him once or twice."

"But you *do* know he was harassing Mr. Vogler personally?"

"I heard something to that effect."

"When you spoke to him, how did he seem to you?"

"Concerned. Worried about his daughter, naturally."

"Was he tense?"

"No more than you or I would be in his situation."

"Angry?"

"I can see where your questions are leading, Detective. I'm not a psychologist, but I highly doubt that he was homicidal." There was mild sarcasm in his voice. "Why do you assume it was someone Jake knew? Maybe it was a burglar. And if it *was* someone who knew Jake, it could have been a business acquaintance."

"Could be. We're checking into all that." He paused. "Someone mentioned a support group that you started, Rabbi Markowitz. Can you tell me a little about it, please?"

"Basically, it's composed of *agunot*, women like Deena who are legally bound to their spouses. They share experiences, emotions. The women in the group seem to be benefitting."

"I'd like the names and phone numbers of the group members, please. By the way, where does the group meet?"

"At the members' homes, on a rotating basis. But why do you have to contact them? They have no connection to Jake."

"You're probably right, but I'd like to talk with them."

"Frankly, Detective, I think giving you their names and numbers would be an invasion of their privacy."

"I can get the names some other way, but I'd really appreciate your cooperation. It would save me quite a bit of time, time I could spend looking for Mr. Vogler's killer."

He hesitated, then took out a notebook from a desk drawer, flipped through it, and dictated names and numbers to Ryker.

"Is there a group leader?" Ryker asked.

Markowitz nodded. "Mrs. Rudman."

"How long has she been a—what did you call it?"

"Agunah. Over eleven years." He explained her case.

Ryker whistled. "No kidding. That's pretty tough. Almost like a life sentence. No offense, Rabbi, but can't you and your colleagues get together and change the law or something?"

"We're working on finding a solution to the problem, but it's a slow process. Unfortunately, politics rears its ugly head even in religion. In the meantime, we have to deal with each situation on an individual basis and try to get the husbands to cooperate."

"What about the other women in the group? How long have they been like this?"

"It varies. From several months to several years. The main thing is that the women give each other support and hope."

"So what's your success rate?"

"Not great," he admitted. "Oh, most of the husbands eventually come around; usually, it's a question of a cash settlement. That sounds ugly, and it is. I can't really count those as successes, not when the woman has been virtually forced to pay blackmail. Sometimes, the *get* is tied to a custody battle. Those cases can be more difficult. And then we come across a man whose motivation is just spite. With men like that, who knows when they'll see reason?"

"If ever," Ryker said quietly.

"If ever." He sighed. "But we like to think positively." He seemed lost in thought.

"In your opinion, Rabbi, was Mr. Vogler one of those men?"

"I didn't say that." He was obviously annoyed.

"So would you count Vogler as one of your success cases, Rabbi? Mrs. Vogler *is* free, isn't she?"

"That's a crass way of looking at it, Detective! No, I certainly don't count it as a success. A man is dead. How can anyone count that as a success?"

"The killer can," Ryker reminded him.

* * *

"The boyfriend's name is Michael Benton," Moran told Ryker and Stollman on Sunday morning. "Dr. Michael Benton. He lives in an apartment house on Holt near Olympic."

"A medical doctor?" Ryker asked.

"Psychologist," Moran said. "I talked to the manager and some neighbors yesterday. They all think he's a hell of a nice guy. Quiet, keeps to himself most of the time, but friendly. Always pays his rent on time, that kind of stuff."

"Any female visitors?" Ryker asked.

"The manager—Mrs. Lupisco—says she's never seen any. Except for his mother and sisters. He introduced them when he moved in; they were helping him unload boxes. But they don't come often. They live in the Valley."

"Did you talk to Benton himself?"

"He wasn't in. That was about ten in the morning. The manager said he goes to synagogue every Saturday morning and sometimes doesn't come home all afternoon. He told her he gets invited out to lunch after services. Anyway, I called his apartment off and on all day, but he wasn't home. I figured I'd go over there this morning and have a chat."

"Could be he just didn't answer the phone during the day," Stollman said. "Orthodox Jews don't answer the phone or use electricity on the Sabbath. My grandfather was real strict about that. This Benton guy sounds Orthodox, too."

"Makes sense," Ryker said. "From what Ann Douglas and the rabbi said, Vogler wasn't religious when he met his wife, and they had some pretty heavy problems because of it. Mrs. Vogler would be pretty dumb to make the same mistake twice."

"Which rabbi are you talking about?" Stollman asked.

"I met with this Rabbi Markowitz last night." He described their conversation. "He's got strong opinions on this *get* business. According to him, what Vogler was doing was criminal, and Markowitz wanted to help put a stop to it."

Moran grinned. "The Jewish Equalizer, huh?"

"Something like that." Ryker smiled. "He said he'd be willing to do whatever it took to get Mrs. Vogler her divorce."

"What did he mean by 'whatever it took'?" Stollman asked.

"I asked him that. He assured me he hadn't been planning

anything illegal. He *did* tell me that according to Jewish law, someone like Vogler can be whipped.''

''Thirty lashes, huh?'' Moran said.

''Actually, I think he said forty.'' Ryker grinned. ''I also asked him about the women in this support group he started.''

''Did you get their names?'' Stollman asked.

Ryker nodded. ''Markowitz wasn't happy to give them to me. And he thinks I'm wasting my time. He's sure the killer was a burglar or some business connection.''

''Not the beautiful ex-wife?'' Moran asked. ''Sitting around, waiting for her ex-husband to let her off the hook?''

''Markowitz says no way is she involved.''

''What about her father?'' Stollman asked. ''He's Orthodox, right? So he sees his daughter getting involved with another guy, but they can't get married. And he's not stupid. He knows that sooner or later, they'll get tired of waiting, and they'll start living together and then boom!—excommunication.''

''Come on, Hank!'' Moran laughed. ''You've gotta be kidding! That's a motive today? Tell him, Sam.''

''I don't know, Tom. They're very serious about their religion. That plus the daughter's miserable, and Vogler's harassing her with phone calls and doing God knows what else.''

''I thought Novick had an alibi,'' Moran said. ''You checked it out with the assistant manager there, didn't you, Sam?''

''I spoke with her on Thursday. She said Novick came in that Sunday afternoon around three and stayed for almost two hours. She didn't remember exactly what time he left. I'll have to call her again, pin her down. It could be important.''

''Where's the convalescent home?'' Stollman asked.

''On Melrose and Sweetzer.''

Stollman said, ''And Mrs. Pearson said she saw a man entering the house at five-forty. So even if Novick left the home at five-ten, he could've made it to the Sherbourne house by five-forty.''

''With time to spare,'' Ryker agreed. ''It could work.''

Moran said, ''And he knew about the gun. Hell, it's his!''

''Shit! I forgot to tell you guys,'' Ryker said. ''Mrs. Vogler called me last night. She found the gun in her hall closet, says she probably didn't check carefully. I picked it up and dropped it off downtown. I'll ask Zeke to run a ballistics test first thing tomorrow.''

"You think he'll get it done so fast?'' Moran asked. "You called in one favor last week on the bullet Kanata extracted.''

"I'll give it my best shot. No pun intended.'' He grinned.

"So it was in the closet all the time and she just didn't see it?'' Stollman shook his head. "I don't know.''

"Could be. Which means that if Novick is the killer, he had access to another gun. Because if he took the gun and killed Vogler with it, he wouldn't return it. He wouldn't want to stick his daughter with a smoking gun, and he knows that we know it's his gun.'' He paused. "Unless he figured we'd believe the daughter's story about misplacing the gun and wouldn't check it. Or maybe he thought if he cleaned the gun, we wouldn't be able to run any conclusive tests. The same reasoning would fit the boyfriend, too.''

Moran said, "I guess that lets Mrs. Vogler off the hook, right? She's not about to give us the gun if she used it to kill her ex-husband.''

Stollman said, "Maybe the killer returned the gun to direct attention away from himself. I'm thinking about Kasden.''

"Or from herself," Ryker said. "Ann Douglas. She certainly wouldn't lose any sleep if Mrs. Vogler had to explain how the murder weapon happened to be in her house. Anyway, there's no point in trying to figure this out until we get the ballistics report. With any luck, that'll be some time tomorrow.''

"So now what?'' Moran asked. "We sit around waiting?''

"Not exactly. First, I have the names of those women in the support group. Tom, I'd like you to tackle those.'' He handed him a list. "There are five regulars, excluding Mrs. Vogler. See if they know anything about Vogler and Novick.''

"Any of them cute?'' Moran grinned. He scanned the list. "Most of them live within a close radius. Should be easy to see all of them today. But I want to try the boyfriend again.''

"Okay. Hank, we have Kasden's books and the bank statements. Let's go over those now, see if we can find any discrepancies, anything suspicious. If it's too difficult, we can send it down to Parker Center; they've got some accounting experts there. But I thought we'd give it a try first.''

"Okay with me. By the way, the Vogelanters called. Their rabbi said they can come today to check their son's effects if it's important. They said they'd be here some time after noon.''

Moran said, ''Sam, no word yet from the Futrells—they're my last name on the open house list, remember? I'll try them again today. They've gotta come back some time. Oh, and I spoke to George. He's feeling better, says he'll be in Monday.''

''Glad to hear it.'' Ryker drummed his fingers on his desk.

Stollman said, ''What are you thinking about?''

''That we still don't have Kasden's or Novick's prints.''

''And Dr. Michael Benton's prints,'' Moran added quickly. ''Don't forget the boyfriend.''

''Right. I'd like to get that wrapped up so that we can eliminate them.''

''Or find a positive identification,'' Stollman said.

After two tedious hours and four cups of black coffee, Ryker pushed himself away from his desk.

''I don't know about you, Hank, but I need a break.'' He groaned, kneading his forehead.

They had begun with the firm's books and the bank statements for two years ago and worked through July of last year. So far, nothing, aside from an obviously clerical error in the amount of $3.26. Hardly earth-shattering news.

''I'm doing okay, Sam. I'd like to keep at it. I'll finish last year, then quit for a while.''

''Maybe we don't know what to look for.''

''I don't think that's it. We just haven't found anything yet.''

''Maybe we won't.'' Ryker took his jacket and slung it over his shoulder. ''If anyone calls, I'll be back in about an hour.''

Some birds had had a picnic on the windshield of his car. Ryker turned on the ignition and activated the windshield mister, but a flashing message on the dashboard informed him that the water level in the mister was too low. The dry blades smeared the droppings across the windshield.

''Shit!'' he exclaimed, then laughed aloud at the ironic aptness of his expression.

In the trunk he found a spray bottle filled with Windex and a semi-clean rag that he had stored for just such an emergency. He cleaned the windshield with deft strokes.

Less than fifteen minutes after he'd pulled out of the precinct parking lot, he found the house on Fuller. There was one car in the driveway. He parked his car, walked up the path, and rang the bell. He heard heavy footsteps approaching.

"Who is it?"

"Detective Ryker, sir. I called, but the line was busy." It was a lie, but Novick couldn't know that. "There are a couple of things I have to ask you."

Max opened the door but didn't invite Ryker in. "This is a bad time, Detective. I'm drowning in paperwork, and I have a meeting with the children of a new resident. If I'll have five minutes in between to breathe, I'll be lucky."

"This won't take long, Mr. Novick."

"Any other time, really. Just now, I can't."

"Tomorrow, then?" Ryker asked pleasantly.

"Tomorrow, fine." He was about to close the door.

"Let me give you my card." He removed a wallet from an inner pocket of his jacket, took out a glossy card, and handed it to Max. "Call me and let me know what time is convenient."

"I will." He glanced at the card and turned it over. "You gave me the wrong card, Detective." He smiled. "This is for a video rental store." He returned the card to the detective.

"Sorry." Ryker was clearly embarrassed. He slipped the card into an outer pocket and checked his wallet. "I thought I had one left in here."

"It's okay, Detective. I can call information. It's only twenty-five cents."

"Not necessary. I've got thirty cards in a holder I carry with me. Could you hold this a minute?" He handed the wallet to Max, searched in a pocket, found a small vinyl card case, and selected one card. "Here you go." He handed it to Max and took back the wallet. "Please call me tomorrow. It's important."

"It's a promise." Max closed the door.

Ryker walked back to his car, the wallet now in an evidence bag that he'd whipped out of his pocket as soon as Novick had shut the door. Sitting in his car, he retrieved the card from his other pocket, careful to hold it by one corner, slid the card into another evidence bag, and slipped both bags into a large envelope. He grinned widely with satisfaction.

It wasn't three 7s on a Vegas slot machine, but it wasn't bird shit, either.

23

WHEN RYKER RETURNED, STOLLMAN WAS STILL SCRUTINIZing the cramped figures on the pages of Kasden's ledger books and comparing them with the bank statements.

"Find anything?" Ryker asked.

"I'm still on October. There was a small irregularity in August of last year, but I don't know if it means anything."

" 'Irregularity.' I'm impressed. You sound like a bona fide accountant. What was it?"

"A check was made out to the firm on August 18th for $5,300. A deposit from a buyer named Leader. That check wasn't deposited in the bank, but two weeks later, Kasden deposited a personal check for $5,300 in the bank. So I guess it all balances. I just couldn't figure out why there was that gap."

"Is there a deposit receipt?"

"Yeah. It's dated the 18th, too."

"Call a realty firm and check it out. Maybe it's okay."

"I will. By the way, you just missed the Vogelanters."

"Did you show them their son's stuff?"

Stollman nodded. "You were right about the watch, Sam. They noticed right off that it was missing. Seems that Novick gave his son-in-law a Rolex when the young couple got engaged. According to his parents, he loved it. Wore it all the time."

"Anything else?"

"Nothing that they noticed. The good news is, the watch was inscribed on the back—"To Jake, from Max and Pearl." That'll make it easy to spot if it's been pawned. I put out the word on the streets that we're looking for it."

"Good work." Maybe it'll show up. Maybe it *was* a robbery."

"Maybe. I know a couple of guys who'd kill for a Rolex!"

"You talking about me?" Moran asked, joining them. "Who has a Rolex?"

Ryker told him about Volger's watch. "You're back early. Did you check out all those women?"

"A couple of them weren't home." He checked his notebook. "I figured I'd start with Hollywood and work my way back here, but I'm saving the best for last. Okay. Susan Bergman. Real cute, and built, too. She just graduated."

"What do you mean?" Ryker asked.

"Her husband's giving her the religious divorce. She was real up front with me, told me it was costing her old man $100,000. Seems her family's loaded, so it's no problem. From what she heard about Vogler, he was a real creep."

"Anything specific?" Ryker asked.

"Nope. She knew about the calls he was making. I got the impression that as much as she's sorry for Mrs. Vogler, she's all caught up with the fact that she's out of her own mess."

"That's human, I guess," Ryker said.

"Next, Magda Feroukhim. American, kind of dumpy, married to an Iranian. Didn't say much. Basically repeated what the other women said. They all felt sorry for Mrs. Vogler, aren't too upset that Vogler's dead. But why should they be?"

"What about the Rudman woman? She's the group leader."

"She wasn't home. Neither was the Presser woman. I'll go back later and try them again."

"Okay. So that's it?"

"One more. Miriam Kalinsky. Pretty, in a serious kind of way. She wasn't exactly thrilled about talking to me, but she was very pleasant. She's the only one so far who seemed upset by what happened—'he died so young,' that kind of stuff."

"She felt sorry for Vogler?" Stollman asked, surprised.

"Kind of. Thought he was misguided but that eventually, he'd have come around. She *did* tell me something interesting, though. Apparently, Vogler tried to rape his ex-wife." Moran looked pleased with his announcement.

"When was that?" Ryker said.

"About a month ago. She doesn't remember the date. Actually, she didn't realize she was telling me something we didn't know. We were talking about Vogler's phone calls— Mrs. Vogler told the group about them—and I said it's too bad Mrs. Vogler was so frightened that she had to get a gun. So this Kalinsky woman says she never liked the idea of the gun, but she couldn't really blame Mrs. Vogler for getting one. 'Especially after what happened,' I said, meaning the calls. So she says right; if Vogler tried to force himself on his ex-wife one time, he could try it again. Apparently, the only reason he didn't succeed is that the women came to Mrs. Vogler's house that night for a group meeting.''

"And she still feels sorry for Vogler?'' Ryker asked.

"I asked her that. She thinks what he did was awful, but she really believes he was disturbed, not malicious.''

Ryker said, "I wonder if Novick knew about this. Maybe that's what he meant when he told Vogler to keep his hands off his daughter.''

"Sure sounds like it,'' Stollman said.

Moran smiled. "The boyfriend knew about it, too.''

"I'm surprised he volunteered that,'' Ryker said.

"He didn't. I told him we knew about it, asked him why Mrs. Vogler didn't report the incident. Clever, huh?''

"Why didn't she?'' Stollman asked.

"According to Benton, she thought it would lessen her chances of getting her religious divorce.''

"What else did Benton say?'' Ryker asked.

"He admitted he's involved with Mrs. Vogler. I told him we know he was at Vogler's apartment late Saturday night— I said the doorman remembered his name.''

"Liar.'' Ryker smiled approvingly.

Moran grinned. "He was surprised, but he didn't deny it. So then I told him the neighbor complained about the noise, and Benton admitted that he and Vogler were really going at it.''

"Does he have an alibi?'' Ryker asked.

"Not solid. He and Mrs. Vogler had a date, but he had to cancel for a patient.''

"On a Sunday?'' Ryker asked.

"He claims it was an emergency. Says he was with the patient from five-thirty until eight. By the time he got home, it was after eight-thirty. And before that, he spent the afternoon doing his laundry in the basement of the apartment house where he lives.''

"Did anyone else see him?'' Stollman asked.

"He doesn't remember.''

"Did he give you the name of the patient?'' Ryker asked.

"He refused. Says it's privileged information. I tried to

push it, but he wouldn't budge. I told him we could get a subpoena, and he said, fine, go ahead.''

"Did he sound worried?''Ryker asked.

"I couldn't tell. Anyway, I told him we wanted him to come in so we could get his prints. Since he was in Vogler's apartment—that line. He said he'd come by some time today.''

"You sound disappointed,'' Ryker said.

"I guess I am.'' He grinned. "I would've liked it better if he'd balked at the idea.''

"Maybe he knows he didn't leave any prints because he wore gloves.'' Ryker smiled. "Speaking of prints, I got Novick's.'' He told them about his ruse. "Between the wallet and the card, I think I got some good partials of his right hand.''

"That leaves Kasden,'' Stollman said. "We'll probably have him come in when we finish the books. We can print him then.''

"Right. Let's get at it. Hank, call that realty office and check out what you found. Then finish last year. Tom, let's take the first half of this year. I'd like to finish this today.''

"What about the other women in the group?'' Moran asked.

"They can wait. I have a feeling we're going to find something in these books. If we do, we can bring Kasden in tomorrow. I'd like to ask him a couple of things.'' He smiled.

Deena knew she wouldn't hear anything about the gun for several days. Ryker had explained that the scientific investigation division—SID, he'd called it—didn't work on weekends. But every time the phone rang, she jumped to answer it. Not that she was worried. She was positive that she'd simply overlooked the gun.

Max and Pearl came by Sunday morning. Pearl prepared a late breakfast and watched approvingly as Deena dutifully finished a healthy portion of eggs and two slices of toast.

"It's delicious, Mom.''

Pearl smiled. Deena thought her mother's color had improved somewhat, and her breathing seemed less labored.

Deena waited until Pearl left the kitchen to go to the bathroom. Max was sitting at the breakfast room table, reading the Sunday *Times*.

"I found the gun, Daddy. It was in the hall closet. I probably just didn't search carefully.''

Max looked at her. "Good. You told the detective?"

"Yes. He came last night and picked it up."

"Why? But I thought—never mind."

"It's just routine, Daddy. He has to rule it out as the murder weapon. I'm so relieved, aren't you?"

Pearl came into the room.

Max stood up. "Let's go." He folded the "Opinion" section.

"So soon?" Pearl asked.

"Stay if you want. I have to go into the home."

"I'll be okay, Mom. Really. Go with Daddy. Anyway, I'm behind in my studies. I thought I'd read a few chapters today."

Pearl looked a little hesitant, but she left with Max.

The phone rang several times during the day.

Brenda DiSalvo called. "I just heard from Marv Cooper. Talk about surprises! Anyway, when you're ready, come in and we'll figure out where you stand."

And Magda called to say that she'd planned to come over but had come down with the flu. She hoped Deena understood.

Sandy and Alan came by in the early afternoon with Jonathan. Sandy found some measuring cups and Tupperware bowls, and Jonathan played with them contentedly in the den.

Deena told them about finding the gun.

"That's great!" Sandy exclaimed. "Isn't it, Alan?"

"I thought you looked everywhere," he said to Deena.

"You sound just like Michael."

"Sorry. I'm just skeptical by nature. But I hope you're right. Then you can put this whole mess behind you."

They didn't stay long—Jonathan had to have his nap—and they were walking out the door when Michael showed up. They stayed on the porch, chatting, until Jonathan began tugging impatiently on Sandy's hand.

In the house, Michael kissed Deena lightly. He handed her a box. "I brought you some donuts to keep you occupied."

She groaned. "You know I have no will power! Anyway, are mourners allowed to binge?"

"Jake would have wanted it this way," he said solemnly, then grinned.

The phone rang. Deena picked up the receiver. "Hello?"

"Deena? It's Elaine."

"Elaine?" She looked at Michael and shrugged.

"You're probably wondering why I'm calling. First of all, of course, I wanted to find out how you are. Faye's been keeping me posted, but I thought I'd call myself."

"That's very nice of you."

"Good. That's good. Listen, Deena, Susan just called me. It seems a detective stopped by her house and asked her all about the group and what we knew about Jake."

"Really?" She wondered how the police had found out about the group, and what they thought they would learn from talking to its members. Just routine, she figured.

"The thing is, they'll probably come by here too. Which is fine. But I don't want to tell them that I talked to Jake."

"When did you—oh, you mean at my house?"

"No, I mean the time I saw him at that restaurant. Remember? It wasn't a big deal, but frankly, I'd rather not go into it with the cops. Okay?"

"They haven't asked me anything about the group."

"But they will. When they do, please don't mention this. I know it sounds dumb, but the last thing I need is to have some cops checking into me. Kenny would just love that!"

"But what if they ask me if you ever talked to him?"

"Say you don't know. I already talked to Susan about it. She agreed. Okay?"

"Okay, I guess."

"Well, I have to go. I'm glad you're doing okay, Deena. Maybe we'll get together after all this is over. Take care."

"What did she want?"Michael asked after Deena hung up.

She related the conversation. "Funny, I'd forgotten all about that confrontation she had with Jake." She described it.

"What's she so nervous about?"

"She's a pretty nervous type anyway. Didn't you see how upset she got the night she paid me a *shivah* call?"

"Oh, was that Elaine? I didn't connect all the names with the faces. Yeah, she was pretty nervous."

"I think it's the idea of having the police question her. I'm not exactly thrilled having them poking around, either."

"Neither am I."

"What do you mean?"

"A Detective Moran came by to see me today. My apartment manager told me he asked her a few questions, too."

"What did he ask you?"

"He knew we were seeing each other, Deena. I didn't

deny it. And he asked where I was Sunday. I explained about our canceled date. They want me to have my fingerprints taken.''

"Why? You've never been to Jake's apartment."

"I don't know." He shrugged. "Routine, I guess. I told them I'd do it today. Deena, they knew about the phone calls. And that Jake attacked you. I'm surprised you told them."

"I didn't tell them. Why would I do that?"

"So who did? Not your father. He'd be crazy to tell them. Who else knew about it?"

"Sandy and Alan? But they wouldn't say anything; anyway the police haven't talked to them. Reuben called me last night after you left and told me that Detective Ryker had been there. But Reuben wouldn't volunteer something like that, either."

"Oh, well, there's no point trying to figure this out. The thing is, the police know."

"I think we've got something!" Stollman said. "I called a realty firm, and the broker I spoke to said that what Kasden did is highly unethical. According to real estate law, a deposit check has to be deposited in the bank immediately. If it's too late to do it on the day of the transaction, then it has to be deposited by the next working day. A two-week delay is definitely not kosher. Also, he said a firm's books always have to be available for an audit by the Real Estate Board.''

"So he was fooling around with some buyer's money, huh?"

Stollman nodded. "This broker said it's called 'co-mingling of funds.' Grounds for having your license revoked by the Real Estate Commissioner."

"REC." Ryker leaned back in his chair and smiled.

"Glad you could make it, Mr. Kasden," Ryker said at ten o'clock on Monday morning. He extended his hand, but Kasden ignored it. Ryker looked at the man standing with Kasden. Late forties, average height, moderate build. Three-piece flannel suit, tortoise-framed glasses, briefcase. A lawyer.

"This is my attorney, Bryan Tischler." Kasden spoke in clipped syllables.

"Detective Ryker." He shook Tischler's hand.

They sat around the detective's desk. Ryker turned on his tape recorder.

"I asked you to come down here this morning, Mr. Kasden, because we've found some irregularities in your firm's books." Ryker's tone was pleasant and unhurried. He pulled over a light manila folder, opened it, and took out a sheet of paper.

"On several occasions you received monies from prospective buyers but did not deposit them immediately in the appropriate bank account. Your name, by the way, is listed as the salesperson on the deposit slips, along with your signature. Beginning with August of two years ago, we found twelve incidents of that nature. In addition, a $70,000 check, received by you from Mr. Murdoch in July of this year, was *never* deposited in the bank." He looked at Kasden, who was staring grimly at the wall beyond Ryker's head. Beads of perspiration dotted his upper lip.

"There are also several major bank withdrawals not reflected in your firm's books, Mr. Kasden. These withdrawals began in October of last year and continued up to the present. Some of the monies were returned to the bank account, but there's still a discrepancy to date of a rather large amount— $286,000. Most of that belongs to the Murdoch account, although several accounts seem to be involved." He replaced the paper in the folder. "I'd be very interested in hearing your explanation for all of these . . . irregularities, Mr. Kasden."

Tischler said, "Detective, my client admits that he has improperly used funds entrusted to him. He found himself in rather desperate circumstances and behaved foolishly. He deeply regrets his actions. It was always my client's intention to return the money he had appropriated. He expects to make full restitution in the very near future."

Ryker smiled at both men quizzically. "And how does he plan to do that, Mr. Tischler?"

"Mr. Kasden assures me he will be receiving a substantial settlement within a matter of weeks. Once these parties have been reimbursed, we're confident that they will sign releases indicating that they do not plan to file charges against Mr. Kasden. With that in mind, and in view of the fact that this is my client's first offense, I hope the district attorney's office will dismiss the charges against him."

"We're talking about grand theft, here, Mr. Tischler. Your client embezzled almost $300,000—more, if you count the money he 'borrowed' and then returned. It's the D.A.'s decision, but I think Mr. Kasden's looking at a minimum of one year in county jail plus probation. And that's if every one of those clients is willing not to file charges. I wouldn't count on Murdoch, you know. From what I've heard, he's not exactly the forgive-and-forget type. If Murdoch or someone else decides to prosecute, you're talking minimum two years in state prison.''

"I feel confident that we can get all concerned parties to drop charges. Once they are reimbursed, of course.''

"As of today, though, your client is not in a position to repay anyone. Is that correct?''

"He will be shortly.''

"Are we talking about the insurance money, Mr. Tischler?''

"Yes.''

"That policy is with Fidelity Mutual, Mr. Kasden, right?''

"Yes.'' His voice was strangled. He was sweating profusely now, the moisture glistening on his almost bald head.

"I just wanted to make sure we were talking about the same policy. See, I got these from Mr. Vogler's safe deposit box. Very interesting.'' He withdrew some folded documents from the manila file and showed them to the two men. "I didn't know that people usually took out partner's insurance.''

Kasden spoke quietly. "In our business, we don't have merchandise or some other tangible commodity. What we have is our name and—'' he coughed—"good faith. So we thought it would be a good idea to protect each other in case one of us died. Unfortunately, it turned out to be good thinking.'' He mopped his forehead and the nape of his neck with a handkerchief.

"So you were insured for $450,000.''

"That's correct.''

"And how much is it with the double indemnity clause?''

"I don't know exactly! You make it sound like I ran to the phone the minute I found out Jake was dead!''

"Are you saying you didn't contact the insurance company?''

"I called. I had to tell them about Jake's death, didn't I?''

"And you didn't ask them about the money?''

Kasden avoided Ryker's eyes. "I asked them. Are you happy, Detective? You want to make me into a villain here, and I don't know why. I've admitted to the misappropriation of funds.''

"Embezzlement, Mr. Kasden. Grand theft."

"Whatever. But what are you saying, that I'm happy Jake's dead? 'Cause if you are, you're crazy! I loved that man!"

"What about the double indemnity? Whose idea was that?"

"It's standard."

"Not for violent death. I spoke to Sid Wyman, your insurance agent. According to him, you're the one who insisted on amending that clause to include violent death. Generally, it just pays off on accidental death."

"I don't remember that."

"Wyman remembers it very clearly. He says it was just a few months ago. He also says that's when you changed the policy from $250,000 to $450,000. So with the double indemnity, you'll be getting a check for $900,000. Not too shabby, Mr. Kasden."

"The firm was growing. And with the dollar fluctuating, I thought we needed extra protection. Jake agreed."

"Mr. Wyman says you've been calling him about five times a day about the insurance money. He said you sounded anxious."

"Of course I'm anxious! I need the money to pay back Murdoch and the other clients!"

"I doubt they'll pay until Vogler's murder is solved. How would you have paid them back without the insurance money, Mr. Kasden?"

"Listen—"

"I'm going to have to ask Mr. Kasden not to answer any more questions, Detective," Tischler interrupted quickly. "I sense that we're straying from the embezzlement charges. Do you intend to charge my client with something else?"

Ryker smiled. "Not at this time. But let me be frank. We're investigating the murder of Mr. Kasden's partner, and I'd be lying if I said your client isn't under suspicion."

"You think I killed Jake? You son of a—"

"Shut up, Ben!" Tischler put his hand on Kasden's shoulder.

"We have reason to believe that Mr. Vogler was aware of Mr. Kasden's activities, was worried about them, and was contemplating reporting Mr. Kasden to the Real Estate Commissioner. In view of Mr. Kasden's financial difficulties, and the substantial insurance settlement he can expect because of Mr. Vogler's death—well, I think it's pretty clear. We're pursuing that and other lines of investigation."

"I didn't kill him, Detective! You have to believe me."

"What do you plan to do now?" Tischler asked Ryker.

"We're going to book your client on grand theft. I assume you'll be arranging for bail?"

"Immediately." He turned to Kasden. "It shouldn't be more than five to ten thousand. I hope to have bail posted before the end of the day. Ben, don't say anything to anyone."

Kasden nodded. His face was ashen.

Humpty Dumpty had a great fall. "In the meantime, Mr. Kasden, I'll have someone take you to be booked. And printed."

When Ryker returned to his desk after taking Kasden to the jailer, Stollman was waiting for him.

"Zeke called," Stollman said. "I don't know what magic you have, but he got the ballistics test results for you."

"What did he say?" Ryker asked.

Stollman told him.

"No shit!"

Deena was reading a text on tax law when she heard the front doorbell. She hurried to the entry hall.

"It's Detective Ryker, Mrs. Vogler. May I come in?"

She opened the door and invited him into the living room.

"I just got the ballistics test results. The gun you gave me was not used to kill your ex-husband."

"I knew it was all a mistake." She smiled, almost giddy with relief. "You're sure?"

"Absolutely. Every gun barrel has unique markings—lands and grooves. A bullet is made of soft lead, and when it's fired through the barrel, those markings are embedded on the bullet."

"So can I have the gun back?" She would return it to Max. She never wanted to see it or any other gun again in her life.

"I'm afraid not, Mrs. Vogler. You see, the gun you gave me isn't the murder weapon. But it isn't your gun, either."

"It's my father's. I thought you knew that."

"It isn't his gun, either. We checked the registration."

"I don't understand. Whose gun is it?"

"Now that's a good question, Mrs. Vogler, but I have no idea. You see, this gun isn't registered. To anyone."

24

DEENA COULD HEAR HER HEART BEAT IN THE SILENCE. "THIS is impossible." She shook her head. "There has to be a mistake. I know the gun I gave you is mine. I recognized it immediately."

"I'm sure it looked exactly like yours, but there are thousands of handguns with the same exact color, size, and shape. We ran the serial numbers of the gun you gave me through a computer listing. That gun isn't registered."

"Computers make mistakes. Can't you run it through again? I'm sure you'll see that this is the gun my father gave me."

"The computer *did* find the registration of your father's gun. The serial numbers are different."

"But I thought all guns have to be registered."

"They're supposed to be. But sometimes a gun dealer will sell a piece and not register it. For the right price. It happens all the time. The fact is, we have a major problem here. Obviously, somebody took your gun and replaced it with another one. The way I see it, that means your gun—your father's gun—was used to kill your ex-husband. That's the only logical explanation. Why else would someone have switched guns?"

Deena wanted desperately to argue with him, to refute his calm statement, but how could she? He was absolutely, terrifyingly right. She felt as though he'd slapped her.

"Why don't we sit down," Ryker suggested. "I'd like to ask you a few questions."

"Right. I'm sorry." Deena automatically sat on the cushionless seat where she'd been sitting all week. She noticed Ryker's puzzled look, was instantly annoyed with herself. The last thing she needed was to have to explain to a police detective why she was sitting *shivah* for Jake.

"This is part of Orthodox tradition during mourning. You're probably wondering why I'm doing this, though."

"No, I get it. Rabbi Markowitz explained that according to your religion, you were never divorced, so that makes you a widow, right? Under the circumstances that must feel weird."

"Weird" was an understatement. "It's almost over."

"Mrs. Volger, we know your ex-husband was refusing to give you this religious divorce, and that you and he weren't on the best of terms. I have to be honest. As a detective, I'm bound to consider you as a suspect. You had constant access to your gun, and you could've easily replaced it at any time with another gun, and then 'discovered' it when it was convenient."

"But I couldn't have bought another gun! Even if I knew how to get an unregistered gun, aside from going to the funeral, I haven't left the house since I found out Jake was killed. I'm not allowed to leave during the seven days of mourning. It's too bad you didn't have someone tail me; he could've verified that I'm telling the truth." She didn't notice the quick smile that flickered across Ryker's face.

"You could have had someone buy a new gun for you."

"Then why would I call you up and give you the gun? That doesn't make any sense!"

"Maybe you figured we'd run a ballistics test, rule out the gun, and return it to you without checking to see if it was your original gun. That's probably what the killer thought."

"I think I should call my lawyer. I don't think I should answer any more of your questions."

"Relax, Mrs. Vogler." He smiled. "I probably shouldn't be telling you this, but somehow I don't see you as the killer. But that's my personal opinion—naturally, we'll have to check into all your actions thoroughly."

"Detective Ryker, I know you found out that Jake was harassing me, that he attacked me. So it would be silly for me to say we had a normal divorce. The truth is that I hated him." She hesitated. "Once or twice, I wished he would die. But I didn't kill him. I'm not sorry he's dead, and maybe that makes me a horrible person, but I didn't kill him."

"I believe you." Her face was flushed, her green eyes bright, intense; he realized again how pretty she was. Vogler, he decided, had been a real ass for cheating on her. "But whether your ex-husband was a wonderful guy or an A-one bastard, it's my job to find his killer. I need your help to determine who had access to your gun and entry to your house.''

She didn't answer.

"I know this is difficult for you, and I can't force you to answer. I *will* get the answers, though, one way or another.''

"All right.''

"Good. Let's start with your parents and get them out of the way. When was the last time they came to your house before Mr. Vogler was killed?''

"They come all the time. I can't remember exact dates.''

"Try, please.''

She thought for a moment. "They were here the Friday before. They came to drop off some Sabbath food my mother prepared. She likes to cook for me.'' She smiled nervously.

"And have your parents been here since the murder?''

She nodded. "The night before the funeral—that would be Wednesday—and Thursday night, along with some other people. It's customary to visit the mourner. They were here yesterday, too. They know this is a difficult time for me.'' She braced herself for his next question: *How did your father and your ex-husband get along?*

"I see.'' He scribbled some notes. "Okay. Let's move on.''

That's it? She was weak with relief, careful not to show it.

"By the way, how did you come to find the gun Saturday night? I forgot to ask you.''

She hesitated. "Actually, a friend of mine found it. Michael Benton. I think one of your detectives spoke to him.''

"You're a little more than friends, as I understand it.'' Ryker smiled. "Any plans to marry?''

None of your damn business! "We haven't discussed it.''

"Dr. Benton knew about the gun? And where you kept it?''

She nodded. "He didn't like the idea of my having it.''

"And was he here before the murder?''

"He comes over frequently.''

"So aside from Saturday night, he's been here other times since the murder?''

"Yes. But Detective Ryker, he's the one who found the gun. And he thought right away that someone had taken it and replaced it. As a matter of fact, we argued about it, because I kept insisting that I just overlooked it all along.''

"He could've put it there just before he 'found' it. And he could've been arguing about it just to throw you off, Mrs. Vogler. Have you considered that?"

She hadn't. Now that Ryker had mentioned it, she still didn't want to think about it. But she knew she would.

"I understand that your ex-husband and Dr. Benton had a serious confrontation. Came to blows, did they?"

"You mean in the restaurant? Jake was acting ugly, and childish. He hit Michael." She still remembered the stares. "It was so embarrassing. But how do you know about that?" Had the manager called the police? Probably. He would have heard about Jake's death.

He'd been guessing about the blows. "We hear things. People call the station." He could have told her the truth, that he hadn't known a thing about the restaurant scene, but he didn't have the heart. She looked so appealing, so vulnerable. He was getting too soft, he decided. "And then there was the Saturday night before the murder, at Mr. Vogler's apartment."

He watched her face. She looked blank but recovered quickly. He realized she knew nothing about Benton's visit.

"Right. Michael told me about that." She smiled. "He was just trying to get Jake to leave me alone. Michael is a very nonviolent person. He's a psychologist. He teaches people how to deal with their feelings."

"My mother has a saying about shoemakers going around with torn soles. Maybe it's easier to show people how to control their feelings than to control your own." He paused. "I understand you two were supposed to go out that Sunday."

"Yes, but Michael had an emergency. A patient called him."

"But he came over later?"

"No. By the time he came back, he was exhausted."

"Does that happen often—emergency sessions, I mean?"

"Once in a while." Never before. Why do I think I have to lie to protect him? she wondered miserably.

"Okay. Not too painful so far, right?" He smiled. "I understand you belong to a support group for women in your situation. Do they meet at your house sometimes?"

"They met here once."

"When was that?"

"The Tuesday before the murder. That was the day I think someone broke into my house, Detective."

"I don't think an anonymous burglar would return to your house and replace your gun with another one, do you?"

"I guess not." She felt silly for having mentioned it. You're grasping at straws, she told herself.

"So did they all know about the gun?"

"Yes. And they knew where I kept it. Detective, this is silly. You can't think that one of them is involved."

"It's unlikely, but we have to check everyone. Were these women here after the murder?"

"Some of them."

"Could you tell me who was here?"

"Faye Rudman. Miriam Kalinsky. Susan Bergman." She thought for a moment. "And Elaine. Elaine Presser. That's it."

"Were they here once or several times?"

"Faye was here more than once. We're pretty close. The others were here Thursday night."

"Now I want you to think very carefully, Mrs. Vogler. Did all of these women have an opportunity both to take the gun and to replace it with the second gun? Please take your time."

"I feel very uncomfortable doing this, Detective."

"If they're not involved, they have nothing to worry about. In any case, I'll be asking them all the same questions. Did the women use your bathroom, for example?"

"I didn't keep track of who used it or how many times."

"But each one could've gone to your bedroom and taken the gun from your nightstand without being noticed?"

"I suppose so."

"Dr. Benton found the gun in the entry hall closet, right? Let's check these names one at a time, okay? Mrs. Rudman. Did she have an opportunity to put the gun there?"

"Probably. Detective Ryker, *everyone* had an opportunity to put the gun there. This isn't proving anything."

"Just bear with me, please. What about Mrs. Presser?" She nodded.

"Mrs. Kalinsky? Mrs. Bergman?"

"I told you, Detective. Everyone."

"What about Rabbi Markowitz?"

"You've got to be kidding!"

"I have to ask."

"He was never here before the murder. We always met at

his house or at his synagogue. He *did* come to the house the night before the funeral and Thursday night, too. I didn't notice that he had a gun with him, but maybe he had it under his hat.''

"Okay." He smiled. "What about Ben Kasden? Did he know you had a gun?''

"Ben? As a matter of fact, he did. After Murdoch's men intimidated me, he was worried. I told him about the gun.''

"Was he here before the murder?''

"He came over a few days after that incident with Murdoch's men. That's when I told him about the gun. But he didn't stay long. I don't remember if he came another time.''

"And after the murder?''

"Well, he was here with everyone else on Thursday night. I think you should know that Ben and Jake were extremely close, Detective.'' Why was she defending him? He'd embezzled funds from the firm, had put them all in jeopardy.

"On Thursday, was he alone in the entry hall at any time?''

"I don't know. Things were pretty hectic.'' She hesitated. "He did come back after everyone left. He wanted to discuss some personal things with me, and I guess he was alone in the hall for a few minutes.'' She wondered suddenly what Ben had told the police. Funny, but he'd completely slipped her mind.

"I understand that you're a partner in your ex-husband's firm. Were you aware of any problems going on in the office?''

Obviously, he knew. But she didn't know how much. "I'm not sure what you mean, Detective.''

"Mr. Kasden admitted to me that he's been embezzling money from several clients. Did you know anything about this?''

Her face reddened. "He told me about it Thursday night. That was the first I heard of it. I was horrified.''

"But you didn't call the police.''

"He was my friend, Detective. And he promised he was going to return all the money within a short time. I didn't know what to do. Michael thought I should call you, by the way.''

"Do you think your ex-husband knew about any of this?''

"I have no idea.'' She hesitated. "He *did* tell me about an earlier incident. Ben borrowed some money from an account. Jake was furious and told me that if Ben ever did anything like that again, he'd report him to the Real Estate Commissioner."

"That's very interesting."

"But it has nothing to do with Jake's death, Detective."

"Maybe. Are you aware that Mr. Kasden and your ex-husband took out life insurance naming each other as beneficiaries?"

"No. I had no idea."

"Quite a substantial sum, actually. The policy had a double indemnity clause. Since Mr. Vogler died of unnatural causes, Mr. Kasden will get $900,000. Interesting, isn't it?" He smiled.

"Very." She was stunned. Was that how Ben planned to solve all of his problems? Was that the "sure thing" he'd told her about? And when had he decided it would be a sure thing—before or after Jake's death?

"Mrs. Vogler?"

"Excuse me? I'm sorry; I didn't hear what you said."

"I asked you if anyone had a key to your house."

"My parents have a spare key. I have one to their house, too. And I think my in-laws still have a key."

"You never changed the locks? Not even after your ex-husband attacked you?"

"I kept meaning to, but somehow I never got around to it. I *did* have a chain on the front and side doors. And Jake knew I had a gun. I made a point of letting him know about it, especially when he started making those phone calls."

"Did your in-laws know about the gun?"

"I don't know. Jake may have told them. But I can't believe you're asking me about them! They're Jake's parents!"

"I have to consider everyone, Mrs. Vogler. They seem like nice people, by the way."

"They are. I feel terribly sorry for them. Especially for Ida. That's Jake's mother. She doted on him."

"He wasn't so close to his father?"

"They got along. But Joe, Jake's father, was upset that Jake wasn't giving me the divorce."

"Touchy situation. Looks like this *get* business made a lot of people unhappy, huh? So who else had a key?"

"That's it, I think. Oh, and my next-door neighbor. We thought it would be a good idea if each of us had a set of keys to the other's house. In case we ever got locked out."

"So let me get this straight. There were a couple of people

who had keys to this house, but they couldn't have come into the house without your knowing it because you say you never left the house all week. Is that correct?''

"Well, almost correct. I went to the funeral Thursday morning. And I spent the weekend at my parents' house. Mourning isn't permissible on the Sabbath.''

"How long were you gone?''

"I left here around four-thirty on Friday afternoon. I came back around seven-thirty Saturday night.''

"By the way, what about your ex-husband? Do you think he still had the key to this house?''

"I guess so. Unless he threw it out. But Jake couldn't very well have put the gun back.'' This was one trick even *he* couldn't have pulled off, she thought.

"Not exactly.'' Ryker grinned. But Ann Douglas could have, he thought, pleased with the information. He stood up. "Well, Mrs. Vogler, I really appreciate your help. I know this wasn't easy for you, but I hope you understand that it was necessary.''

Deena followed Ryker to the door.

"If you think of anything I should know, even something that may seem insignificant, please give me a call right away.''

"I will. Detective Ryker? I forgot to ask you. Were there any fingerprints on the gun?''

"Not one. But I wasn't really surprised. Are you?''

After Ryker had left, Deena walked slowly into the den and slumped down onto the floor. Three-quarters of the puzzle was finished, but she had no desire to look for any missing pieces.

She didn't want to think, to examine the possibilities like a cast of characters in a play. She had to talk to someone, someone safe. She tried Alan, but his secretary told her he was in court. Reuben was out, too. His soft-spoken wife apologetically explained that on Monday afternoons, he taught a Torah class for young businessmen in the area.

"Is it urgent?''

"Yes. Please ask him to call the minute he gets in.''

But when the phone rang, Deena didn't pick it up. What if the caller was one of the people she wasn't ready to face?

What Ryker was suggesting was impossible. She couldn't believe that someone who had sat in her living room or in the intimacy of her den, someone who may have hugged her, commiserated with her, assured her that everything was going to be all right, had taken her gun, used it to kill Jake, and replaced it with another weapon.

But what else could she believe?

It was worse now than when her gun had been missing, far worse. Because all that time, she'd hoped that it would miraculously turn up, or—and she had liked this even better, had clung to it with grim tenacity, a life preserver bobbing in a raging sea of disaster—she had embraced the idea of the stranger invading her house.

But Ryker had effectively squashed both possibilities.

Now she was left with the truth.

"Kasden's out on bail," Stollman said as Ryker approached his desk.

"That was quick. How much was bail?"

"Ten grand. By the way, I took a copy of Kasden's prints downtown and gave it to the lab boys. How was your meeting with Mrs. Vogler? She must've been a little surprised, huh?"

"More than a little. She was blown away. Unless she's a damn good actress, she doesn't know anything about the gun or the murder. Where are George and Tom?"

"Out for a late lunch. They should be back any minute."

"Okay. As soon as they're back, I'll fill all of you in on my discussion with Mrs. Vogler."

"Anything interesting?"

"Maybe. Lots of alibis to check out."

"Shit."

When Moran and Lewis returned, Ryker, checking his notebook occasionally, related his conversation with Deena.

"So where does that leave us?" Lewis asked. He sounded congested, but had insisted he was feeling better.

"With lots of legwork," Ryker said. "We have to follow up on all these people. Mrs. Vogler admits she doesn't have an alibi, but that in itself isn't suspicious. Why would she?"

"What about Novick?" Moran asked. "Did you check again with his assistant manager?"

"This morning. She can't be sure what time Novick left; she knows it wasn't before four-thirty, because he had a meeting with some relatives of a patient at three forty-five, and it lasted awhile."

"But that still leaves Novick wide open," Stollman said.

"Definitely," Ryker said. "Kasden was there, too, after the murder—twice, if you notice. He could've put the gun there."

"But from what you said, he didn't have an opportunity to take Mrs. Vogler's gun before the murder," Lewis said.

"I know. That's a problem. But maybe he got the gun somehow. Hell, maybe *he* was Mrs. Vogler's burglar."

"I thought you wanted Ann Douglas for that role," Lewis said. Ryker had told him about her visit the previous day. "She could've borrowed Vogler's key, taken the gun, and returned the other gun when Mrs. Vogler was away for the weekend. She could've called the house to make sure no one was home."

"Maybe," Ryker said.

"Anyway," Lewis said, "I can't believe Kasden killed Vogler. You should've seen him when I told him Vogler was dead, Sam. The man fell apart."

Stollman said, "Come on, George. If he killed him on Sunday, he had three days to practice his act for the police."

"Yeah, well so did Mrs. Vogler. Not that I think she did it. I told you all along I don't think she's the killer."

"Does Kasden have an alibi?" Stollman asked.

"He claims he was home with his wife," Ryker said. "I haven't talked to her yet, but even if he wasn't, what are the odds she'll say so? We'll have to check into everyone. Tom, the bad news is you have to go back to the women you talked to yesterday. You didn't ask them about alibis. We can probably forget Feroukhim, since she hasn't been at Mrs. Vogler's since the murder, but we may as well be thorough."

"Okay."

"Also, check out the boyfriend's alibi. I'll call the D.A.'s office about getting a subpoena if Benton still doesn't want to give you the name of the patient he says he was with."

"Right."

"Tell you what. I'll talk to the Presser woman and to Mrs. Rudman. Hank, check out the rabbi's alibi. He says he was with a study group all afternoon. Call him and get the names of the people in the group. Be diplomatic, okay? We don't need him calling the chief of police. And call the Douglas woman. Ask her if she can remember talking on the phone with someone in the afternoon, stuff like that. Try and pin her down."

"Got it."

"Also, call the Vogelanters. Tell them you forgot if they mentioned being home that Sunday, in case the son tried to call them—something along those lines. I don't want them to think we're checking their alibis. And see if they were home all day Friday and Saturday."

Stollman asked, "You don't really think the father could have done it, do you, Sam?"

"Not really. But he had a key; he may have known about the gun. We have to check him out."

"But when would he have put the gun back?" Stollman said. "I told you; they're not supposed to leave the house during the mourning period. And they're strictly Orthodox. They don't drive on the Sabbath."

"They came here to check the son's stuff, right? If the old man killed his son, I don't think a religious rule would keep him from protecting himself, do you? But if it makes you feel any better, I don't think he did it. Even though he was acting a little strange."

"Okay."

"Also, tell him the doorman mentioned he was visiting his son the week before the murder. Ask him why he didn't tell us."

"You think he was there?" Stollman asked.

"Maybe. And I'd like to clear up those other visitors. I don't like loose ends."

"What about me?" Lewis asked.

"It's your first day back; go home a little early. You still don't look great. Don't worry; we won't solve the crime before morning." He grinned.

The phone rang. Ryker picked it up. "Detective Ryker."

"Detective, this is Ann Douglas. I wanted to know what's happening with the investigation."

"We're following several leads, Miss Douglas."

"Are you making any progress?"

"Definitely. Nothing I can tell you about, though. Sorry; it's still confidential."

"Detective, there's something I forgot to mention the other day. Mr. Novick offered Jake a cash settlement for the divorce—$75,000."

"Really?"

"Yes. Jake turned it down. He said Novick was furious."

"I see."

"I thought you should know."

I'll bet you did. "We'll check into it." After he had hung up, he repeated what she'd told him.

Moran said, "So Novick was desperate. And if Vogler wouldn't take money for the divorce, maybe Novick figured his daughter would *never* be free."

"I feel sorry for her," Lewis said. "I mean, if it's her old man or boyfriend, either way, she loses."

25

SOMEHOW, DEENA KNEW IT WAS MICHAEL.

She was in the kitchen preparing a salad when she heard the side door bell. She opened the door and let him in.

"I tried calling you a few times. No one answered."

"So?" She went into the kitchen.

He followed her. "So I was worried. And curious. I thought maybe Ryker had gotten some information about the gun."

"He did." She rinsed the lettuce leaves and slapped them onto some paper towels she'd prepared. "It's not my gun."

"You mean the murder weapon isn't your gun? Well, I guess you were right. You must've misplaced it."

"That's not what I said, Michael. Ryker checked the serial numbers on the gun I gave him. It's not my father's gun. And it's not the murder weapon." She tore the lettuce and tossed the pieces into a wooden salad bowl on the counter.

"So what does that mean?"

"You figure it out. You had all the answers before."

"What's the matter with you? I come over because I'm concerned about you, and you snap at me the minute I step into the house. And why can't you look at me instead of fussing with that damn salad!"

She whirled around. "Why didn't you tell me you went to see Jake Saturday night? Why did I have to hear it from Ryker?"

"Is that what this is all about? Look, I'm sorry you're

upset. But nothing happened. I went up, we argued, and I left. That's it.''

"Then why didn't you tell me?''

"There was nothing to tell. And I'd knew you'd worry.''

"Well, I wish you had said something. I told Ryker I knew about it, but I'm not sure he believed me.''

"So what? Why are you making such a big deal about this?''

"It's not just this, Michael. He knows about the fight you and Jake had in the restaurant. Don't ask me how, but he heard about it. And he implied that he knows we're serious about each other. He asked if we planned to get married.''

"So?''

"So you have a good motive for killing Jake. And you still haven't told me where you were Sunday night.''

"How many times do I have to tell you? I was with a patient.''

"But you won't say who it is.''

"I told you; it's confidential. I told the detective the same thing.''

"I'm sure he must have been real impressed.''

"If he gets a subpoena, I'll give him the information; until then, I won't say anything about it. Not to the police, not to you. I'm sorry, but this is important to me.''

"Well, it's important to me, too. Can't you see that?''

"Frankly, I can't. I don't understand why you keep bringing this up. What do you need, an affidavit saying where I was?''

"Maybe.''

"Are you saying you don't believe me?''

She didn't answer.

"You know, I don't believe this. You're treating me as if I committed a crime just because I won't tell you the name of my patient.''

"It's not that. It's . . . everything. The gun, everything.''

"What are you saying, that you think I killed Jake? I thought we went through all that.''

"I know. But first you won't tell me where you were on Sunday night, and then I find out you had a fight with Jake on Saturday night. And there's a different gun in my closet.''

"But I found the gun. Why would I point it out to you?''

"You could be trying to divert attention from yourself. You

could've figured that the police would test the gun, find out it wasn't the murder weapon, and drop the whole thing.''

"Who put that idea into your head? Ryker?'' He saw her expression. "It *was* Ryker, wasn't it?''

"That's not the point.''

"Well, I didn't do it. Look, I know you're having a hard time, and I can see how this gun development can throw you, but you have to make up your mind whether or not you trust me.''

"I want to believe you. I don't really care if you did kill Jake. I know that sounds crazy, but that's how I feel. I just have to know the truth. So I can figure out what to do.''

He put his hands on her shoulders. "Deena, as God as my witness, I did not kill Jake. I swear it. I should've told you about Saturday night; it was a mistake to keep it from you. And about Sunday night, I was with a patient from around six-thirty till eight-thirty. She was threatening suicide, and I finally had her admitted to a hospital. But I can't tell you her name.''

"But you'll tell the police if they get a subpoena.''

"Yes.''

"Okay.'' She tried to relax. "Ryker wanted to know who had access to the gun and the house.'' She repeated their conversation. "So it has to be someone who was here before and after the murder. And that means it's someone I know, not an anonymous burglar.''

Michael was silent for a while. "Have you considered the women in your support group? Maybe one of them freaked out and killed Jake to rid herself symbolically of her own husband.''

"Are you serious?''

"I don't know. It's possible. You tell me.''

"Well, forget Magda. She wasn't here after the murder.''

"Okay. Who was?''

"Michael, come on.''

"No. Let's eliminate everyone we can.''

"Okay.'' She sighed. "Well, you can forget Susan, too. She's getting her *get*. Her father's paying off her husband.''

"So maybe she resents having to pay blackmail. What about the woman who called you the other day?''

"Elaine?''

"Yeah, Elaine. Why was she so nervous about the police knowing that she met Jake?''

"I told you. She's always nervous."

"Was she in the entry hall alone?"

Deena thought for a moment. "Yes. Remember when she stormed out of the room? She said she needed a cigarette, and she wouldn't want to smoke in front of—" She frowned.

"In front of what? Why'd you stop?"

"Elaine gave up smoking a month ago. We've all been encouraging her." She looked at Michael. "But maybe she started again, when she heard about Jake's death."

"Maybe. Okay. What about Faye? She's been in this boat for eleven years, right? Maybe she just snapped."

Deena shook her head.

"I know you two are close, but you have to be objective."

"No, it's not that. Faye couldn't have done it. She was with her in-laws all afternoon and evening."

"So where does that leave us?"

"Nowhere," she said glumly.

"You think it's your father, don't you?"

She sighed. "I don't know what to think."

"Talk about it. You won't feel any worse; it might help you sort out your feelings."

"It isn't very complicated, Michael. My father hated Jake. He knew Jake tried to rape me; he knew about the phone calls. He was in the house often. Obviously, he knew about the gun."

"But you really think he would've killed him?"

"Maybe he didn't mean to kill him. Maybe he only wanted to frighten Jake into giving me the *get.*"

"I don't know your father well, but he doesn't strike me as someone who would take a gun and threaten someone with it."

"But he was so angry, Michael. And so worried about me. And about my mother."

"Okay. But it's not like the police have any evidence against him. Were there any fingerprints on the gun?"

"No."

"So the gun in itself doesn't prove anything. Who else had access? Have we mentioned everyone?"

"There's Ben Kasden. By the way, Ryker said Ben confessed to embezzling funds. I'm glad it didn't come from me."

"He did? What else did Ryker say?"

"He said that Ben and Jake had partners' insurance. Ben's going to get a lot of money. I think Ryker said $900,000."

Michael whistled. "People have killed for a hell of a lot less, Deena. So that's how he was going to repay all the money he took! And Ben was here Thursday night. Twice. And I left him alone in the entry hall for a few minutes. He had plenty of time to put the gun in the closet! Don't you see what a strong motive he had to kill Jake? With Jake alive, he faced going to jail; with Jake dead, no one would have to know a thing. Why didn't you mention this earlier?"

"I considered him. But when could he have taken my gun?"

"Maybe he was the burglar you told me about."

"You told me that was my imagination."

"Well, maybe I was wrong. You don't remember him coming over any time before the murder? No social calls? No business to take care of? Papers to sign?"

"I don't—wait a minute." She concentrated. "He *did* come over to the house recently. He had some papers for me to sign. Quarterly tax stuff. I don't know exactly when, but it was definitely before the murder."

"Are you sure?"

"I don't know why I forgot about it, Michael, but I'm positive! He was here. And I remember now. We were in the dining room, and he told me to look at the papers, and then he asked me if I had some aspirin. I offered to get him some, but he insisted on doing it himself. It's all so clear to me now!"

"So was he gone long?"

"I don't know. I was busy checking the papers."

"Call Ryker."

"I don't know, Michael. What if it's not connected? Ben could have been getting aspirin, just like he said."

"That's for Ryker to decide, Deena."

"You're probably right."

"What is it? Why are you hesitating?"

"It's just that with the embezzlement and the insurance money, this is going to make Ben look very suspect."

"That's not your problem, Deena."

"I know. But what if he's not involved? Ryker will think Ben is guilty because of the other charges."

"Listen, Deena, you have to face facts. You've known Ben for a long time, and he's always been great. But until last week you would never have believed that he stole from his clients. If he stole out of desperation, who's to say he didn't kill for the same reason?''

"I guess.''

"Your problem is that you don't want it to be anyone you know. I can understand that. Well, I didn't do it. So unfortunately, as far as I can see, that leaves Ben and your father.''

"I'll call Ryker.''

"So what do we have, guys?'' Ryker said. "Hank?''

"The rabbi checks out. I spoke to three men in his group. They can vouch for him from early afternoon through the evening services at the synagogue.''

"Didn't they break for supper?'' Moran asked.

"They had refreshments after the study session, and stayed with the rabbi in the synagogue until eight.''

"So that's that,'' Ryker said. "I never really considered him anyway. What about the Vogelanters?''

"You were right about the father. Mrs. Vogelanter was out of the room for a few minutes, so I had a chance to talk to him. He did go to see his son the Saturday night before the murder. He admitted he was angry with his son for not giving his daughter-in-law the divorce. He went to his apartment to reason with him.''

"What about Friday and Saturday?''

Stollman said, "I spoke to a couple of neighbors. They told me people were visiting the Vogelanters all weekend. It would've been hard for the old man to leave the house.''

"But not impossible. We may have to check further.''

"I also called Ann Douglas. She was really pissed. Said she didn't have to answer my questions, that she came to you with information—all that shit. The bottom line is she says she was home the whole time, but she has no way of proving it.''

"So she's still a possibility. Tom, what did you learn?''

"The Feroukhim woman spent the day with friends in San Diego. She gave me their name and phone number. I called and they confirmed she was there from around eleven in the morning till nine. They went to Sea World, the zoo. The works.

"Next, Susan Bergman. She's the one I told you about last time—she's getting her divorce, remember? She was with her parents all day. I checked. Then, at night, she and a friend—

male, by the way—went to dinner and a show. She gave me the name of the guy; he wasn't in when I called, but I'm sure he'll confirm what she said."

"No surprises so far," Ryker said.

"Nope. That leaves Miriam Kalinsky. She teaches a Sunday Hebrew class from two to four. A babysitter watches the kids during that time. After the class, she took the kids to visit some friends; then they all went out for pizza. They got back around seven-thirty. She spent the evening doing homework with her kids, putting them to bed. By the way, I asked the women if they had contact with Vogler. I forgot to do that yesterday."

"And?"

"They all said the only time they saw him was the night he attacked his wife. But that's a little funny."

"Why?"

"Well, Mrs. Kalinsky said that Mrs. Presser and Mrs. Bergman had met Vogler another time."

"So why wouldn't the Bergman woman remember?" Stollman asked.

Moran said, "Maybe she just doesn't want to get involved. A lot of people are like that. Anyway, she has a solid alibi."

Stollman said, "Sam, what about Benton? Did you talk to the D.A. about getting a subpoena?"

"No go. First we have to show probable cause. I paid Benton a visit, by the way, figured I'd try pressuring him, but he wouldn't budge."

Moran said, "How do you read him?"

Ryker frowned. "Hard to say. He sounded apologetic, but who the hell knows? Maybe he's a good actor. And I met with Faye Rudman. Talk about sad cases. The woman has been in this limbo situation for eleven years. Husband's in a private institution; paranoid schizophrenic."

"Jeez!" Moran muttered.

"Anyway, I asked her about Vogler. She admitted she didn't think much of him, but said she always thought he'd come around eventually. I asked her about the night he attacked Mrs. Vogler, by the way. She said it was awful."

"What's this Rudman woman like?" Stollman asked.

"Classy. Pretty, in a tired kind of way. She was nervous, but so are most people when the police come asking questions."

"So where was she, in the park with her kids?" Moran asked.

"No kids. She was with her in-laws. They live in Beverly Hills. Seems she had to go over some financial papers with them, and once she got there—around two, she says—they persuaded her to spend the day. She didn't get home till around nine. I checked with the in-laws. They confirmed her story."

"What about this Mrs. Presser?" Moran asked.

"Now *she* was nervous. And she seemed in a real hurry to get rid of me. Practically didn't want to let me into the house. Then again, I could hear her kids in the background; maybe she didn't want them to be frightened."

Moran asked, "So what's her story? Divorce-wise, I mean."

"Seems her husband remarried, a civil ceremony. She's real bitter about that, let me tell you. She thought Vogler was a creep, but I got the impression she thinks most men are creeps."

"Except for you, right, Sam?" Moran smiled. "I'm sure you turned on the old charm."

"It didn't work. She didn't even offer me water."

Moran asked, "Did you ask her if she saw Vogler more than once? I'm curious, after what Mrs. Kalinsky said."

"She only mentioned the time at Mrs. Vogler's. I think we'll have to check that out."

"Does the Presser woman have an alibi?"

"She says she was home doing some gardening and going through some closets. Typical Sunday, I guess."

"Where were her kids?" Moran asked.

"With her ex-husband and his new wife. It was his Sunday."

"So no alibi," Moran said. "Interesting. And she had access to Mrs. Vogler's gun, and she could've put the other gun in the closet, right?"

"Right," Ryker said. "But she doesn't seem likely."

The phone rang. Ryker spoke for a while, then hung up.

"That was Mrs. Vogler. She just remembered that Kasden was at her house before the murder. It seems he brought over some business papers for her to sign. And she says he needed some aspirin, insisted on getting them himself."

"She just remembered that?" Moran asked.

"I know what you're thinking. I'm wondering the same

thing. She's trying to get us off her father and her boyfriend. On the other hand, she could be telling the truth."

"What's your gut feeling?" Stollman asked.

"That I'm hungry." Ryker smiled. "I forgot to eat lunch."

A plainclothes detective from burglary walked over. "Any of you guys interested in talking to someone named Futrell? Their call got transferred to our division by mistake."

Moran jumped. "I'll talk to them." He turned to Ryker. "That's the couple from the open house. They were away on vacation, remember? I left a note at their house the last time I stopped by." He left with the other detective.

When Moran returned a few minutes later, he was grinning.

"What?" Ryker asked.

"This could be something. The Futrells were at the open house around three-thirty. The husband remembers the time because he kept checking his watch. Seems he had to pick up his kid from soccer practice at four, and he didn't want to be late. Anyway, when they were there, someone stopped by to see Vogler, and they had a few angry words."

"Who?" Ryker asked.

"Hold on." Moran was enjoying himself. "The Futrells were kind of embarrassed, so they walked into another room, but they couldn't help hearing what the man was saying."

"Come on, Tom. Get to it," Stollman said.

"Okay. The man said he had to talk with Vogler, and Vogler told him he couldn't talk. 'You of all people should know better than to bother me right now,' Vogler said, or something like that. He told him to come back later, after five. The Futrells said he was kind of short, more than a little overweight. Very round, they said. And almost completely bald."

"Kasden?" Ryker said.

"Sounds like it. We can get a picture of Kasden and have them identify him. So what do you think? Is Kasden our man?"

"Looks like a definite maybe," Ryker said. "Where do we get a picture? He's been booked, but I don't want to use a mug shot; that would prejudice the Futrells, and the judge would throw the case out in two minutes."

"We can check through Vogler's stuff," Stollman said. "Maybe he's got some pictures with Kasden. Or ask Mrs. Vogler. There must be a shot of him in their wedding album. He was the partner and from what I understand, a close friend.''

Ryker said, ''Good thinking, Hank. Call her now, okay?''

''Okay.'' Stollman got up and walked to his desk.

''The only thing is,'' Ryker said to Moran, ''even if Kasden was at the house at three-thirty, and Vogler told him to come back later, that doesn't mean he did come back. He could've decided to talk to Vogler the next day. We'll have to show the picture, if we find one, to Mrs. Pearson, too.''

''Yeah, maybe her cat can identify him.'' He grinned.

The phone rang again. Ryker picked it up quickly. ''Ryker.''

''Sam? Marty. This is your lucky day. We have a positive match on the prints you guys dropped off with some prints we found at the Sherbourne house.''

''Let me guess.'' Ryker smiled. ''Ben Kasden?''

''Right. That's one of them.''

''What do you mean, 'one'?''

''We have another positive match. Max Novick.''

26

''WHERE'D YOU FIND THE PRINTS, MARTY?'' RYKER ASKED.

''Kasden's were on the faucet in the main bathroom. Novick's were on the light switch and switch plate in the bedroom where the body was found. I have to hand it to you, Sam. The prints you got on the wallet and card were damn good. You oughta think about becoming a detective.''

''Right. Thanks, Marty.'' He hung up and turned to Moran and to Stollman, who was approaching the desk. ''SID matched prints on Kasden and Novick.''

''No shit!'' Moran exclaimed. ''Now what?''

''My money's on Kasden,'' Stollman said. ''The man had to be desperate what with all the money he embezzled and Murdoch breathing down his neck. And the description Tom got from the Futrells sounds exactly like him.''

"I don't know," Ryker said. "I agree about the description, but at least Kasden had a reason for being there. It was his firm; he could've been stopping by to talk business with his partner. I can't think of a reason for Novick to be there. And he didn't admit he was there when I talked to him."

"Would you?" Stollman asked. "He was probably afraid he'd look guilty if he admitted he was anywhere near the area."

"Maybe. But he has motive, opportunity; he could easily have picked up the gun."

"You want me to forget about getting Kasden's picture?" Stollman asked. "I talked to Mrs. Vogler; she said okay."

"No, we have to check Kasden out, too. Try to get a picture that has Kasden *and* Novick. As a matter of fact, do that right now, okay? Mrs. Vogler will be more cooperative before we question her father."

"Okay. What's next?"

"I think I'm going to have to bring Novick in."

"You're going to arrest him?" Moran asked.

Ryker sighed. "Yeah, I am. Otherwise, I can't force him to answer any questions. I think I can show probable cause."

"You don't seem so happy," Stollman said.

"I like the guy. He was uncooperative as hell, but there's something about him. I was kind of hoping Kasden was our man."

"But you still think Novick did it?"

"I still think he did it. Everything points to him."

"George isn't going to like this one bit," Moran said.

"Why not?" Ryker asked.

"You promised him you wouldn't solve this case tonight."

By the time the judge signed the warrants, it was six-twenty, and it was almost twenty minutes later when Ryker pulled up in front of the house on Fuller. Moran and Stollman were with him.

Ryker rang the bell and waited.

Max opened the door. "Detective. I know why you're here. I promised to call you and I didn't, right? I'm sorry; I got so busy, I didn't even have time to call my wife. So what can I do for you?"

"Can we come in, Mr. Novick?"

"Of course. Please." He stepped aside to let them enter

and closed the door behind them. "So. Now. I hope this won't take long, because my wife said supper will be ready in about twenty minutes, and she doesn't like for the food to get cold. She just went next door for a few minutes." He smiled.

Ryker took a folded paper out of his inner pocket. "Mr. Novick, I have a warrant to search the premises. You can accompany my men while they search, if you like."

"So search, if you want. What you expect to find, I don't know."

"We'd like to start upstairs."

Max led the silent procession to the second floor. The detectives searched all the rooms efficiently and methodically, poking expertly through closets, emptying pockets, purses, drawers, medicine cabinets, shoe boxes. Everything. When they finished, they were meticulous about returning every item to its proper home.

When Pearl came back, she found them opening the china closet in her dining room. She stared at the men. "Max?"

"It's nothing," he told her. "They're just checking something out. Go in the kitchen; I'll be there soon."

She left the room obediently, but cast an anxious backward glance at the strangers who had invaded her home and were touching her things.

"Nothing here," Moran told Ryker.

"What other rooms are there downstairs?" Ryker asked Max.

"A breakfast room, the kitchen. You want to check the pots, go ahead. I think my wife made stew tonight." He tried a smile, but it was stillborn.

"What else?"

"A powder room. And a den."

"Let's check the den first," Ryker told Moran and Stollman. He waited politely for Max to lead the way, a host held hostage by his uninvited guests.

There were books and photographs, other memorabilia. The detectives looked behind the gilt-edged, leather-bound volumes of a set of *Britannica,* behind an equally impressive collection of texts with foreign-looking letters.

"Hebrew," Stollman said in an undertone to Ryker.

In a cabinet beneath the bookshelves, Moran found a midnight-blue velvet bag adorned with multicolored embroidery stitches forming a crown surrounded by two lions. He started to open the zippered closure.

"This is a religious article," Max said. "My *tefillin*. I don't know how to translate this, but it is very, very holy. I use it to pray every weekday."

"Phylacteries," Stollman said to Moran and Ryker.

"We'll be careful," Ryker said.

Moran opened the bag. Inside was a fringed prayer shawl, a small prayer book, and another, smaller velvet bag with identical embroidery. He unzipped the pouch, gingerly withdrew the cowhide-encased boxes, and set them on the den table.

"Sam," he called quietly.

Ryker walked to him with quick steps and looked inside the pouch. Careful not to smudge any prints, he pulled out a gold watch and a folded packet of $20 bills. The watch was a Rolex. He looked at the back. "To Jake, from Max and Pearl."

"Mr. Novick, do you want to explain how these items came to be in your possession?" Ryker asked.

Max stood speechless. His face, sagging and drained of color, was gray putty.

Ryker withdrew another document from his pocket. "Mr. Novick, I have a warrant for your arrest for the murder of Jake Vogler. I'm going to take you in for questioning."

"Can I—" He cleared his throat. "Can I call my lawyer?"

"Yes."

Max walked with aged steps to the phone, picked up the receiver, and held it without dialing.

"Mr. Novick," Ryker prompted, "please make your call."

"Right. I couldn't think for a minute." His fingers shaking, he flipped through the alphabet tabs in a black address book on the table near the couch and found the number he wanted.

"Alan Krantz, please." His voice was hoarse. "Max Novick." He listened. "I'll hold, but tell him it's an emergency." He waited a moment. "Alan? The police are here. They just arrested me for Jake's murder." He turned to Ryker. "My lawyer wants to know where you're taking me."

"Wilshire Division on Venice."

Max repeated the information into the phone. "Right. Okay. No, I won't say a thing." He hung up and faced Ryker.

"You're going to have to come with us now, Mr. Novick."

"Can I take a few things with me?"

"I'm afraid not."

"I need my *tefillin*. And my *tallis* and prayer book." He pointed to the articles that Moran had placed on the den table.

"I don't think the jailer will allow you to take them in. I'm sorry, but they're very strict."

"Can you ask them? Please? It's very important."

"Your lawyer can talk to them. Maybe he can get your rabbi to call. But frankly, I doubt that they'll cooperate."

Max nodded. "I'll ask my lawyer. One thing. I don't want my wife should be too upset. Do you have to put on handcuffs? I know in all the television shows they always put on handcuffs."

"It's policy."

"It's not like I'm Charles Bronson, right, Detective?" Max smiled grimly. "I'm not going to run away. If you have to, you can put them on in the car."

Ryker hesitated. "Okay. I think we can do that. You'd better tell your wife you're going now."

"One more thing, Detective Ryker. I don't want to leave my wife alone. She's not well, you see. Could I call someone to stay with her?" His eyes were imploring.

"One call," Ryker agreed.

Max picked up the phone, hesitated, and dialed. "Deena? It's Daddy."

They met in the interrogation room, a small cubicle that seemed devoid of air and compassion. Max and Alan sat across from Ryker. A stenographer sat in a chair near the desk. Stollman stood lounging against the far wall.

Ryker officially began the session by identifying himself by name and rank and stating the date and Max's full name.

"Mr. Novick, I've already advised you of your rights, is that correct?"

Max nodded.

"Please say yes."

"Yes."

"Are you prepared to make a statement at this time, Mr. Novick, concerning the charges against you?"

"My client will answer certain questions in regard to the charge against him," Alan said.

"Mr. Novick, we have conclusive fingerprint evidence that

proves that you were at the crime scene. Can you explain that?''

Max looked at Alan. Alan nodded. ''I was at that house, but I didn't kill Jake. He was dead when I got there.''

''What time did you get there?''

''I'm not sure exactly. I think it was around five-thirty.''

''Did you go in immediately?''

''No. I sat in my car awhile.''

''Why is that?''

''Why? I don't know why. I was trying to figure out what to say to Jake. I wanted to make him see that he was ruining his own life, not just Deena's. I didn't want to fight, just to convince him.''

''So how long did you sit in the car?''

''I don't know. About five, ten minutes. I can't say.''

''Did you see anyone leave when you were going in?''

''I didn't see anyone leaving when I was going in, no.''

''When did you pick up the gun from your daughter's house?''

''I never picked up the gun. I gave it to her weeks ago, months maybe, and I haven't seen it since then.''

''Mr. Novick, when we searched your home we found certain articles that we believe belonged to Mr. Vogler and were on his person when he was killed. Can you explain how they came into your possession?''

''No comment,'' Alan said.

''The watch we found is identical to a watch described by the Vogelanters as one you gave to Mr. Vogler. The inscription on the back reads 'To Jake, from Max and Pearl.' ''

''No comment,'' Alan repeated.

''Did you have an argument—is that what happened?''

''I told you, Detective; Jake was dead when I got there.''

''When I questioned you several days ago about the last time you saw Mr. Vogler, you lied to me, didn't you?''

''No, Detective, I did *not* lie.''

''I'm afraid you did, Mr. Novick. You told me that you hadn't seen Mr. Vogler since the week before his death.''

''That's not what I said, Detective. I told you that the last time I *talked* to Jake was a week before he was killed. But that's not a lie. How could I talk to him when he was dead?''

''This isn't a funny matter, Mr. Novick.''

''I'm not joking. I was very careful in what I said to you, Detective. I don't lie.''

"You were harassing your son-in-law, Mr. Novick. With phone calls, letters. Bothering his clients."

"Yes." He nodded.

"Did you ever threaten to kill him?"

"I don't remember doing that."

"We have a witness who says you threatened Mr. Vogler."

"If you have a witness, you have a witness. Maybe I said I wanted to kill him; people say crazy things when they're angry. Sure, I didn't like him. It's no secret. But kill him?" He shook his head. "No."

"Where did you get the other gun, Mr. Novick?"

"What other gun?"

"The one you put in your daughter's entry hall closet."

"I think you're trying to confuse me, Detective. I don't know of any other gun, and again, I'm telling you I never took the gun from Deena's house."

"What if I told you that we have your fingerprints on the gun that killed your son-in-law?"

"Then, you'll excuse me, Detective, but I would have to say that you're lying. Because it can't be."

"You wiped them off?"

"I never took the gun. Period."

Ryker sighed. "All right. That's enough for today." He got up, opened the door, and asked the guard to take Max back to his cell. "You can go now," he told the stenographer.

"What about bail?" Alan asked when they were alone.

"No way. Not in a homicide. He'll probably be arraigned within forty-eight hours."

"What's the D.A. going for?"

"I'd say you're looking at murder one. It was obviously premeditated."

"All you have is circumstantial evidence. My client claims he's innocent."

"Come on, Krantz; they all do."

"I believe him."

"Good. I hope you do your best to get him off." He stood up to show that the interview was over.

"What about his religious articles? It's imperative that he has them to pray."

"I'll tell you what I told him. Have a rabbi or two call up and apply some pressure. Don't quote me on this, but you can threaten to go to the papers and get some headlines about freedom of religion. That always gets them going."

"Thanks. I'll get on it right away."

"Good luck." He meant it.

"So what did you think?" Stollman asked Ryker when they were back in the squad room.

"I don't know. The evidence is pretty damning. It puts him at the scene of the crime. I bet we find Vogler's prints on the money." They had handed the cash over to the latent print unit.

"The thing is, I can't figure out why he didn't dispose of it. I mean, I figure he took the stuff to make it look like a burglar did it, right?"

"That's the way I see it," Ryker said.

"But he must've realized that if we ever searched his house, we'd find the stuff."

"That's the point, Hank. He probably thought we'd never search his house. Finding his print on the switch plate was lucky. For us, that is. Without that print, the judge would never have signed the search warrant."

"Novick claims Vogler was dead when he got there."

"Of course he'd say that. He has to say something. He can't deny he was there, can he? Not with his prints there."

"So why don't you sound convinced?"

"I don't know. It's nothing I can put my finger on, Hank. Something's gnawing at me, but I don't know what. I'll tell you one thing that bothers me. He says Vogler was dead when he got there. That could be bullshit, but then again, I've been trying to figure out all along why Vogler was still there so late."

"What do you mean?"

"Well, look at the time schedule. The last couple signed in at the Open House at four-forty. Figure they stayed fifteen, twenty minutes. A half-hour, tops. That's if they were really interested. So that means that by five, or the latest five-ten, Vogler was finished. Why did he stick around? I mean, how long would it take him to pack up his stuff and get out? He'd been there all day; I would think he'd want to relax, have a drink."

"I see what you mean."

"And Mrs. Pearson said she was in and out of her kitchen from before five till the time she saw someone—we'll assume it's Novick—going in the front door. That means that someone could've gone in between five and the time Novick arrived.''

"Are you saying you think he *didn't* kill him?''

"No, I'm not saying that. I just don't like the gap. I want to find out what Vogler was doing in that half-hour. If Novick's lawyer is smart, he can convince a jury that someone other than Novick *could* have killed Vogler.''

"Maybe our time frame is off, Sam. Maybe someone came in without signing the list.''

"Good point. We should've thought of that. Let's call the last couple, see if they remember someone coming in after them.'' Ryker checked his notes. "Here it is. Corcoran. Issac and Julia.'' He dialed and waited for someone to answer. After identifying himself, he spoke for a few minutes and hung up.

"Well?'' Stollman asked.

"As far as the wife remembers, they were the last ones there. They stayed till almost five. Not conclusive, but it's something. I don't know what, though. I forgot to ask you, Hank. Did you get the pictures from Mrs. Vogler?''

"Yeah. Sorry; with all the excitement, I forgot all about them. I went there while you were getting the warrants. She was very cooperative. Wait a second. I left them on my desk.''

He came back with a manila envelope and pulled out two pictures. "These are some of the proofs, so they're smaller, but you can still make out the faces clearly. Here's one with Novick and Kasden and some other guests. Here's another with Kasden and his wife, Vogler, and Mrs. Vogler.''

"Show them to Mrs. Pearson in the morning, will you? See if she can identify Novick or Kasden. Then go to the Futrells.''

"Will do. What are you going to do now?''

"I'm going home. It's been a hell of a day. I plan to sit in front of the television with my wife and watch some silly sitcom and forget all about this damn business.''

"I'm sorry it took so long,'' Alan told Deena after she let him in. "I know how anxious you must be.''

"Where's my father?''

"Let's sit down.'' He steered her into the breakfast room. "Tell me what's happening, Alan.''

"It's not good. They police found your father's fingerprints at the crime scene."

"Oh, my God!"

"That's not all. They had a search warrant, and they found a watch and some cash that they think belonged to Jake."

"How can they possibly know that?"

"They have to check the money for Jake's prints, but the watch has an inscription from your parents. It's a Rolex."

"My parents gave that to Jake when we got engaged. He always wore it." Her tone was hushed with despair. "But what did he say, Alan? How did he explain it?"

"That's the problem. He refused to tell me anything. He swears he didn't kill Jake, but he won't tell me a thing about the watch. I told him he's burying himself if he doesn't tell me the truth, but he won't budge."

"You have to make him tell you, Alan."

"I'll keep trying, but I think you know how stubborn he is. Look, tomorrow I'll try to arrange for you to see him. Maybe you can convince him to talk to me."

The front doorbell rang.

"You sit," Alan told her. "I'll get it."

He returned a minute later with Faye, who moved quickly to Deena and hugged her.

"How did you know?" Deena asked.

"Michael called. He said he was here at your house when your father phoned."

"I didn't even hear him. I guess I'm a little out of it."

"I don't know what to say. I never thought it would come to this! God, it's so awful! How's your mother doing?"

"She's asleep in my bedroom. Her doctor came and gave her a sedative. Michael picked her up and brought her here after my father called. He thought it would be best."

"I think he's right," Alan said. "Is Michael here now?"

"He left for a while, but he's coming back soon."

"I don't want to leave you alone," Alan said.

"I'll stay," Faye said. "I planned to, anyway."

"Good. I have some things to take care of. I want to call a few rabbis and get them to pressure the police department."

"Why?" Deena asked.

Alan explained about the *tefillin*. "Ryker suggested that the rabbis call."

"I'll bet he's real concerned," Deena said.

"He's only doing his job, Deena. You have to admit that the circumstantial evidence looks pretty bad for your father."

"What do you mean?" Faye asked.

Deena explained about the fingerprints, the watch, and the money. "And I don't think I told you about the gun."

"What about the gun?" Faye asked.

"Remember I told you Michael found the gun Saturday night? Well, it's not my father's gun."

"How can they know that?" Faye asked.

"They checked the serial numbers. The gun I gave Detective Ryker isn't registered. Do you see what that means?"

"I guess so. But it *is* only circumstantial. They can't convict someone on circumstantial evidence, can they, Alan?"

"I wish I could say it's never happened."

"Something will turn up to prove he's innocent, Deena," Faye said. "You'll see."

"I hope you're right. Can I ask you something, Alan?"

"Sure."

"I want the truth. Do you think my father did it?"

"No, I don't. But he's not helping his case by refusing to tell me the whole truth."

"But why isn't he talking? It doesn't make any sense!"

"It does if you look at it from one point."

"What's that?"

"Well, I figure that he took the stuff to make it look like a burglary. That's pretty obvious. But the only thing that could explain his not talking is that he did it not to protect himself, but to protect someone else."

"Who?"

He looked at her. "I think that's obvious, Deena. You."

27

AT THREE-THIRTY ON TUESDAY, BEN KASDEN WAS ONCE again sitting across the desk from Ryker. Once again, his attorney was at his side, holding his client in check with invisible reins.

"I know this was short notice, Mr. Kasden," Ryker said. "I appreciate your cooperation."

Ryker had fully expected Kasden to snort with resentment, but the man, definitely subdued, was wearing contrition like an ill-fitting suit that constricted his movement.

"I want to help you solve Jake's murder; I really do."

"Mr. Kasden, we have conclusive evidence and eyewitnesses who place you at the Sherbourne house on the afternoon of October 29th, the day that Jake Vogler was killed. Any comment?" The Futrells had positively identified Kasden in the photo that Stollman had shown them earlier that morning.

"Listen, Detective—" Kasden began eagerly.

Tischler put a restraining hand on Kasden's arm. "Are you placing my client under arrest?"

"Not at this time." Ryker smiled at both men blandly.

"Then he doesn't have to answer your questions."

"Bryan, I want to answer him! I have nothing to hide!"

"Ben, I think it would be in your best interests if you said nothing right now."

"I know what I'm doing." He faced Ryker. "You're right about my being there. I wanted to talk to Jake about Murdoch. But that was at three-thirty, and when I left, Jake was as alive as you and I are. If you're wondering why I didn't tell you about it earlier, well, it was a dumb mistake, because I know you're wondering whether I'm telling you the truth right now. And I guess I don't blame you. But I am.

"The truth is—and I'm ashamed to admit it—I had so many other problems going on that I didn't want to get involved, and seeing as how I knew I left Jake alive and well, I didn't see the harm in not telling you I'd been there.'' He fixed Ryker with an earnest gaze that the detective found mildly repellent.

"The witnesses also overheard Mr. Vogler asking you to return after five. And we have another witness who saw a male of your description entering the house after five.''

That was as general a statement as Ryker felt he could get away with. Mrs. Pearson had been unable to make a positive identification of either Kasden or Novick from the pictures.

"No way! No way can you place me at the Sherbourne house twice that day, 'cause it simply didn't happen. I decided to leave it till Monday morning. Ruthie and I were home. Ask her; she'll tell you—and not 'cause she's my wife. You want to know the truth? This is a little embarrassing, but okay.''

He smiled with the boyish candor of someone who was caught with his pudgy hand in the cookie jar and crumbs on his lips. "We rented a couple of X-rated movies at the video place. We figured what the hell, we're alone in the house— our daughter's back East in some fancy college. If we're not adults now, when will we be, right?''

"I have the receipt from the video place, and I can tell you everything we saw, if you don't believe me. But between you and me, it wasn't what I expected, you know what I mean?'' He grinned and shook his head in conspiratorial disappointment.

And that was it. Ryker had no way of telling whether Kasden was telling the truth—the man could have seen the video at any time, and the receipt was proof of nothing. But it didn't matter, and they both knew it. Unless Ryker found someone who could place Kasden at the Sherbourne house after five, Kasden's alibi would remain as unshakable as granite.

Ryker didn't fare any better with Novick. He met with him again on Tuesday morning, but despite the detective's efforts to trap him into inconsistencies, Novick didn't deviate one inch from his original statement. And he still remained stubbornly silent about the watch and the money—money which, according to SID, had definitely been handled by Vogler.

"I don't know why you're picking this thing to death,'' Moran said to Ryker after Kasden had left with his attorney. "We have Novick in custody with a clear case against him.''

"I told you why. I want to sew up that thirty-minute gap. It bothers the hell out of me. I don't want to be tripped up by it in court."

"Figure it this way," Moran said. "The last couple left at five. But Vogler doesn't know that no one else is going to show up, right? So he sits around, looking pretty, in case a prospect comes along. Then, at around five-fifteen or five-twenty, Vogler decides to close up shop. We know he removed the pennant, right? And he went around collecting stuff to put back in his little blue tote. So let's say he's finished by five-thirty. Then he takes a cold soda from the fridge and relaxes in the air-conditioned house before he goes out into the sweltering heat."

Stollman grinned. "God, Tom, you could have been a real Hemingway with that final touch."

"Glad you like it. Seriously, doesn't it fit, Sam?"

"Maybe. What the hell, you're probably right. I'm just disappointed about Kasden. I mean $900,000—that's some motive! He's such a weasel, and he's slipping right out of our hands."

"Maybe his wife did it," Moran said. "Maybe Kasden told her that Vogler was going to turn him in to the commissioner, and she saw her spending money going up in smoke."

"Maybe," Ryker said, 'but I doubt it. Mrs. Pearson said she saw a man. In any case, they're giving each other alibis."

"What's with the embezzlement charge?" Stollman asked.

"From what I hear, Kasden's lawyer is running around like crazy trying to get all these releases signed. When I saw him this morning, he said he's 'cautiously optimistic.' I don't think he's tackled Murdoch, though."

"Will the insurance company pay up?" Stollman asked.

"Not yet. They're waiting to see what happens with the murder case. But with Novick in jail, Kasden looks pretty confident. He sure didn't seem all that worried just now."

"So if he's not the killer, he gets all that money." Moran sounded miserable. "It doesn't seem fair. Even if he ends up spending a year in county, he comes out better than all of us."

"It's the American way," Stollman said. "Get used to it."

"Speaking of the American way," Moran said, "some rabbis pressured the chief into letting Novick use his prayer stuff."

"Yeah?" Ryker said. "Well, why not. Doesn't hurt anyone."

"Of course, a guard's with him all the time," Moran said, "making sure he doesn't use those straps for anything irregular. And he's getting some kosher food, too. Some organization is sending in meals that are wrapped and sealed."

"I knew Orthodox Jews eat only kosher," Ryker said, "but even in jail?"

"Uh-huh," Stollman said. "They're very strict about it."

Ryker said, "It's strange that a man with that kind of religious conviction would kill someone, don't you think? I guess he was desperate. You know what? I don't know what I would do if someone tried to mess up my kid's life like that."

"You wouldn't kill, Sam," Stollman said.

Ryker shrugged. "I sure as hell hope not. Anyway, enough philosophy for a squad room, right? You guys leaving?"

"I am," Moran said. "See you in the morning. And cheer up, Sam; maybe Novick will be a little more talkative."

"By the way," Moran said, "I filled George in on what's been happening. He picked a fine time to have a relapse."

"I told him he came back too soon," Ryker said.

"I'm going, too," Stollman said. "Before I forget, Sam, the Vogelanters called when you were interrogating Kasden. They want to know if they can have their son's effects. I said they probably could, since everything's been printed. I told them you'd call. I left the message on your desk."

"I'll take care of it. See you in the morning."

Ryker shuffled among his papers until he found the slip Stollman had left. He called the Vogelanters and promised them that barring any unforeseen snags, they'd receive their son's possessions within a few days.

There really wasn't much to give them. The financial papers might be important for the lawyers and the accountants. The watch had to stay in evidence; he'd told that to the Vogelanters this morning at their apartment, had shocked them with the news of Novick's arrest, had watched their faces crumble with disbelief into a thousand tiny wounded fragments of hurt and betrayal.

The eel-skin wallet was nice. Ryker picked it up, rubbed his hand along the baby-soft skin. Maybe he'd hint to Linda about getting him one for Christmas. He opened the wallet, looked at the handsome, living face of Jake Vogler protected by a slightly scratched, clear plastic sleeve. There was no way of knowing what had lain behind those smiling gray eyes.

From the compartment where the bills would have been (if Novick hadn't removed them; stupid of him), a pink folded paper protruded like a slip peeking out past the hemline of a skirt. Ryker looked at it, then drew it out like a rabbit from a hat.

He had no idea what it was doing there.

He knew with a thudding certainty that it had not been there when he'd first seen the wallet lying beside the twisted body, when he had tentatively poked it open with his key, his hands careful not to disturb the evidence of a violent death.

He opened the paper and saw that it was a computerized receipt dated October 29. He called directory assistance, requested the number for the store whose name was printed in dot matrix characters at the top of the paper, and dialed the number that a computerized voice chanted twice over the phone. He spoke briefly with a salesperson and hung up.

He picked up the phone again and was connected with SID.

"Who went out with the crime unit to the Sherbourne house?"

Someone went to check. "That would be Denise Brady and Raymond Kelly. You want to talk with one of them?"

"Please." He waited with impatient patience, drummed his fingers on his desktop.

"Raymond Kelly here."

"This is Sam Ryker, Wilshire Division. I'm in charge of the Vogler homicide. I understand you were with the crime unit sent out to the house."

"Right." The voice was alert, instantly nervous. "Something wrong?"

"I'm not sure. I have a wallet here that belonged to the deceased. Do you remember it? Black eelskin."

"Yeah, I remember."

"There's a pink receipt stuck in here that I didn't see before. Can you tell me how it got there?"

A crackle of static. "I guess I put it there, Detective."

"May I ask why?"

"I found it next to the body; I assumed it fell out of the wallet. Did I do something wrong?"

There were several things Ryker wanted to say; instead, he replaced the receiver softly in its cradle and cursed.

In the morning, Ryker told Moran and Stollman about the wallet.

"What's the big deal?" Moran said. "So the guy put the receipt into the wallet. Where's the harm?"

"Look at the date." He handed it to Moran, who showed it to Stollman. "It's dated October 29. The day of the murder."

"So?" Moran asked.

"That store doesn't open till twelve noon on Sundays. I checked. So if Vogler was conducting an open house that started at twelve sharp, that means he'd be setting up at least fifteen minutes before that. So how the hell did he end up with a receipt from a store that opens at twelve?"

Moran said, "So you think it's the killer's receipt?"

Ryker nodded. "I know what you're going to say—that Novick could've accidentally dropped it. You're probably right. But it's evidence we should've had all along."

"You don't think he dropped it, do you?" Stollman said.

"I'm not sure. Let's say I have some doubts. This is a paint store. Look where it is—not even near Novick's neighborhood. If he wanted to get some paint, why wouldn't he go to a place near him? There are plenty of them around."

"Maybe he stopped on the way to see Vogler," Moran said.

"Yeah, sure. He figures he'll be in the neighborhood anyway when he goes to kill Vogler, so why not pick up a couple of cans of semi-gloss."

"Maybe he got to that side of town early and didn't want to just hang around," Moran said. "So he went to a store. It could've been any store; he just happened to pick that one."

"What about Kasden? Where does he live?" Stollman asked.

"I looked it up," Ryker said. "On Camden. Not far from the store. The lab couldn't raise any prints, by the way."

"If you're thinking about other possibilities, what about Benton?" Stollman asked. "He's close by. And we still don't know if his alibi holds."

"True."

Moran said, "So what are you saying? Novick *didn't* do it?"

"I can't say that. But I want to follow up on this."

* * *

Ryker slipped his car into one of the angled parking slots in back of Standard Brands. He occasionally came here to buy house paint, hardware, or posterboards and art supplies when one or both of his daughters needed them for school projects. He walked in, showed his ID to a saleswoman who looked at him suspiciously, and checked out the prices of latex exterior paint while he waited for the manager.

"Hi. Can I help you?" a woman's voice inquired.

He looked up into a smiling dark, pretty face whose eyes had been made unnaturally serious by his visit.

"I'm Detective Ryker. I'm investigating a homicide that took place on Sunday, October 29th, not far from here. I'd like to ask you some questions about a customer, if that's okay."

"October 29th; that's ten days ago. I don't know if I'd remember much. Do you have the customer's name?"

"No. Just a receipt."

"Well, that won't tell me much. And I'm not sure how we'd go about finding out which salesperson helped this customer."

"I brought some pictures. I thought maybe you and your staff could take a look, see if you recognize anyone."

She looked at him dubiously. "All right. I'll call over a couple of the salespeople at a time."

"Thank you."

She left and returned with a tall, lanky tow-headed young man and a painfully thin, carroty-haired young woman whose shoulder blades almost sliced through her yellow cotton blouse.

Ryker took out the first picture, the one with Novick and Vogler and Kasden standing to one side. The manager shook her head, passed it on like a peace pipe to the others. Nothing.

The detective took out the photo with Kasden, Jake, and Deena. He watched expectantly as the three took turns studying it. There was no recognition, only apologetic shrugs.

"Can we try the rest of your staff?" he asked the manager.

She sent two angular young men who wore identical stone-washed jeans and sweat tops with amputated sleeves. One in gray, the other in white. The vacant expression in their eyes was identical, too. Ryker passed around the pictures, but there wasn't so much as a flicker of response.

"Do you remember anything unusual happening on a Sunday, about ten days ago?" Ryker asked.

"I don't work Sundays," White Top said. He sidled away.

"Like what?" Gray Top asked.

"I don't know. Anything." Ryker looked at the manager. "You want me to ask the others, right?"

"I'd appreciate it."

She was gone for a few minutes, and when she came back it was with the skinny girl.

"I don't know if this is what you mean, mister," she said, "but I was workin' here the Sunday 'fore last, and somebody knocked over a whole double display of colored pencils. Took me most of an hour to get 'em all sorted out again."

"Could you look at these pictures again, miss, to see if one of these men is the one who knocked over the display?"

"Who said anything about a man? This was a woman did it. She was so jittery, I'm surprised she didn't knock over half the store. So then she apologizes and buys four dozen pencils that she probably doesn't know what to do with." She looked at him. "Is that it?"

"Yes. Thank you." He thanked the manager, too, and left before he was tempted to buy some caulking tubes for his bathrooms so that the trip wouldn't have been totally worthless.

It was only the next morning when Ryker was reading the stenographer's notes of Novick's interrogation that he realized what had been nagging him for over two days, like a tickle demanding to be scratched.

"Listen to this," he told Stollman and Moran. " 'I don't lie.' It's from the notes from my talk with Novick on Monday."

"So?" Moran asked. "Give the man a Boy Scout award."

"That was in response to my statement that he lied to me when I first questioned him about Vogler's death. See, I checked my notes, and Novick is right. He never told me that the last time he saw Vogler was the week before he died. He was careful to say that it was the last time he *spoke* to Vogler."

"What's your point?" Moran asked.

"I'm getting there. So I checked my notes again from Monday's session. I was looking for a similar *truth*, you see, something Novick said that would let him get around the truth without actually lying.''

"Are we to assume that you found it?" Stollman asked.

Ryker nodded, grinning. "I asked Novick, 'Did you see anyone leave when you were going in?' and he answered, 'I didn't see anyone leaving when I was going in, no.' Get it? What he *didn't* say is that he didn't see someone leaving *before* he went in. Like when he was sitting in the car.''

"Come on, Sam," Moran said. "This is reaching.''

"No, it's not, Tom," Stollman said. "I can see what Sam's getting at. And the question is," he said with mounting excitement, "who did he see leaving, right?''

"Yeah. But a better question is, why is Novick protecting this someone who was leaving the house with a dead body in it?''

"His daughter. It's got to be his daughter," Moran said.

"Maybe,"Ryker said. "Or—and I think this is a more interesting possibility—maybe he *thinks* it's his daughter, but he's not a hundred percent sure. See, he doesn't see a face, but he knows it's a woman. And he can think of only one woman who would want Vogler dead.''

Stollman said, "So he takes the watch and the cash to throw us off. But he can't explain *why* he has to throw us off, 'cause then he'd be implicating someone else. But why does he hold on to the stuff? Why not dump it?''

Ryker said, "Because if it turns out that it *isn't* his daughter, he can give the stuff to the Vogelanters. I can see him thinking that way. And remember, he probably didn't think we'd search his house.''

"So who is this woman?" Moran asked.

"We have to be thorough. It could be the daughter, but I don't think so. It could be Ann Douglas. She doesn't have an alibi, and she had motive and opportunity. Or—and this may sound far-fetched—it could be the Presser woman. She's the one I told you was so nervous when I went to question her, remember? She doesn't really have an alibi either. And she gave me the impression that she didn't exactly love men.''

"Is she the one whose husband remarried without giving her this religious divorce?" Stollman asked.

"I don't know," Ryker said. "I'll have to check my notes.''

" 'Cause if she is, I could see a motive. Maybe she figures

she's getting even with her husband by killing Vogler. We could check with a psychologist, see if it makes sense.''

Moran said, ''Sam, we never followed up on what the Kalinsky woman said—you know, that the Presser woman and that other one met Vogler. That's because Novick was arrested. Maybe we should check into that a little more.''

''Right, but first let's check out Mrs. Presser's alibi. If it holds, there's no point checking out the other angle. And I want to go back to the store, this time with pictures of these women.''

''Why?'' Moran asked.

''One of the salesgirls told me about some woman who knocked over an entire display. Maybe it's her. Maybe she was nervous 'cause she was planning on confronting Vogler. I don't know why I didn't think of checking into that more in the first place. Somehow, I was locked into Kasden. Or Novick. I wasn't thinking along the lines of a woman. Dumb.''

''The problem now is where to get a picture of these women,'' Stollman said.

''We have a photo of Mrs. Vogler,'' Ryker said. ''That's why I don't think she's the one. Because she was in one of the pictures I showed around, and no one recognized her. Mrs. Kasden is in the same picture, by the way.''

''But you asked them to look for men, didn't you? That makes a difference,'' Moran said.

''You're right. I may have; I don't remember. So we'll have to show them those pictures again before we can eliminate Mrs. Vogler and Mrs. Kasden. Tom, why don't you do that right now. Also, I'm not sure, but there must be a picture somewhere of Vogler with Ann Douglas. Let's check his stuff again.''

Stollman said, ''There's one other person we haven't considered at all. Mrs. Novick.''

Ryker was about to say something but stopped. ''Okay.'' He nodded. ''I'm listening.''

''She had access to the gun as much as her husband did; she had the same motive. According to her, she was home all day by herself. How come we never thought of her?''

''I don't know.'' Because she seemed so frail, so helpless?

''What if Novick thought he saw his *wife* leaving the crime scene? He'd certainly do everything he could to protect her.''

''Yeah, he would. But I don't know . . .''

Moran said, "I think Hank's got a point, Sam. We'll have to check her out, too."

"Okay. But that means we'll have to get another picture with her in it. I don't feel like asking Mrs. Vogler for it. Maybe we'll find one with Vogler's stuff."

"What about the Presser woman?" Moran asked. "How can we get a photo of her?"

"I haven't figured that out yet," Ryker said. "But I'll think of something."

28

THE FIRST THING DEENA DID ON WEDNESDAY MORNING WAS to strip the house of its coat of mourning.

She went from room to room, removing and refolding the sepulchral white sheets that had hidden the mirrors. And when she was finished, she tiptoed quietly into the bathroom, past the still, sleeping figure of her mother lying in what Deena would never again have to think of as Jake's bed.

It was strange meeting her face after a week's absence. She looked paler, she thought, her cheeks a little drawn. But then, what had she expected? She had been quarantined by death.

Her hair lay on her shoulders, limp and dull, and although she'd sponged herself throughout the week (that much was permitted), she felt as though she were covered with an invisible veneer of grime and grief that she had to shed.

She undressed quickly, turned on the shower faucets, and embraced the almost hot water like a returning lover. For minutes she stood under the braided transparent stream that plastered her hair to her scalp; then, adjusting the shower head, she let the jets of pleasantly stinging water play with her body, leaving her skin blush-red wherever they caressed her.

She felt glorious, forgetting everything for the moment as she abandoned herself to the water, but when she began attending to the practical business of soaping her body and shampooing her neglected hair, she remembered with sharp suddenness her mother lying in her bed, her father trapped behind bars. What was he doing now? she wondered guiltily. Quickly, she rinsed her hair and shut off the water.

Pearl was still sleeping, snoring lightly. She had all too eagerly taken another Valium, and Deena worried briefly whether her mother would manage to face the coming Max-less nights and days without some kind of tranquilizer to soften the jagged edges of reality. She would have to.

Careful not to wake Pearl, Deena removed a skirt and a pair of flats from her closet; a bra, panties, cotton socks, and a sweater from a dresser; and returned to the bathroom to get dressed. She decided to let her hair dry naturally. With a last glance at her mother, she stole out of the bedroom, walked quickly to the kitchen, and picked up the phone.

Alan had nothing new to report.

He had seen Max on Tuesday afternoon, but Max had firmly refused to discuss the damning evidence the police found in his *tefillin* bag. And when Alan had suggested that Max's self-destructive behavior was a misguided attempt to protect Deena, Max had angrily informed him to stop playing psychologist.

"He still doesn't want to see you, Deena," Alan said now. "I'm sorry. I don't think it's because he's embarrassed. I think he's just convinced somehow that you're involved."

"But he doesn't have to worry about me! Ryker practically said that I'm not under suspicion. Didn't you tell him that?"

"I did. Maybe he thinks Ryker's saying that to get you off your guard." He sighed. "Who knows? Look, I'll be seeing your father some time today; maybe he'll see things differently."

She turned on the radio, had a yogurt for breakfast, and hoped her mother would be waking up soon. Deena would make her some breakfast and coax it with maternal patience past her reluctant lips. After that, Deena would go to UCLA. She felt guilty about leaving her mother alone in the house, but she couldn't afford to miss any more classes. And she'd arranged to have Sandy come over with the baby to keep Pearl company.

Last night, after changing into her nightgown, Deena had deposited her mourning uniform near the side door. Now she opened the door, picked up the discarded brown dress, and went outside to dump it into one of the large trash bins. As she was coming back into the house, she heard the front doorbell.

Probably Faye, she thought, and hurried to answer. She had been a vigilant friend throughout this ordeal, offering hope and understanding.

It was Ryker.

"Can I come in?" His face was inscrutably serious.

"Why are you here?" she asked with uncharacteristic bluntness.

"This is important. I have to talk to you."

She stepped aside and allowed him to enter but made no move to leave the entry hall.

"Can we sit down somewhere?"

"I don't understand why you're here. Your job is finished, Detective." She underscored his title with unconcealed derision. "You've saved the city from a vicious criminal."

"I can understand how you feel, Mrs. Vogler."

"No, you can't! How can you possibly know what it feels like to have a father in jail?"

"All right, I can't know. But I can imagine it must be pretty painful."

"What do you want, Detective?" she said tiredly. "Why don't you just tell me and leave me alone?"

"Mrs. Vogler, I need your help."

She looked at him as though he'd propositioned her. "My help? I think I've already helped you enough, don't you?"

"Look, I'm taking a risk by telling you this, but I have a feeling that your father may be innocent."

"What do you mean?"

"A couple of things have been bothering me, little things. I can't really go into all of it, but I'd like to follow up on them and see where they lead."

"If you had your doubts about my father, why did you arrest him in the first place? Or is there a quota to be filled on homicide arrests like there is on parking tickets?"

"Mrs. Vogler, you know about the fingerprints, about the evidence we found at his house. And he had a strong motive and easy access to the gun. What choice did we have? And I didn't come up with this other stuff until after I interrogated him." He was surprised and somewhat annoyed with himself. Why was he defending himself?

"How do I know you're not just trying to trap me into making things look worse for my father—who, for your in-

formation, is innocent, in spite of what things look like!''
From the minute Max had been arrested and had denied his
guilt, Deena had believed him without reservation.

"You're just going to have to trust me, Mrs. Vogler.''

"Frankly, that's a lot to ask.''

"True. Then again, I'm trusting you. And if you help me,
and I'm right, we may be able to prove your father's inno-
cence. I'm not promising, by the way. I just have a strong
hunch.''

"All right.'' She led him into the living room and sat down
on the couch. "Sit down.''

Ryker sat on a folding chair. "It's clear to me that your
father took the watch and money to make it look like Vogler
was killed by a burglar because he's trying to protect you.''

"Detective, my lawyer figured that out two days ago.''

"Okay. But I have reason to believe that your father thought
he saw you leaving the crime scene.''

"That's impossible! How could he think that? I was nowhere near there!''

"But he doesn't know that. I think he saw a woman—I'm
not sure who—leaving the house, and he jumped to the conclusion that it was you. That's why he felt he had to protect
you.''

"So how does that help him? The woman could be anyone.''

"Not really. That doesn't make sense. It has to be someone who knew your ex-husband, not some stranger. I have
some ideas, and I need your help to see if they're valid.''

He told her about the receipt in Jake's wallet and about the
woman in the store. "This is confidential,'' he warned. "I
could lose my badge for telling you this.''

Deena nodded.

"My theory is that she dropped the receipt when she
opened her purse. Maybe she went to get a tissue to wipe
some prints or something. I don't know for sure.''

Deena had listened raptly, had allowed herself to feel the
first glimmer of hope. "You said you have some ideas as to
who this woman is. How do you know it's not me?''

"We checked. One of my men went to the store this morning and showed your picture around. No one recognized you,
and the salesperson who told me about this other woman
definitely eliminated you.'' No one had recognized Ruth Kasden, either.

"I guess I should be relieved."

"I guess." It was his first smile since he'd arrived. "I'm looking into two possible suspects. One is Ann Douglas."

"Ann Douglas! Why would she want to kill Jake?"

"Maybe she found out he had no intention of ever marrying her." Ryker told Deena briefly about his meeting with her, about his theory that she knew about the gun and could have used Vogler's key to Deena's house. "Her alibi is weak. I spent an hour at Vogler's apartment this morning until I found a picture of her. I'm the only one who met her, you see."

Ann Douglas, Deena admitted to herself, sounded like a plausible idea. A wonderful idea. "You said there was someone else." Do I get to choose? she wondered.

"Right." He looked at her carefully to see her reaction. "Elaine Presser."

"That's ridiculous! Why would she kill Jake?"

"Before I get into the why—and I'll admit it's just a theory—I should tell you that she doesn't have an alibi."

"I don't either. Lots of innocent people don't."

"Right. But you didn't give us a fake one. Mrs. Presser did. She said she was home all afternoon, but I spoke to her ex-husband this morning, and he says that's not true."

"How would he know?"

"See, their kids decided to sleep over at his house that night, so he took them back with him to her house to get some overnight stuff. They got there around a quarter to five, but she wasn't home. They waited for almost an hour, then left."

"How does he know what time it was? Maybe he's confused." Was she defending Elaine or trying to convince herself Ryker was wrong?

Ryker shook his head. "He said he knows the time because the kids have a favorite show on at that time, and that's what they were watching while they where waiting. Of course, none of this is conclusive, but you have to admit it's interesting."

"But I still don't understand why she would do it."

Ryker shrugged. "I'm not a psychologist. But isn't it possible she hated her ex-husband for the way he was treating her and projected that hate onto your ex-husband? Let me ask you something we're unclear about. Did she ever meet your ex-husband?"

"Yes. At a restaurant. They had some words." Should she tell him? Should she betray the confidence of a member of the exclusive sorority she'd joined? Suddenly, she remembered why Ryker was here, remembered her father. "Elaine called me a few days ago. She asked me not to mention that she'd run into Jake; she said she didn't need the police bothering her and the kids. I believed her."

"No reason why you shouldn't have. I need a picture of her. Without connecting her to the receipt, I don't have any evidence; hell, I'm not even sure she's the one! I thought you might have a picture of her or know where to get one."

"As a matter of fact, I do. One of the times we met, Susan Bergman brought a camera. She's quitting the group, you see. Her husband's giving her a divorce. Anyway, she wanted to take a group picture, and we all thought, why not? She has one of those cameras with a little timer that lets you delay the snap, so she's in it, too."

"Can you get a copy without making her suspicious?"

"I don't have to. She gave everyone a copy. I'll get it."

She was back a minute later and handed him a color photo of the group. "This one is Elaine." She pointed to her. *I am fingering her, she thought.*

"I know. I met her." He stood up.

She walked him to the door and opened it.

"Thanks," he said.

She didn't know what to say, so she said nothing.

Ryker entered the store. This time the tall, lanky young man was at the front register, and he went to get the manager.

"One of your men was here this morning," the manager informed Ryker with a hint of impatience.

"I know. I'm sorry we keep bothering you, but it's very important. I have some other pictures, and I wanted to know if I could show them to the thin girl I talked to on Tuesday."

"You mean Ginny? Okay. I'll get her."

She was back in a minute with the girl, who looked even thinner, if possible, in a body-hugging knit top. Ryker handed the first picture to her and waited while she examined it.

She shook her head.

"What about these?" He handed her the other two.

She looked at one, then studied the other. "Yeah. That's her."

He hadn't realized that he'd been holding his breath until he expelled it.

"She was walkin' around the place, up and down the aisles. Kept checkin' her watch. I remember 'cause I was sure she was gonna knock something over, the way she was touchin' everything without really lookin'."

"You're sure about this?"

"I just told you I am, didn't I?"

He pointed to Elaine's grinning face. "You could testify in court that this woman was here on Sunday, October 29th?"

She looked at him. "Not this one. Who said anything about this one? I never saw her before in my life." She jabbed at the face in the picture. "This is the lady I'm talkin' about."

After waking up late, Pearl had insisted on going home to take care of a few things. "I can't stay here forever," she had told Deena. "I'll be fine."

Deena had reluctantly driven her home, and when she returned, she stood in the kitchen, washing the few breakfast dishes she'd left in the sink.

Her mind was on Ryker. She wondered what he was doing, what he'd learned. It was fascinating how he'd pieced together an entire theory (and she prayed to God he was right) from a little piece of paper that the killer may have dropped.

She tried to imagine the killer's face when the police confronted her with evidence that placed her at the side of Jake's just-dead body. Ann Douglas? Elaine?—she admitted to herself that she didn't really care anymore, as long as her father would be exonerated.

It was almost comic, really, that an ordinary receipt could have such monumental significance just because it was lost. Everybody lost receipts. Just two weeks ago, she'd spent an hour searching through several purses for a sales slip for a denim skirt.

Why did that sound so familiar? she wondered suddenly. When had she . . . ?

"*. . . I have . . . some things to return, if I ever find the receipt . . .*"

Her heart lurched. Her world and the plate she was holding slipped out of her hands and came crashing down together.

She dialed quickly, but the line was busy. She left everything on the floor, grabbed her car keys from the hook, and ran out the side door. It was a short drive, but her mind raced with the Honda until she turned the corner and pulled up in front of the split-level house.

The driveway was empty.

She ran up the pathway and pounded on the front door, pounded and yelled. She was still pounding when Ryker came up behind her.

"She's not here," she said to him listlessly. "The phone was busy; it's probably off the hook. I just figured it out," she added. "I didn't trick you. I thought it was Mrs. Presser."

"What are you going to do?"

"I think we'd better open the door." He pulled out his wallet, took out a credit card, and jiggled the lock open. "Maybe you'd better wait out here."

She nodded.

Ryker was back within a few minutes. "No one's inside. Looks like she packed some bags." He went to his car, leaned in, and picked up the hand radio unit. "This is Ryker. Wilshire Division. Put out an APB on a female Caucasian—" he turned to Deena, who had followed him, trancelike, to his car. "What kind of car does she drive?"

"A Buick, I think. Dark blue."

He repeated the information into the radio. "She may be armed. Her name is Faye Rudman." He listened intently. "Okay. I'm holding." He waited. "What? Yeah, I'll wait."

Ryker and Deena stood, not looking at each other. A few minutes later, the radio crackled. Ryker listened, then nodded. "Yeah. Yeah, I got that."

He faced Deena. "They got a call about a half hour ago. She crashed into an embankment heading east on the San Bernardino Freeway."

29

DEENA SAT WITH REUBEN AND RYKER ON THE BRIGHT OR-
ange vinyl seat in the corridor several feet from the nurses'
station.

Strange benchmates, she thought.

Michael had gone to buy some tea for her, some coffee for
himself and the two other men. She had called Reuben first,
as soon as she arrived at County General; he'd come almost
immediately, his eyes flooded with anguish. Michael had canceled his last three appointments.

The waiting was difficult.

Deena watched two grim-faced nurses rushing by in a rus-
tle of gray-white polyester, their rubber soles squeaking on
the linoleum tiles. A janitor worked carefully around their
feet, his stringy mop slapping the floor in wide, soapy cres-
cents. Along the hall an elderly man inched his way, one
hand pushing a chrome pole from which an IV unit was gently
swinging, the other clutching the back opening of a short,
faded hospital gown that exposed the tops of his knobby
knees.

She had accepted a ride from Ryker, had sped with him
with legal recklessness so that she could reach the hospital
sooner and wait longer to find out whether Faye would sur-
vive.

Ryker had been in contact with headquarters throughout
the ride but had learned very little. Paramedics had pulled
Faye's unconscious but still breathing form from her
accordion-pleated car. She had been thrown into the steering
wheel and suffered apparent damage to her chest and abdo-
men; they had no way of determining the extent of the internal injuries.

"They found a package on the floor in the front," Ryker
had told her. "Addressed to me. It's probably your gun."

Deena had nodded wisely.

The young, bearded resident who had spoken to them before was approaching, his stethoscope flapping against his white jacket. They stood up quickly.

"How is she doing?" Reuben asked.

"Not great. She's pretty weak. She has several fractured ribs, a pneumothorax—that's a punctured lung—but it seems to be under control. We're not sure whether her spleen is ruptured; an abdominal tap didn't show anything, but we'll probably have to do a repeat later. She also has chest pain, irregular pulse—we're worried about myocardial contusion. It doesn't look good. I'm sorry."

"Can she answer some questions?" Ryker avoided Deena's eyes and the recrimination he knew he would find in them.

"She's conscious," the doctor told Ryker, "and for what she's been through, she seems pretty lucid. I don't know for how long, though, because her blood pressure isn't steady. She's pretty heavily sedated, too, because of the pain."

"Can I see her?" Deena was surprised by how clear her voice sounded to her own ears. She had expected it to be as muffled as her thoughts.

"Are you family?"

"Yes." She looked at Ryker defiantly. *Blood sisters.*

"Okay, but just for a few minutes."

"I'm afraid I'll have to come along," Ryker said.

The three walked down the corridor and entered the emergency area. Deena looked resolutely ahead, afraid to trespass on the private dramas unfolding behind the beige curtains that partitioned the long room into cubicles.

Faye was on a bed in a middle cubicle, her arms neatly positioned at her sides. One thin plastic tube was anchored to her nostrils, another to the vein above her right wrist; a third, camouflaged by a sheet, disappeared into her chest. Medical apparatus stood in readiness on either side of the bed.

"I'll be back in a few minutes," the resident told them. He drew the curtain closed behind him.

Deena approached the bed. Ryker stood a discreet distance away.

"You know, don't you?" Faye asked. Her eyes looked cavernous against the unnatural pallor of her skin.

Deena nodded.

284 of 304 Rochelle Majer Krich

"I didn't know if you'd come. I'm glad you did." Her voice, always husky, had a raspy tone that sounded eerie against the muted percolation of the oxygen rushing through the tube.

Deena gently squeezed her hand.

"Did they find the gun?" Faye asked anxiously. "I was going to mail it to the police, along with a tape. To explain. So they would know I did it."

"They have it. Don't worry."

"I'm sorry about your father. So sorry. I hoped the police would think a burglar killed Jake. I realized after I left that I should have taken something, but I wasn't thinking clearly. When Michael told me they arrested your father, I wanted to die."

"It's okay. Don't talk."

"No, I have to tell you. I have to explain. I know everybody thought I was strong. Reuben did. And maybe I was; I did get through eleven years. The first few years I woke up every morning and said, maybe today. Maybe Alex will be sane enough to set me free. I called his doctor all the time; he finally got annoyed. 'Mrs. Rudman,' he said, 'we'll let you know if there's any change.' So I stopped calling. And after a while I stopped hoping. Sometimes, it took me hours just to choose what clothes to wear to get through the day. Sometimes, I never left the house at all.

"Then I met Reuben, and we started the group. And even though I didn't feel there was hope for me, it helped to talk, to share my feelings, to know that maybe I was helping someone else. Doing something. And every time one of us got her *get*—like Susan, Susan was a wonderful thing, wasn't it?—I felt it was worth it." She smiled and closed her eyes for a moment.

"I hated what Jake was doing to you—the phone calls, the attack, the spite. He seemed to be getting angrier, losing control, and it frightened me. Alex used to call me and hang up when I answered, did I ever tell you that? I think he was trying to trap me with the boyfriends he thought I had. And everyone kept saying that Jake was getting worse. Like Alex. Crazy, everybody said. Jake is acting crazy. And even if he wasn't really crazy, I knew he wasn't going to give you your *get*. He said so, and I believed him. And

I didn't want you to end up like me. No one should live like that.

"I don't know when I first thought about the gun. I think it was when the phone calls started. And then he tried to rape you, and he didn't seem to care what anybody thought. He just wouldn't listen. Not to your father, not to Reuben. So I knew I had to do something; somebody had to—you see that, don't you?

"I didn't intend to kill him.

"I called the office to find out where he would be Sunday. I had your gun, of course; I took it the night we met at your house. I just wanted to scare him, to make him stop hurting you. He was surprised to see me, but he knew who I was. I told him I wanted to talk to him. We went into a back room, and I pulled the gun out of my purse and held it with both hands and pointed it at him. 'This is just a warning,' I said. 'I can find you any time. Give Deena her *get* and leave her alone.'

"He laughed. He called me names. 'Interfering bitch,' he said. Other names, ugly names. 'You won't do it,' he said. 'You don't want to rot in jail.' I told him about Alex. 'I have nothing to lose,' I said. 'It's just a different kind of prison.'

"But then everything went wrong. He was supposed to be scared, you see. But he started coming toward me, grinning, and then he was standing right in front of me, and his hands were on mine, and I knew he was going to try to get the gun away from me, and I couldn't let him do that.

"I heard a loud noise, and he had this funny look on his face—you know, like he was surprised? And he slipped to the floor. And he was dead. I know, because I checked. I took out a mirror from my purse and put it under his nose to make sure, but it didn't fog up. I would have called an ambulance if it had. I think I would have." She paused again.

"There was a lot of blood. I didn't know what to do first, but I couldn't call the police. They would never believe me— how could I explain the gun? So I tried to think of all the places where I might have left fingerprints, but I gave up. But I wasn't really worried, because I just walked into the house and found him in the hall. And I didn't think anyone would connect me with him. I called Jake's office the next day so they wouldn't look for him. I muffled my voice with a scarf.''

"Rest a little," Deena said. "We can talk later."

Faye shook her head. "Let me finish. I didn't know what to do about the gun. I couldn't put it back, because I knew the police would check it. So I bought another one. I went to several gun dealers until I found one who was willing to sell me an unregistered one for $800. I didn't know about the serial numbers. I was shocked when you told me later that the police could check that. So I put the gun in your closet that Friday when I stopped by after seeing Alex. I really did go to see Alex. I'm not sure why.

"I knew the police would be talking to all of us, because of the gun; it was just a matter of time. So I told my in-laws that I spent the afternoon with a man, and I warned them that if they didn't want poor Alex's name ruined when everyone found out, they'd better tell the police that I was with them all day. Of course, they agreed; I knew they would.

"I never thought your father would be involved. Because I knew I killed Jake, you see. I had no idea your father was there after me. And then he was arrested! And he had the watch, and the money, and Alan seemed to think the police had a pretty good case. I should have turned myself in, but I couldn't; I just couldn't.''

"It was an accident, Faye," Deena whispered. "You didn't mean to kill him."

"Do you think the police would have believed me? Sometimes, I'm not even sure what the truth is. Maybe I did want to kill him all along. I'm not sorry he's dead; I'm just sorry about all the pain I caused you. Sitting *shivah,* the funeral— I know how you hated that, and it was all my fault."

"You were just trying to help me, Faye. I know that."

"I couldn't let your father sit in jail. But when I thought about being in prison, I knew I lied when I told Jake it wouldn't matter. Eleven years was enough. And then I thought, maybe the doctors will think I'm crazy. And they'll put me away somewhere, like they put Alex away. Another prison. So this morning I packed a few things and decided to run away. I don't know where. But I left the gun. And a tape. I didn't to a very good job of running away either, did I?''

"Don't think about anything," Deena urged. "Right now, you have to concentrate on getting well."

"Why?" An ironic smile. "So I can spend my life in jail?"

"That's not going to happen, Faye. You'll get a good lawyer; you'll see. Everything will be all right." *And they lived happily ever after.* Deena looked away.

The resident poked his head through the curtain. "She should be resting."

"I'd better go," Deena said. "I'll be in the hall. I won't leave."

"I don't want you to blame yourself for any of this, Deena. I didn't do it just for you. I did it for me, too. Because somebody had to put an end to this craziness, don't you see? Reuben is trying, but I don't know . . . I just don't know . . ."

"I'll be right here. Try to sleep."

"I am tired," she admitted. Her eyes fluttered. "How did you know?" she asked suddenly.

Deena told her about the receipt the police had found.

"That's funny." She sighed. "I wasn't even worried about it. It's really funny, isn't it?" She smiled weakly and closed her eyes.

Deena slipped her hand away and walked quietly out of the cubicle. She didn't wait to see if Ryker followed.

30

MICHAEL WAS ALREADY OUTSIDE WAITING IN FRONT OF THE chapel after the service when Deena came out. She walked over to him, crying softly. He held her tightly.

"What happens now?" he asked, stroking her hair.

"Reuben spoke to Faye's mother this morning. She wants Faye to be buried near her, in New York. She's planning on having another service there. Reuben's going to accompany the body on an afternoon flight."

Yesterday they had stayed in the hospital for hours, had watched a new shift take over, had seen the smiling nurses automatically rearrange their faces into sick-bed sobriety the minute they walked past the elevator doors.

When they finally saw the bearded resident once again, his leaden gait telegraphed the news before he reached them.

"It was like a heart attack," he told them. "A result of the myocardial contusion. A bruised heart from the injury to her chest."

A bruised heart, Deena had repeated to herself.

"I spoke to Ryker," Michael told her now. "He's here, you know. It was nice of him to come to the funeral." He'd spotted the detective standing at the back of the chapel.

"I guess. He didn't have to."

"He told me to tell you that your father will be released some time today. He thinks Alan can get around a charge of obstructing justice."

"God, I hope so!"

"He also thought you might be interested to know about Elaine's alibi. It seems she was with a boyfriend, and she didn't want her ex-husband to know about it."

"That's ironic, isn't it? I mean, when you think of Faye's alibi? It's just the opposite."

"I know."

"Faye's in-laws are here. Reuben told me. They spoke to him; they want him to hush everything up, about the *get* aspect. So does Rabbi Brodin. The Rudman's intimated that they'd make it worth Reuben's while if he cooperates."

"What did he tell them?"

She smiled. "He wasn't very rabbinic, I'm afraid."

"Good for him!"

"That's what I said, too." She paused. "Michael, I feel so confused. I'm relieved about my father, of course, and happy that this whole nightmare is finally over for us. I've never been so frightened in my life. But then I think about Faye, and about what happened to her, and I feel so selfish."

"I wish I could make it clear to you. It isn't simple."

Nothing was simple. Jake's death had affected all of them.

She wondered how she and her father would handle the awkwardness of mutual suspicion. Would they discuss it, or pretend that it had never existed?

And Michael. She had disturbed the gossamer filaments of

the trust they had woven. And what, she wondered, had that done to their relationship?

"Stop blaming yourself," he'd told her last night; "You were confused, frightened. And no, I don't need time to think about the way I feel about you. Nothing has changed."

Everything, she knew, had changed. For all of them.

But she hoped he was right.

"Do you think it was really an accident?" she asked now. "The crash, I mean? Or do you think . . ."

"Who knows? Obviously, she was distraught. Distracted. Then again, maybe subconsciously, she saw it as her only escape. I really don't know. But I'd rather think it was an accident."

"It's so strange, you know. I just got up yesterday from sitting *shivah* for Jake, and I resented every minute. And now Faye is dead, and I wish there were some ritual I could perform for her. Because she was my friend, and I loved her, and it has nothing to do with the fact that she gave me my freedom."

"I know this is hard for you, Deena. You were so close."

"But that's part of the problem, Michael. I feel responsible, don't you see? If I hadn't talked to her so much about Jake, if she hadn't known how desperate I was feeling, maybe she wouldn't have done what she did. Here I am, free, and I owe it all to her. And she's dead, Michael. She's dead."

"But not because of you, Deena. You can't blame yourself for confiding in her, just as Reuben can't blame himself for introducing you to each other, for starting the group. I think the strain of eleven years was finally too much. There was no way any of you could have known what she would do."

"But I can't just forget about it, Michael."

"Of course not. Because you're right; it isn't fair. It would be so easy if we could just pretend that none of this happened and go on with our lives. But we can't. And it's going to take a long time for all of us to come to terms with this. If we ever do."

He drew her closer into the circle of his arms.

"Reuben spoke so beautifully, didn't he, Michael? About Faye. About the terrible position she was in."

"He really did. You could hear how upset he was."

"You know, I keep thinking about what that resident said when he came over to us last night. It's almost like what Reuben said."

"What did he say—the resident, I mean?"

"He said Faye never really had a chance. I guess she didn't, did she?"

A bruised heart.

"No," he agreed soberly, "I guess she didn't. Not with the way things are . . ."

IF IT'S MURDER, CAN DETECTIVE J.P. BEAUMONT BE FAR BEHIND?...

FOLLOW IN HIS FOOTSTEPS WITH FAST-PACED MYSTERIES BY J.A. JANCE

ELLIOTT ROOSEVELT'S DELIGHTFUL MYSTERY SERIES

MURDER IN THE ROSE GARDEN
70529-X/$4.95US/$5.95Can

MURDER IN THE OVAL OFFICE
70528-1/$4.99US/$5.99Can

MURDER AND THE FIRST LADY
69937-0/$4.50US/$5.50Can

THE HYDE PARK MURDER
70058-1/$4.50US/$5.50Can

MURDER AT HOBCAW BARONY
70021-2/$4.50US/$5.50Can

THE WHITE HOUSE PANTRY MURDER
70404-8/$3.95US/$4.95Can

MURDER AT THE PALACE
70405-6/$4.99US/$5.99Can

Coming Soon

MURDER IN THE BLUE ROOM
71237-7/$4.99US/$5.99Can